D0951487

(continued . . .)

"*The Pope of Greenwich Village* and *Family Business* enjoyed commercial success, critical respect, and adaptation to the big screen; *Smoke Screen* promises to follow in their footsteps . . . [an] efficient page-turner . . . Patrick is an expert plotter who never tips his hand (and holds some fabulous cards)."
—*Baltimore Sun*

"*Smoke Screen* was worth the wait."
—*The New York Press*

Praise for Vincent Patrick

"Vincent Patrick, like George V. Higgins, Mary Gordon, and John Gregory Dunne, mines territory rarely encountered in modern fiction." —*New York Times Book Review*

Also by Vincent Patrick

The Pope of Greenwich Village
Family Business

Smoke Screen

Vincent Patrick

AN ONYX BOOK

ONYX
Published by New American Library, a division of
Penguin Putnam Inc., 375 Hudson Street,
New York, New York 10014, U.S.A.
Penguin Books Ltd, 27 Wrights Lane,
London W8 5TZ, England
Penguin Books Australia Ltd, Ringwood,
Victoria, Australia
Penguin Books Canada Ltd, 10 Alcorn Avenue,
Toronto, Ontario, Canada M4V 3B2
Penguin Books (N.Z.) Ltd, 182–190 Wairau Road,
Auckland 10, New Zealand

Penguin Books Ltd, Registered Offices:
Harmondsworth, Middlesex, England

Published by Onyx, an imprint of New American Library,
a division of Penguin Putnam Inc.
This is an authorized reprint of a hardcover edition published by William
Morrow and Company, Inc. For information address William Morrow and
Company, Inc., 1350 Avenue of the Americas, New York, NY 10019.

First Onyx Printing, February 2000
10 9 8 7 6 5 4 3 2 1

REGISTERED TRADEMARK—MARCA REGISTRADA

Printed in the United States of America

PUBLISHER'S NOTE
This is a work of fiction. Names, characters, places, and incidents either are
the product of the author's imagination or are used fictitiously, and any
resemblance to actual persons, living or dead, business establishments, events,
or locales is entirely coincidental.

For
Glen and Richard

Prologue

The doctor sat behind the wheel of the Land Rover and watched the three lanky Quioco natives struggle as they poled the big log raft beneath him through a large grove of acacia trees that stood in three feet of water. They were having trouble maneuvering, and finally hung up the raft on a cluster of tree trunks. The technician, seated beside the doctor in the open-top vehicle, cursed softly in Russian—a curse the doctor didn't recognize—then stepped out to help the natives push off. He hadn't been in Africa long, the doctor decided. When they were free and into clear water again the Russian stayed with them, poling the final fifty yards or so to the eastern bank of the river. The doctor remained seated in the Land Rover. He sucked the final puffs from his cigar, then chucked the little stub into the water and watched it move downstream in the slow current. The husky Russian would be good for not much more than tasks like poling, he thought, since he was a poorly trained technician and of only average intelligence. His commitment was suspect, too.

The raft scraped up onto the bank, and the Russian now joined the natives in lashing it hard to two widely spaced trees. The doctor started the Land Rover's engine and drove it forward slowly, in first gear. It made the transition from raft to dry land with barely a jolt, but he kept moving until he was well up on hardpan before killing the engine. He lit a fresh cigar and drew on it with only the smallest sense of accomplishment. They were in Zaire. All very well, but it meant only that the easiest leg of the mission was behind them.

He paid the three Quiocos, then watched them pole into the darkness toward Angola without a backward glance, while the Russian checked that the cans of gasoline and the chests of field equipment were secure. He started the engine, shifted into first, and moved slowly up an incline, away from the water toward foliage thick enough to shield them from any early-morning river traffic. The Russian uncapped a bottle of vodka and held it toward the doctor, who looked at it disdainfully and said nothing. The Russian took a long swig of it, then smacked his lips loudly and exhaled a long, tired sigh. It was a plaintive sound the doctor had often heard from Russians after months in Africa. The Russian waited just a minute before raising the bottle to his lips again and draining a quarter of it in one prolonged draft, after which he sighed once more.

"That's unwise on this continent," the doctor said, as he brought the Land Rover to a stop. They conversed in English—the doctor's far more fluent than the Russian's—unless the Russian was excited or had drunk more than his usual measure of vodka, in which case he lapsed into his native tongue. The doctor understood more of it than he let on.

The Russian smiled, then took another long gulp before tucking the bottle back into its case. He rolled out a sleeping bag a few yards from the vehicle, zippered himself into it, and immediately fell into a deep sleep. The doctor was short enough to lie comfortably on his side across the front seats of the Land Rover, his knees only slightly bent. He covered himself with a thin blanket and asked Saint Theresa to protect him for the next twenty-four hours, an invocation he had managed to make every night of his life since kindergarten—fifty-three years' worth of prayer, often under terribly adverse conditions. It took only a few minutes for him to doze off.

He bolted upright at the Russian's first scream, instantly awake, his head clear and his hands gripping the

AK-47 as he dove to the floor of the Land Rover. There was no sign of humans or animals. The Russian continued to scream and thrash wildly inside his sleeping bag. In the dim, predawn light it took a few moments for the doctor to see that the ground around the sleeping bag was moving. A mass of several million driver ants were foraging on a front twenty or thirty feet wide. The bag itself was barely discernible under a thick coating of the large, black ants. The front would reach the Land Rover in a few minutes. He started the engine, then pulled one of the dozen jerry cans of gasoline from under a bungee cord, unscrewed the top, drenched his legs and shoes and arms and hands with gas, then walked forward deliberately onto the mass of ants.

"Ants!" he shouted in Russian. "Driver ants!" and poured gas all over the sleeping bag and onto the Russian's head. While the Russian continued to scream, both in panic and pain, the doctor unzippered the bag. Ants seemed to erupt out of it like a flow of black lava. He poured the remaining gas onto the Russian's body and dropped the can beside the bag as he pulled him erect. The Russian ran toward the river, bellowing now in a way the doctor had once heard a tethered cow bellow and stomp when overrun by driver ants. The doctor got into the Land Rover and drove gently in reverse for twenty feet or so before turning 180 degrees and heading for the river. Ahead of him, the Russian dove into the water and undressed in a squatting position. The doctor reached the riverbank as the Russian threw his last item of clothing ashore and walked out to shoulder depth, where he scrubbed his body with his bare hands and occasional handfuls of river mud, taking deep breaths then submerging his head and scrubbing his hair while underwater. After a bit he walked out of the water and stood on the bank in front of the doctor. His body, especially his torso, showed hundreds of tiny cuts, which the doctor knew were caused by the ants' very efficient mandibles—he had looked at driver ants under high magnifications. He had also heard village elders describe criminals being executed in years past by tying them to the ground near driver ant nests. The Russian slapped and picked at half a dozen spots on his body.

"These tiny ones—even the scrubbing didn't dislodge the little bastards," he said.

"Those are just heads," the doctor said. "Your scrubbing broke their bodies away. The heads are still biting. A driver ant can have its body severed and the head will continue to work the jaws for hours." He nodded his head admiringly, and added, "You've been attacked by one of the world's supreme predators."

He carried the vodka bottle to the naked, quivering Russian. "The best use for this would be to sterilize those cuts," he said.

The Russian took the bottle with a mumbled curse and lifted it to his lips.

They arrived twelve hours later just outside the tiny village that was their objective. While still a few miles away the doctor tensed expectantly, then made an effort to dampen his optimism. The reports that had reached him in Luanda were no different from the dozen others he had gotten during his seven years in Angola, each of which had proved a disappointment. He kept his hopes high, though, as certain now as he had been each time previously that this would be the one. The Russian slumped in the passenger seat, still demoralized by the ant swarm, and seemed to become uneasy as they got closer. The doctor swung into a wide arc to approach the village upwind.

They came upon the clearing suddenly and stopped at the edge to survey it from the Land Rover. There was the usual arrangement of large straw huts. No activity, no sounds. Dozens of small rodents that the doctor recognized as voles scurried off into the bush, many more than ought to be here. It was a good sign. The Russian pointed downwind, toward thirty or more bodies that lay in a neat row at the far edge of the clearing. Their hands weren't tied behind them and they hadn't been shot. Clearly the bodies had been laid there by villagers who had then run away. The doctor opened one of the equipment chests. He and the Russian pulled on plastic, hooded coveralls, flexible plastic boots that fit over their own, and surgical gloves. They wound several layers of duct tape tightly around the boot tops to form an air seal between boots and coveralls, then did the same gloves-to-coveralls. Finally, they pulled hooded respirators over their heads and wrapped tape around their necks, where the respirator hood ended. The doctor spent long minutes on this seal, knowing it was the most suspect part of his defense. As they left the Land Rover, the doctor, for the first time since leaving Luanda, removed the ignition key. He dropped it unobtrusively on the floor in back. He had doubts about the Russian's nerve.

There were more bodies in the huts. While he examined several of them, the Russian counted the dead. Sixty-eight. The doctor had never seen—had never even read of—symptoms as devastating as these. They had all bled from their eye sockets and had clearly vomited blood uncontrollably. Most of them had no fingernails or toenails, which had fallen off before they died. There were dozens of holes in each body—the skin must have peeled away in patches then actual holes formed through which they had hemorrhaged, holes that from the look of them might easily have been caused by a very aggressive bacterium. He didn't believe it was a bacterium, though. His gut told him that this was a viral hemorrhagic disease, and likely a brand-new one. Ebola, Marburg, Lassa fever—none of them caused actual holes in the skin or this kind of excessive bleeding from eye sockets.

In one of the huts a young woman was still alive, though in a coma. She had all the symptoms that the dead exhibited and was, at the most, hours away from dying. He drew blood from her into two vacutainers then held chloroform-soaked gauze over her nose and mouth until her heart stopped. He directed the Russian to collect blood from the most recently deceased victims, those in the huts. Meanwhile, the doctor performed a hasty autopsy on the young woman. He took a scalpel from his kit and forced himself to pause for a ten-count, to remind himself that this was by far the most dangerous

procedure he would be performing this day. The body
would surely spurt blood that would drench his protective suit, and scalpels frequently skidded off bones to
nick the suit, or worse, pierce his skin—a postmortem
required a heavy hand much of the time. Don't rush, he
told himself, then inserted the scalpel at the sternum and
pulled hard in a straight line down to the pelvis, blood
flooding out and covering his arms and the front of his
suit as he had known it would. He made long, horizontal
slices at the top and bottom of his vertical cut to form
an H, then folded back the two flaps. He shook his head
in disbelief at the devastation. It was like nothing he had
ever seen—an attack unrivaled by anything described in
the literature. Every organ was ravaged, as if an army
of maggots had feasted on it, the liver reduced to the
consistency of jelly. It seemed to be melting before his
eyes. He snipped out pieces of liver, spleen, lymph nodes,
and lung, then cut through for a piece of kidney, and
placed the samples carefully into small, sterile, containers. The terrible damage to her lungs made him hopeful
that the mode of transmission was airborne.

He and the Russian began to pack the samples into
the smallest of three large, nesting thermos bottles. That
bottle would be placed into the next largest one and the
space between packed with flakes of dry ice they would
make on the spot from a tank of carbon dioxide, then the
cover put on the second thermos, which in turn would be
set inside the third, largest one, again the space between
them filled with dry ice. Finally, the nested thermoses
would be sealed inside a plastic bag packed with cotton
toweling that the doctor would soak with bleach. It
would be more than enough insulation for the virus—
and he now had no doubt that it was a virus—to get back
safely to Luanda, where the dry ice would be replaced. In
a pinch, he reckoned, the present packaging would see
the virus safely to Havana.

"I want the blood samples divided now," the Russian
demanded suddenly. "Half and half. In separate thermoses. It's a better way than later." He spoke Russian.
The doctor pretended to understand only part of what

was said—he had pretended from the beginning that his Russian was poor, never letting on that he had lived and studied in Moscow for two years in the early 1970s. It gave him a small advantage in any situation. He rose from his squatting position and asked, haltingly, for the Russian to repeat it, then said that he might have a fourth thermos in the Land Rover, which would allow them to double-pack each of their samples. He went to the vehicle and searched through an equipment chest for a thermos he knew wasn't there, then returned empty-handed to where the Russian was already dividing the vacutainers and sample jars. When he was just behind the squatting Russian he deftly lifted his sidearm from its holster and, saying nothing, shot the Russian once in the back of the head. Moscow would have no need of these specimens, he thought, given the degeneracy they were regressing into. As he dragged the body across the ground and into the hut where the woman's open body lay, he regretted for a moment that his shot had ruined a respirator—they were not easy to come by in Africa—then remembered that he would be off this continent for good in just a few days. While he doused the two bodies and the sides of the hut with gasoline, he allowed himself to anticipate what home would be like after seven years out here. If this virus he was taking with him was new and was all it appeared to be—and especially, God willing, if its transmission was airborne—then this would be a virus of which dreams are made and he would receive a hero's welcome. A very private one but a hero's welcome nonetheless.

I

The secretary of state, Martin Anderson, fingered his page of notes impatiently while he waited for the phone call to end. Sharing the couch with him and skimming his own set of notes was the thirty-five-year-old Jaime Burne-Valera, his troubleshooter for Latin American affairs, a Harvard-educated, second-generation Bostonian acknowledged privately by everyone at State to be Anderson's intellectual superior. His grandfather, Don Guillermo Valera, a Venezuelan poet and political orator whose epic poem, *Song of the Liberator,* was a modern Spanish classic, had befriended and admired José Martí during the revolutionary's long exile from Cuba and later joined Martí in New York City where he helped found the Cuban Revolutionary party in 1893. Don Guillermo, during a weekend speaking engagement in Boston, had been introduced to the socially prominent, rebellious, eighteen-year-old Abigail Burne, an ardent feminist, at an afternoon tea in a Beacon Hill mansion. The couple had checked into the Ritz-Carlton a few hours later and remained in their suite for three days, after which Abigail sent for an Episcopalian minister, a second cousin, who married them in the hotel. Jaime's Latin genes, though outnumbered three-to-one, had acquitted themselves magnificently, in his coloring, hair texture, and an intense but private pride in his centuries-long Castilian heritage.

The President's phone call was approaching the ten-minute mark. Anderson glanced across at the Vice President, whom experience had taught to come forearmed with reading material—he perused an open folder on his lap—then at Tom Crowley, the young adviser who had a tighter grip on the President's ear than anyone else in the White House except the First Lady. What wisdom the holder of the world's most important job might glean from this ambitious yuppie was beyond Anderson. Tom stared blankly at the ceiling, the look of a man who had been through this often and knew of no solution but patience. All four of them studiously kept from watching the President, who, half an hour late because of a lengthened jog, had then taken the call just minutes into the meeting, and now fed himself a slow but steady stream of corn chips from a bowl on the desk as he spoke into the phone. The secretary had alerted the President yesterday that he would be placing what might well be a grade-one security matter on the presidential plate. He hadn't expected to be interrupted by a call about the replacement of a second-level deputy at Agriculture.

"I need to think about it some more," the President finally said. "I want to sleep on it."

He hung up and turned to the secretary.

"You're on, Andy."

"As you know, Mr. President, we've had Burne-Valera here meeting from time to time with Castro's people to see if we couldn't quietly work out a deal on refugees. Well, the Cubans requested a meeting for Monday and Jaime went."

He motioned for Jaime to speak.

"I've always met quietly in my hotel room with Jorge Fuentes, who is very much a second-level deputy in their diplomatic corps, almost precisely my counterpart, in fact."

Tom Crowley studied Jaime intently, and noted his remarkable equanimity in describing himself as second-level. Was it truly a lack of ego? Or supreme self-confidence? Or, most likely, a pose. In any event, it baffled him, since he harbored a constant resentment that the person seated in the President's chair was not himself.

"It was Fuentes I expected on Monday," Jaime continued. "Instead, I was driven to the outskirts of Havana, to an unmarked office in a converted house. A while later the door opened and in strode Mr. Fidel Castro."

It got everyone's attention, especially the President, who blurted out, "Fidel him*self*?" then looked to his secretary of state and said, "You never told me that, Andy."

"I believe I did, sir. You were up to your neck in the Iranian mess."

The President, easily star-struck in any event, asked Jaime, with a touch of reverence in his voice that bordered on obeisance, "What was the first thing he said to you?" It was Crowley's guess he hoped to hear that Fidel had sent warmest regards to the bright young President of the great United States. If so, Jaime disappointed him.

"He informed me that he could recite all of Books Three and Four of my grandfather's *Song of the Liberator* by heart. Then observed that were Don Guillermo alive today he would surely take up residence in Havana."

The President turned to Anderson, annoyed.

"Fidel himself. I wish you had made that clear yesterday, Andy. It puts this in a whole different light." He turned to Crowley and said, "Have somebody locate Millicent. I want her in on this."

As Crowley hurried from the room the President said, "Let's wait till she gets here. There's no point her having to play catch-up."

He reached for a corn chip and then the phone.

Things were off to the usual unfocused start, Anderson thought. The President had only been half listening yesterday.

Tom Crowley dispatched an assistant to find the First Lady, with instructions to inform him when she arrived at the meeting. He didn't return to the Oval Office, knowing that nothing substantive would be discussed until she arrived. He had known yesterday after Anderson's call that she ought to be included but the President had said no, they could call her in if need be. Everyone would now kill twenty minutes until she arrived. This seemed to be how a good part of every day passed, cobbling together things that should have been planned more carefully the day before. Ultimately, though, her presence would be well worth the delay, since no one could better manipulate the President into making a decision, something Crowley had watched her do more than once. Each time it put him in mind of sheepdog trials he had once watched in Maryland in which a single border collie in an open field would circle and dart for hundreds of yards and manage to drive a sheep, without ever touching it, into a small pen—a place it didn't want to enter. Since then, Crowley and a select few sometimes referred to the First Lady as the border collie. Without her nipping at his heels, even a grade-one security matter could sit on the President's plate for a long, long time.

He went into his office and found Linwood Cutshaw, the CIA director, seated comfortably in an armchair skimming a thick report. Crowley wasn't surprised to find him there. It had been planned yesterday during a phone call the President had placed after hearing from Anderson, requesting that Cutshaw bring to this morning's meeting whatever he might dig out overnight bearing on the possibility of Fidel Castro having some major new weapon. The President had then told him who would be attending.

"Will you extend me the liberty of being candid— maybe even blunt—Mr. President?" Cutshaw had asked, sweetening up a Carolina drawl as he always did when speaking to the President.

"You go right ahead, Cutty," the President had said in a sweetened drawl of his own.

"I've worked in this town a long time. When you hear the name Fidel Castro, it has about the same effect as hearing that a girl you've been pokin' has the clap. Makes you kind of suck in a big mouthful of air. Fidel has a long history of burning people in this town. Jack Kennedy underestimated him at the Bay of Pigs and the Mariel boatlift helped cripple Jimmy Carter and a whole lot of other politicians, too. My very own agency was laughed at for years because otherwise sane people here spent a lot of time figuring out how to make the man's beard fall out. A bunch of those people took early retire-

ments, 'cause the beard's just what became public. Over
a drink sometime I'll treat you to some Fidel-schemes
hatched over here that'll curl your hair. Mr. President,
initiatives to deal with Fidel Castro tend to put people
in positions like mine on some damn slippery slopes and
with all due respect to your secretary of state—loyal to
a fault, I'm sure—he's not the man I'd choose to be
protecting my flanks if I ever find myself sitting at a
microphone stutterin' up at a congressional committee.
Which is pretty much where I see that slippery slope
leading to. Naturally, I'll attend the meeting if you tell
me to. But I could speak a lot more openly—I could be
a lot more flexible in the options I lay out for you—if I
met just with you, the First Lady, and Tom Crowley.
That's a group I'd be happy to go behind enemy lines
with."

The President had paused before replying.

"Just be at the damn meeting, Linwood. And if you've
got a problem giving me a hundred percent at all times,
say so, 'cause frankly, I don't need a dog that won't
hunt," is what the President, after he hung up, thought
he should have said. He didn't. Although it had flashed
through his mind that if Cutshaw's monologue wasn't
insolent it was certainly condescending, his natural instincts had caused him to say, "Hell, Linwood, who you
so afraid of up there on the hill?" then laugh for a bit
before adding, "I'd rather have you coming from a comfortable position. You wait in Tom's office and we'll talk
after Andy and the others leave. Just the team you want
to go behind enemy lines with."

Now Crowley indicated the thick report in Cutshaw's
hand.

"Anything good in there?" he asked as he settled in
behind his desk.

Cutshaw glanced up and gave young Crowley a brief,
patronizing smile before returning to his reading.

He's one arrogant son of a bitch, thought Crowley,
even by the standards of Washington.

*   *   *

Half an hour later Tom Crowley's phone rang. The First
Lady was in the Oval Office. Crowley locked his desk
drawers, though he wondered why, as he did so, certain
that Cutshaw could and would pick the locks if he grew
curious. He left Cutshaw to his reading and note-making,
and went into the meeting. The border collie had been
brought up to speed and was listening intently, along
with the others, to Jaime Burne-Valera describe his
meeting with Castro. Her presence already had the President more focused—the corn chips had either been finished or put away.

"He was wearing the fatigues you always see him in,"
Jaime said. "Up close you realize they're tailor-made.
We shook hands and he said that usually he would spend
twenty minutes asking questions about the States. 'I lived
for a few years in Manhattan,' he reminded me. 'On
Eighty-fourth Street. But what I have to say today is too
important. I don't want to diminish it with small talk.'

"When he spoke there wasn't a hint of bluster or pos-
ing. His voice was soft. 'Nothing I say here is meant as
a threat,' he said. 'That isn't my purpose. Also, I don't
wish to convince you of anything. Be clear about that.
Just listen carefully and relay this with great accuracy to
your President. You're to be nothing more than a very
precise messenger. I mean no disrespect in using that
term. Cuba—poor, tiny, beleaguered Cuba—finds itself
able to make extraordinary demands on the United
States, and to have those demands met. This will happen
within weeks. When I present your President with this
dilemma, he won't have much time to respond—days
perhaps—and some of my demands will require him to
have set processes in motion earlier, to have moved political pieces into place, to have suitable public statements
prepared, maybe to have the secret agreement of congressional leaders. If he doesn't do these things in advance, he won't be able to act in time and that will be
a tragedy. I'm not asking today for any response from
your government—I will do that when I do it. This is
simply for your leaders to study. To be prepared for.
And to recognize the origin of an upcoming small disas-

ter that will soon occur in the U.S. There is no way your government would accede to our demands based upon a verbal threat. You need a demonstration of our power first. And you will soon get one, and know exactly from where it came.'

"I started to say that the United States doesn't take kindly to threats but he shut me up. It was the only time his temper flared. 'You haven't been listening,' he berated me. 'Would Cuba's head of state demean himself by threatening a messenger?' He waited for an answer and I said calmly that I assumed not. 'There is no threat,' he said. 'What your President will soon get is an actual demonstration, which will speak for itself. When your scientists study it they will tell him that we have the capability to quietly decimate perhaps forty *percent* of your population, to—' "

The Vice President interrupted, "He used the words 'quietly decimate'?"

"That's an exact translation," Jaime said. "*Tranquilamente devastar.* It stuck in my mind clearly just because it seemed such an odd choice of words."

"What do they want?" the President asked.

Anderson spoke. "He'll want an immediate, complete end of the embargo. Scheduled airline service between Havana and the U.S. Public recognition by the President of his legitimacy as Cuba's head of state. Public recognition of the United States' failed Cuba policy. I would think those are for openers."

The President laughed. "For the price I'd pay for that in Florida, these guys better have a couple of workable H-bombs."

"That's precisely the sense I came away with, Mr. President," Jaime said very seriously. "That he believes he's got something on that scale."

It sobered everyone. After a long silence, the First Lady turned to the President and asked, with some surprise in her voice, "Shouldn't we have Lin Cutshaw in on this?"

The President stroked his chin thoughtfully before answering, which Tom Crowley recognized as a signal for her not to pursue this, a signal Crowley had decoded a year ago. Neither the President nor the First Lady knew he was aware of it.

"I don't want him in too early," the President said. "I'll get to him later." He stood up, signaling that the meeting was over. "Let's all think some more about this. I don't have to say, not a word about this leaves the room."

As they stood, Anderson said, "Just one parting thought. I spent hours yesterday mulling this over. It's just a preliminary thought but I think it's worth putting on the table."

"Go ahead," the President said.

"If they've really got something, these demands aren't as disastrous as they seem at first blush. There might be—"

The Vice President interrupted forcefully, "Let's not even *think* about that. The United States of America cannot cave in to blackmail."

"Meeting these demands would be political suicide," Crowley said.

"I'm not advocating it," Anderson said. "But let's not close any options too soon."

"Let's close this one," the Vice President said. "Right now. Blackmail is an issue we've got to take a stand on."

The President showed a momentary irritation. The Vice President shouldn't have used the "take a stand" phrase, Crowley thought. It cut pretty close to the bone for the President.

The President waved them out, and said, "Let's all do what I just said. Let's all think some more about this."

The Vice President, Martin Anderson, and Jaime Burne-Valera filed out, leaving behind the trio with whom Linwood Cutshaw had magnanimously agreed to meet.

"Bring Cutty in," the President said to Crowley.

Cutshaw started off in his usual preemptory manner, draping his jacket over the back of the couch, then setting a six-inch-high stack of reports on the carpeted floor with just enough of a thud to draw attention to the obvious—that a lot of people had stayed up all night assembling them and that he was the person in the room in command of all this knowledge. He asked for "the details" in the tone that Crowley assumed he must use when seated with subordinates in his office overlooking the wooded countryside of northern Virginia. It irritated the President, who, Crowley was pleased to see, was not going to treat this meeting as an open-ended bull session in which everyone, including the Chief Executive, revealed all. Often, during Oval Office meetings, Crowley mused upon what a healthy thing it would be if the President played poker once a week with cronies, as Harry Truman had—it might accustom him to holding his cards closer to his vest.

"There are no details," the President said. "Just some rumblings over at State about Castro having an important new weapon. Probably all hot air but Andy's concerned."

Cutshaw paused long enough to make the point that he recognized a bald-faced lie when he heard one, and then kept them waiting for a long minute while he scanned the two pages of his own tiny, handwritten notes before laying them down and speaking. "*Important* new weapon. That's what we've focused on. Nuclear's the first thing we analyzed. Chances of that are essentially zilch. It's such a major undertaking to bring in the talent and resources that we would have picked up on it, and there's nothing on the screen of him getting stuff from places like Pakistan or China. So forget nuclear.

"It really leaves chemical or biological. Chemical's far less likely—it requires pretty large quantities of stuff and an elaborate delivery system. If they've got anything—and we believe they well might—it's biological."

There was a silence while they absorbed it; then the President asked, "You believe he might have something?"

"A virus," Cutshaw said.

"How bad is that?" the First Lady asked.

"About as bad as it gets, if they've got the right virus."

"What does 'the right virus' mean?" she asked.

"One way to think about it is a virus as lethal as the HIV/AIDS virus—neighborhood of ninety percent—but one that goes from infection to full-blown disease in maybe a week instead of four or five years, and is airborne, like a common cold or influenza virus instead of needing an exchange of bodily fluids."

"Does anything close to that exist?" the President asked.

Cutshaw nodded. "Indeed they do. And now imagine someone getting that virus"—he slowed his speech and emphasized every word—"into a big, enclosed, crowded space. Maybe right over in the Smithsonian, with its fifty thousand visitors a day. Say only five thousand were to be infected and carry the virus back with them to the fifty states before anyone had a hint there was a problem. Each of them on an airplane sharing recirculated cabin air with a few hundred other passengers who are going to disperse to other planes and other places. Each of those five thousand men, women, and children might easily infect a hundred people just while traveling. And each of *those* people . . ."

He trailed off and gave them the tough, knowing look of a veteran cold warrior who had evaluated a lot of doomsday scenarios in his time. His audience of three were properly affected, the President especially. This was not the kind of problem he had ever confronted.

"You said Castro might really have something like this," the President said. "Why?"

"There have been hints. Airy little rumors over the years in the Miami and Jersey City expatriate communities that a doctor down in the Zapata swamp seemed to be running some funny experiments. There were also rumors from Angola and Zaire that a Cuban doctor might have carried samples of a deadly virus off the continent. Nothing substantial but enough to find their way into reports. Where they just sat, 'cause there's always whispers floating around out there about some new doomsday weapon. Then, last year, the World Health Organization held a week-long virology conference in Copenhagen and the Centers for Disease Control in Atlanta sent four of their virologists. One of them was a fellow with contacts in the intelligence community."

"What's that mean?" the President interrupted. "With contacts?"

Cutshaw studied the three of them for a few moments before answering, his lips pursed appraisingly, as though wondering whether it was prudent to pass this sort of classified information on to the President. Watching him, Crowley found himself more admiring than angry at the man's enormous arrogance. He sensed that the President was intimidated by it, and made a mental note that there were things to be learned from Cutshaw, who now apparently concluded that his audience could be trusted.

"All through the cold war the military conducted research on biological warfare, a lot of it right over at Fort Detrick in Maryland. The CDC in Atlanta kept clear of it. There are a lot of humanitarian types work down there, besides which some of the epidemiological studies they deal with need international cooperation. They never wanted to be tainted with warfare research. This virologist I mentioned was at CDC but he would perform consulting work for Fort Detrick secretly. Literally no one at CDC knew of it. He happens to have what I would call an intelligence mind-set, and let's say a more realistic assessment of the world than most of his CDC colleagues, and so he'll pass things on to us that he thinks are important.

"Well, late one night in Copenhagen he found himself in the hotel bar with some of his European opposite numbers, swapping anecdotes about viral outbreaks around the world. A Russian virologist told a story that took place in Angola in 1989. The Soviets still had people in Angola then. So did the Cubans. Including a doctor—a physician—who had some advanced training in virology as well. He was hoping to get his hands on a virus suitable for warfare and he had a kind of loose information network spread over Angola, Zaire, and Zambia. Apparently he got lucky in '89 and got to an isolated viral outbreak in western Zaire, along with a Russian techni-

cian—the Soviets for years prowled around Africa trying
to latch onto deadly viruses. Hell, we all did. The Russian
never came back from the village. Over the next year or
so the Soviets accused the Cubans of foul play and bad
faith but by then the USSR was falling apart. Gorbachev
was sucking air and there was another closet capitalist
coming out in the Politburo every week on CNN. Castro
saw them as weak and decadent. He ignored them.

"This Russian in Copenhagen believed that the Cuban
had brought back to Havana a virus that was a public
health official's nightmare—something with the charac-
teristics I just mentioned. The Russian's story, the rumors
in the Miami community, the rumors out of Cuba itself,
everything together makes us believe it's true. Castro
most likely has a weapon that's deadly and that we can't
do much about."

Cutshaw next delivered a brief discourse on virology, employing just enough medical and biological nomenclature
to give it an academic gloss that he knew would appeal
to the President. He then took from an envelope a dozen
eight-by-ten, black-and-white glossy photos, and warned,
"As they say on the evening news, this is graphic foot-
age, folks."

He handed them across to the President, and said,
"These were taken in the Crimea in the mid-seventies.
We got them from some of the Soviet files that were
opened up a few years ago. You're looking at victims of
a hemorrhagic virus that hit a small community on the
Black Sea. The Russian virologists who investigated it
believe it's carried by fleas, about like the bubonic
plague. The plague, incidentally, is bacterial."

The President paled but forced himself to examine
each photo at length, as though committing it to memory.
Then he looked across his desk at Cutshaw and said,
"My God." It was the reaction Cutshaw had hoped for,
the reason he had selected the most gruesome photos
from the files. The President had little in his background
to prepare him for a problem like this. The photos were

meant to make the threat, and the need to take action, real for him. They did.

The First Lady and Crowley recoiled from the pictures but managed to get through them all. She was visibly shaken, and sensed that Cutshaw was pleased by it. She had never much cared for him and now his air of superiority from the moment he entered the room, along with her own difficulty in confronting the photos, suddenly angered her. She also believed—correctly—that Cutshaw held the President in low regard, and she resented his presumption that he had to lead her husband by the hand through a course that just might prove too tough for him. That she knew handholding was indeed what her husband needed for this only intensified her resentment of Cutshaw.

"I suppose people in your world learn to treat pictures like these pretty impersonally," she said to him, in a more accusatory tone than she had intended.

"Close to it," he said.

"It must dull your capacity for compassion."

He shrugged that off and said, "I wouldn't know. In my world people don't evaluate one another on things like capacity for compassion. Or empathy, or sympathy, or sensitivity. Not even on self-actualization."

The complete lack of derisiveness in his voice made his needling even more effective.

"What do they evaluate one another on?" she asked.

"Oh. Courage and loyalty and fortitude and devotion to duty. And when that requires dulling your capacity for compassion, you do it. The way a surgeon does it." He gave a deprecatory little smile, and added, "It's not very up-to-date. More a nineteenth-century kind of value system."

She returned the smile, but liked him even less now. His complete lack of defensiveness had made her appear naive rather than morally superior.

Cutshaw moved on to the next segment of his notes. He addressed the President.

"What will Castro do next?" he asked rhetorically, and paused for a long time before answering. "He's going to first lay some set of demands on you. If his virus is as deadly as I believe it is, then he's going to demand an end to the embargo, public groveling, that sort of thing."

The President, and the other two as well, were clearly impressed. Cutshaw basked in the glow for a few moments before continuing with his performance.

"After they communicate their demands? My guess is that they'll conduct some kind of 'demonstration' for your benefit."

It bowled his audience over. The President, with the tone of a student awed by a professor, asked, "How do you *know* that?"

"Because for hours last night I thought real hard on it, Mr. President."

Even the First Lady gave him an admiring nod.

"He'll have to find someplace in the States isolated enough so things don't get out of hand, but where he can infect some people, report it to us, and have our virologists go in and confirm for you that, yes, it's the real McCoy. That means getting the virus into this country and—here's the crucial part—having it in the hands of someone expert enough to dispense it."

"Is it that tough to do?" Crowley asked.

Cutshaw smiled at the young man and slowed his drawl to a snail's pace. "It ain't like broadcasting seed on a still day, Tom. You don't want stuff like this in the hands of some bright lab technician. And they'll be coming here with a detailed plan for a much bigger event if we don't cave in on the demonstration. The Smithsonian kind of thing." He paused to let that sink in, then said, "It's the doctor who Fidel has sent. You can bet on it."

"*Sent?*" the President said. "What do you mean, *sent?*"

"Oh, he's here," Cutshaw said. "Castro wouldn't be talking to the State Department unless the doctor was already here."

He paused again and looked at the President, then said softly, "I assume he *has* talked to State already, hasn't he."

Only the First Lady maintained a noncommittal countenance; the others registered surprise at his final bit of deduction.

"The doctor is here. And the virus, too," he said, then sat back, wanting them to absorb the implications. The President did just that. He swiveled his chair a quarter turn and looked out of the floor-to-ceiling windows. His expression, Cutshaw thought, was that of a man who wished he was somewhere else. After a bit he turned back into the meeting and mused aloud, "What the hell do we *do*?" He looked toward the First Lady and Crowley as he said it.

They looked to Cutshaw, who mulled it over, then shook his head slowly.

"Illegal. Any countermeasures we take will have to be done on American soil. And the law is clear as a bell on that. No CIA. Dulles or Casey would have said, no problem, and assigned fifty agents to it anyway. And everybody would have closed their eyes. The world has changed."

"Christ, there must be a mechanism to deal with this," the President said. "What's the right way to do it?"

"By the right way do you mean the legal way?" Cutshaw asked.

Both the First Lady and Tom Crowley shook their heads, yes, well before the President did.

"Bring in the FBI," Cutshaw said evenly. "They're legally empowered to handle this." After a few moments he added, "But you'll have to close your eyes to two important facts. One, they'll be so busy covering their asses and writing the future PR releases that they'll botch it. Two, by its nature this is not an operation that can succeed without cutting legal corners, and speaking bluntly, the guy who's running the bureau won't do it."

He smiled at the First Lady. "He doesn't have a nineteenth-century value system."

"Maybe we could resurrect Hoover," she said.

Cutshaw pretended to miss the sarcasm and said, "I'd love to. The bastard was blackmailing half the town but hell, that just made him even hotter to cut corners on a piece of work like this. Hoover knew how to come through for a President who needed him. The guy you've got over there now wouldn't let an agent jaywalk on his way to make an arrest. We just may have become a bit too moral for our own good."

"You wanted the attendance here limited so you'd feel free to give me options," the President said. "Give me some."

"There's just one option that makes sense. Because, *it will work.* This project should be subcontracted. Farmed out to a private individual who'll be able to bring the doctor very quietly into a secure environment and through him get hold of the viruses, too. I would personally run the subcontractor. Not another soul at the Agency would know of this."

There was a long silence, finally broken by Crowley.

"Christ, but it sounds like Nixon's plumbers," he said.

"Nixon's plumbers were near morons. Worse, they were amateurs."

"Whom would you subcontract this to?" the First Lady asked. "Who is he?"

"You don't want to know that," Cutshaw said.

She considered that, then nodded her agreement and asked, "What if he's exposed somehow?"

"The very worst that happens is he gives me up," Cutshaw said. "And that's unlikely. If it did happen, I'd claim I was acting on my own. In the larger interest of national security. That part is accurate, by the way."

The President looked miserable. "God, it all just feels like Iran-Contra. I'm sure people sat here and meant well, too."

"Think of the successful stuff," Cutshaw said. "The stuff that worked over the years and never came to light."

"Has *anything* in this town not come to light over the years?" Crowley asked.

"Oh, yeah," Cutshaw said. "The stuff that was subcontracted. And even the ones that went bad—like Iran-Contra—who really got hurt?" He turned to the President. "Judging by the treatment the public gave the adolescent

Marine colonel, if I got exposed for this I just might be the candidate running against you in the next election."

The President smiled.

"It's one of his saving graces," Cutshaw thought, "a fairly ready smile."

"The three of us are going to have to kick this around and then I'm going to sleep on it," the President said.

Cutshaw pulled on his jacket and picked up his pile of reports.

"Do you want to hold on to the photographs while you kick it around?" he asked.

"We've seen them," the President said. He was testy for the first time.

Cutshaw walked across the room and turned in the doorway to address the President. "You can't delay on this, you know."

Before the President's testiness could resurface, the First Lady nodded her understanding of that.

Cutshaw settled into the backseat of the seven-thousand-pound limo that had been stretched just fourteen inches at the time it was armored. It gave him the legroom he needed yet at first glance the car appeared to be a production-line sedan. He told his driver to take the leisurely route to Langley, turned off the gooseneck lamp behind him, and closed his eyes for a catnap, setting his internal alarm for ten minutes, something he had been able to do since childhood. He was now nearly sixty and still it took just a brief nap to refresh him, a faculty his mother had always attributed to military genes passed down from both the Linwoods and the Cutshaws. His maternal great-grandfather had lost a leg leading a charge of the First Carolina Rifles at Antietam, while his own father, a VMI graduate and protégé of George Marshall, had been a brigadier general when he was killed in the Battle of the Bulge. Linwood, an only child, had disappointed his mother by turning down an appointment to West Point, going instead to Harvard for degrees in mathematics and philosophy. A professor there recruited him into the CIA as an analyst in 1957, a week before *Sputnik* was launched. He had never left the Agency.

He awoke ten minutes later. The pile of reports on the seat beside him was a reminder of how impressed the meeting participants had been with his ability to assemble so much data overnight. They had been even more impressed with his certainty that Castro was already talking to State, and his prediction that Castro's next move would be a demonstration rather than a full-scale attack, which was precisely what Burne-Valera had told them earlier. Those feats resulted from a circumstance that Cutshaw had decided to keep to himself—the sequestered Havana office in which Castro had met secretly with Burne-Valera, and in which all planning for this whole top-secret project took place, was wired. The bug had been installed six months earlier by a Havana telephone technician whose relatives in Miami were paid eighty thousand dollars out of Cutshaw's discretionary funds. Late in the day Monday, just hours after Castro had met with Burne-Valera, a transcript of the meeting had been placed on Cutshaw's desk. It had given him all that night plus Tuesday morning to dig out files and analyze the situation before receiving the President's call yesterday for today's meeting. He had taken along a copy of the transcript this morning with the intention of presenting it to the President, even visualizing, during the ride into Washington, the nonchalant gesture with which he would place it on the Oval Office desk, along with a good-ole-boy comment about primitive Cuban security measures, delivered in a heavy drawl. He had relished the drama of that little moment. But the President, while confiding in his self-righteous wife and thirty-something aide, had chosen not to make the head of the Agency a first-team player. His unwillingness even to divulge that Burne-Valera had met with Castro galled Cutshaw. He had decided at that moment to keep his knowledge of the Havana bug to himself. It meant forgoing the President's awe at the Agency's omnipotence but that would be short-lived in any event. Over the long haul, secrecy had its advantages. It would allow him to appear nearly clairvoyant at times, as he had earlier in the Oval Office—a happy circumstance for an intelligence agency head—and it would keep the President in the dark, a situation that Cutshaw believed would best serve both the President and the country at large. The man struck him as incapable of keeping a secret, someone who would, at the least, confide in Anderson and, at the worst, seek advice from his political consultants. To inform the President of the bug would be to hear the morality of it being debated on *Nightline* a week later. As they crossed the Potomac into Virginia he was more than comfortable with his decision—he felt nearly virtuous. He was protecting this President from himself.

The downside to keeping the bug secret—and it gnawed at him more than a little—was that he couldn't pass on the additional knowledge picked up on it since Burne-Valera's meeting. The Cuban doctor was actually still in Cuba, not due here for another ten days. That was to the good—telling the President he was here pressured him to act. But most important, he hadn't been free to inform the President that the virus was indeed already here, brought into the country weeks ago by a Cuban agent now awaiting the doctor's arrival, the virus safely stored somewhere on the East Coast. What the bug had never picked up was, where.

II

Chuck Breslin had his coat on and was halfway across his small office when the phone rang behind him. He stopped to listen as the machine picked up. It was a recently acquired client, George Glasgow, an importer of expensive glassware who was trying to have a proprietary line of hand-painted dinnerware manufactured in Latvia. He had engaged Breslin to deal with the necessary Latvian government officials, a euphemism for paying off the right people the right amounts. While Glasgow told the machine that he was confirming their next morning's breakfast date at the Algonquin, Breslin started to reach for the handset, then decided instead to return the call later. Glasgow's money was important to him but their phone conversations were never brief, and he had only fifteen minutes to walk to his lunch with Lin Cutshaw, who was a great believer in promptness.

Breslin locked the door behind him and took the elevator seventy-eight floors down to the lobby, where the usual weekday group of suburban grade-schoolers waited on line for an elevator to the observation deck. It reminded him, as always, that he was in the Empire State Building and gave him a momentary lift. As a kid playing in the streets of Greenpoint he had been filled with wonder that he lived in sight of the world's tallest building. He would look across the river and try to imagine what the city might look like from the top of it, until, one day, he played hooky from the third grade and found his way along three different subway lines to the building. He had stepped into the elevator with a class from Syracuse and spent hours on the observation deck before returning home after dark to find that a missing-child bulletin was out on him. His father had given him one of the few beatings of his childhood but it hadn't stopped him from returning to the building from time to time. Three years ago, when he opened his one-man consulting firm, he had felt the same child's sense of wonder at being able to sublet two hundred square feet of space in the building.

He walked at a brisk pace east on Thirty-third Street. That Cutshaw had chosen an out-of-the-way, mediocre French restaurant on Lexington Avenue signified a business meeting—the Four Seasons' Grill Room was invariably the director's choice for a New York lunch at which he felt free to be seen with his guest. This could simply turn out to be an offer of work, but Breslin had a nagging fear that it wasn't, that someone in the Agency had gotten onto and reported him. That would bring down Cutshaw's wrath, and God knew what further repercussions. There was no concrete reason to believe that had happened, though—more than likely it was just his own guilt fueling that fear. He hoped that was so, and that it was a piece of off-the-books work Cutshaw was bringing to the table. He liked to think that his services were missed.

He had resigned from the Agency three years earlier, having been bitten, inexplicably, by the money bug, and convinced that a one-man consulting outfit for American businesses wanting to tap into the emerging Eastern European markets could easily become a six-man outfit, able to generate a high-six-figure income for its founder. It hadn't quite worked out. He had drawn $150,000 last year—a living. When he left the Agency, Cutshaw had said that he might sometime be called upon to take a freelance assignment. During his eleven-year tenure Breslin had become a favorite of Cutshaw's and the feeling was reciprocated, though they seemed an unlikely pair, the director the only child of a Charleston family in America since 1690, Breslin, nearly twenty-five years his junior, raised in Brooklyn as the youngest of twelve children. He had slept, for the first three months of his life, in the pulled-out bottom drawer of his parents' bedroom dresser, as had the eleven siblings who preceded

him. His father had worked his entire adult life for Bell
Telephone, handling customer complaints in a Manhattan office where he died at his desk of a heart attack
just a few years short of retirement. At the wake the
family discovered that for forty years even his closest
colleagues had believed Peter Breslin was father to four
children—for reasons of his own he had confided in no
one that there were twelve. Chuck came to believe that
four was the number of children his father had truly
wanted, for he remembered an evening in the early 1960s
when his father, a man who received communion every
Sunday of his life, who sent each of his twelve offspring
to Catholic school, slammed down his evening paper
after reading that the mass would now be celebrated in
English and that liberalization was the pope's order of
the day.

"If they relax the birth control ban now I'll never set
foot in a church again," he had said, then left the room
ready to burst with anger.

Unlike Lin Cutshaw's mother, who had been disappointed when her son chose Harvard over West Point,
Maureen Breslin had been thrilled that her Chuck had
gone straight from St. Francis Xavier High School into
the Army, where he excelled in one of the elite airborne
divisions, after which he graduated City College then put
himself through St. John's Law School at night. For the
eleven years that he then worked for the CIA she, along
with the rest of his family, believed he was employed in
the legal section of the Commerce Department, a job
that required a lot of travel. Despite her old-fashioned
patriotism there were pieces of work that he did during
those years that would have caused her great moral
anguish.

Breslin nursed a glass of red wine. He wanted a second
glass but was deterred by the small bottle of Perrier in
front of Cutshaw, who he knew enjoyed a daily ration
of two or three stiff bourbons but was from the sun-over-the-yardarm school of drinking. They sat at a wall table
and shared a large crock of coq au vin, ordered despite

the waiter's strong recommendation of pig's feet bourgu-
ignon. Cutshaw had taken the opportunity to go into his
good-old-boy mode, explaining to Breslin, "I prefer to
eat a little higher off the hawg than that," then asked in
the same friendly tone, "So tell me 'bout this consulting
work you do, Chuck."

"Overseas investment opportunities. I'm a facilitator."

"A good few of the people who leave the Agency
these days are doing just that. Oilers, we call 'em. You
facilitating anything right now?"

"A little bit. In Riga."

Cutshaw nodded. Breslin had been involved in Latvian
and Lithuanian affairs for a while at the Agency.

"How's business otherwise?"

"Slow."

"What kind of money you bringing home?"

"You must know that, Linwood. To the dollar. You
didn't come up here dumb."

"I didn't have time," Cutshaw said, then smiled. "I'll
run a check when I get back."

It was a lie. He had no intention of doing anything
that might leave even vestiges of a connection between
Breslin and himself.

"I'm managing," Breslin said.

Cutshaw indicated the nearly empty wineglass and
asked, "You ready for another?"

"I'm fine. One's enough at lunch."

They ate silently for a bit, then Cutshaw asked, "How
far out on a limb you willing to go for your country these
days, Chuck?"

"As far out as always."

"Well that's plenty far enough," he said approvingly.
"The assignment I'm looking to lay off on you is a bitch,
plain and simple. It'll make your old days in airborne
seem easy."

Breslin had to keep from exhaling a loud sigh of relief.
This was about work—it had, in fact, been his own guilt
making him fearful of having been discovered.

"This thing is illegal from start to finish," Cutshaw
said. "It's domestic, so we're breaking the law right there

and the operation will be criminal all by itself. You'll be committing a federal felony. Likely a couple of state ones, too."

Cutshaw let that sink in, then added, "Stuff that carries long prison terms."

"Like what?"

"I want you to kidnap somebody."

"Well that sure is a federal felony, Linwood. Where?"

"Right here in New York."

"An American?"

"A foreign national."

"Doesn't sound all that tough," he said. There was a quizzical note in his voice.

"I haven't finished. It gets tougher as it goes along."

"Uh-oh," Breslin said.

Cutshaw nodded. "That happens to be an appropriate response in this case." He motioned to the waiter to refill Breslin's glass and said, "It's written all over your face."

"How well protected is he?" Breslin asked.

"Fair to good. But that's less crucial than this—if his government suspects it's us who've got him, it's a disaster. And they'll be half expecting it. Or something like it. We're going to have to make this look like some run-of-the-mill criminals grabbed him. That he was in the wrong place at the wrong time in what the world knows is a crime-ridden country. It needs terrific cover, and the only cover I see for it is to grab two or three legitimate citizens along with him."

"Some run-of-the-mill criminals kidnap three or four people at once? That's going to play?"

"Not if they're kidnapped for ransom. But I think it'll play if they're taken as hostages in some kind of robbery."

Breslin let out a soft "Whew."

"I said it gets tougher as it goes along."

"You know how much cooperation you can expect from the local cops here. What kind of robbery are you capable of staging in New York?"

"We can't stage anything. This has to be the real McCoy."

Breslin studied him for a few moments, then asked seriously, "Is this for real, Linwood? Or is this some elaborate gag?"

"It's as real as it gets. I'm asking you to *do* an armed robbery. A *real* armed robbery. During which you and your accomplices grab three or four people who you take along as hostages, one of them our target. All of it so bona fide that our target's government truly believes their guy simply ran into a piece of bad luck."

"What kind of robbery?"

Cutshaw hesitated, then said, "A very elaborate one. So elaborate it'll fool the target's government. It's tough but doable. There'll be four of you. Which is another big problem in this scheme. I have to limit it to *the minimum number of operatives*. There'll be no backup, no support people to jump in when there's a glitch. This op can't tolerate a glitch."

"And if someone gets in our way during this? That happens during robberies. A cop. A security guard. Some taxpayer playing hero?"

"You do whatever a robber does in a given situation."

"And if the cop, or security guard, or taxpayer ends up dead?"

Cutshaw said deliberately, "We can live with that."

"Who's 'we'?"

"Me, and the President," Cutshaw said.

Breslin studied his face for a bit. "*This* President said that?"

"Without blinking. I met with him Tuesday morning," he lied. "And I raised exactly that point with him—that people can get killed in robberies. He said we have no choice. I agree with him."

"You and the President might be able to live with a cop being killed but if I get nailed I'm not sure I'll be able to live with it. The death penalty is back in New York."

Cutshaw concentrated on separating the last shreds of chicken from a thighbone.

"Who the hell is this guy, Linwood?" Breslin asked. "What are you going to get out of him that's so crucial?"

"What do you know about biological weapons?"

"Nothing."

"Are you finished eating?"

"Yeah. Why?"

Cutshaw took from his nicely worn attaché case the glossy photos that had thrown the First Lady so off balance. He handed them to Breslin.

"This is what a really virulent, hemorrhagic virus does to its host," he said.

Breslin examined each photo at length. His face remained impassive but Cutshaw could see that the pictures were making an impression. And he hadn't gotten to the children yet. When he set down the photos, Cutshaw waited a bit for the images to sink in before speaking.

"A hemorrhagic virus—if it's airborne—is a terrorist's wet dream. First off, no one even knows an attack has occurred. America just goes about its business. And think about the numbers, Chuck. To infect five thousand people in one day is completely feasible. If each one infects just five other people a day, after four days you've got three *million* victims. *And still no one knows we've been attacked.* A virus able to do that is already in the country. The guy we're after is coming here to disseminate it. We've got to get hold of him. And in a way so no one suspects we've got him, or they'll let some second-stringers set this damn stuff loose in a couple of sports arenas or rock and roll concerts. You got any nieces or nephews who go to rock concerts?"

Breslin considered for a long minute, then said, "Who else am I with on this?"

"You have someone in mind?"

"No. But I want to know who's picking them."

"I am."

"Then that part's good enough. Tell me about the operation."

"Some background. Seven years ago we found ourselves having to confirm someone's identity in one hell of a hurry. We had stumbled onto an Israeli intelligence operative in Los Angeles who was plundering a couple of big oil companies for scientific and industrial data. Mostly state-of-the-art exploration techniques. Nothing much to get excited about—he wasn't even working for the Mossad. One of the Israeli scientific agencies had him on their payroll. We were about to hand it to the FBI, then suddenly discovered he was moonlighting for the Soviets, with an active pipeline into the stealth bomber program at Lockheed, but with nothing provable in an American or Israeli court. Well, the most effective move was to grab him off during one of his regular trips to Mexico City, have him confirm who his contacts were inside Lockheed, then take him out in what would be a mugging gone awry, and let the Israelis figure it all out for themselves. We snared him easily enough in a prostitute's apartment, but then Murphy's Law kicked in. He denied his identity, well enough so the operatives on the scene developed legitimate doubts. Then the safe house they had lined up turned out to be no good. You know the kind of muddle—we might have hold of the wrong man and we had just hours to make a decision. Our target had made two visits to a dentist the year before during a stay in New York. He was under surveillance each time. We decided on the spur of the moment to send two operatives into the dentist's office in the middle of the night. Simple and straightforward. This was a street-level office in a small apartment building on the East Side of Manhattan. No doorman. It should have been a walk. Our guys found the records easily enough, but as luck would have it they stepped out of the office door smack into an off-duty detective on his way to his girlfriend's apartment upstairs. They took a crack at overpowering him but that didn't work out real good— with all their expensive training, they ended up handcuffed together on the floor, the younger guy with a split in his forehead that took eight stitches later that night. They got desperate enough to tell him they were intelligence guys, and because they were only carrying out a couple of X rays he was smart enough to figure that just might be.

"He let them put through a phone call and our emer-

gency supervisor woke me at home. I called the dentist's
office and near begged the detective to hold tight for
half an hour. The man had a sense of humor, because
he told me he was on his own time for one thing and
was pretty anxious to get up to his girlfriend's apartment
for another. He waited, though. And given the media
coverage he would have got out of nailing two of our
guys in a dirty operation, that spoke volumes to me
about his character. I was real close with a Deputy Inspector in the NYPD who I roused out of bed at three
A.M., and did he put his neck out for us. He hustled over
to the dentist's office and talked to the detective. They
let our guys walk. With the X rays. The deputy inspector
I expected it from, but not the detective. You know,
when you're cutting some corners off in real big chunks,
you sure don't want it to go bad in San Francisco or
New York City—you want to be in a small town smack
in the middle of America. Cross the street from the
American Legion post that half the police force belong
to. It made me want to thank the detective personally."

"And was the Israeli lying?" Breslin asked.

"Yeah. We had the right guy all the time. Well, I made
a point of coming up to New York the following day and
buying the detective dinner at Le Cirque and then a
whole lot of drinks afterward at a place in Greenwich
Village he knew pretty well. He was good drinking company—a New York Eyetalian you'd take for a Swede.
We swapped a bunch of war stories. One of them was a
case he had worked on years earlier that caught my attention enough for me to pull all the news clippings on
it when I got back to Langley. It came back to me yesterday while I was scratching my head about how to get
hold of our target without tipping our hand that it's him
we're after. You see, this marvelous bug we've got in
place tells us that our target—a physician, by the way—
will arrive at Kennedy in the wee hours, meet his contact
here, and the two of them will check into a very upscale,
very low-profile, midtown hotel. Lord knows how or why
they picked that particular spot for their night in New

York. Maybe 'cause it's the very last place that a terrorist from the country in question would be expected to stay."

He went into his attaché case and brought out copies of newspaper clippings and magazine articles. He smiled as he handed them across the table, not his tight, cold-warrior, meant-for-effect smile but one that carried genuine delight. The top clipping was a *Daily News* front page.

GUNMEN TAKE $3 MIL
FROM MIDTOWN HOTEL
24 HELD HOSTAGE
FOR 3 HOURS

"It's ballsy, Chuck. About as ballsy as it gets. These guys actually *occupied* the hotel, the way you would on a commando raid. Damn, if four thieves could pull it off, sure as hell we can. And it's so elaborate—hell, it's so *outlandish*—makes you want to do it just because it's there to be done."

"Kind of like Everest," Breslin said flatly.

"Kind of like Everest," Cutshaw said. He seemed to take pleasure in the analogy.

III

Breslin was back at his desk twenty minutes later, copies of the newspaper clippings in front of him. He turned to the *Daily News* story first, which had appeared on page 3.

BANDITS GET $3 MIL AT HOTEL QUINCY

Four well-dressed bandits who arrived and departed in a stretch limousine seized control of the elegant Hotel Quincy at 2 A.M. yesterday and held 24 employees and guests captive for 3 hours while looting nearly 100 safe deposit boxes of $3 million in cash and jewelry.

Chief of detectives John Raggio said that the description of the gang and their methods fit the robberies of two fashionable midtown hotels earlier in the year, the Chichester and the Barnes House, in which $90,000 in cash was taken plus half a million in jewelry.

The 300-unit Quincy on Central Park South caters to socialites and millionaires and has hosted such notables as Winston Churchill, Jean Paul Getty, and Darryl Zanuck over the years.

Guard Greets Limousine

The hotel doors are locked between 1 A.M. and 6 A.M. with a security guard stationed inside the main entrance to admit late-arriving guests. Four additional guards are on duty through the night. A black stretch limousine arrived at about 2 A.M. and discharged three well-dressed men carrying luggage who said they had reservations. Guard George McSwiggan, a retired Yonkers policeman, unlocked the door for them. He then saw that the third man wore a false nose, mustache, and eyebrows. They were followed into the posh lobby by the "chauffeur," who wore a similar disguise.

Handcuffed and Blindfolded

One of the gunmen disarmed McSwiggan while a second handcuffed the desk clerk. A third went off and returned with another security guard. The bandits then rounded up 14 more employees, including porters, bellhops, and maintenance workers. Seven guests, four of them late arrivals, were added during the course of the robbery. All of the captives were handcuffed, their eyes covered with tape, then made to lie facedown on the plush carpets and Persian rugs of a conference room adjacent to the lobby. The bandits repeated over and over, "Don't look at our faces. Don't remember anything. We know where you live, we'll kill you." They took identification from each captive. No one was injured during the robbery.

The bandits located in the cashier's office a list of guests who had stored valuables in the 300 hardened-steel safe-deposit boxes located behind the cashier's desk and concentrated on those of couples and single women. "Those are the ones most likely to contain gems," Chief Raggio said. Throughout, one bandit manned the desk and fielded incoming phone calls.

Gentlemen Bandits

At 3 A.M. Dr. Dieter Schmidt, visiting from Vienna, rang for the elevator on the eleventh floor, where he was leaving the suite of his mother-in-law to rejoin his wife in their eighth-floor suite. Dr. Schmidt said the robber manning the elevator, who wore a Hotel Quincy uniform jacket, pulled a gun and took him back to get his mother-in-law, Mrs. Helga Loewendahl, of Brussels. They then stopped at the eighth floor to pick up Mrs. Schmidt and proceeded downstairs where the three guests joined the handcuffed group on the conference room floor.

As a bandit started to remove a valuable gold locket from Mrs. Schmidt's neck she asked if she could remove the photographs of her grandparents. The bandit then told her to "keep the whole thing. We don't want to damage your pictures."

There was a separate "human interest" box below the main story.

A NICE WAY TO BE ROBBED

Pasquale D'Amico, a porter, expressed the sentiments of many of the captives when he said, "No question about it, these guys behaved like gentlemen. There was no rough stuff. If you're going to be robbed this is the way you want it to be. And they didn't take a dime from any of the workers. Nothing."

Dr. Dieter Schmidt, a guest taken captive during the robbery, said that the bandit who operated the elevator was courteous, however, "he had trouble leveling the car at the lobby. He showed admirable persistence though, and finally got it just right." He added that, courteous as the bandits were, "it was a harrowing experience. It is very scary to lie facedown for several hours never knowing whether something will go wrong during the next moments." Mr. D'Amico agreed, saying, "They weren't carrying guns for nothing."

A follow-up story appeared in the next day's *New York Post.*

INTERPOL ALERTED TO HOTEL QUINCY CASE

Believing the bandits may attempt to fence their loot in Europe, Interpol was alerted to the Hotel Quincy case yesterday. The Police Department has assigned 20 detectives of the major case squad to the case, headed by Detective Captain Michael Unger. Detectives escorted victims yesterday to Cartier and Harry Winston in attempts to identify jewelry taken from their safe-deposit boxes. Some of the long-term guests say they have forgotten what was in their boxes and would require several days to compile a list. Hotel safe-deposit boxes are insured for only $1,000 but many guests have additional coverage on personal policies.

Captain Unger noted strong similarities to the 1970 heist of the posh Blue Lagoon Spa in Miami Beach where thieves netted $2 million in cash and jewelry and shot a hotel security guard, who lost the sight of one eye. Two Boston men were convicted nearly two years later of taking part in that robbery, Vincent (Jimmy) Fiore and Peter

(Buster) Mahoney. Fiore was sentenced to life in prison and Mahoney to 25 years. Both men are still in prison. Two other suspects were arrested in that case but never went to jail.

Time and *Newsweek* had carried articles that added little to the newspaper coverage. Each had played up the gentlemen-bandits angle and treated the robbery in a lighthearted way as an almost welcome change from the crude violence that typified so much contemporary crime. A lengthy piece in *New York* magazine that ran about eighteen months later was the most interesting. Confidential sources had told the reporter that a New York City detective on the case, Dario Tedesco, had tracked down and identified to everyone's satisfaction the leader in the robbery, but never could put together enough evidence for an indictment. Tedesco had declined to be interviewed for the story. Breslin guessed that Tedesco was the detective with whom Cutshaw had been drinking seven years ago—the "Eyetalian" so easily taken for a Swede.

Breslin sat back in his desk chair and looked out upon lower Manhattan from his eight-hundred-foot-high aerie. Low-lying clouds moved from east to west behind the graceless towers of the World Trade Center, which dominated the scene. He tried to visualize one of the towers, with its seventy thousand occupants, toppling over as the 1993 terrorists had hoped, and agreed with what Cutshaw had said when referring to the incident during lunch.

"If those Arabs had ever brought that building down, Chuck, it would have been the worst day this country saw since Pearl Harbor. And believe me, that *still* would have been small potatoes compared with what this doctor's going to do if we don't stop him."

Breslin knew that he would say yes when Cutshaw called. It was a workable plan—ballsy all right, just as Cutshaw had said, but absolutely workable. Cutshaw's final comment had about clinched it for him even before he returned to the office to read the articles.

"You realize," he had said, "this has to be a real robbery. The safe-deposit boxes have to be busted open and there's no way we can return the money and jewels under the table to the victims. Hell, they're insured anyway. The four of you just do what you like with the stuff."

Breslin felt no guilt about netting half a million or so out of this. He would have earned it. More important, money was truly secondary and he knew there was nothing self-serving in that judgment. Had Cutshaw said there wasn't a cent available to pay him for this work, he would have taken the assignment anyway. It had been a real effort to remain impassive while studying the photographs of the Russian virus victims. And if the President felt that the stakes were high enough to justify killing innocent citizens if need be, then it was a job that had to be done. Just as he had when employed by the Agency, Breslin thought of the President as commander in chief, and acceptance of this kind of assignment as answering his country's call.

Cutshaw possessed in full that attribute of the lifelong spook of seemingly knowing another's thoughts and actions from miles away—no sooner had Breslin decided for certain that he would go ahead with it than his phone rang.

"Breslin Associates," he said.

"Short and sweet, Chuck," Cutshaw said.

"Yes."

"Good man. I'll be in touch real soon."

Cutshaw clicked off.

Breslin touched base with George Glasgow's secretary and confirmed their breakfast for the next morning. The Latvian project would now require a little juggling but he was sure it would work out fine. His highly structured, once-a-week love life might also require a little juggling and that could prove to be more touchy. The desk clock read 3:45—time to leave for his Thursday rendezvous, which had been an exciting prospect during the first months of the affair, his first with a married woman. Lately it had gone downhill, though, and as with any relationship he had ever been in that was a hundred percent sexual, it had gone from good to terrible very quickly. Given the choice, he would sooner spend the next few hours at the gym.

He received the usual nod of silent thanks from the doorman as he pressed a folded ten into his hand. At the start of his affair with Lynn six months ago, a single girlfriend had given her the use of the apartment for a few hours every Thursday. His own place was out, since as a matter of course former employees of the Agency were placed under brief surveillance from time to time and Lynn was the last person he wanted to show up in a report. On his first visit he had watched the young, Puerto Rican doorman, whose nameplate identified him as Nelson, go through a sham search for a set of door keys, pushing a drawer full of junk around in circles for a full minute before Breslin pointed to the most prominent item in the pile, an envelope addressed to "Mr. Begley" and marked in the upper left corner, "Ms. Wrabel, Apt. 8F." The delaying tactic was clearly a bid for a tip and Breslin had obliged with a ten, which brought a smile to Nelson's face and the generic "No problem." Breslin had made the tip a regular thing, and had missed only four Thursdays in the past half year, so Nelson was doing all right. Since Lynn would arrive each Thursday ten or fifteen minutes after him and they would leave together a couple of hours later, the doorman knew they were using it for what Lynn liked to call their assignation. Breslin's Uncle Eamon had put in forty-five years as a Manhattan doorman, and so Breslin knew this was a fairly common situation and one in which a doorman felt entitled to a regular tip, almost as an acknowledgment that he wasn't a fool.

He rode the elevator to the eighth floor, and remembered that until last week he had believed Heide Wrabel was coming out a lot better on the deal than Nelson, clearing fifty dollars each Thursday for the use of her place. From the beginning, it had struck him as an odd arrangement for two women whose friendship went back some fifteen years to when they were roommates at Wesleyan, even more so after his snooping—done as a matter of course when alone in a stranger's house—had told him that Heide knocked down a six-figure salary at an advertising agency. The money went toward the cleaning lady, Lynn had explained their first time there, and Breslin had since left the money on the coffee table each week, always the crisp fifty-dollar bill that Lynn had suggested. "Two twenties and a ten looks kind of mercenary," she had said. "A nice, clean fifty is more genteel." It had been okay with him. Compared with what a comparable hotel suite would cost, it was a bargain.

He let himself into the apartment, which was as meticulously neat as always, hung up his coat, and entered the small kitchen where he took from the refrigerator a bottle of Stolichnaya and a dry vermouth, both provided by him. Heide was apparently a nondrinker. He rinsed two stem glasses and set them in the freezer wet, then poured himself a large, neat shot of the Stoli and took it to the living room window, where he stood and looked down for a bit at the dark, fast-moving East River some hundred feet below, his eye caught, as always, by an outcropping of rocks almost directly beneath the window, close enough to shore that it wasn't a hazard to the barges and small boats that plied the river. After a bit, he took in the view looking across the river to Queens and Long Island. Early on, using Heide's binoculars, he had managed to find the roof of his old Greenpoint house, where only one Breslin still lived, his sister Shelagh, ten years his senior. He guessed that most people living with a panoramic view owned binoculars or even a telescope— he had bought both after his first week in the Empire State Building.

Below him a tug moved slowly up the river, pushing two barges of gravel on its starboard side. "Worth a kiss," he thought, as he remembered summer nights in Greenpoint as a fourteen-year-old, sitting on the Java Street pier with his arm around a girl, playing the game they called ferdiddle. Tugboats on the river at night ran a single white light on the mast if hauling nothing; two lights, one above the other, if pushing barges directly forward or on a side; three lights if towing barges astern. If a boy spotted a tug running two lights and said "Ferdiddle" before the girl did, he got to kiss her. He had learned how to kiss that summer, at the river's edge, the lit-up skyline of Manhattan like a cardboard cutout just across the dark water.

Now he sipped his vodka and remembered that for the first five months of his affair with Lynn he would never pour a drink for himself if he arrived first, and he had always arrived first, since she had once told him, with mock coyness and a theatrical southern accent, "It would make me feel tawdry and indecent to sit here waiting for you, Chuck. What would I do? File my nails? Your being here first and waiting for me makes for a more romantic assignation."

It was a bit of a ritual for them. He would chill a stem glass while he waited for her, then mix martinis when she arrived. They would sit on the couch at the large window that overlooked the river and the Queensboro Bridge, exchange one long, intense kiss, prop their feet up on the coffee table, clink glasses, then sit back and consume their drinks leisurely over small talk about the previous week. They never communicated between their Thursday trysts. She spoke during these interludes on the couch as much about her husband, Jeremy Sisler, a workaholic investment banker, as she did about herself. Breslin was never able to figure out why that was, and never felt it would be productive to ask.

After half an hour on the couch they would start to neck in a way he imagined suburban kids once necked in drive-in movies, then work their way into the bedroom for an hour's worth of unpredictable sex. She might be hesitant and low-keyed one week then aggressive and licentious the next, and he had failed completely to pinpoint anything that would give him a clue as to which Lynn had shown up on a given day. The unpredictability added a nice edge to the affair for him but he had also come to see it as a hint of real craziness. She playacted a lot, too, both in bed and before. What tried his patience most was her emotional immaturity, which had surfaced gradually over time. A month ago he had for the first time poured himself a drink before she got there. When she walked through the door and saw it in his hand she had stopped short and asked accusingly, "You couldn't wait?" then sulked for a bit until he asked what was wrong.

"The romance is waning," she had said. "Little things like this are the first signs."

The few minutes of cajoling needed to reassure an adult about something so petty had irritated him.

Often, while they lay on their backs beside one another talking, the sex finished, she would go from subject to subject without making the normal transitions, as though she were free-associating, or analyze someone's behavior from a point of view that struck him as bizarre. He had several times said to himself, "God, she's off-the-wall." And then, last Thursday afternoon, as she had started to cry while recalling some trivial incident in a restaurant and describing a waiter as "deliberately cruel, the way Nazis must have been cruel," the phrase had somehow formed itself in his mind differently. "The woman is absolutely mad," he had said to himself, then turned his head to watch her as she talked intensely toward some distant point far above the ceiling, and realized with a terrible, sinking feeling that he just might be dead right. He wondered if perhaps it ran in her family.

That same day he had left Lynn outside the building and walked to First Avenue, where he stopped for a drink at Billy's, a comfortable bar near Fiftieth Street. Twenty minutes had passed before he realized that his office keys were missing and that they must be back in Heide's apartment. He had walked back to Sutton Place and checked with Nelson that Ms. Wrabel wasn't home yet. The keys had been between the cushions of the couch. As he had turned to go he had scanned the room, as he would a hotel room he was leaving, and did a double take on the coffee table. The fifty was gone. He had looked around on the floor but with no real hope of finding it—knowing from the position of the ashtray that he invariably set on top of it that the bill had been

removed. On his way out of the building he had waited
a minute while Nelson accepted tenants' dry cleaning
from a delivery man, then asked him, "Since we left, has
anybody gone into Ms. Wrabel's apartment?"

Nelson had made his discomfort clear. He had stared
and said nothing, until Breslin took a ten from his
pocket.

"Your girlfriend went back upstairs for a few minutes," he had said, and took the ten.

"Did she ever do that before?" Breslin had asked.

"She always goes back upstairs for a few minutes,"
Nelson had said. "Every Thursday."

He had shrugged, with the same puzzled indifference
that Breslin's Uncle Eamon used to express about the
doings of his tenants, then asked with feigned innocence,
"You not interested in what she does on Fridays?"

It had stopped Breslin cold. He had taken a few moments to answer Nelson's quizzical look with another ten.

"She ducks back upstairs for a few minutes every Friday, too," he had said. "After her and Mr. Gordon
leave."

"Every Friday," Breslin had said, and waited for a
confirmation.

"Like clockwork. Same as every Thursday."

"Mr. Gordon?" Breslin had asked.

"I maybe shouldn't be talking about him, you know?
You suppose to be discreet on this job."

"This is the last ten I can go for," Breslin had said,
and folded it before pressing it into Nelson's palm.

"A guy about your age. Wears better threads, to tell
the truth, but dull. All business. Carries a tashay case all
the time, but he must keep his lunch in it, 'cause the
man don't tip shit."

"How long have they been using Ms. Wrabel's
apartment?"

"Started right about when she did with you."

"And she leaves with him and goes back upstairs every
time," Breslin had said.

"Never fails."

*   *   *

Breslin knew that along with the half million a year her husband brought home Lynn had inherited several million dollars from her grandmother. That she chose to hook a hundred bucks a week from two guys who didn't know they were paying for it, all the while behaving like a love-struck teenager, confirmed for him that she was more than a little bit wacky, and he suspected it went deeper than that. This was some confused set of fantasies she was playing out, and people unable to keep their fantasies in place could be dangerous. The safest thing was to ease out of the relationship as gracefully as possible. There was a time-bomb quality about her and he didn't need a spurned woman—particularly this one—looking to make his life miserable.

The downstairs buzzer rang, which meant she was on the way up. He mixed martinis in a small carafe, the only item of glassware suitable for it, then dropped two olives into each chilled glass and waited until she rang the door chimes to pour the drinks. When he let her in they simply said "Hi" to one another. The demure persona in which she always arrived seemed accentuated today, but he guessed it was last week's revelations making it seem that way. While he put her coat on a hanger he watched her walk down the short hallway to the living room, where she would wait for him to bring their drinks. She wore jeans, hand-stitched and made to measure, almost certainly from a SoHo designer. They must have cost six hundred, he thought, and the coat he was holding another two thousand. She sure wasn't getting anything but emotional mileage out of his fifty a week.

He carried in the drinks and set them on the coffee table, then sat beside her on the couch and entered into the overly long, passionate kiss that she needed each week as an affirmation of mutual lust, and maybe even love. Whichever, it seemed to satisfy her romantic notions of a proper "assignation." He kissed her longer than he had ever kissed a girl on the Java Street pier. She sighed deeply when it was over, then they picked up and clinked their glasses.

"How was your week?" she asked.

"Okay. Better than okay, really. My hand-painted-dinnerware deal is moving right along. George Glasgow's going to have the pleasure of depending on a Latvian management team to produce dishes for him. He has no idea how fast he's going to age."

He sipped his drink, then added in as offhanded a way as he could muster, "Oh, you'll never guess who I ran into today. Your father. We ended up having a quick lunch together."

Her surprise was genuine enough for him to regret for a moment telling her. It was the safest way, though. If Cutshaw did casually mention the lunch to Lynn, her adolescent psyche might easily be bruised by Breslin's lack of confidence in her, enough for her to reveal their affair. Cutshaw himself had actually introduced them just before Breslin's resignation from the Agency, in the lobby of the Kennedy Center during an intermission of *Rigoletto*—Lynn accompanied by her father, Breslin with a woman he dated occasionally. They had spent just a few minutes talking. Then, one Tuesday morning earlier in the year, he and Lynn had found themselves just one step apart on the escalator of F.A.O. Schwarz, each birthday shopping for a nephew. They had begun using Heide Wrabel's apartment two days later, and he had begun having second thoughts not long after, for were her doting, protective daddy to ever discover this affair, it would drive him straight up a wall. That was a position that no one who knew Linwood Cutshaw wanted to put him in.

IV

Dr. Ernesto Rivera turned the VW bug off the black-topped road into a field of gently swaying grass that reached nearly to his eye level. As if from habit the car settled comfortably onto the trail it had created over the years, a pair of ruts in the coal-black soil separated by a strip of flattened grass. The doctor had come to think of it as his driveway, which ran dead straight for a hundred yards before twisting into a severe S-curve as it entered a stand of mangrove trees, after which anything moving on it was out of sight of the little-used road. The mangroves' tangled network of aerial roots always intensified for him the sense of being home in Cuba. He stopped halfway through the S-curve, where a heavy iron chain was stretched across the driveway a few feet above the ground, anchored at its far end to a mangrove root, at its near end to a steel stanchion driven into the ground. The stanchion stood in front of a one-room cinderblock structure, painted green. Fredo, outfitted in his usual fatigues, sat in front of the building, his chair tilted back to lean against the doorjamb, a Kalashnikov semi-automatic lying across his lap. There was no signboard or printed warning of any kind posted. As always, before unhooking the chain from its eyebolt in the stanchion and dropping it to the ground, the sentinel extended two fingers and flicked them up just a few inches, the barely detectable vestige of what had been, in the early days of his assignment, a recognizable salute. For all that it mattered to the doctor, Fredo could have abandoned the pretense of a salute, or any other sign of deference. What mattered was that never, in the past six years, had the doctor found the chain down. He drove on, at the ten-mile-per-hour speed dictated by the now snaking pair of ruts.

He was returning from his weekly visit to Buena Ventura, where he spent each Thursday afternoon at the corner table of a dirt-floor cantina on the outskirts of town, reading the week's newspapers while working his way at a leisurely but steady clip through the better part of a liter of rum. He would begin at noon, drinking Cuban martinis—rum and red vermouth with a twist of lime. Later in the day, as the sun settled onto the horizon, he knocked back generous shots of straight rum. His evening was passed with one or another young prostitute. He was back in his own bed by eleven, where he would enjoy his deepest sleep of the week, eight hours of dreamless, snoring slumber that made the next morning's headache well worth it.

He lived in a simple cinderblock house built for him upon his return to Cuba—a living room, one corner of which served as a kitchen, a study, and a bedroom the size of a monk's cell. There was an outhouse nearby. The years in Africa had been harsh enough to make these quarters seem luxurious. This part of Cuba, the Zapata Peninsula, on one side of which was the Bay of Pigs, was nearly all swamp and thinly inhabited. The prevailing wind was from the south and so he had situated the laboratory a thousand feet north of his living quarters, a very minor precaution but he had incorporated every minor precaution he could, believing that all those things added up. Working with a hot, lethal virus in the high-tech, money-is-no-object installations of the United States or Europe was dangerous enough—his primitive conditions demanded even more attention to detail. He had given himself every edge possible, a practice he had followed all his life and that had proven itself once again in this case. After six years of handling the virus daily with the most makeshift equipment and unsophisticated safety measures, he had all but completed his work and was still alive. There were few scientists with the enormous discipline to have done that, and he took great

pride in it. He attributed it to his many years of
soldiering.

He entered the living room with an unopened bottle
of rum in hand, the first time since moving in that he
had brought liquor back from Buena Ventura and into
the house. He poured half a glass and, because he was
thirsty, added ice cubes from the refrigerator in the corner, then leaned against the small countertop, more
woozy than he generally was after his weekly outing. He
surveyed the room's Spartan furnishings and realized that
in just a few days, when he left this place, he would not
only miss it but would likely never see this room, these
few pieces of furniture, again. The same sense of sadness
he had felt during his final few days in Africa flooded
his chest. It occurred to him now, as it had then, that he
had reached an age where, along with the pleasure of
some new experience came the realization that it was for
the very last time, an age where several occurrences each
day reminded him that his own days were numbered,
that the end of his life was not very far off. Ten years,
perhaps? Not much for a fifty-eight-year-old, but it was a
realistic estimate. Had he pursued the comfortable career
envisioned by his parents, a wealthy physician-to-the-rich
in Rio or Buenos Aires, he might now be looking forward to twenty-five more years, but the life he had chosen had burdened his body with a heavy debt. It would
soon come due. He had fought off two bouts of amoebic
dysentery over the years, suffered from an occasional
attack of malaria, and still carried the hepatitis-C virus,
whose antibodies continued to attack his liver, picked up
from blood given him in Angola in 1979 during an operation to remove shrapnel from his stomach. His shattered
spleen had been removed in that operation.

He swirled the glass of wine in his hand and knew that
short of a violent death it would be the chronic hepatitis
that would do him in. Several years ago here in the compound, he had performed a liver biopsy on himself, a
procedure that called more upon the soldier in him than
the physician. He had marked with a pen the proper spot
between the ribs on his right side, used his left hand to

hold a three-inch-long needle on the mark, then grasped
a brick in his right hand and smacked it against the needle, driving it in several inches through the rib cage, holding his breath throughout. The tip of the needle was then
just shy of his liver. He had screwed on a syringe of
saline fluid and injected enough of it to clear the needle
of tissue and cartilage, then pounded it in to its hilt with
the heel of his hand, an easier task than the first drive
through the rib cage, embedding the needle in his liver.
He had quickly drawn up the syringe plunger until he
had a needle full of liver to be expelled later onto a
slide, a cylinder the size of a toothpick, which he had
fixed in alcohol and sliced into the thinnest possible
disks. Those were stained and put under a microscope.
He had biopsied himself again a year ago and so he
could see the amount of liver damage that had occurred
over a four-year period. The bands of scarred tissue told
him that he was in the early stages of cirrhosis, but it was
proceeding slowly. He considered himself lucky. Almost
perversely, he considered having contracted the hepatitis
virus in the first place as a piece of luck rather than a
calamity—had the mortar wound come five years later
almost certainly it would have been the HIV virus trans-
fused in the six pints of West African blood. He had
always had his share of luck, he thought, then reflected
on his innate inclination to consider a pernicious disease
of the liver as a piece of luck. He suddenly smiled,
though he was alone in the room, as he happened to
focus on the glass in his hand. It was, quite precisely,
half full.

He had been raised in an elegant Havana household
whose servants deferred to him from the age of two, at
which time he spoke in well-formed, lengthy sentences,
the only child of a mother whose bearing hinted at her
conquistador ancestry and a father who ministered to
Fulgencio Batista and most of the high officials in his
government, delivering their babies, curing their gonor-
rhea, sending them off to the appropriate European or
American specialists when need be, terminating a mis-

tress's pregnancy, always with the requisite discretion. He had twice, in the wee hours of the morning, been called to a suite in the Hotel Nacional to prescribe for Meyer Lansky's diarrhea. For Ernesto's first communion the pensive and often melancholy little boy was given an exquisite, 300-power microscope handcrafted in Switzerland. He was precocious enough to be accepted into the University of Havana at fourteen as a biology major, by which time he spoke and read fluently both English and German. The summer before he entered college, the summer of his entomology phase, had been spent with distant relatives in the rural, eastern end of the island, where late one afternoon while cycling back to his cousins' hacienda with a saddlebag full of beetles in collection jars, he heard long bursts of gunfire in the distance. Ten minutes later he had nearly run over the leg of a wounded man crawling across the road into a field of sugarcane. He had got off the bike and studied the fatigue-clad man briefly, then for reasons he could not have explained pulled him far into the field, where he had dug two bullets from his back with a Swiss army knife. Open trucks carrying soldiers and searchlights that swept the fields passed them several times. Ernesto had stayed beside the wounded man through a rainy night and fed him leftovers from a picnic lunch he had carried on his beetle-hunting expedition. In the morning they were found by the man's comrades, who thanked Ernesto profusely. Their leader had embraced him and said, "We're going to topple this government. I won't forget what you've done."

It was July 26, 1953, a date that Fidel would take as the name of his movement, and only eleven fighters and Fidel himself escaped from their unsuccessful raid on the Santiago de Cuba army outpost. Ernesto finished college four years later, a fully committed Marxist, and joined Fidel in the Sierra Maestra, where he became so close to Che Guevara, the renegade Argentinean physician whose Christian name was also Ernesto, that he came to be called Cheito. On January 1, 1958, he marched into Havana with Fidel and his troops, their revolution won, and discovered that his parents had prepared days earlier to flee the city for Spain. The night before their departure their throats had been cut while they slept and everything of value taken. The killers had never been officially identified but over a period of years Ernesto pieced together and followed up leads, cajoled and bought information when possible, and called upon Raul himself to have several of the regime's jailers extract information from prisoners who had it to give. A Batista police lieutenant known as El Peso Pesadeo—The Heavyweight—assigned to watch over and escort the Riveras to the airport, had murdered them, then escaped to Miami along with hundreds of other Batista officials. Ernesto had obtained a small photo of El Peso Pesadeo, and had carried it in his wallet ever since.

At the urging of Che himself, Ernesto had become a doctor, ironically fulfilling the first half of his late parents' hopes. He then specialized in virology. The professors, the school, the whole impoverished system, drained of talent and resources by the endless stream of emigrants flowing ninety miles north, were so unequal to his talents that he was, in fact, self-taught, and it had weighed on him sometimes that had he been studying in the States he would have access to fine minds and equipment, and opportunity for recognition on a great, sweeping stage whose footlights burned so much more brightly than those of the tiny island. While his mental gifts inspired reverence in those around him, his admirers were unable to appreciate truly what they were revering and somehow that was worse than no recognition at all—they knew that he was the best in their league but he alone knew that not only did he belong in an entirely different league, but he would have excelled in it. What he had often longed for in those years was an audience who knew just how fine a performance they were applauding. At certain moments the phrase "pearls before swine" came to mind and left him feeling disgusted with himself, at one point in his studies so guilty about his feelings toward those ordinary minds around him that he left the island for six months to carry a gun once again with Che, first in the Belgian Congo and then in the mountains of Bolivia. He had been one of the ragtag, exhausted handful of fighters run to ground and surrounded by government troops on a sunlit October day in a valley beside the sleepy town of La Higuera, the very last comrade in arms to exchange words and an embrace with the man he had come to love. The following day he had lain hidden just a hundred yards from the tiny village schoolhouse where the wounded Che was held captive, and watched through binoculars as a Bolivian colonel and an American CIA agent—an expatriate Cuban—questioned him. The big, open window of the schoolroom afforded a perfect view, a neatly framed picture, of everything that occurred within, including Che's unceremonious assassination in the early afternoon by a Bolivian Army lieutenant. Straddling one of the little wood desks, arm extended, the young officer had fired three pistol shots into Che, who stood at his ease just a few feet in front of him, head tilted up a bit in self-confident defiance. Ernesto, along with five other surviving Cubans, had made his way home, with the vision of Che's execution seen ever afterward in his mind's eye as a Goyalike etching, framed by the large, open window of the schoolhouse. Back in Cuba, after seeing the photos of government troops triumphantly exhibiting Che's body to the world, he had supplemented his revolutionary ardor with an intense craving for vengeance.

He bit off the end of a fresh cigar and lit it, then settled into a sagging but comfortable armchair to sip rum and treat himself to a rare few hours of reverie in which the unrelenting mental discipline of his life was furloughed and his thoughts allowed to wander freely wherever they liked, in any disconnected way they liked, fueled by the alcohol. Memories surfaced, of his dangerous five-year dance with the submicroscopic killer that he had borne to this swampy patch of land so fittingly close to the Bay of Pigs—his own tiny predator, a parasite of sorts, but a parasite that didn't feed off or even live off its host. This vicious little creation needed a suitable host only so that it could replicate itself, but once a host was entered woe to every tissue cell in it, as he remembered from the autopsies in Zaire and the dozen or so death-row political prisoners trucked to him over the years to be infected and subsequently autopsied.

For all its deadliness he had never come to hate his virus, since he wasn't, as was usually the case with virologists, searching for ways to destroy it or even protect against it, but rather for ways to understand its limitations and its needs, the environments in which it could thrive and those in which it wasn't comfortable. He had sought to learn what his virus *wanted,* because he and the virus had the same goal—for it to amplify itself into very large quantities. It was, after all, his ally, the most powerful ally Cuba had in today's world, and yet it was an ally with whom he had been unable to relax for even a few moments during their long dance.

As part of his meticulously kept research notes he had christened the virus Kaongeshi-Zaire, following the profession's custom of using the name of the river nearest the discovery site, though he had been sorely tempted to put his own name on it. Pride had kept him from calling it the Rivera virus, the certainty that when his notes were someday published—posthumously for sure—the big leaguers, the American and English and French virologists, would smile condescendingly at a third world egotist's desperate hunger for recognition, which in a small way would diminish what he knew to be his own remarkable piece of scientific work.

He refilled his glass to his imaginary halfway mark and stepped outdoors into the kind of perfect Cuban night the remembrance of which had often made his heart ache with homesickness while lying on the hard, dry earth of Angola. A light breeze off the Caribbean rustled the lush vegetation. The air was clear and the absence of city lights intensified the moon and stars. He drew deeply on his cigar and looked skyward and recalled that on his first night back in Havana, after so many years of seeing the night sky from southern Africa, the familiar positions of the constellations from Cuba had given him as much

a feeling of being home as had the faded Latin colors of
the houses, the ever-present music, the sweet language
of his childhood all around him. He had drunk in Cuba
that first week back—reveled in it—and let himself wonder for just the briefest of moments, with a perverse
touch of admiration to leaven his despair, how anyone
could hope to convert a nation of Latinos into willing
Communists. He had never entertained that question
about the Angolans.

He indulged himself in memories of obstacles overcome in the early days of setting up the laboratory—the
challenge of acting as design engineer and construction
foreman, the need, because of the damned blockade, to
scrounge for even the most basic items. His first order
of business had been the construction of a building that
could be made airtight, with smooth interior surfaces easily scrubbed down. A heavy-duty marine shipping container the size of a trailer truck had been found for him
and steel partitions welded in to divide it into three separate compartments, each with a bulkhead-type door leading into the next one, the first compartment to serve as
a dressing room, the second an air lock, the third as the
laboratory itself. Every crack and pinhole in every wall
had been filled with weld and ground smooth, then the
entire inside coated with several thick layers of epoxy
paint. Finally, smoke had been blown in under pressure
to test for leaks.

Each compartment was vented with a thirty-inch pipe
that passed through the ceiling and rose vertically for a
few feet above the roof before making a right-angle turn
to run horizontally for fifty feet—three fat, black tubes
stretching downwind side-by-side that even now, as he
looked at them in the near distance, made him think of
huge sipping straws inserted into his marine container.
At the outlet of each pipe was an exhaust fan that ran
continuously, pulling air out of the compartment it
vented, the fan always struggling because it was a bit
starved for air. He had designed the inlet openings in
the compartment to be not quite large enough to feed
the fan the air it wanted. This kept the compartment

always at a slightly negative pressure—any leaks would carry air from the outside world in, never the other way round. An airborne virus floating anywhere inside the compartment either attached itself to some surface or was inexorably sucked up into a microfilter that covered the inlet of the vent pipe. In the remote event that a virus found its way through some flaw in the filter, it then had to travel through the fifty-foot horizontal run of pipe, on the inside of which he had mounted banks of ultraviolet lamps. He remembered how enormously difficult it had been to procure all those components, how the arrival of microfilters or epoxy paint from Canada after months of waiting carried the same sense of victory that winning a firefight against a superior force in Africa had.

From where he stood the end of each pipe bathed the vegetation near it in a thin haze of ultraviolet light. If one were to stand directly downwind of the fans it would be a more dramatic sight—three distinct, thirty-inch-diameter circles of intense ultraviolet light in the midst of tropical vegetation. He had never stood directly downwind of the fans. Now he was suddenly tempted to do so but knew immediately that he wouldn't. It was the liquor prompting him to a meaningless act of defiance—too much drinking always brought out the bellicose teenager in him, but he never gave in to it. Some piece of his mind always remained sober enough to recognize it for what it was and restrain him.

He lay in bed and thought ahead to the next nine days. His biggest concern was for the virus waiting for him in the States—was Angel Sosa caring for it properly? He would feel much more comfortable were he himself bringing in the virus, but he would be entering the States on a doctored Venezuelan passport, and thus go through Customs. Angel Sosa had crossed into the States illegally months ago, carrying a small quantity of virus with him. He pointed out to himself that he no longer had control over it, and was then able to erase it from his thoughts. The ability to do that had been invaluable through all his years as a soldier. There would be plenty to occupy

him in the next nine days—research animals to be eu-
thanized and incinerated; the hot lab to be thoroughly
sterilized with hundreds of gallons of bleach and UV
light; virus to be placed into long-term, frozen storage
here at the compound with the necessary security and
backup generators; and, of course, the completion of his
neatly handwritten research notes, which he believed
would find their way into a major collection after his
death. Most important was his one true labor of love,
the editing of his diary.

He had started a diary right after the day, forty-two
years ago, that he had met Fidel and Che in the sugarcane field near the Santiago de Cuba army post, and
had kept it religiously ever since, more certain with each
passing year that it would find a home eventually in ar-
chives of the great Cuban Revolution. From the beginning his expectation of historical recognition had hinged
on the diary. Now, with his scientific triumph in hand, he
foresaw it as a valuable resource for a future biographer.

In fact, he maintained two diaries: One was contempo-
raneous, accurate because it rarely lay unwritten in for
more than a few days at most. He thought of it as his
rough version. The second was the official diary for pos-
terity; he considered it simply a polished version of the
rough, though he chose to maintain precisely a one-year
lag time for entries. His procedure was to sit at night
and record the day's events accurately in the rough diary,
then turn to the earliest entry—which would now be one
year old—make additions or deletions he deemed necessary, then enter the revised material into the official
diary. The year-old original pages were then destroyed.
He had begun that procedure early on, after discovering
that the normal, one-book method of diary keeping could
prove humiliating when entries were reread a while later.
He felt that having a year's worth of subsequent events
before making an entry into the official diary made for
less awkward biographical material.

Now, staring at the ceiling, he called up in his mind
the familiar vision of this future biography's dust jacket.
A microscope and an AK-47 would be superimposed

over a full-length photo of his young self taken in the
Sierra Maestra, a photo he kept in a clear plastic sleeve
inside the official diary. The title would read, *The Life
of Ernesto (Cheito) Rivera, Soldier-Scientist.* This mission
to the States would be the crowning achievement of his
career—Cheito the Soldier applying the fruits of Cheito
the Scientist's labors to make the most arrogant, powerful country on earth a supplicant. He knew very well that
huge numbers of casualties would make for the high
point of the book. Yet Fidel himself had explained to
him not a month ago that if the demonstration in the
United States, the infecting of just a handful of isolated
Americans, convinced the American President to accede
to Cuba's demands, then the big one, the infecting of
many thousands designed to escalate exponentially,
would be called off. He had left that meeting with a
hollow feeling, caused less by the possible loss of his
autobiography's high point than by what the decision said
about Fidel. Forty years of no soldiering was too long
for any revolutionary. The steel in Fidel, God bless him,
had softened—this was not the man he had known in
the Sierra Maestra. Earlier that day Fidel had told a
Canadian journalist that he was preparing to do joint
ventures on the island with European real estate firms,
explaining his newfound position by saying, "I don't particularly like capitalism but I'm a realist."

After the meeting the doctor had walked on the Ma-
lecón and later meandered around Havana, studying the
tourists, the prostitutes, the Diplostores. Everyone doing
business but only with the longed-for Yanqui dollar.
"The revolution is over," he had thought, "waiting for
someone to pronounce it dead. Only these Fidelistas who
haven't eloped don't know it." He had sat on a low stone
wall and stared out at the Morro Castle, remembering
the sacrifices he had made in Angola, having to fight
back tears for one of the few times in his adult life,
chewing on Fidel's easy phrase, "I don't particularly like
capitalism but I'm a realist." *Particularly.* This from one
of the great Marxists of the century. This mission he was
being sent on was a desperate effort to breathe new life

into the Revolution's corpse. A doomed effort. Even if
his demonstration caused the United States to grant Fidel's handful of demands, it was too late.

He asked Saint Theresa to protect him for the next
twenty-four hours, then started to doze. The dust jacket
of his book was replaced in his mind's eye by a vision
of the New York skyline and hordes of cabs moving
along a wide street, images garnered from old newsreels
and magazine photos, and stories told him as a little boy.
His parents had loved New York—his mother especially—visiting it for ten-day stays half a dozen times in
the 1940s, and returning with souvenirs for him. For
years a small metal replica of the Empire State Building
had stood on his bureau. Now he was about to indulge
himself materially for one of the few times in his adult
life—the one night that he and Angel Sosa were scheduled to spend in New York would be at the elegant hotel
of which his mother had spoken so well and so often.
He had an odd yearning to see if their little gift shop
still stocked replicas of the Empire State Building.

He would be there in about a week and would follow
the plans laid out by Fidel—conduct a demonstration
project in a little town a few hours north of New York
City that Angel had selected. It was his duty as a soldier
to carry out that mission. Since his last meeting with
Fidel, though, he had often asked himself, "What would
Che do if he were to arrive in America in possession of
the Kaongeshi-Zaire virus?" Cheito was certain of the
answer. Che had understood vengeance, and so did
Cheito, soldier-scientist. The imperialists who had in-
flicted so much pain on Cuba over the years—so much
unnecessary pain and humiliation—deserved justice. Deserved casualties on a huge scale. Far beyond some demonstration in a hamlet in upstate New York. Whatever
the results of that demonstration, the big one was going
to happen.

V

Teddy Tedesco swung his comfortable, ten-year-old Caddy off the Jersey Turnpike onto the southbound lanes of the Garden State, pushed a Tony Bennett cassette into the deck, set the cruise control at sixty, and settled in for the dull but restful two-hour ride to Atlantic City. Since retiring from the department six years ago he had driven this route every Tuesday, to a part-time job so sweet that when it had fallen into his lap he had described it to colleagues as a godsend. And they had seen it as just that, since it allowed him to do what each of them dreamed of—go out on half pay just as soon as he had his twenty years in with enough income to live comfortably. During his last weeks in the detective room they had envied his God-sent casino job with cynical cop humor that he had parried by commenting blandly that God rewarded virtue. He had seen no reason to confide to them that this godsend, like most, had consisted only of opportunity dangled before him—it had been up to him to reach out and grab it fast.

For a year or so before his twentieth anniversary he had mulled over the possibility of staying on but finally concluded that for cops of his stripe, who had gone on the job to play cops and robbers and lock up bad guys and were known to their colleagues as first-through-the-door cops, the conventional wisdom in the department was dead-on—get out with your pension the day you've got your twenty in, before some piece of bad luck takes it away from you. His twenty years of service above and beyond, including a bullet in his stomach while still a beat cop that had kept him in Bellevue for weeks, a

slashed cheek and neck while working undercover nar-
cotics, citations for heading up three major cases over
the years including the biggest hotel robbery in history,
and finally, a deserved reputation as one of the very best
first-grade detectives in the department—with only 120
cops holding that rank on a force of 38,000—none of it
would matter if late in his career he was unlucky enough
to make a judgment call from which the media felt they
could wring a story of misconduct with enough drama to
hold viewers or sell newspapers. Below deputy inspector,
you were quickly offered up as a goat if the public clam-
ored for a sacrifice, and the bosses down at One Police
Plaza simply chalked it up to "the system" no matter
how good a cop they knew you to be. Worse, they
seemed to take a perverse pleasure in it. Teddy believed
that it confirmed their own deeply held certainty of life's
unfairness, a conviction that was the near-inevitable result of a lifetime spent as a cop. The brass also believed,
deep down, that the goat very likely deserved what he
was getting—not for the stated crime but for a dozen
others they assumed he had got away with earlier in his
career. A narrow, mean view of life, Teddy thought, that
came from the hundred-year domination of the department by the Irish, who knew that we are all sinners and
must pay for it sooner or later. It was a sentiment he didn't
share, not least because he had been raised Italian, among
people who also believed we are all sinners but that there
is no good reason not to get away with it forever. He
knew very well that only the civil-service-mentality cops,
the summons writers who slouched through a whole career by wearing blinders when they walked the streets,
could afford to stay on after twenty years and build up
their pensions further. Teddy had had to get out, but
that meant living on his thirty-two-thousand-dollar-a-year
half-pay pension or going to work as a square badge
on the security staff of a department store, a depressing
prospect. It had been a quandary. And then the godsend
had arrived, though it hadn't looked like that at first.

He had just come off a four-to-midnight shift and was
eating a late dinner alone at a favorite Italian restaurant

in the West Village when the owner, Lorenzo, hurried across the room to his table and whispered that the kitchen help thought there was a prowler in the basement.

"Maybe you'll take a peek downstairs, Teddy? You know how a couple of squad cars flashing lights outside can hurt the register, no?" he had asked, then added a thin film of Neapolitan soft soap. "I'll tell Samantha I never saw such courage in my life."

Teddy hadn't wanted to risk his life rooting out some crackhead in a dim basement. He had wanted to dog it, but he was a regular in the restaurant and sometimes dated one of the waitresses, Samantha, a tall young actress from Minnesota for whom his tough New York detective image was the big attraction. With Lorenzo on his heels he had reluctantly descended the stairs into the building's basement, his heart thumping and his hand resting on his holstered revolver. A nervous Lorenzo had asked, "Wouldn't it be a good idea to take your gun out, Teddy?"

"No," Teddy had told him. "If I jump a second too soon and shoot some eighteen-year-old who didn't shoot first I kiss my pension goodbye. Doesn't matter if his rap sheet's as long as your arm. And if the gun he's carrying is a toy I'll be in front of a grand jury for a criminal indictment no matter how real it looked. I'm better off taking my chances getting shot."

At the bottom of the stairs Lorenzo had decided he could be of no further help and would stay on the steps while Teddy looked further. A noise from behind neatly stacked cartons of imported tomatoes sent Lorenzo upstairs and caused Teddy to grip his gun tighter, though he still didn't remove it from its holster.

"Police," he had said evenly, then repeated it with more authority.

A frightened, skinny, seventeen-year-old kid with all the earmarks of a Manhattan private-school product had stepped out under one of the sixty-watt bulbs that hung from the ceiling and asked not to be shot. The sidewalk trapdoor had been left unlocked by a porter taking out corrugated cardboard for a garbage pickup and the kid had gone down the ladder on a dare from his friends to see if he could steal a bottle of liquor.

"Your porter must be very new to America," Teddy had said to Lorenzo dryly. "You better tell him he can't leave a cellar door open in New York City."

Lorenzo had nodded gravely as Teddy turned to the boy and said, "If this was thirty years ago I'd give you one of those kicks in the ass that make you limp for a week and send you home. But now your parents would sue me and the city and the restaurant and whoever manufactured the shoe I left in your ass, so I've got to run you in. First, though, I'm going to finish my steak pizziola."

He had handcuffed the kid to a pipe and finished his meal, during which he decided that if, when he returned to the cellar, the boy was contrite and respectful he would keep him out of the criminal justice system and bring him home to his parents instead, with a recommendation that he be sentenced to ten weekends of washing dishes and mopping floors for Lorenzo. Over a snifter of Cordon Bleu that Lorenzo pushed on him he had felt virtuous about his handling of the situation. It was community policing at its second best—the only more constructive treatment would have been the old-fashioned kick in the ass.

Teddy had been surprised to learn that his prisoner was Scott Pralt, the adopted son of Conrad Pralt, who, on name-recognition surveys of New Yorkers always scored higher than the mayor and beat out even the President on polls restricted to high-school students. Pralt was a highly successful young egomaniac who presented himself as a self-made billionaire despite it being common knowledge that he had inherited his retailing empire intact while still in his early twenties. The only valid claim the man could make about his own contributions to his success was that he hadn't squandered his inheritance, and had reluctantly let his widowed mother convince him to invest in Atlantic City hotels and casinos early on. Given his enormous ego and mediocre intellect these were no small accomplishments. Of people like Conrad Pralt, Teddy, as a child, had often heard his father say, *"Lui debbe dare grazie a Dio ogni sera che il suo padre e nato primo di se,"* which meant, "He should thank God every night that his father was born before him."

Young Scott was already known to the public as a child who had run away from his father's eighteen-room Central Park South triplex at age fourteen and was then caught shoplifting a CD at Tower Records a month after being returned home. The boy was a favorite of the supermarket tabloids. Because he had been adopted by Pralt in infancy, the tabloids often speculated about where his "bad genes" had come from. They, and the mainline media as well, would have had a field day with Teddy's arrest of troubled-little-rich-kid Scott Pralt. No one knew that better than Lorenzo, who, when he learned Scott's identity, cried out that he was cursed— how else explain his own stupidity in having Teddy check the basement quietly, instead of dialing 911, which would have brought police cars with flashing lights to his restaurant, television cameras close behind. Realizing that it was still not too late, he had offered Teddy free meals for the rest of his life if he would turn the boy in.

"This could make me well," he begged. "It's the next best thing to having a big-shot mafioso shot dead in my dining room."

"Shame, Lorenzo," Teddy had said. "Mafiosi come to your restaurant and you hope they get killed while they're eating?"

"As soon as I kiss their cheek and seat them, I run into the kitchen and pray to Saint Jude for it, Teddy. Facedown in their pasta. Why not? They got to go sometime, and God willing it happens here I'll have a line around the corner forever. And the more blood gets splattered around the busier I'll be. You can't get a table in Umberto's since the day Joey Gallo got clipped there."

Conrad Pralt had been effusively grateful to Teddy, who had no idea then that Pralt was in the process of negotiating, with holders of $300 million worth of junk bonds, a conversion to class B stock in one of his casinos. Any negative publicity, even something as irrelevant as his adopted son's arrest, could hurt him where it hurt most. He had poured for himself and Teddy glasses of Johnnie Walker Blue Label, a Scotch that Teddy had not only never tasted but had never heard of, then led Teddy out onto his sixty-foot-long terrace that overlooked Central Park and asked what he could do for him.

Teddy had bristled, not at the obvious offer of money, which was almost de rigueur for someone in Pralt's position, but for the patronizing tone and the arrogant, ramrod posture he assumed as he sipped his Blue Label Scotch and surveyed Central Park as though it were his backyard.

"I didn't do it for you," Teddy had said. "Matter of fact, when I decided to give the kid a break I didn't even know his name. If I had known right away it was your kid, I would have locked him up."

"I take it you don't like me," Pralt had said with apparent pleasure.

"I don't have an opinion. Look, if people found out I cut some slack for an ordinary middle-class kid, it would be no problem. But your kid? They'd crucify me."

"So why didn't you change your mind when you learned who he was?"

" 'Cause the kid still deserved the break. I had made my mind up and I would have been embarrassed for myself if I backed off."

There had been an added element in Teddy's decision that he had preferred to keep to himself. When Scott Pralt had identified himself, Teddy's first reaction had been to cover himself and book the kid, then he had remembered clearly an old tabloid front page, a picture of Scott over the lead—ADOPTEE FROM HELL? CONRAD PRALT AGONIZES OVER BAD-SEED STEPSON. Teddy had a soft spot for adoptees.

"You still haven't told me what I can do for you," Pralt had said in his most patronizing tone.

"You can send the kid to work for Lorenzo for the next ten weekends so I didn't waste my time. And you can say thanks. That's more than enough. I'm a cop, not hired help."

Pralt had mulled that over for a minute, properly impressed with Teddy's integrity, then shook his hand and thanked him with genuine sincerity. Later, he had had him investigated by the people on his casino security staff who ran background checks on potential employees. Two weeks before Teddy's twentieth anniversary a surprising, unsigned invitation for a "late night Blue Label on the terrace" had arrived at Teddy's home.

The first thing that had struck him upon seeing Pralt again was the man's changed demeanor—Pralt's great pleasure with the effects of hard work on his son's character had extinguished all but a hint of condescension. Teddy found him nearly likable, from the opening "Pour yourself a drink, I'll be off this call in a minute" to his enthusiastic recounting of Scott's newfound work ethic.

"I swear, you turned Scott's life around," he had said. "And by keeping me out of the papers you saved me more money than you'd ever guess. Well, I know how to pay for value received."

Teddy had sipped his drink and waited to see where things were leading.

"You're eligible to retire on half pay in a couple of weeks. I'm told someone in your position can use a part-time job. Well, I can put you on in Atlantic City. I want you to drive down there, meet with George Klewski, my head of security, let him explain our operation to you, then you write your own job description. I mean that literally—tell me what you would like to do in this organization and what hours you want to work. Give me one day a week for a thousand bucks." He had let it all sink in for half a minute, then added, "You're a fool if you pass this up. It's a lifetime contract."

He had wasted no time in meeting with George Klewski, an overweight ex-lieutenant from the heyday of Rizzo's combative Philadelphia PD. From head to toe Klewski had the look of a cop with a hundred excessive-force complaints in his folder, the cop who, coming on duty, might stop to whack a suspect although he had nothing to do with the collar. Klewski had felt threatened by Teddy and responded as he would have on a South Philly street corner—by trying to establish dominance. He had pretended to study for the first time the background report his staff had put together on Teddy.

"Dario Tedesco," he had said, pronouncing it Dairy-o, then studied Teddy's face for a few moments and added, "Nobody would ever take you for a wop."

"No? Why is that?"

"You look too light for a wop. And kind of delicate."

"You wouldn't be the first one to make that mistake, George. Now you . . . I'll bet nobody ever took you for anything *but* a Polack."

Klewski's face had hardened and Teddy decided to straighten him out right away.

"It's not having a neck that gives you away, George. That, and the trouble you have reading. It's not Dairy-o, it's Dario. But anyway, people call me Teddy, and that one you ought to be able to pronounce. Ted-dee. Just sound it out and remember that the *y* is pronounced like an *e*. You'll get it down if you practice it a lot."

Klewski had reddened and tapped the report.

"Hotshot New York detective, huh? One day a week for a thousand bucks? You must have nailed Pralt banging a twelve-year-old boy to shake him down for this deal."

"Why don't you ask Pralt? I'll give you his home number."

"Fuck you."

"Listen, George, this is private industry, not a rank-and-file department where people have to kiss your fat Polish ass because you're a lieutenant. You try to hurt me around here—you back me into a corner—and I'll fucking bite. Capeesh? So why don't you give me a tour of the place like you're supposed to and we can get out of the schoolyard here and practice getting along with each other."

* * *

Klewski's comments about his non-Italian looks had been old hat to Teddy, who had first defended himself against the charge in the fourth grade at Our Lady of Mount Carmel, a Bronx grammar school around the corner from the Arthur Avenue tenement in which he grew up. The tenement, the school, the entire neighborhood, had been as close to being 100 percent Italian as any place could be in America, purer by far than Little Italy in Manhattan, which had long been contaminated by tourists and eventually became more Chinese than Italian. Teddy grew up on streets where long rows of unskinned rabbits and lambs hung in butcher shop windows, and grocery stores stocked olive oil in nothing smaller than gallon tins. In the hallways of his tenement he heard Sicilian or Neapolitan dialect more often than English, and the very old people in the neighborhood spoke Italian so exclusively that as a little boy he believed it was a consequence of growing old—along with becoming frail and wrinkled and forgetting the names of children, you forgot how to speak English. His looks were so glaringly out of place in that world that as a nine-year-old he had asked his father why he didn't look like everybody else.

"Who says?" his father asked through a mouthful of tripe marinara.

"The kids."

"Anybody tells you that you punch them in the mouth."

"Why?"

" 'Cause they shouldn't say that. Your mother's from a hill right near Naples and my family came here from Sicily. You tell them that. Then you punch them in the mouth."

His mother had said nothing—she understood fewer than a dozen words in English and had long ago decided that those were more than enough. Teddy had eventually punched a lot of kids in the mouth but mostly for other reasons. He had grown up, though, smelling a rat. He was culturally Italian to the bone but he realized, as he got older, that his mirror didn't lie—so many recessive genes couldn't possibly have expressed themselves no matter how many invasions Sicily had endured over the centuries. Through troubled, teenage years he had been too busy running wild on the streets of the Bronx to question his parents, though later in life he would wonder how much his fighting and outright lawbreaking was due to his confusion about who he was. Always lurking in the back of his mind through adolescence was the question whether he hadn't been fathered by a backdoor visitor and why, if it were so, Gaetano hadn't killed or maimed his mother—for sure he could see in Teddy's face the same evidence the rest of the world saw. Then, while he was in Vietnam as a twenty-year-old Marine, having been given by a Bronx Criminal Court judge a choice of joining the service or doing an indeterminate prison sentence of zero to eighteen months for assault, his parents had been killed in an accident on the Bronx River Parkway. Ten years later, as a young detective, his world had trembled beneath him when his wife of five years, Maggie, coldly gave him the choice of resigning from the job or the marriage. Twist and turn as he did over the next six months, she had finally cornered him, and he had unhappily broken up the marriage rather than leave the job. The loss of her large family—five siblings and half a dozen uncles, all with families of their own, every one of them living on Long Island—affected him enough for him to become interested again in his own origins. He had dug through scrapbooks and letters to piece together his family background and then talked to childhood neighbors on Arthur Avenue and neighbors from Bensonhurst, where his parents had lived for a few years right after the war, before he was born in 1948, and even neighbors in Boston where they had lived briefly. Over the years he had constructed a scenario that he would lay a hundred to one was true, but without the kind of hard evidence to finally make the case.

His father, Tommy Tedesco, had been christened Gaetano Tedesco in Monterey, California, in 1920, a son of Sicilian immigrants, the only one of five children to survive childhood. He had run away from home at fourteen and made his way across every state of western and mid-

dle America working as a day laborer, carnival roust-
about, and jack-of-all-trades when he could, begging at
farmhouse doors when he had to, and stealing when he
was desperate. In 1940 he had joined the Army and
found himself, four years later, in Italy, where he met a
pretty, seventeen-year-old Neapolitan whose entire family had been lost in an Allied bombing raid. They had
returned to America as husband and wife and settled in
Bensonhurst, Brooklyn, where Gina gave birth to a boy
they christened Dario. There were enough birth compli-
cations to make another pregnancy impossible, and the
baby died before the year was out. A short time later,
very suddenly, the Tedescos relocated to Boston where
they moved into a tiny apartment. With them was an
infant named Dario. They spent less than a year in Boston and then returned to New York, where they took
the small one-bedroom apartment on Arthur Avenue in
which Teddy lived until he left to join the Marines.

Teddy had verified all of those things as fact. What he
could never be certain of was where and how he had
been acquired. For nearly twenty years he had been convinced that Gaetano and Gina had either bought or stolen him. Then, just a month ago, he had received a note
from one of the Bensonhurst neighbors he had last talked
to twenty years earlier, Joe Cutolo, a now-retired brick-
layer. He was one of the very few people Teddy had
interviewed to whom he had confided his purpose, since
Cutolo himself was adopted and sympathetic to Teddy's
mission. As a young man in Bensonhurst, Cutolo had
been friendly not only with Gaetano and Gina Tedesco
but also with a priest then in the local parish, a Father
Donald Gangemi—Father Donny to neighborhood children and adults alike—who had baptized the newborn
Dario Tedesco, then, just months later, buried him. The
priest had been transferred to a decaying parish in Lawrence, Massachusetts, shortly after the funeral, when rumors proliferated in Bensonhurst about an affair with an
attractive high-school art teacher, a Miss Manning. Joe
Cutolo had kept in touch with Father Donny these forty-
or-so years, driving up each summer with salamis and a

mortadella on what was known as Father Donny's Pressing Day, to take part in the priest's annual production
of a fifty-gallon batch of homemade wine. Over a late-
night bottle of the previous year's vintage, the now-aged
priest had let slip that not long after his arrival in Lawrence he had discovered an infant on the rectory steps
and passed the boy on to a family rather than turn him
over to the state for placement in a foster home. Cutolo
believed that it had been Teddy found on the rectory
steps and given to the Tedescos.

Teddy had heard all this just four weeks ago. Now,
cruising on the Garden State to Tony Bennett's rendition
of "It Had to Be You," he was surprised at himself for
not having rushed north to question the priest the day he
had heard about it—in a small parish setting there was a
real chance the priest would know, or at least suspect, who
had left a baby on the rectory steps forty-seven years ago.
Maybe, after twenty years of grappling with the mystery
of his origin, he had become comfortable with having
been bought or stolen and didn't want to deal with this
new possibility of having been abandoned. If so, it was
one more sign of his early middle age. He mulled over for
a bit which of the three possibilities he would prefer, given
the choice, and could only be sure that last on the list
was to have been stolen. The choice between having
been sold by his natural parents or abandoned by them
he couldn't make without knowing the circumstances.
Were they unmarried? Teenagers? Poor? Sick? Emotionally disturbed? Simply uncaring? His father married? His
father unknown? Drug addicts? His mother a hooker
who never aborted him in time? Just two people too
selfish to raise their child? The possibilities were endless.
He knew. He had chewed on every imaginable possibility
for nearly a lifetime and was never quite able to swallow
his mouthful or spit it out, knowing all the while that
none of it really mattered anyway. He was who he was.
Whatever he might find to be true—bought, stolen, or
abandoned—the following day he would be no different.
Popeye's favorite line beat a tattoo in his mind as he
drew closer to Atlantic City, but in spite of it, he realized

that he wanted desperately to know who his biological parents were.

Deciding what to do about this new development was the second of only two minor problems in his otherwise comfortable existence—his more important decision was what to do about the boredom that for six years now, since he had retired, had felt like a debilitating disease and more recently felt as though it were terminal. He hadn't foreseen when he left the job just how much he would miss playing cops and robbers.

"You're going to need it, Teddy. I don't care how sweet a deal you fell into," Roger Cochran had said over a beer in Donoghue's a week before Teddy cashed out. "You feed off the job a lot more than you know."

Cochran was a sixty-year-old lieutenant who was going to be forced against his will to retire in five more years.

"Sleeping late and working one day a week and taking home more money than ever and I'm going to miss what, Roger? Reading Miranda rights to the shit stream of New York? Rapists? Murderers? Pedophiles? Which ones would you say I'll miss most?"

"You'll miss the action."

Teddy had shrugged that it was possible but unimportant.

"And the action's just the least of it," Cochran had said.

"You got the cop mentality down pat, Roger? You know what makes us all tick?"

"Forty years on the job. Twenty-two of them as a lieutenant," Cochran had reminded him.

"Okay, so what am I going to miss more than the action?"

"Locking up the bad guys. Taking them off the streets. For your kind of cop, Teddy, that's what the job's really all about."

"You think there's some appropriate violin music on the jukebox for this?" Teddy had asked. "Sounds like part of a commencement speech at the academy."

"That's a veteran's response. Solid cynicism, the standard cop defense mechanism."

"Where'd you zero in on that?"

"We covered it in a psych seminar at John Jay."

"But underneath we're all caring, nurturing guys, is that it?" Teddy had asked.

"No. But God forbid we're accused of being do-gooders and we quick put on our strongest suit of armor—cynicism. Like you just did. This is one of the most worthwhile jobs in the world but we'd rather say we're in it for the adrenaline rush than we want to help people and lock up bad guys. Part of the macho shit we all buy into."

"You learn that at John Jay, too?"

"Same seminar. It was on cop suicides," Roger had said. "Wait and see if I'm not right."

Cochran had proved to be right. After a few years of retirement Teddy had become bored enough to take up skydiving, which he stuck with in desperation for nearly a year, until he admitted to himself that free-falling thousands of feet was doing nothing for him because it was meaningless. What he needed to cure his boredom was what Cochran had predicted—action in the cause of something worthwhile. The cop side of cops and robbers.

Just before ten o'clock Teddy walked across the casino floor to the boardwalk entrance to take his usual break. He had made it a rule from his first night in the town never to leave Atlantic City without spending at least a few minutes savoring the ocean breeze and looking out at the Atlantic, and he had not missed doing it once, no matter the weather. Generally, late in the evening, he took a ten- or fifteen-minute stroll. The weather he stepped into on this night promised to turn nasty soon; perhaps the start of a squall, the wind was blowing off the water in gusts powerful enough to stop him in his tracks for just a few seconds. His face was suddenly covered with a fine mist that he thought for a moment was rain, until he tasted salt on his lips and realized that it was spindrift blowing across the deserted boardwalk. He bent forward into the wind and walked across to the railing, opposite the casino entrance, intending to stand for just a few minutes rather than stroll the boardwalk. The ocean at its roughest always enthralled him and now he pressed hard against the railing and listened to the surf pound and breathed deeply. Implausibly, during a brief calm spell, a voice close behind him called, "Teddy." He turned, and after a few moments recognized the man approaching, hand outstretched, to be Linwood Cutshaw, who, at the end of a long night of drinking seven years ago in Greenwich Village, had told him, "You ever need a favor, Teddy—I owe you one." He shook Cutshaw's hand.

"What the hell brings you down here?" Teddy asked.

Cutshaw looked around in a purposefully exaggerated way, then gave his most conspiratorial smile. It promised Teddy everything he had been yearning for these past six years.

"Hell, Teddy," he said, "I came down to talk to you," then leaned closer to keep some completely improbable passerby from overhearing them, and added, "if we can have one of those conversations that after it's done, never took place."

Teddy felt a rush but kept his voice very even.

"Fire away. You want to go indoors?" he asked, and indicated the casino.

Cutshaw smiled, and asked, "How many video cameras you people have running in there?"

"Eleven hundred and forty, exactly."

"Let's stay out here in the fresh air."

They stood beside one another and looked out at the ocean quietly for a bit before Cutshaw spoke.

"That hotel robbery you once told me about? The Quincy?"

"What about it?"

"The stuff I read on it said you were sure you knew who did it but couldn't get enough evidence to indict."

"True."

"Who is he?"

"Frank Belmonte. Frankie Rocks. Career heist guy."

"Is he good at it?"

"He planned the Quincy, he ended up with maybe half

a million out of it, and I could never make a case against him. I put away his three accomplices, but not him."

"You know him?"

Teddy smiled. "Hell, I owe him a hundred bucks."

Cutshaw waited for more.

"Me and Frank played cat and mouse for a long time," Teddy said. "Serious as it was, both of us got a kick out of it, too. And nobody ever got hurt on one of Frankie's capers, so I didn't have that real obsession to lock him up that you get with the sadists or the psychos. During the investigation the two of us had a standing date every Friday morning for coffee and biscotti in a pastry shop on Elizabeth Street. Lambiasi's. We'd spar with each other—I couldn't put together near enough to indict, but I knew he'd done it and he knew I knew. We kind of took to each other—we had a lot in common. Same age, and he was raised on the Lower East Side, same kind of neighborhood I grew up in. We even knew some of the same people—guys both of us had run across when we were kids. Anyway, I bet him a hundred bucks I'd get an indictment on him but I never did. And I never looked him up to pay him."

"How'd you like to look him up now?"

"What do you want with him?"

"I want him, along with three people I provide, to rob a hotel ten days from now."

Teddy felt himself gulp, but managed to sound unimpressed.

"You going to put him on Uncle Sam's payroll?" he asked.

"No. He's got to believe it's a bona fide robbery."

"And the other three?" Teddy asked. "They're your people?"

"Two of them are. The third one is you. If you're interested."

Teddy's heart speeded up.

"A good cause?" he asked.

"The best."

"Can I say no, after I hear it?"

"Of course."

"Shoot," Teddy said, with the relief of a prisoner set free. Had Cutshaw said it was work for the devil, he thought, his answer would have been the same.

Cutshaw ran it down for him—including the photos of hemorrhagic-virus victims—then said, "You'll hit it off fine with Jay Garrick. He'll lead the operation. He'll also have available any amount of front money you'll need— I mean *any* amount, Teddy, 'cause this thing has to be done right. You'll like the fourth man, too. Chuck Breslin. You'll meet Garrick in just a few minutes. He'll be the only one on the crew isn't a New Yorker. The big question is, can you convince Frank Belmonte that it's a bona fide robbery? That you're a cop gone bad?"

Teddy smiled. "I should be embarrassed to say it, Linwood, but it won't take much selling to convince Frankie that I went bad. He used to say that he could never understand what a guy like me was doing being a cop, anyway."

At about ten o'clock, Klewski, whose niece in Buffalo would turn fifteen next week, sauntered into the hotel gift shop in search of a T-shirt. As he examined a stack of them near the window fronting on the boardwalk he caught sight of Teddy walking out of the casino. It didn't surprise him, since he had long ago noticed Teddy's habit of taking a late-night fresh air break. What did surprise him was to see another man step out of a nearby doorway and follow Teddy to the railing. They shook hands. It looked to Klewski like a prearranged meeting. Why, he wondered, would the hotshot, overpaid Dario Tedesco arrange to meet someone on the boardwalk? He would watch this further.

"I'm going to let you two talk," Cutshaw said as Teddy shook hands with Jay Garrick, a man in his early thirties who had almost surely played college football. "Teddy knows the objective. Including who we're grabbing off, and why."

"How tough is it going to be?" Garrick asked, as Teddy watched Cutshaw stride across the boardwalk.

"The crew who did the Quincy weren't rocket scientists. And the ones who did get nailed, it was well after the robbery. Fencing jewelry. That's how those cases usually get broken. Belmonte planned it perfectly, and he'll be with us on this one."

"We'll have to make the hostage-taking look like a last-minute thing. We can't let Belmonte in on that part of it."

"I had kind of figured that," Teddy said dryly.

Klewski, still in the gift shop, had not got much of a look at this big, young man who had been introduced to Teddy at the boardwalk rail, replacing the older man, who seemed to have headed back toward Pacific Avenue. For sure, they were doing business out there, Klewski thought. Then, unexpectedly, the man beside Teddy turned to face the casino, obviously wanting his back to the wind, while Teddy remained facing the ocean. Klewski saw an opportunity and seized it. He picked up a Kodak disposable camera and said to the clerk, "Josie, I'll be back in two minutes to pay for this," then hurried through the door that opened into the lobby and across a hundred feet of carpeting to the casino entrance on the boardwalk. The two of them were in the same position, with Teddy's back to him and the stranger facing him. They were a full fifty feet away, but with the lights of the casino and boardwalk signs illuminating the stranger's face against the dark background of the ocean, plus the magic of a really good enlarger, Klewski, after six years of an arm's-length, grudging armistice, believed that he just might stick it to the wop yet.

"What we want to avoid at all costs in there is violence," Garrick said. He listened for a few moments to Teddy's assurances that Belmonte was not a violent guy, then ceased hearing him, suddenly focusing his attention on a squat man in a suit jacket directly across in the casino doorway who was taking pictures of—what? The dark ocean in the background? What the hell was there to shoot except Teddy and himself? And Teddy's back was to the camera. The squat man could only be taking a picture of him. Someone investigating Teddy, most likely, which meant there could be more to Tedesco than he would have guessed. The squat man may well have caught Lin Cutshaw on film, too. And then again, Garrick knew, the picture taking most likely meant nothing—the kind of minor coincidence that turns up so often on clandestine assignments. This was just a tourist wanting a nighttime shot of beach and ocean. He hoped.

They parted company with a handshake fifteen minutes later. Foremost in Garrick's mind as he left Teddy was the squat man with the camera, who had disappeared after the picture-taking. A light, driving rain had begun to fall, joining with the heavy winds to turn the weather worse, and Garrick would have liked to hurry to the car, where Cutshaw waited for him, but he exercised the self-discipline to do the prudent thing—take a walk on the boardwalk.

He walked east, past the Steel Pier and the Showboat, onto what was a nearly mile-long stretch without a casino or a store open for business. Garrick considered the odds of anyone but himself out strolling the boardwalk to be astronomical. Ten minutes into his walk he slowed, stopped indecisively, then turned and barely paused before continuing at a brisk pace back toward downtown Atlantic City, retracing his path. Through the windswept rain he saw, a hundred yards ahead, a figure walking toward him. He was disappointed—he had wanted the squat man with the camera to be a harmless tourist. Just twenty feet apart and it was clear that the walker intended to continue on by him at a steady clip, head down and face turned slightly away both from the wind and from Garrick. Garrick motioned toward him and called out, "Excuse me!"

The man had little choice. He came to a stop and looked up. It was Klewski.

"Are there any more casinos the way you're heading?" Garrick asked. "I came down this way thinking I'd find one."

"The Showboat's the last casino on the boardwalk," Klewski said. He took the opportunity to study Garrick's face. He searched his memory, trying to ID the face before him, running backward in time through his Atlantic City years, through Philadelphia. Nothing. Klewski's near squint through the rain betrayed his interest in Garrick's identity.

Garrick flashed the smile he had perfected as a teenager selling magazine subscriptions door-to-door in southern California.

"Why do I think we know each other?" he asked. "You ever work in Richmond? Reynolds Aluminum, maybe?"

"I'm from Philly," Klewski said, pleased to open up a conversation. "You come up from Richmond to gamble?"

Garrick laughed. "I've got no stomach for gambling. If I lose twenty-five dollars in the machines I'm sick for a week. No, I came up to visit an old buddy who works in one . . ."

Garrick shot him directly in the heart just once with a silenced Glock. He recognized Klewski's look of complete surprise as his arms flew up and he staggered backward from the force of the shot, then fell flat on his back on the boardwalk. Even the pros exhibited just that expression when it came out of nowhere, and this one, who had stopped so easily and started to answer his questions so openly, was clearly not a pro. He crouched beside Klewski and patted him down until he found the camera and his wallet, concerned for a few moments for his own shoes, until he realized that the blood flowing off Klewski's torso didn't form a puddle as it would have on solid ground, but ran down into the gaps between the boards and dripped to the sand below. He saw an ankle holster, revolver still in it, and shook his head in disapproval.

As Garrick drove across the expressway, Cutshaw, beside him, said solemnly, "Our first casualty of this operation, Jay. And it's an American civilian."

Garrick nodded, but didn't take his eyes from the road in front of him.

The battle was now joined, Cutshaw thought—the Cuban doctor had claimed his first victim. And certainly not his last. Cutshaw knew that before he had the Cuban in hand, more Americans would need to be sacrificed. That was a source of quiet satisfaction to him. Casualties were hard evidence that a war was being fought, and the most agonizing casualties, the innocent American civilians who had to be sacrificed by their own people, like the one lying faceup in the rain on the boardwalk, were proof that the stakes were huge and the rules of engagement so brutal that few commanders were able to step up to the plate and do what he, Cutshaw, was doing. The young man beside him was a victim, too, in just a slightly lesser way, forced by terrorists to sacrifice a fellow American. None of this was work for summer patriots. And it was not work for people who couldn't improvise decisively on a moment's notice, he thought, which was one of Jay Garrick's great strengths. They had come down to Atlantic City prepared for Jay to use the Glock on Tedesco if, unexpectedly, he had turned down the assignment. He was sure that eventuality had never occurred to Tedesco, just as it must never have crossed his mind that there might be more to the robbery plans than what was told him. Cutshaw marveled that someone could be as sharp and street-smart as Tedesco was, yet remain so naive about situations like this one, never considering that the more righteous the cause, the more willingly leaders sacrifice operatives if necessary. He was not that much different from the squat man following a stranger in a desolate setting and, as Garrick too had marveled while telling him, leaving his gun on his ankle. "You wonder why the man bothered to carry it," Garrick had said. In Cutshaw's experience that naïveté was common among blue-collar city kids, New Yorkers far more than anyone, for they grew up as what they would later in life describe as "street kids," a term in which they took great pride. They banded together in gangs, either actually or emotionally, shutting out and sneering at the world around them but learning to trust their fellow street kids. They developed a code that prized loyalty, and never saw what a weakness that was—that it was, in fact, the ultimate naïveté. They grew up believing that they were part of the most cutthroat, jaded city in the world, while, in fact, like modern Dead End Kids, they were no more a part of that city than the most provincial Iowan. The most jaded throat-cutters had all been born elsewhere and had come to New York as young adults to practice their trade. Loners, unburdened by a code of loyalty, never sneering at the larger society but striving instead to be part of it. Tedesco and Chuck Breslin, another New York street kid, had that naïveté in common. He would guess that Frank Belmonte, career heist-man, was afflicted with a severe case of naïveté as well. It was not an uncommon ailment among lifelong thieves.

Cutshaw glanced at Jay Garrick, whose lightly tanned, cheerful face was impassive as he kept the car just under the legal speed. Garrick, he knew, had been raised in the heart of the San Fernando Valley.

VI

At a few minutes past 10:00 A.M., Frank Belmonte crossed to the east side of Elizabeth Street and descended the three concrete steps that led down to the front door of Lambiasi's Pasticceria. As always, he peered in through the glass-paneled door for a moment before entering. Everything seemed in place, including Gennaro, the seventy-year-old, onetime fast-moving bantamweight who spoke fewer than a dozen sentences a day and now stood, as he had every morning at this time for fifty years, dozing with open eyes in front of the ornate, brass espresso machine that had been brand-new when the Lambiasis opened their doors in 1910. Frank stepped into the deep, narrow store and walked past a long line of display cases filled with trays of pastries and biscotti, and nodded at Gennaro, who had awoken when Frank entered. Gennaro's body remained stone-still but his head tilted almost imperceptibly toward the rear of the store to alert Frank that someone was waiting for him in one of the booths.

It was Chicky Dhiel, a lifelong thief from Yonkers with whom Frank had once shared a cell in Attica. They had gone through the riot together. Since then their paths had crossed only occasionally but they felt the bond of two combat veterans who had survived the same tough battle, in this case the five-day siege and fifteen-minute onslaught in which forty-three people were killed. The last Frank had heard, a year or so ago, Chicky was doing time somewhere in the Midwest.

They smiled and shook hands, keeping it cool and low-keyed.

"You look good, Chicky. Healthy."

"I been lifting weights."

Frank's face registered mild surprise. "I never heard. Where?"

"Joliet. Joint is a real shithole."

"I always done my time in New York," Frank said. "I never been out of state." He rapped his knuckles on the plywood booth.

"Well, hope it stays that way," Chicky said. "I'll tell you, if I thought I'd do my next bit somewhere like Illinois, I'd go to work in my brother-in-law's garage."

"What was the pinch?"

"Two security guards grabbed me in the service stairway of one of those high-rise condos on the lake in Chicago. I was carrying tools."

Frank nodded his understanding and said, "It happens," but would have bet that Chicky had been drinking or doing coke, or, most likely, both, and had been wandering the condo without a plan hoping that somewhere along the way opportunity would greet him. It was why he had found excuses not to work with Chicky on the two occasions he had been approached.

"What did they hit you with?" he asked.

"A nickel. But I wound up doing just thirteen months. Less than my minimum. Eighty of us got cut loose together, displaced by menaces to society. I'll tell you, Frank, this ain't the worst time to be knocking off fancy apartments. There's not enough room in these joints, and they're locking up so many violent felons that guys like us do bargain-basement time. And with this three-strikes-for-violent-felons shit, it can only get better."

Gennaro arrived and set a cup of caffe latte in front of Frank, something he did every morning without being asked.

"You want something?" Frank asked Chicky.

"They got plain American coffee?" Chicky asked.

"Bring us a brown coffee," Frank said to Gennaro.

As Gennaro walked back toward the counter, Frank adopted a businesslike tone for the first time and asked, "So what brings you this far south of Yonkers, Chicky?"

"I knocked over an apartment in Riverdale last week. Small potatoes. It's a little embarrassing to even talk about it, Frank, but I only been on the street three weeks and I got to get a stake to get rolling. Anyway, there's a guy in Long Island I been fencing my stuff to since I'm a kid but he's out of circulation. I was hoping you could move the stuff for me. As a favor, one Attica vet to another. You want to take a slice out of it, that's fine, too."

Frank kept from groaning aloud. He was paying the price for being unusually closemouthed—unlike most cons, who exaggerated their crimes, he had never confided to fellow prisoners, even to cellmates like Chicky, that he worked very big-league jobs. Acquaintances like Chicky thought of him as just another one of them, at most one notch up, and Frank liked it that way.

"What do you have?" he asked.

Chicky took out a knotted handkerchief, undid it quickly, and spread it on the Formica tabletop. Frank did little more than glance at it all—an engagement ring, three cocktail rings, a man's signet ring, a brooch, a necklace, and a pin.

"What did you bust into, Chicky, a homeless shelter? This is a pile of shit."

"I told you it was a little embarrassing. But the engagement ring looks good, Frank. You got a loupe on you?"

"I don't walk around with a loupe in my pocket. But I don't need a loupe to know what you got here. Do yourself a favor and go pawn this shit, 'cause the cops won't spend ten minutes looking for it. I wish I could help you, Chicky, but to be honest, this is ridiculous."

Frank watched him reknot the handkerchief and realized that Chicky had to be desperate even to show him this stuff.

"You need a few dollars?" he asked.

Chicky's shoulders sagged with relief.

"Jesus, Frank, a hundred, a hundred and a half, would give me a toehold right now."

Frank knew that with a hundred-and-fifty-dollar loan,

Chicky, if desperate, could convince himself to come back in two weeks and ask for more. Three hundred, and Frank wouldn't see him again until he could repay the loan. That could be forever. As Frank peeled off three hundreds that he could ill afford just then, he remembered that Chicky Dhiel had always been a decent guy—an unlucky, untalented career thief who really ought to take a job in his brother-in-law's garage but never would. He was, for Frank, a kindred soul who had stood naked and shivering directly in front of Frank, one of a thousand naked, shivering inmates lined up single file on the windswept yard of Attica in the hours after the riot. Frank suddenly remembered a mole the size of a quarter on one of Chicky's quivering, hunched-up shoulders. He peeled off two more bills and handed Chicky five hundred.

"I can't say when," Chicky said as he took it.

"I didn't ask," Frank said.

Teddy walked into Lambiasi's at a few minutes before eleven. A heavily tattooed young couple, unmistakable methadonians, were laying in their day's supply of sweets, pointing through the display case glass at cannoli and sfogliatelle and biscotti that Gennaro was boxing. Teddy wasn't surprised that the old man hadn't picked up on the current practice of placing a Baggie over the hand as a disposable glove—Gennaro still handled everything with his bare fingers. Very little ever changed in Lambiasi's. He walked past the bent-over couple to the booths in the rear, where Frank Belmonte looked up from his *Daily News* crossword, broke into a smile, and stood to shake Teddy's hand.

"How the hell are you?" he asked.

"Good," Teddy said, and handed him a crisp hundred-dollar bill. "I owe you that, if I remember right."

"You remember right," Frank said as he took the hundred. "Now I'm only out four hundred for the day."

Teddy looked at him quizzically but got no further explanation, as Frank continued to smile.

"Sit, Dario," he said, then squeezed Teddy's shoulder,

an unusual display of affection for him. He called out to Gennaro to bring Teddy an espresso and some pignoli cookies, which he remembered, correctly, as Teddy's favorite, then said, "You know, I'm surprised at myself, being so happy to see a cop."

"I've been off the job six years," Teddy said. "I retired."

"I heard. I also saw you in one of the Atlantic City joints a couple of years back, moving around the casino. I didn't want to put you on the spot or anything, talking to me. I clocked you for a security guy."

"You were right."

"So what brings you down here?" Frank asked. "Besides the pignoli cookies."

"I have a proposition for you."

Frank looked at him skeptically, then said, "You know me too well to think I'd rat somebody out, no, Teddy?"

"Absolutely. Besides, I'm out of the business of collecting information. This is an offer. To do a piece of work."

Frank's voice retained a prison-yard flatness. "Legal?" he asked.

"No."

Frank took a long sip from his cold cup of coffee.

"What kind of work?"

"The Montclair Hotel. In about ten days."

"A suite? You talking about cracking a hotel suite?"

"The whole place," Teddy said. "A complete takeover. Like the Quincy."

Frank absorbed that, then nodded his head slowly in a mixture of wonder and respect for a few moments before saying, "Madonna me. When you go for the horse you go for the cart, huh?" He was quiet for a few more moments, then asked, "Why?"

"Because there'll be a Belgian national checking in who'll put ten million bucks' worth of uncut diamonds in one of the safe-deposit boxes." He leaned forward for emphasis. "Better yet, the way he came into these diamonds, he's not going to be able to report them missing after the robbery. *No one will ever be looking for them.*"

It made the impression that Teddy had hoped it would. Fencing loot was the most vulnerable part of a robbery like this. Frank had instantly realized that they could literally throw away all the other jewelry, the cut stones that would remain identifiable even after being pulled out of their settings, and safely sell off uncut stones for very close to their market value over a few-year period.

"Is this an inside tip?" Frank asked.

"Do I look dumb enough to work with a guy inside?"

Frank shrugged apologetically. "So where'd you come by this?"

"A few weeks ago a casino security guy suspected that two high rollers might be doing a drug deal. I spent a day and a half eavesdropping. Some of the suites are set up for that."

"Bugged suites in Atlantic City. Who would've guessed," Frank said dryly.

"It turned out not to be drugs but diamonds. Ten mil worth."

"Uncut," Frank said. "That's like a dream."

"Uncut."

"And if your tip is bad? If this guy don't check in? Or checks in with nothing but lunch in his briefcase?"

"The boxes are so loaded we *still* walk away with millions," Teddy said.

Frank sipped his coffee and thought about it for a bit, then said, "When I asked, why, Teddy, I meant why *you.* Why are *you* taking this kind of shot?"

" 'Cause I'm tired of being poor. And working in a casino teaches you just how poor you are."

"I know it's easy to count what's in the other guy's pocket," Frank said apologetically, "but you can't be starving, Teddy. You went out on half pay, no? Plus, you're knocking down some kind of salary in Atlantic City, even if they're underpaying you. And twenty years carrying that piece of tin in your pocket—you must've scored a *couple* of times. Enough to put something away in a little box."

"Between you and me, Frank, I filled up a *big* box from my years on the job. I went overboard when I first went to Atlantic City. I went for the whole boodle."

"Jesus Christ," Frank said. "Even a solid guy like you gets hooked? Fucking gambling—it's like heroin."

"I spent three years in Gamblers Anonymous meetings. So that's not going to happen again. A week ago they gave me notice in the casino. The end of a nice, easy gig. I'm not about to go to work pinching Wal-Mart employees who're ripping off a couple of hundred a year in merchandise. Or like a guy in my squad who retired when I did, bodyguarding rich Arabs who come to town for a few months. But after two weeks a lot of the Arabs decide New York's safer than they thought so they fire him. The only way he can work steady is to have a buddy phone in anonymous threats once a week to the Arabs who hire him. Then they keep him on. I won't live like that, Frank. I have too much pride. I'd sooner put my neck out once, for one big heist, and then live well for the rest of my life."

"You're just planning this thing, Teddy? Or you're going in?"

"I'm going in."

Frank gave a small, admiring nod. "I always had you figured for balls. Who else do you have lined up?"

"Two more guys," Teddy said. "And here's the beauty part. Neither one is a career thief. You'll be the only guy along who even has a record. You realize what a plus that is, Frank? You happen to be a great exception to the rule that career thieves are fuckups. They gossip, they brag, they get greedy, they get drunk or coked up. They imagine some disrespect you paid them so they brood for a while then drop a dime on you for it. They get busted on a mopery charge and make deals and the people they deal are their partners on a big score who wind up doing fifteen to thirty to save the rat a six-month bit. It's why cases get broken."

Frank thought of Chicky Dhiel, and knew that most *good* thieves were only a notch above Chicky. He said sadly, "Everything you say, Teddy—it's right on the money."

"These two guys aren't fuckups," Teddy said. "Both ex-military types. Rangers. Special Forces. Tough and cold as ice and trained for just this kind of operation. Both loners, so a week after this happens every bum in the city won't know who did it. And both disciplined— they sit on their share of the stones for a year, and not a day less. This is a dream team, Frank. And we need you to open the boxes."

"How sure are you of the ten mil in uncut stones?"

"Go to sleep on it," Teddy said.

Frank smiled. "You know how many times in my life I been told to go to sleep on something and I did, then kicked myself later?"

"Who were the guys saying it?"

Frank thought for a moment, then agreed. "You got a point there, Teddy. That's an important point. Why don't we look this thing over?"

They decided to cross the street to Frank's place, where he would put on a suit and tie to blend in nicely at the hotel. Teddy had come properly dressed. As they stepped off the curb in front of Lambiasi's, Frank moved his hand in a greeting and said, "Hey, Wong," to a young Chinese guy passing by.

"Herro," the Chinese guy said, with the outsized, any-thing-to-please grin that Teddy decided gave him away as an illegal.

"You know him?" Teddy asked Frank after they passed him.

"No, I just call him Wong. He's been in the building next to mine a couple of years now. Nice guy. Always a big smile."

"What's your guess?" Teddy asked. "Is he legal?"

"Forget about it," Frank said. "But who the hell cares. These people work like you never saw and they don't bother nobody."

A hundred feet down the street they stopped in front of an eighty-year-old, narrow tenement.

"I'll be ten minutes," Frank said and disappeared into the building for a few seconds before reappearing suddenly and holding the door for Teddy.

"Come on up," he said apologetically. "What the hell have I got you waiting on the sidewalk for?"

As they trudged up the stairs, Frank said, "I live with my mother. She's not in such good shape. Diabetes, heart, six or seven other things, every one of them life threatening. She's in her eighties."

"She had you late, huh?" Teddy said.

"In her forties. I was the last."

"Where are the others?"

"There were five of us, all boys. We lost my brother Pete in Vietnam. My brothers Bobby and Tommy were both soldiers with the Lucchesi family. They got clipped ten years ago in the same hit. The only rumors I heard was that it was a junk deal went bad. Sounded accurate, they were both up to their ears in *babanya*. The only one left besides me is my brother Lou and he's got six more years before he's eligible for parole on a fifteen-to-thirty he's doing in Pennsylvania for a lousy hijacking that went sour 'cause the driver had a heart attack. Louie's sixty-one."

He paused at the third-floor-front apartment to find keys, and said, "The Belmontes don't run in such good luck."

"What happened to your old man?"

"Stroke. Dropped dead when I was six, unloading a truck."

He led Teddy through the door, which opened directly onto the kitchen of the tiny apartment, whose layout, and even more, the aroma of olive oil and garlic that permeated the kitchen, caused a wave of nostalgia for his Arthur Avenue childhood to engulf him. Yet something about the room was jarringly wrong. It took a few moments for Teddy to recognize that the entire kitchen had been redone in the most elegant, expensive way— hand-painted country tiles from Italy covered the walls and floor; countertops were marble; the six-burner Garland range was a top-of-the-line industrial model; the cabinetry was enameled in a high-gloss, pastel peach; the pots hanging from a rack were wrought copper. The kitchen belonged in an Upper East Side town house featured in *Architectural Digest.* A window framed in handcrafted moldings opened on a dim airshaft and gave a view of a dingy brick wall just four feet away. Teddy followed Frank into the small living room. A striking Persian rug lay on a floor of beautifully grained wood set in a parquet pattern.

"It's Brazilian rosewood inlaid with some American wormy chestnut," Frank said when he noticed Teddy admiring it. "Don't ask what it cost. The guy who laid it restored some floors in the White House when Jackie O. redid the place."

He pointed and said, "Clock the baseboards."

Teddy saw that they had been done in a faux marble, with veins and shadings·painstakingly painted in.

"The guy who done it did the baseboards in the Hermitage," Frank said. "In Russia. Lays on his side on the floor with tiny little camel-hair brushes in his teeth, like Michelangelo must've done that ceiling in the Vatican. A hundred and ten bucks a running foot. After I watched him, I thought he's underpaid."

"What do you think he got for it in Russia?" Teddy asked.

"Forget about it. I asked him that right away. He got *un gatz* is what he got. Guy was doing a double dime for political crimes in some joint in Siberia makes Attica sound like the Rainbow Room, when the big shots at the Hermitage tracked him down and cut him loose to do their whole place. He lives in Brighton Beach now. These baseboards are beautiful, no, Teddy?"

"They're unbelievable," Teddy said. "This whole place is. You must have a half a million in here."

"You're low."

"So not for nothing, but why put it into a tenement on Elizabeth Street?"

"My mother would shrivel up and die in a week if I took her out of the neighborhood."

"Who owns this building?" Teddy asked.

"My mother. Her and an old widow in the apartment behind us are the only Italians left in the building. All the rest are chinks."

The furniture was ornate but very expensive and beautiful to look at. If the kitchen belonged uptown, Teddy thought, this room should have been in a small villa overlooking Florence. In fact, the front of the room looked out onto Elizabeth Street, through two windows whose inside sills were marble. A hassock was in place at one window, a pillow on the sill. Teddy was sure that Mrs. Belmonte spent seven or eight hours a day there, forearms leaning on the cushioned sill, watching the street below her and missing nothing.

She entered the room from the bedroom, an old Neapolitan woman wearing black. She would have put on black for her husband's wake thirty-five years ago and worn black ever since. There was no sign of the frailty Frank's words might have implied, but Teddy had been raised around too many old Neapolitan women to have expected any.

She jerked her head toward Teddy and asked, "*Che e?*"

"He's a friend of mine. Dario," Frank said.

She gave Teddy a slow hair-to-shoes examination and up again, then said to Frank, "*Lui non sembra Italiano.*"

"Of course he's Italian. Didn't you hear his name?"

She shrugged, to inform the two of them that she knew when she was being lied to.

"*Io sono mezza Siciliano e mezza Nabolidon, signora,*" Teddy said, and nodded respectfully.

She smiled sardonically, as Frank disappeared into one of the two bedrooms.

"You're not from the neighborhood," she said.

"I'm from the Bronx."

She gave no sign that she had ever heard of the Bronx.

"You want a coffee?"

"*Grazie,* Mrs. Belmonte. That would be nice."

She motioned with her head for him to follow and led him into the kitchen, detouring for a moment to the front window, where she glanced down at the street as if to check that all was well. In the kitchen she lit a burner and slid a half-full coffeepot onto it, then set out two cups. While they waited for it to heat, she studied Teddy, then asked, "You're married?"

"No. I'm a bachelor."

"My Frankie, too. But what's a matter with the two of you?"

As she poured each of them a warm black coffee she said, "Can I tell you something? I never had a grandchild. Five children and not a single grandchild. Not one."

"I'm sorry for you, Mrs. Belmonte," he said.

"Frankie's my last chance for it. Marry anybody, I tell him. Let her have a baby, then pay her and get divorced. I never thought I'd say that but we're living in new times here. Divorce is no big deal. I want to see a grandchild christened. Capeesh, Dario?"

"Yes."

"Then tell Frankie he should do it."

Frank entered the room snugging up his tie.

"Tell Frankie he should do what?" he asked. "Make sure he don't get gravy on his suit and tie?"

He kissed his mother on the cheek and winked across the table at Teddy.

"You got a clean handkerchief in your pocket?" she asked.

Frank went back to get one. She said to Teddy, "You look like you got more sense than my Frankie. Look out for him, Dario, huh?"

Teddy gave her a reassuring nod as Frank returned, folding a pressed handkerchief to fit his hip pocket.

Frank left the house carrying a briefcase of black, hand-tooled leather, which, along with his conservative suit and tie, gave him a lawyerly look.

"That case is a good idea," Teddy said as they got into a cab on Mulberry Street. "It gives us a nice business look."

"It does even more than that," Frank said. As the cab headed uptown, he opened it for Teddy's inspection. It held a camcorder, rigidly mounted to a support structure of narrow, aluminum brackets that was riveted to the case itself. The end of the case that faced forward when Frank held it in his hand had a pattern of circular leather pieces on it, some raised, some indented. One of them was actually an opening to accommodate the camcorder lens. Between the pattern of tooling and the darkness of the leather, the lens wasn't easy to see even when Teddy looked for it. A flexible cable ran through the handle, which allowed Frank to start and stop the camcorder with a trigger.

"High tech," Teddy said, with genuine admiration.

He gave Frank a brief rundown. Never having been past the front door of the Montclair, Teddy had spent a few hours the day before boning up on it. It was on Fifty-fifth Street just west of Park Avenue, a three-hundred-unit hotel completed in 1912 whose beaux arts facade now made it a designated landmark. It offered no special weekend rates or deals of any kind, had never acquired an 800 number, and advertised in only half a dozen of the most upscale magazines, with a single-column inch that simply said, "The Montclair Hotel, New York City," set in ten-point Times Roman. The smallest unit was a junior suite at $600 a night. Rates rose steeply after that, peaking at $5,500 a night for the Presidential Suite, first occupied by William Howard Taft. The last President to stay was officially listed as Dwight Eisenhower but it was believed by many to be the hotel Jack Kennedy had unofficially used for his tryst with Marilyn Monroe on the night she sang "Happy Birthday" to him at Madison Square Garden. Teddy took that with a grain of salt—he had heard it rumored about half a dozen Manhattan hotels, spread, he was sure, by hired PR people.

More than half of the occupants were permanent residents, many of them for twenty or more years, aging grandchildren of multimillionaires whose legacy had been invested wisely for generations, people whose names were completely unfamiliar to the public and who liked it that way. Montclair permanent residents undoubtedly maintained the lowest average profile of any rich New Yorkers. It prompted Teddy, as he gave some of this background to Frank, to ask why he and his crew hadn't done the Montclair instead of the Quincy fifteen years ago.

"You know something, Teddy?" he answered sheepishly. "I never even heard of the joint."

At Frank's suggestion they had the cab drop them at the corner of Fifty-fifth and Park, so that he could go in alone, ten minutes early for the lunch reservation that Teddy had made in the hotel's small restaurant.

"I'll sit in the lobby with a newspaper and get the feel of the place," Frank said. "Meanwhile, you mope around the block and see what you can see. You never know."

Teddy watched him enter the hotel, then walked slowly down Park Avenue past the two office buildings that occupied the block. He wandered into the lobby of each and glanced over the directories, which listed the usual assortment of midtown businesses. Nothing stood out as unusual. Nothing on Fifty-fourth Street or Madison Avenue stood out, either. He stopped for a cup of coffee before entering the Montclair, where his attention was caught by the six-foot-four, 240-pound, uniformed doorman, an alert thirty-year-old who wasn't cast in the usual doorman mold. Teddy wondered if the eleven-to-seven doorman was the same type.

It was a fairly compact lobby. Frank was seated on a settee located almost directly across from the registration desk. He had his briefcase on the cushion beside him, the lens facing the desk, with the cashier's and concierge stations likely in its field of vision as well. Teddy walked across the lobby to Frank, who stood to shake hands.

"Sit for a minute and watch," Frank said. "And remember we should be talking to each other."

Teddy joined him on the settee and asked, "Did you clock the doorman?"

"Yeah. The worst. All the makings of a hero. But I doubt the doorman we'll be contending with is going to be a linebacker. The graveyard shift's too dull for a big young guy like that."

"What's it look like here?" Teddy asked.

"I can't believe this joint. It's a total time warp. There's old ladies walking through this lobby ought to be stuffed and put on exhibit someplace. You *smell* money when they walk by, like some kind of perfume they leave in their wake. The most important thing is the boxes, though, which I peeped a few minutes ago. They're in that little room behind the cashier's station there." He smiled. "They've picked up that nice look stainless steel gets after a lot of years if it's maintained the way it's supposed to be. The manufacturers call it a patina. There's a whole wall of boxes. I zoomed in with the lens so I'll know for sure when we get back, but from here they looked like models from the twenties or thirties. I could pop a hell of a lot of those things in a couple of hours."

They ate lunch in the nameless restaurant, a carpeted room with green velvet banquettes along the walls and prints of English hunting scenes on the walls.

"First take, Frank," Teddy said. "Give me your first take on the whole setup."

"I've got to check into a room for a few nights so I can see what's happening at two, three in the morning. That's when it counts. But first take? Tough, but it could be made to work."

"What's tough?"

"Security. It ain't going to be the usual old men snoozing on a chair. That doorman's the tip-off. But we'll see. We'll see. The only real open question is whether we take it from the inside, the outside, or both."

"What's your guess?"

"We probably take it from both. Two inside, two out. But I'm not sure."

"How fine do you like to plan?" Teddy asked. "How detailed?"

"Not too fine, Teddy. Guys get carried away with planning. And it's usually got nothing to do with the heist— these lunatic planners turn out to just be control freaks. I shared a cell with one of them once, a Puerto Rican from Bridgeport. A bright guy—taught me Spanish, and people tell me I use almost no slang when I speak it. Used to tie his girlfriend's hands to the bedposts when he was on the street, so that tells you something. He drew these perfect little maps of places he was going to knock off along with charts—fucking time charts—that listed what everybody on the job would be doing every minute. Told me it guaranteed success.

" '*Guarantees* success?' I asked him.

" 'Absolutely,' he says. 'I been doing it for years and if your charts are to the minute, you can't miss.'

" 'Am I fucking hallucinating, Julio?' I asked him. 'Or are we having this conversation in a prison cell? *Both* of us.' Guys in the joint *hate* to be reminded that they got themselves there. This guy got so pissed off we didn't talk for a week, and believe me, Teddy, if you've ever lived with a broad and not talked for a week it's easy compared to doing it where you can't slam a door and take a walk around the block. With a cellmate you're never more than six feet apart. Stewing. You're an arm's length away while he's sitting on the crapper and believe me, when you're mad at somebody that's hard to take. The thing that . . ."

He brought himself up short and said, "What the hell am I talking about doing time for? How'd I get started on this?"

"I asked you how fine you like to plan," Teddy said.

"As you might've guessed by now—not too fine. Except for the first few minutes, especially if we take it from in and out both. Two teams of two. Then you need some real coordination until the security people are neutralized. CIA kind of planning."

Teddy couldn't resist carrying the CIA reference just a bit further. "How would the CIA handle a job like this if they were running the whole thing, Frank? Would they be better at it than a team you could put together?"

"Forget about it. You ever follow any of the stuff comes out about that crew? They screw up all the time. Give me three good heist guys any day. And you know something else? Even what you said earlier about thieves—they gossip, they're undisciplined, they rat you out sometimes. It's true, but I'd still sooner put myself in their hands. All those fucking spies are untrustworthy. They fuck their own people. I watched some of those CIA guys testify to Congress on the C-SPAN channel. They got no face. They lie all the time, Teddy."

Teddy said nothing. Watching Frank munch his club sandwich and remembering Mrs. Belmonte's plea for him to look out for Frank, he felt a twinge of guilt at bringing Frank into the kidnapping under fraudulent circumstances, but was able to dismiss it when he considered that at the end of the day his lies would mean nothing—Frank would walk away with a lot of money and Linwood Cutshaw would have his Cuban. There would be no harm done.

During the cab ride back to Elizabeth Street, Teddy said that he would have cash for expenses in hand the next day, so that Frank should check into the Montclair immediately.

"Who's fronting the money?" Frank asked.

"My man from California. Jay," Teddy said. "Whatever we need."

"That's a plus," Frank said. "Nickel and diming it always ends up biting you."

They decided to have coffee, and went into Lambiasi's just after three o'clock.

In the building next to Frank's, almost directly across from Lambiasi's, Mrs. Marchetti, a lifelong inhabitant, climbed the stairs slowly, her friend from Mulberry Street beside her. They paused on the third-floor landing to catch their breath, and listened for a moment to the crying of a baby from the front apartment. "That baby cries plenty for a Chinese. Listen to the weak little voice," Mrs. Marchetti said to her visitor, then lowered her voice even further, though no one could possibly overhear. "The poor thing's got some kind of sickness in its muscles. Never leaves the crib."

"They're nice people?" her visitor asked.

"Nice. Quiet," she said, then lowered her voice and said in Italian, "Illegals, for sure. They're too nice. The husband and wife both—whatever you say to them they smile and look ready to kiss your ass if you want to turn around and present it to them. But if we're going to have Chinese in the building, the illegals are the best kind. They behave."

Inside the front, third-floor apartment Jimmy Eng turned for a moment from his perch at the window over-looking Elizabeth Street and said to his partner, "Catherine, give me a break. That baby's probably been crying long enough."

She walked across to the little table beside the door and clicked off the cassette player. The apartment became quiet.

"Someday you'll make a lousy father," she said.

He didn't respond. His attention was caught by something in the street below.

"Frank Belmonte just got out of a cab," he said. "He's with that same guy he was with this morning."

"The guy trying to sell him the jewelry?" she asked.

"The second guy. The one who wants to rob some-place uptown with him."

"What is it, an apartment?"

"I don't know. The bug hardly picks up the booth Frank sits in. And, sweetheart, we don't want to know. Our warrant doesn't cover Frank Belmonte. We're not going to blow this bug and a RICO indictment against the whole Tommy Ross crew to give some local robbery to the New York cops."

He turned away from the window after Frank and Teddy entered Lambiasi's, and motioned to Catherine not to bother turning on the reel-to-reel, then said, "When I passed them this morning, Frank gave me his 'Hello, Wong number' and I gave him my Chinese-laundry 'Herro.' And the smile. I swear, there are days I think that if I have to smile at another wop I'll choke."

"You could always ask to go back to immigration in-vestigations," she said.

"Thank you, but I doubt I'll request that transfer. I've yanked enough people away from sewing machines and woks to last me a lifetime. This organized-crime work is classier." He stood up and stretched. "Take the window till I come back," he said. "I'm going to run across for a cannoli. You want something?"

"Six weeks on the Riviera."

As he went out the door, she said, "Don't forget to say 'Herro,' and smile."

"Fuck you, Catherine," he called back in a loud whisper.

VII

Frank Belmonte rang Teddy's downstairs bell at 7:30 P.M., on schedule. He believed that he was arriving at the start of a four-man meeting but, in fact, Jay Garrick and Chuck Breslin had been in Teddy's apartment for nearly an hour planning that part of the operation about which Frank was to be kept in the dark—the taking of the two Cubans and whichever two solid citizens seemed best at the time. Teddy buzzed him through the downstairs door then opened the apartment door and stood just outside it, on the tiny landing, and watched Frank climb the flight of stairs up to the first floor.

"Hey, Teddy," Frank said, and held out his hand.

Teddy shook it and led him into the apartment.

"Am I the first one?" Frank asked.

"The two of them have been here maybe five minutes," Teddy lied as they walked to the living room.

Garrick and Breslin were standing. Teddy made the introductions.

"Frank. Jay. Chuck."

They shook hands and sized one another up. Each of them assumed a businesslike demeanor.

"You guys say hello," Teddy said, and headed for the kitchen. "There's drinks in that long cabinet. I'll get something for us to pick on."

He started to remove the Saran Wrap from a plate of roasted sweet peppers on the kitchen countertop but decided they would be better warmed to just a little above room temperature. He put the plate in the microwave and punched in twenty seconds. While the peppers rotated, he cocked an ear toward the living room. Gar-

rick and Breslin were running down brief curricula vitae
for Frank, following the story they had set up earlier
with Teddy, that both were Special Forces veterans with
a handful of West Coast burglaries under their belts,
brought in from L.A. by Teddy to do this piece of work.
Jay Garrick truly was a Special Forces veteran, and
Teddy had warned him not to play up any violence in
his past since Frank wouldn't work with a partner likely
to hurt someone gratuitously. Garrick and Breslin were
both able to speak knowledgeably about burglaries because each had done some for the Agency—jobs similar
to the dental office burglary of X rays into which Teddy
had stumbled seven years ago.

He removed the plate from the microwave, lifted off
the Saran Wrap, and touched the back of his index finger
against the peppers to test for warmth. They were fine.
It occurred to him that what had started out as a meeting
he was reluctant even to hold in his apartment he had
somehow managed to turn into an informal meal for
four. He always felt compelled to put out food when
someone came into his house, a result of his Arthur Avenue upbringing, and so he had stopped by Sal Anthony's
market that afternoon meaning to pick up nothing more
than a pound of Gaeta olives and a wedge of fontina
cheese. But the olives were flanked by a platter of roasted
peppers and another of grilled eggplant and zucchini slices,
both of which had caught his eye, and the tray next to
the eggplant held bite-size pieces of chicken and sweet
sausage panfried in olive oil that looked like it would go
well. Before leaving the counter he had added a pound
of stuffed mushrooms to his basket and on his way to
the register had picked up two long loaves of Italian
bread. It hadn't surprised him—he could never get out
of the store with only what he had come for. It had
occurred to him as he paid the cashier that in the case
of Breslin and Garrick, the one of them Irish and the
other from a California suburb, his careful selections
would likely go unnoticed.

Teddy transported plates to the coffee table in several
trips, then joined the others, who were already picking

at the food. Breslin had poured himself a small vodka on the rocks, Frank a Scotch, and Garrick had opened a small bottle of Pellegrino water. Teddy poured a Scotch on the rocks for himself.

"What did I miss?" he asked.

"Nothing," Garrick said. "We were just bullshitting till you got here." Then he nodded toward Frank and said, "You're the man we're banking on for planning the inside stuff, so why don't you kick it off."

Frank popped several of the olives into his mouth as he started to speak. "I just spent three nights in the place and came and went at all hours so I got the layout and the routine down pretty pat," he said, then unfolded a legal-size sheet of white paper and smoothed it out on the coffee table.

"I sketched in the ground-floor level. Rough. This ain't anywhere near to scale—I'm not too big on precision planning."

"Why's that?" Garrick asked. There was a note of disapproval in his voice strong enough to tell Teddy that Garrick was an ex–Special Forces officer rather than a grunt.

" 'Cause the more precision and the more exact the timing and the more everybody starts using some kind of super plan as a crutch, the worse it all fucks up when a monkey wrench gets dropped into the works," Frank said.

Garrick wasn't ready to give it up so easily. He said, "But if everyone is absolutely precise, and carries out his part to the split second, then no one drops a monkey wrench into the works to begin with."

Frank didn't treat it as a disagreement. He seemed to consider Garrick as simply less experienced than himself, someone who hadn't studied the subject in sufficient depth. He smiled tolerantly and said, "The monkey wrenches don't get dropped into the works by the guys doing the job. God drops the monkey wrenches in."

No one spoke for what seemed to Teddy to be minutes, the only sounds the city noises that came in as background hum through the closed windows and Frank's soft sucking of the last shreds of chicken from a short piece of thighbone he held in his fingers. He flashed Teddy a little "thumbs up" on the chicken and sausage as he licked his fingers.

Chuck Breslin broke the silence.

"You mean fate?" he asked Frank. "When you say, 'God drops the monkey wrench,' you mean *fate* plays you a dirty trick?"

Frank shook his head no, and said, "Fate don't drop monkey wrenches into your life. God does."

A firmness in his voice, a quiet self-assurance concerning God's behavior, discouraged each of them from pursuing the subject further. Teddy suddenly recalled several instances during the fourteen months he had investigated the Quincy robbery in which Frank had offhandedly referred to God. Could it be the man was religious? It was something he would explore with him at some later date, Teddy thought, as Frank pointed out on his map the small room adjoining the manager's office, just off the lobby, in which employees and unexpected arrivals would be handcuffed, gagged, and blindfolded.

"What's the size of that room, and how many detainees you expect we'll have to put in there?" Garrick asked.

"It's about fifteen by fifteen, with a couple of couches and armchairs," Frank said. "The manager uses it to meet with anybody who's important. As far as how many people are going to end up in there?" He kept track on his fingers for all to see as he totaled them up. "The doorman goes in right off the bat. There's two security guys go in. There's the desk clerk. There's two porters and a possible emergency handyman. There's one eleven-to-seven bellhop for room service and a half-assed cook in the kitchen for any three A.M. orders of stewed prunes or whatnot. Figure we could easily get six late-arrival guests, say four singles and a deuce. How many's that?"

"Fifteen," Garrick, Breslin, and Teddy said together.

"Right," Frank said approvingly, and Teddy realized he had asked the question only to check their arithmetic.

"Allow three more oddballs off the street. That's eighteen."

"What kind of oddballs?" Garrick asked. His voice carried a tone of annoyance that seemed to be directed not toward Frank but toward the oddballs themselves, intruders with no right to be in the operation.

"Who knows?" Frank said. "Some limo driver looking to take a piss. A Con Ed guy checking out a gas leak. Don't be surprised if a fucking UFO lands on Fifty-fifth Street and a couple of extraterrestrials march into the lobby. Murphy's Second Law."

"Murphy has a second law?" Breslin asked.

"Yeah," Frank said. "The first law everybody knows—anything that can go wrong will go wrong. Murphy's Second Law says that several things that can't possibly go wrong will also go wrong. And it happens all the time, I'll testify to it."

"So after your limo driver and your extraterrestrials, who else?" Garrick asked.

"Figure a possible three more. Guests from upstairs who wander down to the lobby for one thing or another."

"Like what?" Garrick asked.

"You wouldn't believe what very rich people expect at two in the morning," Frank said. "Aspirins, writing paper, Tums, a safety pin. They could want the bellhop to give them an enema, for Christ sake. They manage to lock themselves out of their rooms. They want a dripping faucet fixed right away because it's keeping them awake. Their TV set goes dark. They hear little noises and they're convinced there's a mouse in the closet. And once one of them gets a bug up his ass about something and starts calling down to the front desk you've got to handcuff the bum and throw him in with the others or you'll never get a minute's peace. They're persistent, the rich."

"We're up to twenty-one in that room," Garrick said. "Are they going to fit?"

Frank nodded. "Nice and easy. They're not sitting in

armchairs—they go facedown on the floor. You know we'll need two dozen sets of handcuffs for them."

"I'll handle that," Garrick said. "You don't have to do anything on that end. I'll have plenty of adhesive tape, too."

"Gaffer's tape," Frank said. "Professional gaffer's tape. Stagehands use it. It costs but it's better. And don't skimp on it. Bring a dozen rolls."

Garrick nodded, then asked, "What size glove do you wear?"

"Ten," Frank said.

Garrick jotted that down.

"What kind of tools do you need?"

"Forget it," Frank said. "I bring my own. You know we'll need luggage to carry when we go in."

"I've already got it."

With what seemed to Teddy as some reluctance, Frank asked about guns.

"I've already got them," Garrick said. "Glocks. With silencers."

Frank nodded his approval. "Good choice. You want them big enough to persuade people you're serious," he said, then looked from Garrick to Breslin and asked, "Neither of you are into icing somebody or bashing them around for no reason, are you?"

They both shook their heads no.

"The quieter and smoother it runs, the happier we are," Breslin said.

"And we're agreed that any females get tied up, nobody so much as gives them an affectionate pat on the ass, yes?" Frank said.

"Jesus," Garrick said with great disgust, "what kind of people have you worked with?"

"All kinds," Frank said. "I don't know about California but I can tell you that here on the East Coast, when you put together a heist team you often attract a bad element."

Frank took another twenty minutes to run through his loosely laid plans, during which Jay Garrick several times was palpably annoyed at the lack of precision. He said nothing, though, and Teddy guessed that he was reluctant to probe Frank's monkey-wrench philosophy further.

Breslin and Garrick had collaborated on what Garrick called the peripheral planning—everything until they entered and after they left the Montclair.

"Chuck and I will be the inside guys," Garrick said. "We'll be in the hotel for the better part of two days and two nights, so employees are going to get good long looks at us. Before we check in, we'll both put on some pretty elaborate makeup."

He looked pointedly at Breslin and added, "Which will *always* be fully in place except in the privacy of our rooms."

"You think it'll help much?" Frank asked.

"I'm good at it," Jay said.

Teddy knew from the earlier meeting that, in fact, they would be transformed by a Hollywood makeup artist Cutshaw often used.

"You two," Garrick said to Teddy and Frank, "won't arrive until the robbery begins, so you can go in wearing latex hoods. I'm not talking those cruddy celebrity masks you see in the tourist shops. These you won't even notice at twenty feet."

Frank nodded.

"The safest way for the outside guys to arrive," Garrick said, "is as a late-arrival guest and his driver. It means pulling up in a limo. We already have it. A Caddy. It was stolen in Connecticut and I've had a mechanic go over it from top to bottom. It won't give us any problem. The plates and registration sticker are New York."

Frank interrupted. "You're not going to wait till the night of the heist to grab plates? And what kind of registration sticker you talking about?"

"With today's copying equipment, forging a registration and a window sticker is nothing," Garrick said, pleased with the opportunity to show Frank how planning ought to be done. "And we make up dummy plates. We vacuum-form them out of plastic. It's only a couple of hours' work and once they're painted and dirtied up, a cop would have to feel them to know they're fake. We duplicate the plate off an identical Cadillac, so even if a cop runs a check through his car computer it comes up fine." By way of reassurance he added, "The state inspection sticker on the windshield? We duped that, too. The VIN plate on top of the dash? Done. This car will stand up to anything short of someone examining serial numbers on the block and chassis."

Teddy saw that Frank was literally wide-eyed.

"Are you telling me the registration is a duplicate of someone else's?" Frank asked.

"Exactly."

"How'd you even get hold of one to copy?"

"I've got a computer whiz back in California who hacks into any motor vehicles department in the country whenever he feels like it. None of them are very secure."

"Jesus Christ," Frank said.

"I like to guard against things going bad over foolishness. Like getting stopped for some minor violation and not having a proper inspection sticker on the windshield. People get brought down over things like that all the time."

"Tell me about it," Frank said flatly. "It's called mopery."

He motioned to all that he was about to finish off the last slice of grilled eggplant unless someone wanted some of it. Teddy had had his eye on it for the past few minutes.

"Frankie. *Mezza*," he said, and Frank cut it in half with his fork, scooped a few slivers of sun-dried tomatoes onto it, then passed it across the table to Teddy. The two of them chewed their pieces of eggplant happily while Garrick described for Frank the staging area they would use before and after the robbery.

Teddy listened to Jay Garrick lie. Garrick said that he had procured the ground floor of a small, century-old tenement on Thirty-ninth Street off Ninth Avenue, the southern part of Hell's Kitchen, a neighborhood with a mixture of industrial lofts and what was once called slum housing. Whatever character the neighborhood may have once possessed had long ago been destroyed by traffic-clogged approaches to the Lincoln Tunnel and overhead ramps carrying buses to and from the Port Authority Terminal. The neighborhood's impersonality made it ideal for their use. Garrick gave the impression that they were using a ground-floor apartment, but Teddy knew from the earlier meeting that what Garrick had procured wasn't an apartment at all but what had once been a street-level storefront in a small tenement, used for years to provision dozens of mobile hot dog stands that would be pushed out by immigrants each morning to posts on midtown sidewalks, then returned at night. Part of the storefront had been converted to a garage large enough to accommodate small vans of incoming provisions. It was that feature Garrick had deemed a necessity for a staging area—a garage into which they could actually drive, so that the hostages would not have to be transferred on a street or in an alleyway.

In the earlier, three-man meeting, Garrick had pointed out that the limo in which the two outside men would pull up was unsuitable as a getaway car, since it needed to accommodate what he called the four ops plus four hostages. They couldn't, of course, tell that to Frank.

"The problem is," Garrick now explained, "since the limo has to be left at the curb for hours, there's a small chance—but a very real one—of it getting towed."

Frank nodded, and said, "You don't have to convince me. Billy Bats did twelve years for armed robbery 'cause when him and his partner—a kid from Jersey City, an apprentice—when they come running out of a smash-and-grab jewelry heist that they kept under *four minutes* they stood on the sidewalk and watched their getaway car rolling down Second Avenue on a hook."

"The evening of the robbery," Garrick said, "Chuck here will park a small van with commercial plates on it across from the hotel. The signs on it will be for a plumbing company and there'll be an Emergency Call card on its windshield. We'll use the van for our getaway."

"Nice," Frank said. "Who's on the wheel?"

"Chuck is," Garrick said.

"How far away from this Thirty-ninth Street apartment are you going to ditch the car?" Frank asked Breslin.

Garrick answered for him. "Just a few blocks is fine. When they find it so close to the tunnel they'll think we switched cars there and headed for Jersey."

Teddy watched Frank, who seemed to buy it readily enough, pop a small chunk of fontina cheese into his mouth and bite into a piece of Italian bread. Teddy, too, was partial to fontina. It occurred to him that normally he would have considered himself one of three cops in the room hoodwinking a criminal, and never given a second thought to where his loyalties ought to lie. Now, he felt a twinge of guilt about lying to Frank and realized that the New-York-Italian-American-blue-collar values that he shared with Frank as much as he did their taste in food were more intense than the cop values he shared with Garrick and Breslin.

Garrick proposed that the four of them drink to "a smooth run."

They did.

"And a vault full of jewels," Frank added, and lifted his glass.

As they drank to Frank's toast, Garrick made momentary eye contact with Teddy. In that instant a flicker of self-satisfied amusement in his facial expression managed to convey the idea that he and Teddy were conspirators against the naive Frank Belmonte, who believed that this robbery was all about jewels. The effect on Teddy was as though Garrick had whispered, "This dumb guinea who believes in a God who drops monkey wrenches ought to be stomping grapes in a southern Italian vineyard." Teddy suddenly felt as though he was betraying one of his own, but consoled himself with the thought that once the robbery was done and Frank went home with what might well be a million or so in stones, he would have no gripe about the deception and would never learn of it anyway. There would be no harm done.

VIII

Angel Sosa swung his rented Buick Park Avenue out from under the el into the outside lane of Jerome Avenue, negotiated the narrow corridor between parked cars and steel columns for half a block, then turned into the Tip Top Used Cars lot. It was indistinguishable from the scores of others that stretched for a mile in the shadow of the el—fifty polished cars on display, each with a price drawn in bold brushstrokes of Bon Ami on its windshield. Overhead, hundreds of red, white, and blue plastic flags flapped noisily on lines radiating from a large sign that guaranteed, in both English and Spanish, instant credit for all who entered. Angel stepped out of the Buick and peered through the grimy window of the shack that served as an office. El Cid, the stunningly colored, one-eyed gamecock he remembered from visits to the lot five years ago, stood on a tall filing cabinet against the rear wall. Head held triumphantly high, chest out, he was the consummate cock-of-the-walk, his one remaining eye so piercing and determined that had the taxidermist placed the bird's right leg atop a stuffed, prone pit bull one would have believed it possible. His steel spurs shone. They had been chromed and hung on a chain upon the rooster's retirement, during which he had enjoyed free run of the lot and even the sidewalk of Jerome Avenue, along with frequent visits to the cages of receptive hens. When he died of old age in this very shack and was then mounted beautifully by a taxidermist employed at the Museum of Natural History, the spurs had been put onto his legs. The brass plaque that Angel remembered was still at the bird's feet. It read, EL CID, 11 AND 0. 1977–1987. HE BOUGHT TIP TOP.

"He still looks good, no?" a voice behind him asked softly.

Angel turned to see the squat figure of Flocko, his big, hard belly swaddled in an expensive suede safari jacket. He had once told Angel that his nickname, Flocko, was given him as a teenager in his Puerto Rican village because he weighed under a hundred pounds and every rib was visible. As he matured, his metabolism changed, along with his income and appetite, and he did more than fill out, he ballooned up to two-twenty, but the nickname stuck. They shook hands, and Angel noticed that the garnet-and-diamond ring Flocko boasted of having won on a side bet at an early El Cid bout still adorned his pinky.

"When did you get back?" Flocko asked.

"Couple of months."

"You here for long?"

"Not too long."

"How is Havana?"

"Falling apart, to tell the truth. It's great for the tourists. Cheap. You should visit."

"I've been out of the Bronx twice and I got here thirty years ago," Flocko said. "How's New York look to you?"

"Rich."

"You were here what last time? Five years?"

"Three."

"Never thought of defecting? When they called you back?"

Angel smiled and said softly, "No."

"Commitment," Flocko said, and nodded approvingly, then stepped into the tiny office. Angel followed. It was even more cramped than he remembered. Flocko took a holstered revolver from a drawer in the filing cabinet and laid it on the desk.

"Right to spec. Smith and Wesson thirty-two. Clean as the day it left the factory. Absolutely no history. This fellow's never been fired in anger."

Angel slid it from the holster, hefted it, flipped open and spun the cylinder, then peered through the barrel at the light. It looked and felt good. He handed Flocko four $100 bills, then took the hollow-tip cartridges he proffered and loaded the revolver deliberately. Flocko watched him, then, uncharacteristically, asked a question that was inappropriate.

"You always worked with a twenty-two, Angel. Silenced. Why the change? And you never used an ankle holster."

Angel was about to behave as though Flocko had never spoken, then softened for the moment.

"This one's strictly defensive. A twenty-two's no good for that."

He glanced up at the wall clock just over El Cid's head. Almost six. The flight was due in at 3:00 A.M. and to be on the safe side he would allow an hour to get out to JFK. It gave him eight hours to kill. He would call Stephanie to see if she was available for a last-minute dinner and maybe more. Among the handful of upscale New York women he had dated during his previous thirty-six-month tour of duty, she was the only one he had missed after returning home to Cuba. It had taken him by surprise, the fond memories of her he had unknowingly carried back to the island. It had surprised him even more that the memories were stronger and sweeter two years later, when he was about to return to the States on this present mission. Surprisingly, she engendered first and foremost memories that were asexual—an unseasonably cold October weekday when they walked hand in hand through snow flurries in the nearly deserted Bronx Zoo; later that day espresso and cannoli at a corner café on 187th Street; a perfect morning spent circling Manhattan on a tour boat after he said it would be his first time around, a white lie meant to give her pleasure; the smooth feel of a satin blouse on the inside of his forearm when he laid his arm across her shoulders on the windswept deck of the Empire State Building, that visit truly his first. Small, pretty, soft-spoken, and deceptively strong-willed, she was a forty-year-old widow who taught fifth-graders in an overcrowded Upper West Side public school. She lived alone in London Terrace, a group of ten or so sixteen-story, red-brick buildings from the 1930s that occupied a square block on West Twenty-third Street.

Contacting anyone was against the rules, and since crossing over from Canada three months ago he had obeyed the rule, despite being within walking distance of her apartment for much of that time. Now, on the last day he would be on his own, he deserved a small reward for a job well done up to this point. He wanted to test his memories of Stephanie against reality, and if reality measured up, then perhaps, when this mission was over, he would sit down and think anew about his future. For now, he would simply tell her he was passing through New York on his way to somewhere. As for the little broken rule, there would be no harm done.

At exactly nine-thirty Jay Garrick rose from his armchair and walked across the plushly carpeted living room of his junior suite to stand beside the telephone. He moved deliberately, in a way meant to attract Chuck Breslin's attention. Breslin leaned a bit closer to the television set and pretended not to notice. For the past few days he had spent too many hours with Garrick, who was proving to be the most difficult cohort he had ever worked with. Arrogance was a common characteristic of Agency people but Garrick was so overbearing that it bordered on hostility. More important, there was a mean streak in him, a pleasure in violence that came through those few times that he sat back in one of the suite's overstuffed armchairs, put his feet on the coffee table, and recounted wet-work he had done for the Agency or as a Special Forces captain on clandestine runs into Laos and Cambodia. On every assignment his immediate superior had been a total asshole who would have botched things completely were it not for Garrick's presence.

The phone rang one minute later. Garrick used the remote to mute the Yankees-Angels game in which Breslin, to discourage conversation, pretended to be more engrossed than he was.

He said, "Hello?" into the phone, then leaned with it close enough to Breslin for him to hear Linwood Cutshaw's soft voice on the other end asking for, "Mr. George Berger, please."

"Speaking," Garrick said.

"This is Dr. Prause's secretary. The doctor will be able to keep his appointment. He is on his way to New York. Expected to arrive just after three A.M."

"Fine," Garrick said. "Thanks for confirming."

He hung up and produced one of his smug little smiles for Breslin, who was now looking at him but darting involuntary glances at the mute television every few seconds, meanwhile marveling at Garrick's ability to derive so much satisfaction, what appeared to be so much outright pleasure, from the promptness of a telephone call. The man thrived on split-second adherence to an elaborate schedule. Breslin had at first considered it some kind of anal compulsion but quickly came to see it as an even more fundamental weakness—a security blanket Garrick used to insulate himself from the great fear of failure. Pulled up over his head, it shut out the myriad things that could go wrong, any one of which would wreck the operation. His neurotic need for precision was simply a way to ward off total panic. No matter how meaningless in itself, each tiny goal met, even a planned telephone call that arrived within a minute of its scheduled time, provided reassurance that all was well, that success was in sight, that the plan was working, that he, Jay Garrick—once, as he had unhappily let slip to Breslin, an obese, only child living in a fatherless tract house under the high-voltage power lines that passed over Ventura—was in complete control, as part of an organization that was omnipotent.

"Our man's in the air," he said. "Nonstop to JFK."

"He traveling alone?" Breslin asked.

"So far."

Garrick looked at his watch.

"What time did you tell Teddy you'd call?" Breslin asked.

"Nine-ten to nine-twenty," he said, then explained further. "I needed the ten-minute window. Nine o'clock departure in Caracas isn't the same thing as here. They're on mañana time down there."

Breslin was barely paying attention. The reality of their situation was sinking in. It was going to happen. Another five hours and they would pull out guns and take over the hotel, and hope that none of the thousand things that might go wrong would. His stomach did a few turns. He looked across at Garrick, whose new face took some getting used to. Since the two of them had checked in thirty-six hours ago, they had never left their rooms without the elaborate disguises constructed by Cutshaw's makeup artist. Garrick wore a dark wig that changed his hairline radically, plus a full mustache. Woven-in hair had doubled the size of his eyebrows. A set of colored contact lenses had turned his irises brown. Since he was in his own suite, he had removed the pads from inside his cheeks and tiny, plastic hoops from inside his nostrils, both of which, when in place, added thirty pounds to the weight that would be estimated from a police sketch. Breslin looked into a nearby mirror. His own cheek pads and nostril inserts were in place. Looking at his reflection in full disguise, Breslin believed he could pass his mother at a slow walk and go unrecognized.

Garrick dialed the number of a pay phone at Second Avenue and Fifteenth Street, where Teddy waited. It must have rung only once, Breslin thought, as he listened to Garrick say, "The schedule is perfect. There are no changes."

Garrick hung up, aimed the remote at the television, and restored the sound.

"Who's winning?" he asked.

"Five-two, Yanks. Top of the seventh. You an Angels fan?"

"I could care less. Watching baseball's about as exciting as watching dominoes."

"It's just too subtle for born and bred Californians,

Jay," Breslin said. "I've been at a couple of games in Dodger Stadium. There's maybe twelve fans in the whole park who really understand what's happening on the field at any given moment."

"Well I'm not one of them," Garrick said, and used the remote to turn the set off entirely, then sat across the coffee table from Breslin. He took his carefully drawn diagram of the hotel from his pocket and opened it out.

"Let's go over this one more time," he said. "From first move to last."

Teddy turned his key in the lock and called out, "Frank. It's me," as he swung open the door and entered the apartment. Belmonte was where Teddy had left him twenty minutes earlier, seated on the very edge of the couch cushion, hunched forward over the coffee table, intent upon a game of solitaire. Teddy set his bag of groceries on the unused corner of the table.

"You made a food stop?" Belmonte asked, as he turned up a king, couldn't find a vacant slot for it, and set it out as a new, eighth column.

"You already got seven columns," Teddy said.

"So now I got eight," Belmonte said. "I thought you retired."

"I forget sometimes."

"Is our space shot on schedule?"

"To the minute. We're to pull up half a block away, as close to two o'clock as we can get."

"You ever ask the master planner what happens if one of us has to take a leak during this heist? Do we call it quits and go home because we blew our schedule?"

Teddy preferred not to pursue any discussion of Jay Garrick. He said nothing and began unpacking the bag of groceries. Belmonte turned up another king, agonized for just a few moments, then started a ninth column. He paused in his game for a bit, his mind clearly not on the cards, then looked up at Teddy.

"Something about this guy, Teddy. I worked with a

lot of oddballs in my time, but there's something about this guy."

Teddy decided he had better respond. He kept it low-keyed, with a tiny shrug, and said, "Hey, the guy likes precision. What am I going to tell you?"

Belmonte shook his head thoughtfully, then said, "I've been around thieves my whole life. Thousands of them. Worked with them, hung out with them, done time with them. Hell, I've studied them. The real control freaks I can count on one hand. Thieves are fatalists, Teddy. Fatalists or cowboys. They got to be. Every heist or burglary is a crapshoot, 'cause the bottom line is you've got to hope God don't drop the monkey wrench in. Your buddy Jay don't fit the profile of a habitual. He's what a guy doing social-science research would call an anomaly." He paused for a moment to turn up another card, then added, "An anomaly means he's so far out of the usual pattern that—"

Teddy interrupted, "I know what it means. You know, I never took you for a scholar, Frank."

"Don't get touchy," Belmonte said.

"I'm not touchy."

"Yes you are. 'Cause I thought you might not know what an anomaly is. But that don't mean I think you're stupid, Teddy, I just ain't sure how well read you are. You were a cop for twenty years. With all due respect to the city's finest, I don't see an awful lot of them competing on *Jeopardy!* And as far as me being a scholar—the truth is I got strong scholarly instincts. I just keep them nice and quiet, since the circles I move in don't always prize deep thinkers."

"So you're a closet intellectua¹," Teddy said.

"Not far wrong. If I had been raised maybe five miles north of Elizabeth and Hester—say Park and Seventy-ninth—I'd be settled down in some nice little college town now. Professor Belmonte. Sitting in a leather armchair in my book-lined study. Teaching eight or ten hours a week, publishing some original research every so often in a heavyweight intellectual journal. Couple a times a year be one of those talking heads on *MacNeil-Lehrer.* Be a nice life."

"Not for nothing, Frank, but I have a tough time seeing you in your leather chair, puffing on a pipe."

"Fuck the pipe. They're filthy. I always see myself standing on a stepladder in my study. To get at a book way up on top. One of those beat-up, dark mahogany ladders that roll along on a rail. Like they had in shoe stores when we were kids, and in the big reading rooms at the Forty-second Street library."

"You'd have a Ph.D., I assume," Teddy said.

"This day and age you can't work without one."

"What would your field be?"

"Criminology."

"When the hell did you get interested in this kind of stuff?"

"It was always there, lurking under the surface, but it really came out ten years ago when I was doing a nickel up in Auburn. I finished what I needed for a high school diploma, then I got into one of those college programs for prisoners. Figured it would be good for the parole board. I had fifty credits done by the time they cut me loose. Three-point-six average, and that's from Syracuse University, not some Mickey Mouse diploma mill. Majored in psych. What I found out is I got a real aptitude for academic shit. Our asshole politicians have killed that program since then."

"You didn't keep it up when you got out?"

"Nah. Not even on my own. I can only really concentrate when I'm in the joint. On the street I got no mental discipline. Even my everyday reading habits deteriorate. Forget about Hermann Hesse or dipping into a little Gurdjieff after dinner—I find myself reading the same crap everybody else reads. I did one course at the New School for Social Research up on Twelfth Street. The Urban Deviant as Middle America's Scapegoat, it was called. Taught by a Middle American would faint if he ever came within three feet of a serious deviant, even a rural one. The school actually has a lot of heavyweight faculty but the atmosphere's not very academic. Maybe half the student body are dilettantes."

"So it's all this expertise that tells you Jay is an anomaly," Teddy said.

"Teddy, this guy just called you on a pay phone instead of that phone in front of you, no? Tell me, why? Who the hell is going to be tapping your phone *now*? Maybe *after* the heist you come under suspicion. Not before. He's paranoid is what he is. This guy is worse than my mother and I don't have to tell you what she's like."

Teddy knew. His own mother, like all mothers in the neighborhoods he and Frank came from, had taught him from an early age that the world was ready to swallow up the unwary at every turn. "The minute you set foot outside the door you're in danger," she used to warn him in Italian. "Don't trust nobody."

Teddy looked at his watch. "A little more than four hours before we go in. You going to eat some of this food I bought?"

Belmonte put down his cards and helped Teddy take containers from the bag and set them onto the table, oohing and aahing softly at delicacies he especially liked and happily announcing them by name as he removed the top of each container and recognized its contents, in tones of approval meant to compliment Teddy on his choice. "Bocconcini. Parmigiano-Reggiano—nice and crumbly. Stuffed artichoke. Pasta fazool. Fusilli with broccoli rabe." He started plucking the artichoke, eating it with both hands, scraping two leaves at a time against his bottom teeth. Teddy picked at the room-temperature fusilli-and-rabe, and watched Frank enjoy his food. He felt that his own heartbeat was stronger and faster than usual.

"Was everybody this laid back just before the Quincy robbery?" he asked.

"First of all, this ain't just before the robbery, my friend. When you and me are in the car on the way to the hotel and a patrol car stops for a light right next to us and the cop riding shotgun looks us over for a few seconds longer than you think he ought to and the gun you're carrying is pressing into your stomach—that's just before the robbery. And you'll be scared shitless, Teddy. Like the song says, on that you can rely. Even more scared than me, 'cause this is brand-new stuff for you. Your first time out."

"I haven't been sitting behind a desk the last twenty years, Frank. I tiptoed through a lot of dark hallways with a gun in my hand. Not knowing who might pop out of a door and take a shot at me."

"Not the same. The badge makes all the difference in the world. With a badge you got a right to be there—you're *supposed* to be there—and that takes a lot of fear away. This time you'll be there as an outlaw. The whole system is against you. Out to get you. Whatever happens, you're wrong and the only way you succeed is to get away clean. Outwit everybody. It's you against the world and you know what kind of odds those are. Believe me, Teddy, your neck's never been out as far as it's going to be in a couple of hours."

Angel unbuckled his ankle holster and slid it, along with the .32 it held, under the driver's seat before stepping out into the damp night air and the 100-decibel roar of a jet taking off. This was his first trip to Kennedy in years and so he paused to take in the scene for a few moments—the huge, lighted semicircle of glass in the near distance that was the International Arrivals Building, the procession of headlights circling nearby, sparse but nevertheless present even at this hour, as were the dozens of parked cars surrounding him, all of them late models. During the day and evening, he knew, this lot would be filled to capacity with cars—$20 million or $30 million worth—enough to stock the bleak children's wards of Cuba's hospitals with many months' worth of badly needed antibiotics.

He walked across the parking lot at a leisurely pace. Ahead, a silver Mercedes limousine waiting near the entry to the pedestrian walkway brought to mind a rainy night five years earlier when he had driven Fat Reuben Higuera's month-old silver Mercedes from a deserted industrial street in Red Hook to the long-term parking lot at Kennedy, with Fat Reuben comfortably arranged in a fetal position in the car's generous trunk, leaking very little blood from a single .22-caliber entry wound at the base of his skull. Angel had been attached to the Cuban mission to the United Nations at the time, carrying the title agricultural specialist, but was actually second-in-command of the mission's elite, six-man security force. From the beginning of that thirty-six-month assignment he had passed up opportunities to earn money by smuggling goods into Cuba on trips home or selling information to the CIA or to the zealots in Miami. He wouldn't betray the revolution. But a contract from a Colombian drug dealer in Jackson Heights to eliminate a Colombian drug dealer in Brooklyn carried no moral implications. The work had paid $15,000 plus whatever he might find in Fat Reuben's pocket, on his wrist, and clasped around his twenty-five-inch neck—$10,000 in cash and nearly that in jewelry, as it happened. Before completing that tour of duty in New York he had put three more Colombians into the trunks of their cars and established an account in a Cayman Island bank, his son's name on it as well as his own.

Angel felt no guilt about this, for while he would never betray the revolution, he was a realist. Years ago he had seen clearly that Cuba would someday soon be back in the hands of the capitalists, at which time his then twelve-year-old son ought not be starting the post-Fidel race with his ankles hobbled. It was why he had contracted to put Fat Reuben down. At the start of his tour of duty five years ago he had sat in his East Side apartment one night and watched, on a Spanish-language television channel, Cuban-born *gusanos* in Miami cry out publicly for the chance to run the soil of their beloved homeland through their fingers one last time before they died, beside them their successful sons in business suits yearning for the chance to run Cuban soil through their own fingers for the first time. Left unsaid was the desire of both fathers and sons to own the rich Cuban soil that ran through their fingers, along with the tobacco and cane that grew so well on it and the factories that processed its output. Sadly, he knew they would. That was where the world was heading in the near term. Only some overwhelming twist of fate could prevent Cuba from entering the next century without a vestige of the socialist ideals that had driven it since 1960. The irony was that if this mission on which he was engaged was successful—as he believed it very well might be—it would likely result in an even quicker return to capitalism. During his three years of living in the States he had traveled extensively—though travel was limited by law the restriction was generally ignored. He had acquired the ability to see his own country from a distance and was convinced that were the blockade to come down, were trade to resume—most important, were the Cuban people exposed to hordes of Yanquis and the luxuries with which they lived—the socialist structure would quickly tumble. It had happened in the USSR and it was happening in China, and neither of those peoples had the innate tendencies toward individualism and free expression that Cubans did. He had not expressed this fear to Cheito when they met—it would have been seen as a lack of faith in the Cuban *guajiro*. He had accepted the mission for the chance to see Stephanie and decide his future. Which he had now done. After the dinner and the hour of lovemaking, the reality of her presence had proven better even than the memory of her. He would stay in the States when this mission was over, after buying his now seventeen-year-old son's passage off the island. That could be done these days, for low-profile citizens.

He entered the Arrivals Building and lingered for a few minutes at the Plexiglas partition that sealed off the public from the Customs area to watch a planeload of passengers from Warsaw, their flight nearly six hours late, step into the United States. Several of them were greeted by family groups of ten or twelve with joyous howls upon the émigré's appearance on the other side of the Plexiglas, which quickly alternated with wails of aching sadness for lost years and whatever family tragedies were evoked, then great bear hugs and tears when the new arrival emerged into the public area. Angel had entered the country several times through these very doors during his tour at the U.N. mission, returning via Mexico from brief trips home. In the intervening years nothing about the terminal seemed to have changed but the Plexiglas, which had become cloudy and scratched. The place was, if anything, even more run-down now. He wondered, as he often had in the past, how a country so rich and technically capable could take so little pride in its public places. Disney World, which he had visited once, was far more impressive and better maintained than this small-scale, shabby portal to the world's single superpower.

He walked to one of the small Arrivals screens and found that VASP flight 800, a charter from Caracas, was now due to arrive at three-fifteen, just half an hour ahead of a Tel Aviv arrival. There were perhaps a hundred people in the terminal, most apparently waiting for the Warsaw-flight passengers dribbling through Customs. He needed a place to sit, and took an escalator up to the sprawling second level. It felt like a suburban American mall, with a fake Dutch tavern competing side by side with a coffee shop meant to look like an outdoor café, both closed now. The only open business was a long, stainless-steel counter-showcase at which he ordered a plain bagel with cream cheese and a container of coffee, which he carried to a tiny table for two that gave him a good view of the arrival area below. Both the coffee and the bagel were as good as any he had tasted in his three-month stay.

He was here illegally this time, having used a flight from Havana to Mexico City, an Aeroméxico flight to Ottawa, traveling under his own name with a diplomatic pouch that contained sealed vials given him by Cheito. The security assigned to him from the embassy in Ottawa had known nothing of his cargo, only that Angel was to be shepherded over the border into the United States. They had crossed at Massena, a small town on the New York State side of the St. Lawrence River where the security man had turned back and Angel had boarded a bus for the ten-hour ride to Albany, then three more hours to the Port Authority terminal in Manhattan. A one-bedroom apartment had been rented for him on Eighty-first Street near Amsterdam Avenue, just around the corner from the Hayden Planetarium. As ordered, he contacted no one from the Cuban mission. Before leaving the island he had spent a day with Cheito, who had given him a crash course in how to propagate the virus into larger quantities. Two of the small vials Angel had carried contained virus in a saltwater buffer fortified with DMSO; another two contained an intestinal mucosal cell line that Kaongeshi-Zaire found especially hospitable. Producing sufficient ready-to-go, virus-laden solution in a makeshift bathroom laboratory had been dangerous but straightforward enough, given his education as a chemical engineer.

He drank the last mouthful of coffee from the cardboard container and savored the aftertaste, then rose and walked to the nearby Arrivals screen. VASP flight 800 was still due at three-fifteen. He checked his watch, a handsome knockoff of the numberless Movado watch, bought for fifteen dollars from a Senegalese vendor outside the Museum of Natural History during his first week in New York. Two-ten. He yawned, and stretched his arms over his head, and realized that his body would welcome a soft bed in this incredibly expensive hotel Cheito had insisted upon. In the late morning he would indulge himself in an elaborate room-service breakfast before driving north, providing it wouldn't offend the good doctor's Marxist sensibilities.

IX

At 1:50 A.M. Frank Belmonte pulled the Cadillac out of the East Fifteenth Street parking space it had occupied all day and drove up First Avenue at a steady thirty miles per hour, in perfect synch with the staggered traffic lights. There were few cars on the road. As they entered the short underpass near the United Nations, Teddy, in the rear seat of the limousine, drew a deep breath and exhaled slowly, remembering Frank's warning earlier that this was the point at which nervousness would set in. Butterflies that had lain dormant in his stomach now began to flutter. He fingered the latex hood on the seat beside him. A wig fixed to its top, along with a tight fit and realistic flesh coloring, made it barely noticeable at a casual glance. He sat back and tried to relax, knowing that his stomach would calm down the moment he walked through the door of the Montclair into some physical action.

They turned onto Fifty-fifth Street and made the lights at Second and Third avenues. They had to stop for the light at Lexington.

"How you doing?" Frank asked without turning.

"I'm good. How about you?"

"Feels like Christmas morning when I was a kid."

"You really get off on this stuff, huh?" Teddy said, a bit surprised.

"That's why I've been doing it all my life, Teddy. And you know something? If I had an exact list of what's waiting for us at the Montclair, half the fun would be gone. It's what I might find in the boxes that does it for me. If there was just a pile of jewelry sitting out where you could see it—behind a piece of glass, say—I'd be bored right now. It's working on each box, chiseling it open, feeling it give, then sliding it out and lifting the cover. It might be empty or it might have a thirty-carat flawless river diamond sitting in it—maybe a mil retail. That's the beauty part of this kind of heist."

He was talking faster than usual.

The light changed. Frank crossed Lexington and glided into a long stretch of empty curb on the north side of the street just before the corner of Park.

Teddy checked his watch, and said, "Almost two."

They peered ahead into the next block. The Montclair was a few hundred feet ahead, across the generous width of Park Avenue, on the south side of the street. Lights set in the underside of the massive, cast-iron canopy that extended out to the curb illuminated a wide swath of sidewalk and the plate-glass doors of the lobby. Teddy saw that a van was parked near the hotel entrance—the getaway vehicle, he guessed—with plumbing-company signs printed on it. Just beyond the van, at a darkened restaurant adjacent to the hotel, two private sanitation workers heaved black plastic bags from a huge pile at the curb into the rear well of a compactor truck.

"We wait for them to move, no?" Frank said.

Teddy nodded.

"That Belgian must be sleeping like a baby," Frank said. "Long flight like that."

Teddy said nothing. Garrick had called in a reservation a few days ago in the name of Luc Kiant, then later canceled it at Teddy's suggestion. He worried that Frank would be on edge throughout the robbery and possibly even balk at leaving if he believed the diamond-laden Belgian might still check in at any minute.

When the truck pulled away, Teddy opened his cell phone and dialed. After a few moments he said into the mouthpiece, "Everything's fine. Let's proceed," then hung up. Another cluster of butterflies joined the fliers in his stomach and he wanted things to move quickly now. He caught sight of Frank's face in the rearview mirror. He looked absolutely happy.

* * *

In the living room of suite 623, Jay Garrick closed his cell phone and checked his Breitling watch, simply to see how close they were to their schedule.

"Five-past-two," he said to Breslin, with obvious pleasure, then picked up his room phone and punched the zero key. Unlike every other luxury hotel in the city, which had long ago placed beside each room phone a lengthy menu of services, each with its own two-digit number, the Montclair maintained the simple, old-fashioned zero for anything a guest desired. In fact, it was more than the affectation that newcomers sometimes took it to be. Long-term residents of the hotel thrived on just those touches. A two-digit code smacked of the impersonal, modern world that lay beyond the Montclair borders, whereas a simple zero had about it the sort of homey quality for which they were more than willing to pay through the nose. There were old women in the hotel who for the past thirty or forty years of their lives had never dialed anything but a simple zero, and never failed to have their every need met. They were invariably the women who also chose to continue using a rotary dial phone.

Garrick listened to the phone downstairs ring only once before it was picked up.

"Front desk. This is Peter. How may I help you, Mr. Berger?"

"There's a television in room six-twenty-one that's blasting. The gentleman refuses to turn it down."

There was a long pause, then, somewhat tentatively, "That's Mr. Layton's room, sir?"

"That's correct," Garrick said.

"Ah, I was under the impression that you and Mr. Layton had checked in together? Into adjoining suites?"

Garrick spoke in a tone of controlled anger. "That is not your concern, Peter. He refuses to turn down his god*damned* television and it's disturbing me. Do something about it. Now."

He hung up the phone firmly, then said to Breslin, "We're under way."

Garrick inserted the little plastic hoops into his nostrils and the cheek pads into his mouth. They walked through the connecting door into Breslin's suite. Breslin carried his room phone across to the television, which was set on MTV, and turned the volume up the moment the phone rang. He lifted the handset, said, "Yes," then a few moments later, with the carefully enunciated speech of a drunk, said, "Hey, Peter. At nine hundred a night I'll play this as loud as I like. And if Mr. Berger has a problem with that, tell him for me to go fuck himself."

He hung up. Garrick stepped into the dark bathroom, which was very close to the hallway door. In just a few minutes there was an authoritative, four-rap knock on the door. Breslin opened it.

One of the two security men who worked the eleven-to-seven shift faced him, the big, soft-spoken Italian American in his mid-forties whom Frank, during his three-day stay in the hotel, had immediately made as a retired cop.

"We've had complaints about your television, Mr. Layton."

Breslin looked around in apparently drunken confusion and managed to scan the hallway. It was empty. He did a sudden about-face, walked unsteadily to the set, and turned the volume higher. The ex-cop never hesitated. He strode across the room and pressed the off switch. When he turned to speak, he found two silenced Glocks pointed at his eyes.

"On the floor facedown. Now!" Breslin said.

He did it immediately, arms outstretched. Garrick knelt on his back and pressed the barrel of his gun directly into his ear while Breslin hurriedly closed the door, then patted down their prisoner. He removed a revolver and a walkie-talkie, then quickly tore off a long strip of gaffer's tape and stuck it across the cop's eyes and completely around his head. He wound it tightly.

"Listen close," Garrick said. "I will kill you in a minute if you don't cooperate. Give us a list of every employee on duty and where they are. If I find you've left one out I'll pull this trigger." He pressed the barrel harder against the cop's ear. "Clear?"

"Yes."

Garrick had about him an experienced air. Breslin could easily picture him doing this in some candlelit Vietnamese hut, his knee on the back of a man, woman, or child.

The cop spoke earnestly. "There's my partner, Jerry. He's walking the hallways and stairwells. He's hotheaded but don't let it get to you, please. He's a good kid. There's the night manager, Peter. He's at the front desk. There's the elevator operator. Doubles as the bellhop so he could be anywhere, but he's never away from the elevator for long. There's the doorman. There's two porters. One of them is cleaning the fourth-floor carpet now. The other one I don't know where he is. There's a cook in the kitchen. That's it."

"When's the next employee due to arrive?"

"The whole next shift. About a quarter to seven."

Breslin and Garrick exchanged a look of approval. It matched their own list.

Garrick handed the cop his walkie-talkie. "Get your partner up here. Tell him it's not an emergency but to come up right away. Is that clear?"

"Yes."

"What's your name?"

"Anthony."

"Are you going to be smart about this, Anthony?"

"A thousand percent."

Garrick pressed the Glock harder against his ear and said, "Go ahead."

Anthony explored the walkie-talkie with his fingertips until he found the right buttons, then just before he activated it, said, "I'm Jerry's boss. Anytime I call him I start by asking where he is."

Garrick studied the blindfolded Anthony for a few moments then said, "Whatever's usual. You know what we need, Anthony. Make it work. I'm expecting the full thousand percent you just promised."

"Jerry come in," Anthony said into the walkie.

The walkie crackled, "Go for Jerry."

"Where are you?"

"West stairwell. Eighth floor."

"Come on down to six-twenty-one. No big deal but come right away. Over."

"Copy. Six-twenty-one. Over."

Garrick guided Anthony into the bathroom and had him lie in a fetal position on the marble floor, then bound him with two pairs of handcuffs, joining his right wrist to his left ankle, and vice versa. He asked him, did he understand that if there was any report of noise he would be shot? Anthony said yes, after which Garrick sealed his mouth shut with tape, then joined Breslin at the door.

The knock came within a minute.

The hotheaded Jerry did nothing but tremble when the door was swung open quickly and two Glocks extended to within a few inches of his face. Inside the room, after being blindfolded, his trembling threatened to get out of control. Garrick elicited from him a roster of the employees on duty, which matched Anthony's. He, too, didn't know the whereabouts of the second porter. They brought him into the bathroom of Garrick's suite, where they gagged and trussed him up, then warned him about noise.

Garrick and Breslin left the suite, setting a suitcase on the hallway floor beside the door. Breslin was now even more on edge, in spite of the security guards being out of commission. Inside the rooms it had all been contained and private. He and Garrick had controlled the timing. This hallway suddenly felt like the big, wide world where anyone could pop up at any moment. Garrick checked his watch, for no good reason, Breslin thought, since the cell phone he was about to dial had made split-second timing on a job like this a thing of the past. Breslin checked his own watch, however, out of sheer curiosity. It was 2:16. Garrick finished dialing as they reached the bank of two elevators and pressed the call button.

Teddy answered the phone before the elevator arrived. "How does the deal look from your point of view?"

Garrick asked into the phone, then after a few moments said, "Good. Same here. We've just left our rooms and we're getting onto the elevator. Wait for me to sign off. I'll do it when we reach the lobby."

He said nothing more into the phone, which remained silent in his hand while they waited for the elevator. It seemed to take a long time. When it did arrive and the door slid open, it was Brian running it, the redheaded senior citizen who had been on duty the night before. Breslin had talked to him for a few minutes last night and learned that Brian was in his fifty-first year of service aboard these elevators, the last twenty of which were on the eleven-to-seven shift. Hotel policy was for mandatory retirement at sixty-five, but long-term residents had complained so about Brian leaving that management had extended him until his seventieth birthday, which would be next year.

"I'm the only employee it's ever been done for," he had told Breslin, with a touch of pride that he would have denied had it been pointed out to him. He had lowered his voice and said, "Management must've thought I was banging some of these old biddies, the squawk they put up about losing me."

Now he greeted them with a quick smile and a nod. As they descended Breslin asked, "Busy night?"

"So-so," Brian said over his shoulder. "Even what ought to be a slow night, they keep you hopping around here."

He stood at attention close to the controls of the chestnut-paneled car, facing forward in the stance required for most of his career, when he truly had to operate the elevator. Now he simply pressed the same buttons that any passenger could press. He was there, Breslin thought, at worst as an adornment, not unlike the huge arrangement of fresh flowers on the east wall of the lobby, at best as a minor amenity, like one of the roomy, wood-and-stained-glass phone booths in the lobby that sacrificed expensive midtown-Manhattan floor space to insulate its occupants from distractions. His presence in the elevator assured guests that they were seated in as snug and warm

a lap of luxury as could be found in an austere world
where form had long ago been sacrificed to function.
Breslin wondered how the old man came to terms with
it. He remembered that his own Uncle Eamon, lifelong
door opener for the rich, and always properly servile
during working hours, would describe himself dispassion-
ately as a flunky when asked by working-class people
what he did for a living, and refuse to be more specific.

They reached the lobby. Garrick stepped off first,
Breslin close behind, into the long alcove that housed
the elevator bank. Across from them was a small gift shop,
now dark, that also sold newspapers and magazines. They
fell in together, Breslin's heart pounding. He saw that Garrick's jaw was clenched tight. After a dozen strides they
reached the lobby itself, which opened out on their right,
and paused for just a moment to check it out. Everything
was still. The enormous crystal chandelier that lit up a
thirty-by-twenty-foot Persian rug had been dimmed, as
had the half-dozen reading lamps. The shallow alcove
directly across from where they stood housed the four
roomy telephone booths dating from 1910, whose
stained-glass windows were from the Tiffany Studios.
The booths were unoccupied.

On their left was the front desk—literally a desk rather
than the modern-day counter. It was a Victorian partners
desk with armchairs surrounding it so that guests checking in and out weren't forced to stand. A crystal bowl of
wrapped Valrhona chocolates was set on one corner.
Peter, the graveyard shift manager who doubled as desk
clerk, was in the small cashier's office located behind the
front desk. They could see him through the half-open
door, checking what seemed to be a stack of time cards.
There was a desk phone just inches from his hand.

At the street entrance to the lobby, just to one side of
the locked, plate-glass doors, the uniformed doorman
half sat, half leaned on a high stool reading a folded
magazine as unobtrusively as possible. It gave them their
first unpleasant surprise. Instead of the elderly, grave-
yard-shift regular they had planned on dealing with, it
was the young, linebacker-like, three-to-eleven doorman

whom each of them had so quickly taken note of on daytime visits and whom Frank had described as "the worst. He's got all the makings of a hero."

It was no reason to delay, though. Garrick said softly, "Here we go," into the cell phone, smiling—for anyone taking notice, just another businessman pleased with his state-of-the-art communications.

Breslin turned and walked back to the elevator, where old Brian sat on the velvet-upholstered passengers' bench that spanned the rear wall of the car. Eyes wide open, he stared ahead vacantly, thinking of nothing that Breslin could imagine. Breslin handed him a folded five and said he had set a suitcase down in front of 623, an airline carry-on bag with wheels on it, and then forgot to take it. Brian pocketed the five with an appreciative nod and took the car up while Breslin returned to the front desk. His target was the manager. Just before he got there, Garrick began to cross the lobby toward the front door. He managed a nice, easy pace. As he passed beneath the chandelier, about halfway to the door, he saw the black Caddy pull to the curb at the canopy. The doorman saw it at the same time. He set down his magazine and stood, prepared to welcome a late-arriving guest but from habit following the standard procedure of not unlocking the door until the guest had left the car and crossed the sidewalk in full view. Garrick could see that the exterior courtesy light on the Caddy's doorpost was lit, which told him all was well on the street. He quickened his pace. Until he had the doorman under control Teddy and Frank, both now with latex masks on, couldn't exit the car.

Breslin watched from his position near the desk. This was the crucial moment. If something wasn't right they could still abort this mission. Leave now and melt into the night. If Garrick made his move there was no turning back—they had to occupy and keep under control the whole sixteen-story building for hours. He saw Garrick commit himself—his hand come out of his pocket holding the silenced Glock. Garrick pressed it into the doorman's side. Nothing. The doorman was being told to unlock the door but he remained stone still for what seemed to Breslin a long time, challenging Garrick, showing just the stupid machismo they had recognized in him at first glance. Garrick would kill him in another few seconds, Breslin decided, but now that they were committed it was his own turn to go into action. He took the pistol from his jacket pocket and stepped quickly around the big desk, then through the door of the cashier's office, well into the room before the manager looked up from his paperwork and sucked in a mouthful of air. The pen fell out of his hand.

"Follow every order and you won't be hurt," Breslin snapped. "Turn around. Now!"

The manager swiveled his desk chair a 180 degrees and stretched his arms straight up in the air. Breslin blindfolded him with gaffer's tape immediately, drawing on the expertise of Frank Belmonte, who had instructed them to "tape their eyes first. Even before you handcuff them. Nothing makes a guy more helpless than being blind." He now handcuffed the manager's arms behind his back, then taped his mouth and told him to lie face-down on the floor and to keep very still.

From the rear seat of the limo Teddy watched the stand-off between the doorman and Garrick. He wanted to holler over to this *marmalute* whose body was too pumped up for his own good to do what he was told, that Garrick would kill him any moment now. In his years as a cop Teddy had seen very big guys behave this way more than once, especially very big, *young* guys, who often found it impossible to back down to a smaller man, gun or no gun.

Unless the big guy was outnumbered.

Teddy scanned the street in both directions—not a pedestrian in sight.

"Fuck the plan," he said to Frank. "I'm not going to watch that kid die from stupidity."

"A cop is a cop is a cop," Frank said good-naturedly. "Even a cop who goes bad," then himself realized that Garrick could very well pull the trigger, and said, very seriously, "You're right, Teddy. Make a move. We don't need a murder-in-the-course-of rap hanging over us."

Teddy pulled on his latex hood then stepped from the car and strode across the sidewalk fast, pistol in hand, dangling easily at the side of his thigh. A few feet from the glass door he raised the gun in a two-handed grip and aimed it at the doorman's head, the barrel pressed against the glass. The doorman studied Teddy's gun, then glanced disdainfully at Garrick's before taking the key from his coat pocket. It was attached by a short length of chain to a wood ball the size of a walnut. He held it at eye level for a few moments, swinging the ball on its little chain like a pendulum, making it clear that the decision was his to make and he was weighing it. Teddy thought it even money that he would tell Garrick to shove the wooden walnut up his ass. He put the key in the lock instead and pushed open the door for Teddy.

Garrick was quietly furious. He leaned close to Teddy and said, "Are you too damn dumb to follow orders?"

Teddy ignored him. He was focused on putting the doorman out of commission first thing. Twenty years of police work now paid off handsomely as he clicked a set of handcuffs onto the doorman's wrists in a move as fast and practiced as a magician's sleight of hand, a technique he had in fact learned from a professional magician when he was an eager rookie. He had never bought into Frank's blindfold-before-handcuff theory.

Frank, latex hood in place, arrived at the door, a suitcase and a garment bag in hand, the car now parked just past the hotel canopy. The suitcase was heavy—it held his tools. Teddy locked the door behind him and left the key in the lock. Then he and Garrick blindfolded the doorman and led him across the lobby while Frank hurried ahead to where Breslin waited at the elevator for old Brian to come down with his suitcase. Breslin, meanwhile, opened the garment bag and removed a doorman's uniform made to his measure. He changed on the spot, very quickly, tossing the clothes he took off into the bottom of the bag and pulling on the pumpkin-colored pants and jacket that the Montclair favored for making a first impression on guests. As he stood on one leg, the other into the uniform pants, the elevator door opened.

Old Brian's mouth dropped open. A moment later Frank stepped into the old man's line of vision, close enough for the skin-colored mask he wore to be apparent. He simply showed Brian the gun in profile rather than pointing it, so as not to panic him, and spoke softly and sincerely.

"Just relax, pop," Frank said. "You're absolutely not going to get hurt."

As Breslin buttoned his pants and headed for the front door, Brian asked calmly, "What is this, a heist?"

"That's what it is," Frank said.

The old man broke into an expansive smile and lowered his voice. "There's not enough cash around the joint for a weekend in Atlantic City but if you can crack any of the deposit boxes you'll have the biggest score of your career. There's enough jewelry in them to sink a fucking ship."

Frank wondered for only a few moments why the old man was telling him that, then lowered the gun and motioned invitingly toward the velvet-covered elevator bench. Brian sat, and took it upon himself to light a cigarette, then extended the pack toward Frank, who shook his head no. The old man quietly studied Frank's mask, while Frank studied the old man's worn face.

"You wouldn't by any chance know which boxes belong to which people?" Frank asked softly.

"You pick up on a hell of a lot when you work in a place for fifty-one years," Brian said.

"That how long you been here, pop?"

"Brian."

"Brian."

"Fifty-one years in June."

"What kind of stuff you pick up on?"

"A ton of worthless bullshit. But some worthwhile stuff, too. And then some *very* worthwhile stuff. Nuggets. You got to know which is which so you know what's worth remembering."

"Give me an example of some worthwhile stuff, Brian."

"Mrs. Holbruncke, in four-thirteen, is one of the richest people in the hotel. Hell, she's one of the richest people in the city, but hardly anybody knows her name. Fucked her way into two different fortunes and must have been so good at it they were happy to share their millions with her. A seventy-year-old clotheshorse who if she hung all the jewelry she owns on her wrinkled old carcass, she'd have to be carried in and out of here by a team of moving men. That's worthwhile to know."

"And what's something *very* worthwhile?" Frank asked softly. "Give me an example of a nugget."

"The numbers of both her deposit boxes. She needs two."

"You know their numbers?"

"I play them every day in the Pick-Three lottery."

They were both quiet for ten or fifteen long seconds, each aware that the ball was in Frank's court and that he was reluctant to return it.

Brian spoke up. "You been doing this kind of work for a while?" he asked.

"You could say that."

Brian lowered his voice even more.

"Whitey Perkins. Jimmy Butler. J. J. McFee, let him rest. I could name five more like them."

Career criminals, all. Frank had done time with two of them and had actually robbed a Sutton Place penthouse with J.J., dead now five years, when they were both teenagers.

"What about them?" he asked.

"They're my references. I drank with each one of them a hundred times. Jimmy Butler's my godson, for Christ sake. All those guys were raised no more than six blocks from the house I been in for sixty-nine years on the West Side. The heart of the Kitchen, Forty-eighth and Tenth."

Frank paused for just a few seconds, then said, "What do you have in mind, Brian?"

"I give you one of the two winning box numbers. You crack it and bring me half a handful of diamonds. Not a skimpy handful. Then I give you the second winning box number. You got to keep cracking other boxes around hers, too, so it don't look like an inside job."

Frank needed very little time to consider the proposition. He remembered at the Quincy cracking seven consecutive boxes that were empty. On this job, no matter how fast he worked he would never get into more than forty or fifty boxes, so he could easily miss these two jackpots. The old guy's offer was a good deal for both of them.

"We're in business," Frank said.

"Good. Box two-oh-two."

"You got a safe spot to stash them? They could decide to search the whole bunch of you."

"They ain't going to find these."

"You sure?"

"Not unless they X-ray me. These babies are going down the hatch like a handful of vitamins."

Teddy appeared, and pulled Frank out of earshot of Brian.

"You got the big guy neutralized?" Frank asked.

"He's on the floor in the office next to the manager. Jay hogtied him with the handcuffs. You've got to man the desk. Me and Jay are going to round up the last workers."

"How many are loose?" Frank asked. "Three?"

Teddy nodded. "Two porters and a cook."

"Can't Jay round them up alone and you man the desk? Let me get started on the boxes?"

Teddy shook his head. "Let's stick with the plan. You take the desk till the two of us round them up. Then you start on the boxes." He motioned toward Brian, who was still in the elevator. "Let's get him in with the others."

He went ahead to join Garrick.

Frank led Brian to the manager's office, Frank carrying the suitcase of tools, Brian the airline bag he had picked up from in front of their rooms. It held some hotel towels to give it weight. They would be discarded shortly and the empty airline bag used to hold the contents of the boxes.

"Tell the guy who's going to handcuff and blindfold you to go easy, that you've got a weak heart," Frank said to Brian. "And our little deal—it's just between the two of us. The guy running this show is one of those people steps into a pile of horseshit and worries that his shoes got ruined. You know what I mean?"

Brian nodded several times, in a way that communicated a tired, jaded understanding of human nature.

Frank covered the manager's post. He sat at the desk in the cashier's office where a Merlin telephone system had been installed to act as a switchboard for the quiet graveyard shift. The manager handled all telephone traffic except outgoing, direct-dialed calls, including any late-night room-service orders, which he would then pass on to the single cook on duty in the kitchen, whose level of patience and placating skills were believed inadequate for the Montclair clientele.

"Round up these three strays fast—I want to get to work," Frank told Teddy and Garrick as they prepared to find the two porters and the cook, then called to Teddy, "What's this Belgian's name?"

"Luc Kiant is what he used in Atlantic City," Teddy said.

Frank looked through the guest register but could find nothing close to Kiant, then located the reservations book in the desk's top drawer. Mr. Luc Kiant's reservation for earlier in the day had been canceled. "First monkey wrench," he thought. He slammed the book closed, then consoled himself immediately, first with the certainty that these boxes were more than full enough to make this a big payday in any event, and then with thoughts of his good fortune at meeting up with Brian. His consolation lasted only moments—what if the old man's estimate of box 202's contents was simply an elevator operator's pipe dream? In Frank's experience, the Hell's Kitchen Irish tended to be optimists. He checked the page further for any late arrivals and found two—a

Dr. Sosa and Dr. Gomez, arriving together and sharing a suite, and a Mr. and Mrs. M. Woodling of Chicago. He went to the doorway of the office and called across the lobby to Breslin, at the front door, "Two late arrivals due. A pair of men and a couple."

Breslin signaled that he understood.

Since Teddy was wearing a latex mask it was best for him to avoid the hallways. He would take the cook while Garrick went after the porter who was cleaning the fourth-floor carpet. Teddy went through a door next to the cashier's office, which led to the south side of the building, here at street level used by employees only. The decor changed radically, the hallway dimly lit by overhead bulbs enclosed in wire cages. He walked deliberately, gun in hand, as he had so often during his career, but tenser now than he ever remembered. The tightly fitting latex hood caused him to sweat and was a constant reminder that this whole operation was illegal. To keep the entire building under control for another two or three hours seemed more daunting now than it had in the planning stage.

This section was given over to storerooms, locker rooms, the large kitchen, and a receiving area the size of Teddy's whole apartment, enclosed floor-to-ceiling with schoolyard-type fencing. A set of double doors, now locked and alarmed, gave access to the receiving area from Fifty-fourth Street while a door in the fencing, now padlocked, connected the receiving area to the rest of the hotel. He moved further along and saw what he was looking for—a door with light coming from underneath it. Mariachi music played softly on the other side. He used his left hand to softly twist the doorknob both ways while he pressed lightly inward. The door was not locked. He took a deep breath and pushed it open. At a butcher block just ten feet in front of him a medium-built Latino wearing kitchen whites and a hairnet looked up from the leg of veal he was trimming, carving knife in hand, and froze into position when he saw the gun pointed at him. He seemed not at all fearful, and completely unsurprised at the appearance of a masked, armed man standing quietly in his kitchen doorway at two-thirty in the morning. He stood tranquilly behind the butcher block and looked into Teddy's eyes, waiting to see what would happen next, with the quiet dignity and acceptance of life's sudden vicissitudes innate in Mexican peasants. Teddy relaxed—the cook would give him no trouble.

"You speak English?" he asked.

"*Sí.*"

"How much?"

"I understand everything."

Teddy spoke slowly. "You won't be hurt if you do as you're told. I'm going to take you outside and lock you up with the others. Is there anything here in the kitchen that you have to do first? Ovens to turn off? Anything?"

"Just this leg. It must go in the box."

"Forget it," Teddy said, then pointed to a large plate of yellow rice and pinto beans set on an adjacent butcher block. An unopened bottle of Amstel Lite stood beside it.

"What's that?" he asked.

"My supper. I eat in a few minutes. When I am done trimming."

"You want a couple of mouthfuls? You're going to be tied up for hours."

The cook managed a small smile. "No, *gracias.* My appetite left me."

"Put the knife down," Teddy said. "Turn around. Put your hands behind your back."

Teddy handcuffed him and taped his eyes, then checked the ranges and ovens. Nothing was lit. He led the cook out, stopping to survey the room one last time. Everything was in order.

When Teddy closed the door behind himself and the cook, Arturo Martinez exhaled audibly, for the first time in what seemed to him hours. He zipped up his fly—he had been afraid of the noise it might make—and decided to let a few minutes pass before doing anything. He gently lowered the toilet lid and sat down. The eighteen-year-old had crossed into Laredo three weeks earlier and had arrived in New York just eight hours ago. His uncle, who held a bona fide green card, had sneaked him into the hotel through the employees' entrance for the first night of a planned month-long apprenticeship in common kitchen practices, after which Arturo could start somewhere as a prep cook's helper rather than join the horde of food-delivery boys wandering Manhattan on foot or bicycle searching for addresses that often seemed nonexistent. From his position behind the door of the tiny employee toilet he had heard the entire exchange between his uncle and another man, and had understood none of it. It had been an Anglo talking, who must be a boss. He wasn't sure what he should do. He could find his way back to the door his uncle had brought him through and wait on the street, but it seemed safer here. His leg hurt where he had gashed it weeks ago while making his way across a Texas cotton field in the darkness. It was swollen and had turned green. Later, when he and his uncle were back in Queens, he would show it to him. He was hungry, and his uncle had just set out for him a plate of rice and beans and a cold beer, but he was afraid to leave the little bathroom. The lid of the bowl was uncomfortable. He stood and lifted it, then sat down again on the seat itself. It felt better. He wondered why all chairs were not built this way, and settled in patiently for a long wait, listening to the mariachi music from his uncle's cassette player, nervous but happy to be in New York City.

On the fourth floor Manuel Martinez used the toe of his work boot to turn off the cleaning machine he had been running for an hour now across the plush hall carpeting. A mild stain the size of his thumb refused to lift. He reached into the breast pocket of his uniform shirt and took out a small squeeze bottle of stain remover. *Manny* was embroidered in script above the pocket. After three years as a porter he still hated having his name on the shirt. It was far more demeaning than even the most distasteful job he was called upon to do—clearing a guest's stuffed toilet. That happened about once a week, and each time he was so incredulous at the quantity of toilet paper needed by rich Anglos, even ninety-pound old ladies who consumed so little all day, that he would tell his wife about it when he got home. He sensed that she believed he exaggerated.

Now he squatted above the thumb-sized stain and squirted it with fluid. After a minute he started up the machine and continued to shampoo the carpet.

Garrick stepped off the elevator onto the fourth floor and heard the hum of the carpet-cleaning machine from around a corner of the hallway. He walked toward it easily, comfortable because he could pass muster with anyone who might appear, the only oddity about his appearance being the gloves he wore, and even that small incongruity was moderated by a topcoat folded over his arm. His pistol was in his right hand, beneath the topcoat. He neared the end of the hallway, where he had to turn left or right. The noise was coming from the right. He took the turn, into a long corridor with rooms along both sides and a stairway at the end. Twenty feet ahead of him a chubby young Latino looked up from the big wet-vacuum he was using. He pressed the off button with his foot and pulled the machine to one side. Garrick revealed the gun a bit sooner than he had to, still a few strides short of the porter. The porter reacted instinctively. He dropped the hose and whirled around in one motion, then bounded down the corridor toward the stairway. Garrick moved fast but with no sense of panic—he would nail him on the staircase if need be. As the porter neared the stairway door he reached forward, and suddenly Garrick realized that his outstretched hand was reaching not for the door handle but for a small, red fire-alarm box that was fixed to the wall at eye level. A vision flashed across Garrick's mind of guests pouring out of their rooms and firemen in raincoats and boots tramping the hallways. He raised the Glock and squeezed the trigger. The powerful, low-pitched whistle of the silencer filled his ear as the recoil thrust his unbraced hand toward the ceiling. The porter was driven forward as though hit by a car, his face meeting the wall squarely while his outstretched right hand grasped at air just inches below the alarm handle. The back of his head flew apart. His body came to rest on its side at the base of the wall.

"The hollow-nose bullets are everything they're cracked up to be," Garrick thought.

He didn't hurry forward. He didn't move at all, since the porter required no attention. He stood where he was in the still hallway and watched the row of doors for a minute to be sure no one poked their head out. No one did. He saw what looked to be a porter's ring of keys hanging from the lock of a door next to the stairway, which had no room number on it. He opened it, and saw a slop sink, some mops, and a vacuum. He dragged the porter's body into the closet, tossed the long ring of keys onto the landing of the stairwell, then rolled the carpet-cleaning machine to a position under the fire-alarm box, where it pretty much covered the bloodstains on the floor. The wall was a mess because of the hollow-nose, but not worth dealing with.

When Teddy finished gagging the cook he settled him into a comfortable position on the plush rug of the manager's office, then asked each of the other three prisoners if they were all right. The big doorman and the night manager nodded yes. Old Brian, who had been on the floor for just a few minutes, shook his head no. Teddy peeled back the tape from his mouth and asked what was wrong.

"I'm having a panic attack with this fucking tape on my mouth. I got a deviated septum." He snorted several times. "I'm scared I'll suffocate."

"Who deviated it?" Teddy asked.

"A lightweight named Buddy Budinsky. Nineteen forty-six. I knocked the bum out in the fourth."

"Swear you won't make a sound," Teddy said.

"On my mother."

Teddy looked at Brian's seventy-year-old face and said, "Your mother's still alive?"

"So on her grave. Give me a break, huh? All I want is to breathe."

Frank appeared in the doorway and motioned for Teddy to join him. Teddy pointed a warning finger in old Brian's face, then pulled the dangling tape from the side of his mouth, and joined Frank in the doorway.

"Garrick's on the phone," Frank whispered. "Wants to talk to you."

As Teddy started toward the cashier's office, Frank, still whispering, implored, "The boxes, Teddy. We're here for the boxes, remember? We already lost the Belgian."

"Hang on for one more minute," Teddy said, and a moment later picked up the desk phone.

"Anything wrong?" he asked.

"No," Garrick said. "Did you snag the cook?"

"He's on the floor with the others."

"I got the porter on the fourth floor. With a small complication. He panicked and ran. I had to shoot him."

"Oh, shit," Teddy said. His stomach tightened up. He lowered his voice in case Frank was listening near the door, and asked, "Dead?"

"Completely. But it's all under control. All cleaned up."

Teddy's voice exploded in an intense whisper. "How the fuck do you kill a *porter*? A fucking *porter*! What did he do, threaten you with his mop?"

"Calm down. You're losing it, mister. I had no choice; the man tried to pull a fire alarm."

Teddy was silent for a few moments as it dawned on him that Garrick really may have had no choice—those things happen.

"I'm not going to say anything to Frank," Teddy said.

"You're damn right you're not. I'm going to do a floor to floor for the second porter. I'll check back with you in five or ten minutes."

Teddy hung up the phone and held his head in his hands for a bit. An innocent guy was dead. A working guy. For sure an immigrant, legal or illegal, busting his ass to make a life for himself and a family in Nueva

York. This wasn't a bad guy shot dead holding up a bodega or carjacking a woman in a parking lot. This wasn't even a borderline error—an unarmed bad guy shot during a mugging, but at least a bad guy with a rap sheet two feet long. Teddy had been directly or indirectly involved in all those situations and his conscience had never once bothered him. There were greedy people out there who deserved to die, and as for the mugger, armed or not, he was threatening his victim with violence. That made him fair game for a citizen's revenge or a cop's honest mistake in the dark. If a thief didn't want to put his life on the line he should shoplift. No one ever shot shoplifters. But this porter upstairs was a different story. He was truly an innocent bystander.

The sharp clink of metal on metal brought him out of his thoughts. He hurried to the adjacent room of safe-deposit boxes and stopped in the doorway to watch Frank at work. On Teddy's right, the entire wall was made of dull, stainless steel from floor to ceiling. It ran the full ten-foot depth of the room, some three hundred safe-deposit box doors, each with its own three-digit number machined into its face. The boxes in the lower rows were larger than those above. The wall on the left supported a long, highly polished mahogany shelf set at desk height, just deep enough to hold a deposit box. Two sconces and an English hunting print hung above it. On the shelf, lying flat and opened, was Frank's suitcase of tools. Beside it, opened, empty, awaiting the contents of forty or fifty hopefully overladen boxes, was the airline bag brought down by Brian, the towels it had contained now discarded in a pile on the floor.

Frank stood on a leather armchair, working on a box that was at Teddy's eye level. The extra height allowed him to hammer downward and get his weight into it. He held in his left hand a hefty cold chisel, its working edge set against the small protrusion of a hinge. In his right hand was a squat thirty-six-ounce sledgehammer. He brought it down against the head of the cold chisel every few seconds, rising up on his toes with each blow to get extra force into it, working at a fast pace but not hurriedly—one of those ice-in-the-veins thieves who, were he to hear police sirens approaching right now, would gauge their distance, then continue hammering at precisely the same tempo for another half minute or so.

Teddy moved close to the box for a better look. Mechanical work always held his interest.

"Watch your eyes," Frank said. "There's no workmen's comp if you get hurt."

He hit it once more, then pulled the chisel back to let Teddy get a close look. The protruding piece of steel, which enclosed the hinge pin, was sheared off its mooring for half its length. Frank set the blade of the chisel into the groove it had created and continued to hammer.

Teddy read the number on the door: 202.

"How'd you pick this one to start?" Teddy asked.

"You got to start somewhere," Frank said between hammer blows.

Ninety seconds later the pin housing sheared off and fell to the floor. Frank reached across to his suitcase of tools and selected a thirty-inch prybar and a two-foot length of pipe.

"Jimmy," he muttered as he worked the prybar into the narrow opening left where the pin housing had been. He held the length of pipe squeezed between his knees. When the blade of the prybar found a purchase Frank carefully slipped the pipe over the prybar's other end to give himself more leverage. He leaned against it, the bar crossing his body at the bottom of his chest so he was able to get weight against the end of the pipe.

The door popped. Frank pitched forward suddenly and nearly toppled off the chair. The prybar fell to the floor along with the heavy box door. Frank placed the pipe in his hand into the tool suitcase on the shelf. Within the fortified walls of the box, a flimsy, light-gauge metal tray painted blue held the contents. It had a delicate handle of bent wire on its front. Frank slid the tray out, stepped off the chair, and set it on the shelf. Teddy estimated the tray at six inches wide by three high by nearly two feet long. The cover was hinged at the rear so that when Frank opened it the long, narrow cover stood up high in the air and rested against the English hunting print on the wall, and revealed in the velvet-lined tray itself a treasure trove. Diamonds of every size and shape set into necklaces, bracelets, brooches, earrings, and rings—more rings than Frank had ever fantasized seeing in a single box—glittered under the light of the sconces.

"*Madonna me,*" he said softly. "Fast ballpark estimate—six mil retail."

A moment later something in the tray caught his eye.

"That's got to be Bulgari," he said, and extracted a ring. "You can spot his stuff across a room. This is a sapphire. Oval cut. Fifteen carats minimum. It's a gold mount. These diamonds on the side are baguettes and these are called marquises. That Greek did some fucking work."

He peered at the inner surface and said, "There it is. Signed. Bulgari," then replaced it in the box.

Teddy fingered a necklace of pearls. Until this moment he had given absolutely no thought to the money side of the operation. It suddenly occurred to him that if all went well he would soon be sitting on several million dollars.

Frank took the necklace from Teddy's hand and held it up at eye level.

"Beautiful," he said. "Single strand necklace. And these are *big,* silvery pearls. The biggest guy—the one down here, opposite the clasp—is seventeen, maybe eighteen millimeters, and they're just slightly graduated."

He extended it toward Teddy, and said, "Look at it. Skin surface, luster, and color is what matters here, along with size. Plus the real kicker—the color match, pearl to pearl. This is a knockout. Somebody took years to collect this many matched pearls."

He thought hard for a few moments, then quickly explained to Teddy the deal he had cut with old Brian. He ended by saying, "Just in case Breslin or Garrick see me giving him stuff I don't want you guys thinking I'm skimming."

Teddy shrugged, then indicated the tray full of jewelry and said, "Looks like you made a good deal to me."

"He's got to give me the next box number," Frank

said. He picked up the pearl necklace. "Let me see if I can talk him into these instead of diamonds. These are nice and round. And smooth. They'll go down easy. I'm scared this guy's going to scratch his pipes if he starts swallowing diamonds. We'll be doing Heimlich maneuvers in the middle of a heist. I just hope that—"

"Somebody's coming! Someone coming in!"

It was Chuck Breslin calling insistently across the lobby from the front door. Teddy and Frank left the room quickly, closed the door behind themselves, and stepped into the manager's office. The four captives lay still on the floor. They appeared not to have shifted even inches. Teddy cracked the door open enough to view the front entrance clearly. Breslin was off his stool and at the door, one hand on the key in the lock. A cab was at the curb in front of the canopy.

"Say a prayer," Frank whispered, "that the Belgian decided to check in after all."

A man emerged from the cab and turned to help another passenger out, a woman, while the driver carried three pieces of luggage from the trunk to the door, where he set them to one side. When the couple reached the door, Breslin swung it open for them. The man said something to him—clearly it concerned the luggage—then they walked across the lobby toward the front desk while Breslin brought the three suitcases inside and locked the door again.

"Bellman to the front door," Breslin called across the lobby.

The approaching couple were in their forties and well-dressed. Their bearing marked them as members of the monied class, whether American or foreign Teddy couldn't tell yet. They stopped at the front desk, where the woman sat in one of the armchairs while the man remained standing and surveyed the lobby impatiently.

"You can handle them," Frank whispered. "I'll get back to work. And I got to feed that old thief a handful of stones."

Teddy pulled the door open and stepped out. The movement attracted the couple's attention. As he walked around the cashier's counter the woman apparently sensed that there was something odd about his face. A few more steps and her uncertainty gave way to wide-eyed shock when she made out the latex hood. Her hands clutched the arms of the chair and she started to push herself upright.

Teddy pointed his gun at her.

"Sit!" he commanded, as he might a rebellious Doberman.

She obeyed. Her face expressed such surprise and bewilderment that Teddy guessed this was the very first order she had ever been given in her forty-something years on earth.

The man raised his hands of his own accord.

"You won't be hurt if you do as you're told," Teddy said. "Who are you?"

"Morrison Woodling. This is my wife, Jennifer."

He seemed to expect Teddy to shake their hands.

"We have reservations," he added.

"Put your hands down," Teddy said. He taped their eyes and handcuffed them, then led them to the cashier's office. Frank was just leaving the room, on his way back to work. Inside, Brian licked his lips and gulped frequently.

Teddy put the Woodlings on the floor with the others, after patting them down for weapons in the most cursory way, especially Mrs. Woodling—searching female suspects over the years, including a dozen or more street hookers who had assaulted someone, he had always been scrupulously quick and professional. Both of the Woodlings were agitated, and Teddy sensed that they were not only frightened for themselves but for one another. Although trussed and blindfolded they managed to maintain bodily contact with one another, and clearly derived comfort from it. Teddy envied Morrison Woodling his resource, and, as often when he was privy to some minor intimacy that revealed true love in a long-standing marriage, he thought briefly of Maggie, then considered the lonely position he had staked out for himself in life.

X

Cheito drew deeply on the cigar he had lit in the parking lot and looked out the window of the Buick at the litter-strewn roadsides of the Van Wyck Expressway. He had expected something more impressive on a highway leading from the John F. Kennedy International Airport to Manhattan. This landscape reminded him of a third world country, a graphic result of unbridled free enterprise. It gave him a small sense of I-told-you-so pleasure, yet he felt an odd tinge of disappointment, too, wanting everything to be as spectacular as he had always imagined it.

Beside him, Angel Sosa's familiarity with the country was apparent—he drove with great self-assurance. The way Angel handled the car, the way he barely looked out at his surroundings—and when he did his clearly nonjudgmental response to them—his whole comfortable demeanor, suggested to Cheito that Angel knew the States as well as he had claimed. It also suggested that Angel liked it here. And why shouldn't he? Three years spent living in Manhattan as a member of the United Nations mission must not have been hard to take. Cheito had been working on the virus in those years, cooking Spartan meals in his little bungalow in the Zapata Peninsula swamp, putting in long, dangerous hours every day and visiting Buena Ventura once a week. Before that, during the years Cheito had been in Angola, Angel had been a major in the Villa Clara Province Security Forces—another assignment not hard to take.

Now, watching Angel handle the car with such ease, he wondered how willingly the major would help him infect a few hundred thousand United States citizens. Angel believed that only the single, tiny demonstration would take place. That was because Fidel believed it, too, along with whichever other confidants he had brought into the scheme—any number from zero to fifty, Cheito knew from his experience with the man. Fidel and his cohorts were sure the U.S. leaders would fold after the demonstration; Fidel himself had told him that. How could the Yanquis not give in, Cuba's demands being so easy to meet and their effects so painless when compared with the damage a second, wholesale release of the virus would cause? Also, in recent years Cheito had formulated a theory about the kind of man Fidel had evolved into at the dawn of his old age. The fourteen private, leisurely meetings he had had with the ever-loquacious Fidel since returning from Angola had given him sufficient insight into the man so that he now trusted his analysis, radical as it was. Cheito was convinced that Fidel harbored a great secret belief of his own—a belief that the U.S. President and those around him knew very well that Cuba's demands were just, that Cuba had been ill-treated since the beginning of the revolution, that Cuba had never been given a chance, that they knew all this in their hearts but were unable to acknowledge it publicly. Fidel, who at his core had become weak and stupidly naive, Cheito believed, was now an old man who hungered for the love and admiration of every last person on earth—he was a man able to believe in his heart of hearts that the *norteamericano* leaders were decent men who wanted to do the moral thing but were prisoners of their own democratic system, ruled by the whims of workaday citizens ignorant of world affairs. Fidel was, at the end of the day, a leader cursed with the little-boy quality of seeing the world as he wanted it to be rather than how it was, and now, implausible as it seemed, what this great twentieth-century revolutionary longed for was a world peopled with honorable men. Cheito remembered what Mussolini, in his early days as a Communist, had said of Lenin's failure to establish real communism in the Soviet Union—that he was a sculptor working in metal, but the metal proved too hard for him. Cheito believed that in the case of Cuba it was Fidel's hammer and chisel that were too light for the job. Well, Fidel and whichever ass-kissers he had brought into this operation, including this security-force major beside him whose liver was whole and well and not being eaten away as the result of war wounds incurred while fighting *for a cause,* not for personal glory or advancement—a concept unknown these days in Havana—all of them could plan and believe what they liked. He, Cheito, knew there would be a wholesale release *no matter what.* Let the leaders in Washington capitulate if they cared to—he would not grant them a reprieve. They would learn what suffering is. This was his weapon and he would use it as he wished. History would judge him.

"Do you like it here?" he asked Angel indifferently.

"The States?"

"Yes."

Angel pretended to think for a bit, as though he had never considered the question before, then said, "It's okay. If you can learn to close your eyes to the social injustice." He smiled apologetically and added, "The luxuries can be seductive. I got used to them on my tour of duty here."

"The women?" Cheito asked.

Angel smiled again. "They're hungry for romance. They're rich and spoiled but they're forthright—they appreciate a good performance by an accomplished lover. A wealthy widow on Sutton Place, still in her forties, once said thank you to me and sent a bottle of cognac to my apartment the next day."

Cheito nodded as though favorably impressed, and wondered what sort of fool would tell these things to someone he knows has served ten years in Angola. Could he believe it would bring anything but a bitter taste into the mouth of a true soldier? It must be very nice indeed to be on an assignment where one spends whole nights with soft women who then send gifts, but this major had no idea that a true soldier was wont to spit on someone who took pride in being an "accomplished lover." Certainly he had never received gifts from any of the hundreds of young prostitutes he had been with over the years, none of whose faces he could recall. In bed he had never exchanged a word with them, either during or after sex. Certainly none had ever shown appreciation, and the only "thank you" might be given earlier in the evening when he counted out for them the equivalent of three or four American dollars.

"You've had more than a few of them, Angel?" he asked in a tone that invited more discussion of the subject, which Angel warmed to.

"They can be fascinating, Yanqui women. They think for themselves, and that can be annoying at first, but after a while it's more satisfying than banging away at some stupid young girl and the two of you never say a word to each other. My first year here I had a short affair with a thirty-five-year-old girl who made documentary films. Her background and instincts were completely leftist—her grandfather had once run for the New York State legislature on the Socialist party ticket—yet she had come one day to suddenly disapprove of our revolution. Fidel in particular. Her reason? She had seen an old 1960s poster that said, 'If I can't dance you can keep your revolution,' and had what she called an epiphany."

Cheito didn't respond. He seemed to be waiting for more, which made Angel uncomfortable.

"It was adolescent of course," Angel said, "but . . ."

He searched for a word that he didn't find, and regretted having added the "but." His voice trailed off and he pretended to have to concentrate on his driving, hearing in his mind how absurd he must have sounded to a minor legend who had fought with Che in Bolivia. It had been a stupid lapse.

"Say no more," Angel warned himself. "You're treading on dangerous ground."

He had met Cheito for the first time six months ago, just the two of them in a small Havana hotel room far from any government offices. The meeting had gone well enough for Cheito to cut it short after an hour and express his satisfaction with the choice of Angel as his guide and assistant for the mission. Guiding was more important than assisting, Cheito had said, since he could not move safely around an unfamiliar country alone if things took a turn for the worse, not even in the much acclaimed, free-and-easy United States. Looking back, Angel realized they had got on so well because he had revealed little of himself to Cheito. He had wanted a few months in and around New York and so had been eager to sell himself, not yet aware of the details of the mission. He had gone into the interview knowing that it would include a few killings, but not that it involved a virus. There was something distasteful about that—he would prefer to shoot people. Nor had he known that the targets were to be innocent, apolitical civilians. After Cheito had accepted him it was too late to back out, and after hearing that a small demonstration in a place of his choice would suffice, he had been less uncomfortable about accepting the assignment. He had met with Cheito once more, at the macabre laboratory on the Zapata swamp, where Cheito had instructed him in the technical details of working with the virus and setting it up in the States.

Now, after just a few months in the open atmosphere of the States, Angel had let down his guard and shown a side of himself that might not go down so well with the doctor. This damn country did that—it very quickly lulled people into expressing openly any opinion they might hold. He sneaked a glance at Cheito, and saw a mild-mannered man who didn't seem a bit perturbed. It's likely I'm making a mountain out of a molehill, Angel decided.

He remained silent for the next few minutes while Cheito exhaled small clouds of smoke toward the windshield, then extended the cigar and studied it appreciatively for a few seconds, this to give Angel the impression that his passenger—and commanding officer on this mission—was comfortable and contented. In fact, Cheito was already visualizing how he might carry out by himself what he called in his diary "the big one." He had no doubt he would have to do it alone—Angel did not have the steel it required. It would be difficult alone but it could be done. He quickly put thoughts of the big one out of his mind—he was jumping ahead too far, too soon. The wise first move was to learn the details of what Angel had set up for the demonstration in his three months here.

"How much virus have you grown?" Cheito asked.

"All that you wanted. And more," Angel said. After a moment he added, "Much more than we'll need for the eight or ten targets I've picked."

"Victims," Cheito wanted to say. "Not targets, victims. Don't use euphemisms." He said nothing, though, and after a moment asked simply, "Who are our targets?"

"They're perfect for us," Angel said. "Everything you asked for. Isolated. Contained. The works. It took me months of searching, but it paid off. They're what are called in this country cultists, which is precisely what I looked for. Neighbors leave them alone. Shun them, actually. And this little cult is no exception. They're isolated as a group can be in this part of the country."

Angel went on to tell him what he had learned from his research. In the late 1950s, John Carlin, a tenured professor of psychology at Berkeley who had made several hundred LSD trips, resigned from the university to seek the truth. For the next four years he wandered in India and Nepal, returning as empty-handed as he had left but with the makings of a new way of life, an unlikely blending of fundamentalist Christianity, Zen Buddhism, and a belief in the virtue and healthfulness of hard physical labor, a vegetarian diet, and rigid discipline that included caning on the bare buttocks for major transgressions. The Erigena Derivation, as Carlin came to call his ascetical cult, grew to include a thousand or so adherents along the West Coast at its peak in 1968, several hundred of whom lived in a commune that he headed in the Mojave Desert near the tiny community of China Lake. One member of that mother commune in 1968 was a strikingly beautiful twenty-six-year-old Stanford dropout, Febronia Orbelian, who credited Erigena with turning her life around after several years spent in the streets, the crash pads, and the health clinics of San Francisco's Haight-Ashbury. She was then the only living relative of her estranged grandfather, Zareh Orbelian, an Armenian immigrant who during the 1930s in New York had bought up taxicab medallions dirt cheap. By the mid-1950s he had become one of the city's largest fleet owners, with nearly one hundred Sky View DeSotos on the streets at any hour of the day or night. When his heart failed him in 1962, during his grand-daughter's nadir in the Haight, his entire $25 million estate was left to endow a foundation for the promotion of Armenian culture and the furtherance of research on the great genocide. Febronia was mentioned in the will, which specified that "because of her debauched way of life she is to receive not a penny," of the estate. Unknown to her at the time was that a year before his death Zareh Orbelian had established a $5 million trust fund in her name, the existence of which was to be revealed to her on her thirty-fifth birthday. There were six stipulations, which, if met, would require the three trustees to transfer the entire proceeds of the fund to her. If any of the six was not met, the money was to be donated to the Armenian Cultural Foundation he had endowed. None of the three trustees was of Armenian descent. The stipulations were: She must not, on her thirty-fifth birthday, be in prison, a mental institution, or a drug or alcohol rehabilitation facility; she must not be on parole or probation; she must not be awaiting trial for any criminal offense; she must have a permanent address; she must have visible means of support, based upon a legal definition of the term; she must, immediately upon being informed of the trust fund's existence and the stipulations, submit blood and urine samples for drug testing. A refusal to do so or a positive result for any substance whose possession was illegal by federal statute would negate her receiving the funds. If she met all the stipulations the full sum in the trust fund was to be transferred to her immediately, free and clear.

In 1977, on Febronia Orbelian's thirty-fifth birthday, the trustees and a female nurse sat with her at the com-

mune in China Lake, where, of forty surviving members
she had the most longevity. Even John Carlin was dead,
his ashes scattered over the Himalayas. They drove off
a few hours later with a vial of her blood and a small
cup of urine. The following evening, in Los Angeles, they
wrote a check to her for about $12 million, a result of
the conservative investing of Zareh's original $5 million.
Along with the check they delivered a sealed letter from
her grandfather, the contents of which she had never
revealed publicly.

"She used a million dollars to buy three thousand acres
of land in New York's Catskill Mountains," Angel said.
"About fifteen minutes outside the village of Woodstock."

"Why have I heard that name before?" Cheito asked.

"A huge music concert was held near there in 1969.
Close enough to the town to take its name."

"How far is it from here?"

"About a hundred miles," Angel said. "North. I've
rented a house in the town. The equipment is in it."

"All of it?"

"Every item you wanted."

"How isolated are our victims?" Cheito asked.

"Miss Orbelian's three thousand acres are more than
enough to give her and her followers an enormous
amount of privacy. Except for a half-mile stretch along
an unpaved public road, the property is bordered by government land. New York State land. Uninhabited. Much
of it goes on for miles before it gives way again to private
property. There are ten regulars who live there full-time.
Novices come up on weekends to join in and look into
it for themselves, people not yet ready to give up jobs
and friends and become full-timers. They never stay past
Monday. Tuesday or Wednesday night would be best for
us to go in."

"What do these people do with their time?" Cheito
asked.

"They follow a very disciplined regimen. Last month
I spent two weekends there pretending I was interested
in joining. A clock in a tall bell tower they've built sets

a bell to ringing at five A.M. every day. Everyone rises and immediately takes an ice-cold shower. None of their water is heated. They spend the next forty-five minutes in prayer and meditation. Breakfast is quick. No caffeine allowed. No meat, fish, or dairy products allowed. No talking during meals allowed. Then everyone goes off to do hard labor—farming, woodcutting, building or repairs, food preparation and cooking, cleaning. They rotate every month. It's very egalitarian.

"Every hour on the hour until darkness, every day of the week, the big bell rings and all activity stops for three minutes of prayer and meditation. It must be done facing the east. Any infractions of rules governing these P and M periods, as they call them, brings down the most drastic disciplining—caning. It's done in the temple, everyone watching, with a thin, five-foot bamboo rod on the bare buttocks. They draw lots for who must do the caning. It's considered a distasteful task."

Cheito interrupted, "Does it happen often?"

"Once or twice a year, they say."

"You didn't witness it, though?"

Angel smiled. "No. There was a tall, healthy brunette in her early twenties I hoped might be caught shirking her P and M, but she was very diligent."

"Are these people generally sane?" Cheito asked doubtfully.

"Yes. And not unintelligent. Emotionally wounded human beings was my impression, but it's hard to know. They're forbidden to even talk about their backgrounds in any way—you are reborn the day you become an adherent."

"How many are men?"

"Seven," Angel said. "Three women. Febronia is the oldest. Most of the others are under thirty-five."

"When are they all in one place? Indoors."

"Breakfast. Nine of them at the dining room table, one cooking nearby, but it's all part of one huge room—a longhouse, they call it—built of logs, nearly a hundred feet long. All their living takes place in it. The better place for us is their temple. Much more contained, and close to the long house, maybe a hundred yards. They pray and meditate there every afternoon from two to three and every evening from seven to eight. All of them."

"How big a room?" Cheito asked.

"It's octagonal," Angel said, and took a few moments to estimate from memory. "Say a thousand square feet of floor area."

"How high?"

"It's a peaked roof, but it's the equivalent of fifteen feet."

Fifteen thousand cubic feet would work fine, Cheito thought.

"Windows?" he asked.

"None. Just a big double door."

"Any other openings?"

"A chimney. The room is heated in winter—pretty poorly, I'd guess—by a big wood-burning stove."

"We're not likely to be interrupted? Surprise visitors? Neighbors dropping in?" Cheito asked.

"No. No one ever visits. These people are in a category of Yanquis who choose to live, as they put it, 'off the grid.' Nearly all of their type live in the Far West but there are some here in the East, too. Like this group."

"And this place is definitely isolated enough so no one would hear shouts? Calls for help?" Cheito asked.

"No question. The only thing anyone might hear are gunshots, and they would assume it was someone taking a deer out of season. It's not uncommon up there."

"It's not?" Cheito said. He was surprised.

"Local people sometimes do it for food. In a rural bar in Phoenicia—the little town right near our targets—once I heard a fellow quietly brag, 'I keep deer meat on my table year-round.' There's plenty of real poverty in that area. Mixed in with the expensive second homes of people from Manhattan."

Cheito puffed his cigar and looked out again at the filthy roadside. People just a hundred miles from New York City poaching deer to put meat on the table? His own surprise at learning this took him aback, as, on second thought, did his surprise at the unkempt roadside. For years he had read about the shortcomings of North American capitalism. He would revel in it as he mentally nodded his assent and drew comfort from these affirmations of his own beliefs—beliefs for which, if one wished to minimize his sacrifice, he had lived a life of great deprivation. If one were more coolly objective, he thought, he had, in fact, sacrificed his life for these beliefs, as a Trappist monk can be said to have done. Now it occurred to him that for all those years he must have, on some deeper level, assumed that these stories about inequities in the States were exaggerated. How else account for his surprise at meeting up with them firsthand? He wondered—had he been self-deceptive? And if so, then was the self-deceptiveness he believed Fidel guilty of the great weakness that he, Cheito, believed it to be? He decided it was food for thought for another day. A lifetime of soldiering in a revolutionary cause had taught him the danger of philosophical questioning at moments when action was the order of the day.

XI

Chuck Breslin checked the neatness of his doorman's uniform in the reflection of the plate glass, straightened the bow tie, then moved his head so close to the door that his cheek touched the cool glass, which gave him the longest possible view east along Fifty-fifth Street. According to Garrick, the Cuban and his driver were due any minute. It would be a lot less tense if Cutshaw had been willing to assign an operative to tail the Cubans in from the airport, calling ahead on a cell phone with reports on their progress. "The fewer the better," Cutshaw had said.

"Showtime," Breslin thought. Everything they had done until now had been aimed at this next half hour or so. Having checked his own appearance he now turned to examine the lobby, irrationally fearful that some big overlooked gaffe would tip off the Cuban and cause him to turn tail and run. From his vantage point at the entrance the lobby appeared perfectly serene, as it should in these wee hours: the dimmed lights; the unmanned front desk; the figure of Jay Garrick, in bellman's uniform, seated discreetly on a settee looking at a magazine, his legs crossed; Teddy Tedesco, the Nordic-looking Italian American whom Breslin had come to think of over the past weeks as an okay guy, lounging in the open doorway of the darkened cashier's office, one eye on the bound and gagged hostages who occupied the floor, the other on Breslin, waiting for his signal that the Cuban was arriving. When that happened, Teddy was to close the office door and step out of sight into the alcove that housed the closed mahogany door of the deposit-box room.

He thought for a moment of Frank Belmonte, who now practiced his trade with hammer and chisel, a direct descendent perhaps of some Renaissance Neapolitan sculptor, the only one of the quartet blithely unaware that the real purpose of this whole operation was about to play out. Belmonte was the first career criminal with whom Breslin had spent any time and he was still surprised at the man's apparently principled approach to much of life.

Inside the small, windowless room Frank attacked his fifteenth box, striking the chisel in a comfortable rhythm with easy, arm-saving blows that let the sledge do the work. Years earlier he would have found the closeness of the room cozy and reassuring—he had actually liked to work in snug quarters. In recent years though, he had developed a very mild case of claustrophobia, so slight as not to interfere in his everyday living but enough for him to sometimes leave a crowded subway in favor of walking or pass up an elevator if it meant squeezing his way on. It was also strong enough to give rise to an occasional bad dream about returning to a tiny prison cell. This little room was now starting to shrink. It was the only negative thing affecting him, everything else going so smoothly that he sometimes momentarily forgot this was a robbery. That anything might suddenly go wrong seemed preposterous in these warm surroundings. He glanced over from time to time into the open airline bag on the shelf, already more than half full, a jumble of glittering stones and precious metals that looked to him like a children's book illustration of pirate treasure. It was a sight he had often fantasized about. He could see that this would easily net three or four times the couple of mil he had chopped up with his cohorts on the Quincy job. Which made the behavior of this crew even more surprising—none of them ever stuck his nose in the room to see what the take was or finger the jewelry or encourage him to work faster and open more boxes.

These were the least greedy thieves he had ever partnered with.

The stubborn little hinge he was working on sheared off and fell to the floor. He set down the sledge and realized for the first time that he was sweating, and that his right arm was beginning to ache. He lifted open the lid of the box with his usual optimistic expectancy and for the first time all night was disappointed—it was packed with Polaroid pictures of child pornography, nothing more. The photographs revolted him. He quickly slid the tray back into its berth, studied the suitcase of pirate treasure to give himself a lift, and picked the next target, his sixteenth box, at random. One of the oversized boxes on the bottom row. These big boxes were frequently used for documents and so he generally ignored them, but tonight he wanted to crack just one, because, he said to himself, "You never know." This one, he decided, on a hunch. Last box in its row. Something told him it belonged to a drug dealer who stuffed it with bundles of hundred-dollar bills.

He set the blade of the chisel on top of the box hinge and struck it with the sledge. As he fell into his natural working rhythm he found himself humming "Volare," stretching out parts of the phrasing the way Dean Martin had. He pictured the owner of the box alone in this locked room, perhaps just yesterday, transferring banded stacks of bills from an attaché case into the box. The bills were well-used hundreds, the case one of rich, deeply oiled leather, the drug dealer an elderly, frail Chinaman in suit, tie and vest, who packed the box unhurriedly, with great care. He had relatives in the Golden Triangle. Frank calculated as he hummed. A hundred bills compressed were about an inch thick; $10,000 per inch. This ten-inch-wide box, then, would hold $100,000 per row. Call it five rows deep; half a mil per layer. Three layers high. He hit the chisel just a bit harder each time now, and speeded up the tempo of "Volare," and decided that if this box did indeed prove to be full of cash, he would open the one next to it—for sure this Chinaman had more than a lousy mil and a half. As the chisel bit a little further through the hinge with each blow, however, he found himself glancing up from time to time at box 173, a few rows above. It was no different from the others, yet . . . there was something about it. From the moment he walked into the room it had cried out that it was loaded with treasure. It even *looked* like it was. A Persian rug merchant had once said, about a particularly beautiful Tabriz Frank had loved instantly, that the rug was talking to him. Now, box 173 was talking to him. Box 173 begged to be opened.

Teddy felt no butterflies in his stomach even though his senses were on heightened alert. Their Cuban ought to be just minutes away. He glanced down at the seven detainees, as Garrick had christened them, and focused on Mr. and Mrs. Woodling. Garrick had just told him and Breslin that the couple would be the two additional hostages taken along with the Cuban and his bodyguard. Teddy wondered how the Woodlings would hold up. If it was his call, he would take along the desk clerk and the Mexican cook. Why in the world Garrick felt that a female hostage would lend the operation more authenticity was beyond him. It seemed to Teddy that the dead porter in the fourth-floor closet would convince even a very skeptical Fidel Castro that this robbery had been the real thing. Garrick was running the show, however, and Teddy's four years as a Marine and twenty more as a cop had taught him to follow orders. He wondered how Frank was going to react to the hostage-taking. He would raise a hell of a fuss, Teddy guessed, but there would be no time to debate the issue.

"This looks like it!" Breslin called from the door. "A car's pulling up!"

Teddy closed the door of the cashier's office, isolating the detainees, then opened the door of the deposit-box room so quickly that he startled Frank.

"Cut it!" he said. "Guests arriving. Don't hammer again till I say so."

He pulled the door closed and left Frank to wait impatiently, with nothing to do but swing his right arm slowly in a windmill motion. As planned, Teddy stepped into one of the Tiffany phone booths and waited, able to see the front door but unwilling to stick his head out and possibly spook the Cubans. He leaned his shoulder against the wood wall of the booth and waited.

Inside the deposit-box room Frank, no longer focused on his work, felt the windowless walls closing in. He could use a break. He exited the room and closed the door behind himself, then saw Teddy, in the phone booth, wave for him to get out of sight. Frank ducked into the cashier's office, where he sat in the comfortably upholstered desk chair and surveyed the seven figures lying on the floor, none of them aware of his presence. For just a moment he considered kneeling down and whispering in old Brian's ear that all was going well, and asking how Mrs. Holbruncke's pearls were sitting in his stomach, but decided against it. He would just sit and breathe deeply for the few-minute break in what felt like roomy surroundings.

As the car approached, Breslin took from his hip pocket the folded magazine he had kept there for this moment and pretended to be engrossed enough not to notice the car stop at the canopy. From the corner of his eye he watched the trunk door pop up a few inches, released from inside, then the driver emerge and start across the sidewalk toward him. Even from fifteen feet away it was clear that this tall, well-dressed man was a Latin, with a generous portion of Indian genes in his pool—his hair was jet-black, his cheekbones prominent, his eyes wide-set. He was handsome and bore himself with posture so good as to be noticeable. The passenger, who disembarked on the street side and walked around the back of the car, ignoring the unlatched trunk, was much shorter than his driver. Everything about him was less dignified, but especially his bearing, which seemed almost inappropriate for a man of his age. He carried himself, Breslin thought, more like an athletic twenty-five-year-old than like a physician in his late fifties. Only when the driver was close enough to reach for the door handle did Breslin look up from his magazine suddenly,

as though startled, then fumble for his key briefly before
unlocking and pulling open the door.

"I'm sorry, gentlemen," he said as he held the door wide
and smiled. "Long night. You have reservations?"

"Yes," Angel said.

He and Cheito stepped through the door.

"There are two pieces of luggage in the trunk,"
Angel said.

"Bellman!" Breslin called across to Garrick, who had
quickly put aside his newspaper and stood at attention
near the couch. "Luggage in the gentlemen's trunk."

As Garrick approached briskly, Angel said, "I understand you have parking. The key is in the ignition."

"Yes, sir. The garage is half a block down. The bellman will park it for you."

Garrick passed them and went outside to the car trunk.
Breslin left the key in the lock, its little wood ball dangling, and began to lead them toward the front desk,
pausing after a few feet to wait for Garrick, who carried
in two small suitcases and locked the door behind
himself.

"The manager's stepped away from his desk for just a
minute," Breslin said apologetically.

Garrick, bags in hand, reached them. The four men
walked across the quiet, high-ceilinged lobby, Breslin
leading and off a bit to one side so that his back was
not directly presented to the guests, who walked abreast.
Garrick brought up the rear. When they reached the
front desk, Breslin motioned an invitation for the Cubans
to take the armchairs. They did. Garrick set down the
bags then reached into his uniform and extracted his pistol at the same time Breslin drew his. Garrick pointed
his at Angel's head, Breslin at Cheito's. The Cubans registered only mild surprise, and that briefly. Neither of
them gave even a hint of fear.

Teddy, the moment he saw pistols drawn, stepped out
of the phone booth and walked toward them, his own
pistol extended.

"Be smart and you won't get hurt," Garrick said. "This
is a robbery. We'll be out of here in half an hour."

"A *robbery*?" Cheito said disbelievingly.

Teddy and Breslin handcuffed them, then put strips of tape over their eyes. Breslin returned to the front door while Garrick quickly rifled Cheito's suitcases and Teddy patted down the Cubans. He reached Angel's ankle holster, and said, "What's this?" as he removed the .32.

"It's licensed," Angel said.

"You a cop?" Teddy asked.

"No, I carry a lot of money sometimes. This isn't one of those times."

Teddy led the two new prisoners into the cashier's office.

Frank observed silently from his chair as Teddy guided first one man, then the other through the labyrinth of human forms on the floor to an unoccupied space beside the desk. He set both of them facedown, and asked, "Either of you have trouble breathing?"

Both answered no.

Teddy reached into his pocket for the tape, then realized that Breslin had put it in his own pocket. He picked his way across the floor and left the room.

"This is no robbery," Cheito whispered to Angel in Spanish. "It's us they're after. This is a cover."

Frank leaned down to listen closer.

"I'm not so sure," Angel said.

"If we're separated or if something happens to you, where do I find the materiel?"

"The house is in Woodstock," Angel whispered in Spanish. "A few miles from the center of the village. A yellow house on a road called Quarry Lane. A key is taped to the side of the heat pump at the back of the house. The materiel is in the basement."

"Good," Cheito said. "Tell them nothing if you're interrogated."

It puzzled Frank for only a moment—the word "materiel" was unfamiliar—but it could only mean drugs. "Drugs," he thought. "This can only be about drugs," and hoped that his partners were looking very closely at these Colombians' luggage.

Teddy came through the door, roll of tape in hand. As

he taped their mouths shut, Frank quietly rose from the chair and made his way out, pleased to see that Jay Garrick was going through the drug dealers' bags with what looked to be great care.

He returned to the deposit-box room, where he knelt, purposefully exhaled a long, loud breath the way athletes do to relax, then resumed shearing off the hinge of the oversized, bottom-row box that surely contained the elderly Chinaman's one million five. As he hammered, he reflected on the presence in the hotel of both the Chinaman and the two Colombians, and how the average person had absolutely no idea of the constant chicanery taking place all around him, day in and day out, in even the most upscale surroundings.

Teddy, after taping the Cubans' mouths, returned to his post in the open doorway of the cashier's office and checked his watch. Quarter past four. The next forty-five minutes, he knew, would be the most nerve-wracking stretch. They were over the first big hump—their quarry was under lock and key—but now the robbery had to be stretched for forty-five more minutes. Lin Cutshaw, according to Garrick, believed this delay to be the single most crucial element in Fidel buying the robbery as authentic. Cutshaw wanted the news reports to be such that after the two Cubans arrived on the scene and were handcuffed the thieves continued to crack boxes for nearly an hour before deciding to pull out. It was what one would expect in a bona fide robbery.

There was, now, a natural drive to get out of the place before something went wrong. In about forty more minutes Breslin would shout out that there was a problem. A minute later Garrick would rush to Teddy at the cashier's office and tell him, loud enough for all the detainees to hear, that Breslin had spotted a car parked across the street with what were surely plainclothes cops in it watching the hotel. The excited Garrick would be convinced there were cops all over the street waiting to ambush them when they left. The answer was to leave with hostages. He, Garrick, would select Cheito and his bodyguard, and the Woodlings. The detainees left behind would relate just the story Cutshaw wanted.

Breslin was as much on edge as Teddy, for the same reasons. He wished he was free to pace, which always relaxed him, but instead remained half-seated on the night doorman's high stool. He also wished he had a vodka. An occasional pedestrian passed, nearly always directly in front of him since the lights of the hotel canopy made the south side of the street more inviting. Passing cars, few and far between, invariably moved fast, trying to make crosstown lights, with almost no traffic on the streets. Now a car turned into the street off Park Avenue but didn't pick up speed, as he expected. That drew his attention. It crawled toward him very slowly. After just another five yards he recognized it as a patrol car. His heart pounded and he almost stood at attention but caught himself and instead pulled the magazine from his hip pocket and pretended to be immersed in it. He slouched into as loose a posture as he could muster, watching the street from the corner of his eye.

"They're going to creep right by," he thought as they were nearly abreast of the door. Instead the car swerved slowly toward him and pulled to the curb behind the Cubans' Buick. His heart pounded harder. He continued to pretend not to see it.

They gave a quick toot of the horn.

He jerked his head up, paused, then gave a little wave. The passenger side door opened and a big, young, uniformed cop stepped out and started around the car, clearly heading for Breslin. Breslin got off the stool casually, managing to turn toward the lobby for a moment in a natural motion.

"Cops!" he called out. "Cops! Cops!" then turned the key in the lock and pushed the door open even before the cop had reached the sidewalk.

Teddy's first thought was that Breslin's timing was off by forty minutes, that he had initiated the ruse too early. The thought lasted only a moment. Breslin was opening the door, not needed for the ruse. This was the real thing.

Teddy closed the door of the cashier's office and strode quickly to the deposit-box room. The steady metallic clinking of Frank's hammer and chisel suddenly sounded much louder than it had a few moments earlier.

Breslin sized up the approaching cop quickly—late twenties, his hand not resting on the butt of his gun, friendly demeanor. And his partner, sitting behind the wheel, was lighting a cigarette and looking straight ahead.

"Where's John?" the cop asked.

His name tag said STANKY.

"Some kind of stomach bug. They got me out of bed at two A. M. to cover for him. He thinks it's something he ate."

"Maybe someone," Stanky said.

Breslin laughed and said, "I'm Tommy Quinn."

"John Stanky," the cop said, and stepped past Breslin into the lobby. He motioned toward the far end of the lobby, and said, "I got to take a leak. I know where it is."

He walked purposefully toward the front desk. Breslin tensed as he watched the tall, overweight, dark-blue figure shamble across the elegant lobby, holster projecting out cowboy style, walkie and flashlight swinging from his belt. Breslin estimated that fully equipped, Stanky weighed in at 240, maybe 250. He had a seedy look about him, that was going to worsen with time. In ten years he would be a disaster. If the cop saw absolutely no one, as was about to happen, would he question it? What if he wanted to talk to the elevator operator or night manager? What could he, Breslin, do?

Stanky took a left at the front desk and disappeared from sight as he passed the cashier's office. He would pass the deposit-box room next. Breslin waited, and hoped that Teddy and Frank would stay put and that Garrick would keep busy checking on the security guys upstairs.

Teddy again startled Frank, who had just opened an oversized bottom-row box, its tray held upside down in his hand, hundreds of pages of documents scattered on the floor, some still wafting in the air.

"Papers. Nothing but papers," Frank said angrily. "What's the matter with this fucking Chinaman, keeping crap like this in his box?"

Teddy closed the door and whispered, "Cops. Breslin's opening the door for cops."

Frank set the tray down gently.

"They look like they're responding to a call, or what?" he asked.

Teddy shrugged. After a few moments he whispered, "Which Chinaman?"

Frank seemed puzzled for a moment, then dismissed the question with a little wave of his hand. Teddy surveyed the room, visualizing it a few hours from now when a department photographer would be vying for standing room with crime-lab technicians dusting it top to bottom and Major Case Squad detectives tossing off the usual obscene wisecracks about both the perps and the victims. It occurred to him that this was his first opportunity to watch a scene created. The condition of the little room testified to Frank's several hours of hard work. Teddy counted fifteen steel doors littering the floor at odd angles. Their detached, twisted hinges lay where they had fallen in an almost neat row along the wall of boxes. Empty trays lay helter-skelter in a pile where Frank had tossed them toward a corner. Discarded papers and documents covered the floor.

Frank squatted on his haunches and waited patiently for a bit before whispering suddenly, "I hate this. Should we sneak a little peek out there?"

Teddy considered it for a few moments, then shook his head, no.

"Whatever's happening, let it play out," he said. "If it goes bad there'll be a commotion. We'll hear it."

Frank nodded. After a few moments he looked around from his squatting position, at the walls and then the ceiling.

"You realize a prison cell is only half this size?" he whispered. "And the ceiling's lower."

Teddy glanced overhead, then took in the length of the room and mentally cut it in half.

"Thanks for sharing that with me," he whispered.

Breslin shifted the gun in his belt, to be certain both that it was not visible and that he could draw it quickly, then returned to his magazine and did his best to appear relaxed. His eyes darted constantly, first at the cop in the car, then to the end of the lobby, waiting for Stanky to reappear. Garrick appeared instead. He stepped out of the stairwell in the most leisurely fashion into the crucial area around the front desk and surveyed the scene approvingly. He might well have been a prospective buyer of the hotel.

Breslin whistled softly to attract his attention then waved him off with a vigorous hand motion. To Garrick's credit, he never hesitated, just wheeled around instantly and stepped back into the stairwell. Seconds later Breslin watched Stanky's hulking blue figure stride out from the alcove—he must have left the men's room an instant after Garrick managed to get out of sight. Breslin watched the overweight cop pause at the front desk and help himself to a piece of chocolate from the crystal bowl. He munched it as he crossed the lobby, then sucked his fingertips clean just before he reached Breslin.

"It's like a morgue around here," Stanky said. "Where's Brian? And Peter?"

Breslin shrugged and said, "Upstairs, I think. Brian may be sneaking in a nap. Peter's holding a rich old lady's hand, I think."

"A stuffed toilet, for sure," Stanky said, and took a step toward leaving, but stopped and turned in the open doorway. He pursed his lips thoughtfully. "Is Carlos in the kitchen?" he asked.

Breslin shrugged and made a fast decision that if Stanky walked back there, he would lock the door and follow, and take him prisoner in the kitchen—this cop wouldn't swallow another missing employee.

"I guess he is," Breslin said. "I never met the guy."

"He makes a hell of a meat loaf sandwich," Stanky

said. "Thick, like the Carnegie Deli does pastrami. And he puts a nice slice of red onion on it, and heavy schmears of butter on the top and the bottom bread both."

He was quiet for a moment. Breslin could see that he was thinking of the sandwich.

"The hell with it," he said reluctantly, and patted his waistline, then added, "Do yourself a favor, though. Go back and say hello to Carlos. And don't let him tout you onto some fucking burrito."

He walked across the sidewalk and into the street, then paused just before getting in to call across the roof of the car, "Say hello to John for me."

Breslin let out a long, deliberate breath as the police car pulled away.

"It's clear," he called out.

Thirty-five minutes later Garrick motioned Teddy away from the doorway of the cashier's office and whispered that it was time to go. Teddy stationed himself just inside the doorway, where anything he said could be heard well by the detainees. Then Garrick gave the silent "go" signal to Breslin, who called out loudly, "Cops! Somebody come up here quick. There's cops out there!"

Garrick waited a minute, then charged into the cashier's office excitedly.

"He's right," he said to Teddy. "Across the street in an unmarked car. Watching us. They're cops for sure."

Teddy's voice grew alarmed. "What do we do? What the fuck do we do?"

"We go out of here with hostages, that's what," Garrick said. "We take some of these people along. Nobody's going to take potshots at us if we've got innocent people walking next to us."

There was a flurry of movement on the floor as people adjusted their positions. Teddy realized that they were trying to make themselves smaller.

"Take the couple," Garrick said. "That chick is gold. And take two more."

He paused, as though looking over his crop of nine,

then said, "No employees, just guests. Take the South Americans, too."

Teddy pulled the Woodlings to their feet while Garrick pulled up Cheito and Angel. Woodling grunted loudly and shook his shoulders in violent protest until Teddy smacked him hard between the shoulder blades with an open palm. His wife didn't resist. The Cubans allowed themselves to be led from the room calmly. The four hostages were stood in a row near the front desk.

"Take off the blindfolds," Garrick said. "We don't want them stumbling around."

Teddy stripped off the pieces of tape. When Woodling could see, he continuously motioned with his head toward his wife and grunted loudly.

"See what he wants," Garrick said.

Teddy peeled back Woodling's gag.

"Leave my wife," Woodling said. His voice was desperate. "I beg you. I'll cooperate completely. I'll do my best even to help you any way I can. Willingly. Please don't take her."

Teddy felt a surge of admiration for the man. He was about to tell Garrick to leave her—he still felt that dragging a female along for reality's sake was gilding the lily—but decided this wasn't the time to interfere. There would be no harm done, just an hour or so of discomfort on Woodling's part before they were released.

"She goes," Garrick said to Woodling. "And don't cause any trouble. I'll kill you, and her, without thinking."

He motioned to Teddy to tape Woodling's mouth, then said, "Watch them," and walked quickly toward the front door. Teddy stood guard over the four of them, and noticed Mrs. Woodling exchange a look with her husband of, he guessed, fifteen or twenty years. Her expression of quiet, certain pride caused Teddy to envy Woodling once again. When she caught Teddy studying her and her husband, she stared at him defiantly.

Teddy watched Garrick take Breslin's place on the stool as Breslin went outside to move the van into position at the canopy. Once Breslin had the van set and saw that the street was clear, Teddy would pull Frank out of the deposit-box room fast and they would leave with the four hostages. He saw the van pull to the curb just in front of the Buick belonging to the Cubans. Breslin must have motioned that all was well because Garrick signaled Teddy to get Frank. As Teddy walked across to the deposit-box room he looked over his shoulder at the hostages, who never moved.

He swung open the door and spoke fast and urgently. "Out! We're out of here! Now!"

Frank, who was working in an upright position, calmly extended his arms away from his body and released the hammer and chisel from his gloved hands so that they fell to the floor away from his feet, turned to the airline bag on the desk-height shelf and quickly zippered it closed, and stepped through the door to stand beside Teddy.

"Front door out?" he asked, as his eyes went to the gun in Teddy's hand.

"Yeah."

Frank stopped in his tracks when he saw the four hostages standing beside one another, Teddy's gun pointed in their general direction and Garrick, now standing in the middle of the lobby, about halfway between the door and the hostages, with his gun pointed toward them as well.

"What the fuck is this?" he said.

"There's cops all over out there. We're taking these four with us. Insurance. They won't be hurt, Frank, don't worry."

"Don't *worry*? Are the three of you nuts, or what? Let's make a run for it out the back and take our chances. You go out of here with hostages and there'll be SWAT teams and helicopters following us."

"Argue later," Teddy said, and motioned toward Garrick. "He's calling the shots."

"You two. Come on," Garrick said. He pointed at the Cubans.

They walked to him.

"I'll get these two across the sidewalk and into the van," he said to Teddy. "Then bring the couple out."

Garrick smoothly extended the handle of the airline bag and wheeled it behind himself as he marched the Cubans to the front door.

Frank asked Teddy, "He ain't going to take off, is he?"

"He'll stick," Teddy said.

While Teddy and Frank studied the van, as best they could see it, Mrs. Woodling easily managed to get the fingers of her manacled right hand into the long, left sleeve of her blouse and undo the piece of tape holding a key to the underside of her wrist. She manipulated the key in a practiced way to unlock her handcuffs then smoothly slid her freed right hand down into the front of her skirt until it reached her crotch, her eyes never leaving Frank and Teddy. She slipped a Charter Arms undercover .38 special, two-inch barrel, from its holster and brought it out in one continuous motion that was fluid enough to attract no notice. As she clasped it with her left hand to gain the two-handed grip she had been trained to use, the handcuffs dangling on her left wrist clinked loudly enough to attract Frank's attention.

"Teddy!" he screamed.

Her arms were already extended in front of her, elbows locked, the pistol at chest height with just a few more inches of travel needed to bring the sight to eye level as Teddy whirled. He was just ten feet away, facing her squarely but off balance, back on his heels, as the slug exploded out of the barrel. She couldn't risk a head shot and so she placed the shot dead center in his chest, a perfect heart shot. The force of it knocked him backward. Even with the vest, it felt as though someone had hit him with a full swing of a baseball bat. His arms flew out but he held on to his gun. As he lurched backward, he saw her whirl to get Frank. She got off one shot at him as he dove behind the big Victorian partners desk. Her back was turned to Teddy when he squeezed the trigger. His first shot took her just below the neck and drove her forward; his second caught her lower down along the spine, just a few inches above the waist. She sprawled forward on the floor, facedown. Teddy turned to Woodling, still handcuffed, who ran for the front door.

"Frank!" Teddy shouted.

"I'm okay," he said, and rose to his feet. "What the fuck is happening?"

"Let's get out of here," Teddy said.

As they ran to the front door Teddy watched Breslin drive off without looking back. Woodling crossed the street at a near run and headed toward Madison Avenue.

Frank exited the front door first. He stood still for a moment beneath the entrance canopy, uncertain whether to go left or right. Teddy, when he came out, said, "Park is better." They walked to their right, peeling off the latex hoods as they went. Frank, following Teddy's lead, stuffed the mask into his jacket pocket.

"He's robbing us," Frank said. "Your buddies are robbing us. They didn't panic and take off back there, they split with the suitcase 'cause they're going to cut us out. It's not going to happen, Teddy. I ain't going to come up on the short end on this one. What kind of lunatic takes hostages? And he was wrong anyway. Fucking paranoid saw cops outside except they weren't there. And who was that broad? What the fuck was she all about, packing heat in her panties? She looked like a schoolteacher for Christ sake."

Teddy turned right on Park Avenue. They headed downtown at a fast clip along the wide, deserted sidewalk, Teddy scanning the street intensely. He needed time to figure out the fine points, he decided, but there was no doubt that Garrick had set things up for him and Frank to be left dead. The couple were part of Garrick's team for sure. Was Cutshaw behind it? Teddy wasn't sure.

"When we do get a cab," he said to Frank, "remember not to give the driver a good look at your face. A few hours from now there'll be a dozen detectives checking the call sheets of every Manhattan cabby who was in this neighborhood around now. Whoever picks us up is going to be interviewed for sure."

"So maybe we should have him drop us off a couple of blocks from the garage," Frank said.

"Garage?" Teddy said. "We're not going to the garage."

"What are you talking about? That's where the airline bag is. That's where I'm heading, my friend. I didn't put my neck out here so some asshole from L.A. can rob my end."

"We need a place to hole up is what we need, not a showdown at the OK Corral," Teddy said. "What are you going to do, go in there with a gun blazing?"

"If that's what it calls for," Frank said in an even tone.

"What happened to your big commitment to nonviolence? You've been sounding like Mahatma Gandhi whenever the subject comes up."

"I said I didn't *like* violence, Teddy. I said I wouldn't use it on some innocent bystander gets caught in a jackpot he don't belong in. But if somebody wants to piss all over me, I'll shoot."

They were quiet for a bit, then Frank said, "We don't even know for sure that Garrick and Breslin are robbing our end. Maybe they really did panic back there—it happens."

Teddy said nothing. He saw no way out of going to Thirty-ninth Street short of opening up and telling Frank the whole truth. He couldn't do that. By the time they got there, he believed, Garrick, Breslin, and the Cubans would be already gone; they were likely switching vans just about now.

They were nearing Fiftieth Street when Teddy spotted an empty cab on the other side of the center island, heading uptown. He stuck the tips of his pinkies into his mouth and let out a piercing whistle. It made him think, momentarily, of his father, who used to lean far out of their Arthur Avenue tenement window in his undershirt and whistle that way for him—a high-pitched piercing trill that carried two blocks, and was distinct from the summons of every other father in the neighborhood. His father had taught him how to do it. The driver waved that he would make a U-turn but got caught by a red light. They waited patiently at the curb for the light to change.

Frank spoke suddenly, a man just struck by a revelation. "That broad back there—she was somehow part of the drug deal. She was meeting those junk dealers. *That's* why the pistol in her panties."

"What junk dealers?" Teddy asked.

"Those spics. I heard them talking. They had a junk deal going down upstate."

The cab pulled up. As they got in, both of them managed to position their arms and heads so that the driver never had a good, clear look at their faces.

XII

Breslin tapped the steering wheel lightly with his fingertips in an unhurried beat as they waited for the light to change at Fifty-fifth and Ninth Avenue. The carefully timed tapping was part of an intense effort to appear calm, to present himself as a man surprisingly patient under the circumstances, a professional soldier for whom even the most unexpected, bizarre developments during an operation were no cause for questioning higher-ups. He made a point of staring straight ahead, in particular never stealing a sideways glance at Jay Garrick, beside him in the passenger seat.

Even before the van had been fully away from the curb at the hotel, Garrick had indicated the two Cubans in the rear and put a finger to his lips in a sign that he didn't want them to overhear anything. Now, he sat quietly with gun in hand, dangling it comfortably between his knees so that it pointed at the floor, but with his index finger in the trigger guard. He was, Breslin guessed, observing and gauging his behavior. Breslin's eyes darted to his left frequently to check the street behind in the driver's side mirror, each glance accompanied by a nearly imperceptible movement of his head in that direction, just enough movement to register with Garrick, who would, Breslin hoped, see beside himself a man whose only concern was for being pursued by police.

Breslin was, in fact, as scared as he had ever been. He was fairly sure Garrick planned to kill him in the next ten minutes or so. No question but that the woman back there and her partner had been planted by Cutshaw to kill Teddy and Frank—leave them dead in the hotel lobby—though from what he had been able to see from his vantage point behind the wheel of the van, Cutshaw's female had been the one to go. Garrick had shown no surprise; certainly he was in on it. As Breslin continued to tap his deceptive little riff, he tried to answer for himself—and very quickly—why Cutshaw and Garrick had not brought him into their scheme. His years in the Agency had taught him that there might well be an innocuous reason—the usual need-to-know operating procedure. He could hear Cutty softly drawling to Garrick, "Hell, Jay, if Chuck's not needed to eliminate them two, then don't tell him nothin' till it's over. Need to know." The years had also taught him, though, that things might well be more complicated, and the players more dangerous, than they appeared. That Frank Belmonte ought not be left alive, given his ability to someday identify the others, was perfectly understandable. And Teddy, while more reliable than Belmonte, was not an ex-Agency guy, and so everyone would rest easier with him gone, too. But the need-to-know explanation for why he himself hadn't been brought into the scheme didn't feel quite right. Why? Something about Garrick's demeanor told him that he had no reason to change the answer he had given himself just seconds after pulling away from the curb—because he was due to go next.

The light changed. He turned left and accelerated fast enough to catch the green at the corner of Fifty-fourth. His stomach tightened. It would be clear sailing now through staggered traffic lights down to the Thirty-ninth Street garage, only two or three minutes more, and if Garrick did plan to kill him, for sure he would do it in the garage, their temporary safe house on this operation. Likely before he ever got out from behind the wheel. He wished he could pull over for just five minutes and sort things out, but had to settle for driving carefully along nearly deserted Ninth Avenue, needing first to make the crucial judgment required—to trust Cutshaw and Garrick or not. To attribute his fears to paranoia when in fact Garrick intended him no harm, or whether to commit himself to a survival strategy and go on the offensive.

And if he did decide to go on the offensive, he needed to formulate a plan in the next few minutes.

He wanted to believe he was still part of Cutshaw's team, that Linwood would not sacrifice him, that there was no need for action on his part. He wanted to choose the path of least resistance and bathe in the warmth of trust and good feeling. Not surprising, he thought—that was always the case in this kind of situation. As they neared Thirty-ninth Street, he decided that Garrick's silence was a good sign. If Garrick intended to do him in, he would be talking now, constructing some fiction about what had gone on in the lobby, in order to put him at ease. That Garrick felt no need to explain—that he could sit there silently—was enough of a plus to tilt Breslin toward trusting him.

"I've been trying to figure out that mess back there in the lobby," Garrick whispered. "But I believe I know what happened. Once we're settled in the garage, I'll tell you what I think it's all about."

Moments later, as Breslin completed his turn onto Thirty-ninth, he took the remote door opener off the dashboard, then aimed and pressed it. Halfway down the block, on their right, the door began to rise. He slowed, and moved to his left, hugging the curb to give himself the widest possible turning radius. The overhead door was fully open well before he went into his turn, the garage interior lit dimly by a bare hundred-watt bulb that had come on when the door opened. He saw that there would be plenty of clear space on both sides of the van, three or four feet on his left, where there was a wall, and the same leeway on his right, where a Lincoln Town Car sat, facing out. It was the vehicle they were supposed to transfer the hostages into. He made the turn so slowly that the van came nearly to a stop. When the wheels straightened fully he judged that he was some forty feet from the rear wall of the garage, now directly in front of him. He floored the pedal with one hard push of his foot. The van leaped forward. The screeching told him he was laying down lines of rubber in the street. He picked up enough speed so that the front wheels left the ground when they hit the little incline of the sidewalk. The acceleration pressed his body against the back of his seat. He pulled the door handle with his left hand and held the door open a few inches. Just before they hit the cinder-block wall he slid down and to his left, and braced his right shoulder against the wheel, still pressing the pedal hard against the floor. The car hit the wall and gave off the sounds of metal crunching. He saw Garrick's head fly forward against the windshield and the gun drop to the floor. Breslin reached under Garrick's crumpled body and groped along the floor mat for the gun, found it, and felt a surge of relief—he would not die in the next minutes. He thought for one moment of putting a bullet into Garrick's head but could not do it, in spite of his certainty that Garrick had been about to kill him; shooting a CIA operative in cold blood was impossible for him. Instead, he rolled out of the driver's door onto the garage floor and scrambled to his feet, sprinting toward the door even before he was fully erect, then out to the openness of the sidewalk. He turned left and headed for Ninth Avenue as he had planned during the ride downtown. Halfway up the block he felt for the first time a sharp pain in his right elbow. It must have jammed against the steering wheel when he hit. If he got away with only that self-inflicted bit of damage he would count himself lucky. The Cubans suddenly flashed into his mind, and he slowed his pace for several strides. Should he go back? But to do what? Wait for Garrick to recover? He remembered that the Cubans were handcuffed. His die was cast, and the immediate circumstances called for him to look out for number one. Now he needed to get off the streets, to someplace safe where he could gather his wits. He remembered that Garrick's gun was in his hands. It was pointless to keep it; he hadn't used it just a minute before and wouldn't use it now. It was also the gun that had killed the porter. He wiped it clean and tossed it into the dark doorway of a storefront.

*   *   *

When the van surged forward with no warning across the gutter then the sidewalk of Thirty-ninth Street, Cheito was lying among the pieces of plumbing equipment on the van floor. His feet were forward. The rush of adrenaline was familiar to him from the scores of surprise ambushes and firefights he had been through during his years of soldiering. When they crashed into the wall he hit the back of the passenger seat in the best possible way—feet first. He was barely shaken and his survival instinct kicked in immediately—there were no precious moments lost in gathering his wits. He groped around the floor of the van for a short length of two-inch black-iron pipe he had made note of earlier, finally found it, snatched it up in his manacled hands and was on his feet in an instant, crouched because of the low headroom, homing in on his immediate target, Jay Garrick, who was slumped on the floor in front of the passenger seat, head in hands, dazed. Cheito swung the short length of pipe as best he could in the confines of the van. It landed with a dull thud on the back of Garrick's skull. He fell on his side, half on the seat, half on the floor, clearly immobilized, but judging by how he lay perhaps not dead. It was of no interest to Cheito, who wanted his pistol. He felt around for it, the handcuffs slowing him up, but couldn't find it. He was puzzled, and after a bit told himself to give it up, but could not—he had carried a gun and slept within easy reach of it for too many years. Finally, he had to get out and only then thought of the keys for the handcuffs and realized that they were of far more use to him than a gun. He went into Garrick's pockets as best he could but found no key. Behind him, he heard the rear door of the van open, and turned. Angel jumped out, and fell to the garage floor. Cheito went out the door.

"What's wrong?" Cheito asked.

"My knee," Angel groaned. "It cracked against that pile of pipes in the van."

Cheito pulled him to his feet, clumsily, because of the handcuffs. Angel held on to the door for support and groaned again. His knee buckled and he nearly collapsed. He looked at Cheito, who in turn stared appraisingly at the injured leg hovering inches above the concrete floor, unable to bear any weight.

"It's your patella," Cheito said. "A fracture, no doubt. Probably just a hairline but you can't put weight on it." He paused, then added, "For weeks."

"I'll be all right," Angel said. "I just need a minute."

Cheito said nothing.

Angel took a halting step, then stood still.

"I just need a minute," he said. "You go ahead, I'll catch up."

His eyes, fixed on Cheito's face, gave away that even as he spoke he knew it was the babble of desperation.

Cheito moved past him, reached into the van and came out with the same short length of pipe he had used on Garrick. Angel turned and took a step toward the open garage door. Cheito hit him hard on the side of his already damaged knee, then three more times on the base of the skull.

He dropped the pipe, was about to exit onto the street, then realized that his handcuffs were in plain sight and ought to be concealed. His jacket draped over them would do well but there was no way to remove it. Nor could he remove Angel's jacket without first hacking off his hands, and there was no tool with which to do it. He scurried back into the van, reached across the passenger seat, and pulled off Garrick's jacket. It would not only cover the handcuffs, but with luck, a careful search might turn up the key. As he made his way back through the van he looked for a tool that might be of help, fruitlessly, until his eye lit upon the black airline bag. Could it contain tools? He doubted it, and there was no time to look, but the wheels made him realize that walking the streets with the bag in front of him—pushing it—would, along with the jacket, give him a completely natural appearance, a reason to hold his hands together at his waist. He draped the jacket across the chain of the handcuffs and pulled the airline bag out of the van. Something in it clanked, the sound of metal on metal. Tools? His spirits rose for a moment. Maybe he was about to get lucky.

XIII

They had the cab drop them at Thirty-eighth Street and Ninth Avenue, then walked uptown and west for a block and a half, the streets still empty of people. As they neared the garage and saw that the door was open, Teddy put his hand inside his jacket and rested it on his pistol. He had decided during the silent cab ride that if Garrick or Breslin presented a threat he would shoot them, CIA or not. He took out the pistol as he entered the dim room, just ahead of Frank. Seconds later they saw Angel, his head facedown in a small pool of blood.

"Did I tell you this was a drug deal went bad?" Frank said. He opened the back door of the van and scanned the floor.

"No suitcase," he said. "The fucking suitcase is gone."

Teddy walked to the front of the van and saw that it had smashed into the wall. What was that about? Right now it didn't matter and he was able to put it out of his mind. He peered through the windshield and recognized the crumpled form as Garrick, then reached in and felt for a pulse, almost out of curiosity. It was there, and strong.

"Dead," he lied to Frank. "Let's get out of here *now*. Someone could have seen that guy's body and called it in. Come on."

Frank didn't argue. He took a last look around, then hurried out to join Teddy.

They walked downtown, Frank nervously trotting out each thought the moment it entered his mind, constructing a scenario of which he had no doubt. As he repeated it and laid in more detail, he became more convinced that it could have happened no other way. His immediate certainty about something of which he had so few pieces of mushy evidence and even fewer hard facts intrigued Teddy. It was out of character with the Frank Belmonte he had seen to date. He wondered, was this a syndrome of Frank's species of bold, lay-it-all-on-the-line career criminal? A need to commit quickly and exclusively to the first version of reality that occurred to him? Maybe some sort of compulsive decisiveness, the absolute flip side of the inability-to-choose that so often paralyzed people. It might, Teddy thought, be an avoidance tactic—a vaccine against the indecisiveness that would be fatal for a nervy jewel thief.

Frank was sure that the Woodlings had been at the hotel to make a buy from the two Spanish drug dealers. The older drug dealer had planned to screw both his partner, now lying dead behind the van, and the Woodlings. Breslin was in league with him—Breslin willing to screw his own three partners.

"What a score," Frank kept repeating, with as much admiration as anger. "Breslin and the spic make off with a suitcase full of jewels *and* that dead broad's money."

Teddy did not disabuse him of his fantasy, since he himself was not about to reveal all. As for what had really happened in the garage, he didn't know and didn't speculate; he was now on the lam and his concern was to make the best next move. He wondered briefly about the dead Cuban and the whereabouts of the other one, who might well be on the loose. In any event, he had no clue as to how to track him down. That problem was back in Cutshaw's lap, and there was absolutely no percentage in calling Cutshaw on the hot-line number he had been given at the Atlantic City meeting. His own first order of business was finding a safe place to hole up and work out some kind of plan. He couldn't simply turn himself in and explain that his motive had been patriotic, though the thought had occurred to him just seconds after they left the hotel. His patriotic motives would count for nothing, with a dead porter and a dead woman left behind. She was certainly some kind of CIA operative, but that would never come out. Like it or not, he and Frank were a pair now, and their best hope for a safe place lay with Frank; even Teddy's closest friends wouldn't harbor a fugitive from this kind of crime. That this was true, that he finally had not a single person to whom he could turn in dire circumstances, gnawed at him, but he dismissed the thought quickly. He had no time for it now, but it would return, he was sure, in the very near future. Right now, a safe place was needed.

"Where to, Frank?" he said. "We need something completely off the beaten track. Someplace a hundred percent safe."

"I started thinking where we could hole up the minute that twat reached for her crotch," Frank said. "This ain't just a jewel heist anymore."

After a few moments, he said, "I can get us an oceanfront hole-in-the-wall in Brighton Beach."

"Someone we can trust?"

"Someone who won't sell us out for money. Unless it's really a lot. He'll look at the papers tomorrow and figure it was me got the Montclair, but he'll say nothing to nobody, including me, 'cause he'll assume we've already stashed the jewels someplace safe. He'll also figure there's a nice taste for him down the road and he'll be right—we'll throw him twenty-five big ones if we get back our stones."

"He knows you did the Quincy job?" Teddy asked.

"He's *sure* I did it, just like all the wiseguys in the neighborhood, but I never said yes to anybody. I'll tell you though, Sally *will* sell us out to save his own skin, if he's backed into a corner. Welcome to this side of the law. That's about as good as it gets over here."

"The spot we're in, it's a lot better than anything I can do on my side," Teddy said. "Everyone I could go to would turn me in sooner than risk an aiding-and-abetting charge. The couple of friends who wouldn't do it out of fear would do it for moral reasons."

Frank nodded his head in grave understanding and said, "The fucking moralists. The worst. Never even want to hear the circumstances, and if they do listen they got no empathy. I know a lot of people wouldn't stick their neck out 'cause there's no percentage, but thank God I don't know anybody would turn me down for moral reasons."

He spotted a phone nearby and dug through his pocket for change.

Their hole-up was in Brighton Beach, known as Little Odessa since the late 1970s when tens of thousands of Russian Jews saturated the area, drawn by the proximity to water, most of them having come from areas on or near the Black Sea. Frank picked up what he called an emergency key from the counterman in a twenty-four-hour Russian fast-food restaurant just off Ocean Parkway, to whom the apartment owner, Sally, had called ahead. The studio apartment was on the third floor of a drab, six-story apartment house built flush against the land side of the boardwalk. The apartment was rented for a few hundred a month by a lifelong friend of Frank's, a Brooklyn guy, Sally Seventeen, who had been on the fringes of organized crime since age twelve. He was now in his late sixties. Sally had run numbers for years; worked the bars and barbershops of Nostrand Avenue as a street-level sports bookie until long after that neighborhood became completely black, earning the boroughwide distinction of being the last white bookie in Bed-Stuy; run a chop shop in South Ozone Park for six years before being raided and serving seventeen months in Auburn, amazingly, the only time he ever did; brokered small vanloads of cigarettes that carried no state tax stamps, brought up from North Carolina in trailerloads and broken down to five-thousand-carton lots for hustlers like himself; moved bad $10 and $20 bills bought for fifteen cents on the dollar, passing them in newsstands, bodegas, and drugstores, purchasing small items that he threw into the trash basket but getting his hands on the nine good dollar bills given as change—a tough way to grind out a day's pay. For the past few years he had been able to sell advance pirated tests he called "Sats" to legitimate businessmen with mediocre offspring at $1,000 a copy.

Throughout, during those occasional flush times when he was on a rich run and income exceeded his nut and his gambling losses, when he was ahead $10,000 or $20,000 over a sustained three-month period, he put it out on the street at six-for-five, lending it a few hundred at a time to truck drivers, construction workers, waiters. Sooner or later, though, he would lose it all gambling, with borrowed thousands to boot, on which he would then have to pay rather than receive six-for-five.

"Sally never sleeps," Frank had explained to Teddy. "Guy's a workaholic. On the street from early in the morning till late at night. Earning. Always earning. Looking for the next angle. Whatever it takes to turn a buck. And he's a real anomaly for his kind of lifelong hustler. The guy's taken maybe two dozen pinches over the years but only did seventeen months in the joint. That's in a class with DiMaggio's fifty-six-game streak."

"Maybe he got lucky," Teddy had said.

"Over that many years, it's more than luck. This is a guy in the trenches. A street-earner. A guy violates six serious laws *every day of his life.* That many years, a social scientist will tell you it's statistically significant. No, with Sally it's just the opposite. He got lucky just once in his life, while he was passing a batch of fugazy twenties. Bought a Pick-Ten lottery ticket on Chambers Street—strictly to get the nineteen bucks of good change—and caught them all. Along with some other winners. Cashed it in for a hundred thou. *And then* he dropped every cent of it on a three-day weekend in Atlantic City. Sally can just never catch a break."

"He ever consider going straight?" Teddy had asked, in a carefully neutral tone.

Frank had given him a sidelong glance and said, "Typical smart-ass cop remark," then added, "He's one of those guys just don't have the makeup for it. You know the type, Teddy? By the time they're ten years old— whatever ain't nailed down. Even when he was a little kid, Sally would steal a hot stove. His kind all start young. He's what I classify as a constitutional thief. It's just his disposition."

"Sounds like every thief I ever dealt with," Teddy had said.

"You might not have paid close enough attention," Frank had said. "Most career thieves are constitutional, but there's exceptions. Eccentrics, just like in the straight world. Happenstance criminals, who don't really belong in the life. And then there's the casuals—a lot more of them than people realize. Guys drift in, drift out. Go straight for years, then boom—get out there and make a score."

For a while now, Sally Seventeen had been hooked up with the Russian mob in Brighton Beach, starting with gasoline tax scams, branching out when that came to a sudden end. The apartment was a convenient place to stay overnight when need be; otherwise he lived with his mother in Bay Ridge. He rented the little studio apartment under the name Oleg Sholokov, which was on the lease and the mailbox and attracted no attention. The few cheap prints that hung on the apartment walls, left over from the previous tenant, were Russian winter scenes.

Teddy now found himself staring for a few moments at one of the lifeless prints in the early morning light, a winter landscape with a horse-drawn sleigh. The colors were awful. Sally's studio apartment was a fair-size room with faded peach-colored walls that had not been painted for a long time. The ceiling was flaking in spots. Teddy sat across from Frank at a white-porcelain-top kitchen table set flush against the south wall, directly beneath a narrow window whose blind was opened fully. Frank had lifted the window a few inches to admit the pleasant sea breeze. On the opposite, windowless wall an opened-out sofa bed looked as though it had not been closed in years. A small night table and an easy chair were the only other pieces of furniture.

They had decided to proceed step-by-step: reach the safety of the apartment; eat, since both of them were famished, a common aftereffect according to Frank; sleep for five or six hours; then buy the afternoon papers to learn how much the police knew. The morning papers, which would be on the stands very soon, would have nothing.

"We may have left behind all kinds of leads," Teddy had said. "I can pretty much read between the lines. We'll know whether we're under the gun. Whether we can show our faces or not."

It had made sense to Frank.

Spread before them on the chipped tabletop were paper plates and take-out trays of stuffed cabbage, piroshki, blini, dumplings, kasha and sour cream, brought in from the all-night restaurant under the el where they had picked up the key. Each of them wolfed down the food and took long drafts from cold bottles of Brooklyn Lager. Frank indicated the expanse of food and said, through a mouthful of kasha, "It's a good thing Sally's not here. He'd demolish the whole works in a couple of minutes. Nice and easy. Then he might eat the trays, too."

"Sally likes to put it away," Teddy said.

Frank nodded. "Guy could eat a horse and never belch. The Russkies out here love to sit at a table with Sally."

He crammed half a beef piroshki into his mouth and said, "This stuff ain't anywhere close to our cuisine but it gets the job done." He took a long drink of beer from the bottle, and said, "Too far north is their problem. They never had nothing to work with. Cabbage and potatoes and a ton of lard to cook in. What the hell grows in eight feet of snow that anybody wants to eat? None of them cold-weather countries are much better off. What the fuck you going to do with a beet? We were lucky, Teddy—tomatoes and olive oil, a hell of a start. And we invented pasta right away. Ourselves. That Marco Polo story is bullshit."

"You make do with what you got," Teddy said, and dug into the kasha.

Frank nodded approvingly and said, "See? You're a guy would do easy time. That's the attitude you got to have. All the guys who do their time hard, they can't compromise. Life's got to be all their way. Butter on both sides of the bread. You would do your time easy, like me."

"That's comforting to know," Teddy said dryly, and put a spoonful of sour cream onto a blini.

He realized, suddenly, that he was now one of Frank's happenstance criminals, on the lam in the Brighton Beach crash pad of a constitutional thief listening to another constitutional thief's advice on how to do easy time.

"Tell me something, Frank," he said. "What kind of thief are you? Constitutional? Happenstance? None of the above?"

"That's a tough one," Frank said. "A lot of my time in the joint, I've spent trying to answer that." He chewed thoughtfully for a bit. "Deep down, I don't think so," he said. "It's never black and white, but I think with me it was learned behavior." He shrugged. "But then again, maybe not. I could be a constitutional. First thing I remember robbing was from Woolworth's. I was maybe seven. What's weird is, I didn't glom a toy soldier or something—I pocketed a piece of costume jewelry. A ring with a hunk of purple glass on it the size of a dime. It looked to me like it was worth more than any of the toys. So who knows."

Voices carried up from the boardwalk, some thirty feet below, speaking Russian and sometimes Yiddish. Teddy looked out at the gray Atlantic Ocean and the cloudless morning sky above it. These refugees had made a wise selection in Brighton Beach. They had a forty-foot-wide, well-maintained boardwalk to stroll on, with plenty of benches for the sitters, then a two-hundred-foot strip of clean sand, nearly empty of people and blankets at this early hour. Seagulls cried and went about their business at the edge of the Atlantic Ocean. Two blocks from the boardwalk in the other direction was a subway line that delivered a rider into the heart of Manhattan in forty-five minutes, for a dollar and a half.

"Beats Atlantic City," Teddy thought. "By a long shot."

Frank finished his beer, then put his head back and let out a long, loud yawn.

"I need my zees," he said. "It's what a lot of time in the joint does to you. Makes you a creature of habit."

He walked to the open sofa bed, removed his shoes, and lay down, carefully keeping himself on one half of it. After a moment he said, "Teddy, if we roll into each other, don't panic. Fucking Sally's done some job on this mattress. It's like trying to sleep inside a giant soup bowl."

Seconds later Teddy heard his first rumbling snores. Teddy knew that he was not going to fall asleep so fast, and so he opened a fresh bottle of beer and looked out at the wide expanse of ocean. He was still unsure whether Cutshaw was behind the treachery at the hotel or if it was Garrick operating independently. Right now the prudent thing to do was to assume the worst-case scenario: that it was Cutshaw's doing, that Cutshaw wanted Frank and him safely dead, and that he would now do his best to hunt them down. Breslin's role in all of it was a question mark, since he had melted into the night along with the Cuban. Given the Byzantine world in which he operated, Teddy thought, the man might well be working for Castro. He hoped that the news reports would give him more to go on. For now, he decided, he would not open up to Frank with the whole story, not until he had to, if ever.

A ship came into view a mile or so offshore, a freighter that looked too small for an ocean crossing, with containers piled high on both fore and aft decks. It had just passed through the Narrows and was now in the open sea, bound for somewhere he wished he was just then.

XIV

Cheito's decision to turn right immediately upon running out of the garage was completely arbitrary, a mode of operation so rare for him that it took a few seconds for the implications to sink in—that because he had no information to go on and thus no reason to trust his instinct, one direction was as good as the other. He was trusting to luck. His stomach tightened, a familiar warning signal from his body to keep his wits about him. He explained to himself that anxiety was to be expected, that these surroundings were causing it, that everything was so unfamiliar he would often be forced to choose arbitrarily in the days and weeks ahead, that he had better learn to be comfortable with coin tosses, since there was no way to change things.

He walked along the still-dark, deserted street pushing the overloaded airline bag, whose wheels were far too small for easy travel over these sidewalks. The handcuffs threatened to unsettle him. To the point of panic, he thought; another rarity. While under guard on the floor of the hotel office and then in the van, he had hardly been aware of them. Now, as the only obstacle to his being completely free, the handcuffs made him vulnerable in a way he could barely tolerate. He was sure that if the chain joining the two bracelets were just a few inches longer he would be able to relax, and at once saw the absurdity of the idea, yet remained convinced that it was true. Even when wounded on the battlefield, he had never felt so incapacitated and out of control.

He reached the corner of Tenth Avenue and hesitated for a few moments, dreading another arbitrary choice.

When he saw from the position of a passing cab that this was a one-way street, he decided it was better to walk with his back to the onflow of traffic. He turned right. This logical decision, small as it was, gave him a welcome sense of relief and let him think more clearly. First, he must get free of the handcuffs. He scanned the street as he walked, stupidly, he thought, since he realized that were a hacksaw miraculously to appear at his feet, he would have no way to use it. Still, he couldn't stop surveying the sidewalks, which were deserted except for men curled into doorways or loading docks, many of them nestled among huge, black plastic bags bulging with what he thought at first must be their possessions, until he saw several clear plastic bags filled with bottles and cans. These sleeping men were scavengers. It crossed his mind that this was the system the entire world was now eager to emulate.

Overhead signs directed traffic to the Lincoln Tunnel. He remembered from maps he had studied in Cuba that the tunnel went under the Hudson River to New Jersey, and clearly the tunnel was somewhere off to his left. It meant he was heading north, a piece of information he could put to no use, yet was a small comfort—things would fall into place, bit by bit, as they always did if he remained calm. He berated himself for not having made more time to study maps and transportation systems. It was unlike him to be less than overly prepared and not to have considered that any one of a dozen eventualities might befall Angel, putting him on his own. All along the avenue were parking lots, with signs that underscored for him how much a fish out of water he was. One sign read, EVENT RATE, $16.91. What events? Could this be a weekly rate? Why such a strange number? Why not $17.00?

Every few minutes, like clockwork, a tiny convoy of yellow cabs suddenly came up from behind and overtook him. They would continue north at a steady speed and disappear into the distance. Who were they expecting to pick up at this hour? Why travel together that way? Were they truly taxicabs? Ahead, as far as he could see,

the endless line of red lights turned green, one after another. The unfamiliarity of it all disturbed him more than
he had allowed for, and the damn handcuffs intensified
the terrible feeling of being not in control. Although he
was walking on concrete between the vertical walls of
city buildings, this present situation, he thought, was not
different from moving behind enemy lines, unarmed and
slightly crippled, through a shallow arroyo devoid of vegetation. That was a situation he had once survived. The
secret to surviving now was the same as then—to embrace the lack of control, the anxiety, as a challenge. To
welcome it as an athlete welcomes a tougher task. It was
how he had always reacted to adversity, how he had
overcome a pampered childhood to become a hardened
soldier, had overcome obstacles that few scientists could
have in replicating the virus; this was one more opportunity
to triumph. Another chapter in *The Life of Ernesto
(Cheito) Rivera, Soldier-Scientist.* The bar had been set
higher; clearing it required nothing more than great will
and the ability to concentrate, which he knew he possessed.

He berated himself for not having concentrated earlier,
for spending precious time in the van searching for the
pistol instead of searching for the key to his handcuffs.
It had been instinctive to want a weapon, but that was
no excuse. Had he thought clearly back in the van, he
would have seen that the handcuffs would be ten times
the handicap that lack of a pistol would be. It was the
eight-year layoff from soldiering that had led to his blun-
der. He looked around. He was back to soldiering now.

His little self-administered infusion of confidence took
the edge off his anxiety and made him more comfortable.
He suddenly remembered that the jacket draped over his
wrists just might hold the key to his handcuffs. His hopes
rose. Half a block later the deep, poorly lit alcove of a
loading bay presented itself, empty but for several wood
pallets stacked in front of the huge door. He turned into
it, laid the bag flat on the concrete apron, and laid the
jacket on top of it. He went through every pocket, feeling
in the corners with his fingers, then, more from desperation than any real hope of success, felt the lining from

top to bottom. Nothing. He turned his attention to the airline bag. When he unzipped and laid back the flap, his eyes widened. "Plated junk" was his first thought. "Costume jewelry." There was simply too much of it to be real. This was part of the elaborate ruse set up at the hotel to cover up that he and Angel had been captured by FBI agents. He lifted out a large brooch and took a few steps toward the street, where he held it up toward a nearby streetlight. He had looked at a fair number of diamonds while in Angola—these were, he believed, the real thing. The brooch was also too heavy to be junk jewelry—the setting was almost certainly gold. He examined the pin clasp as best he could in the less than perfect light; it was too sturdy and elaborate for costume jewelry. Finally, he had been raised around valuable objects, including jewelry; this piece had about it a beauty, a purity, that costume jewelry never had. The thing was surely worth hundreds of thousands of dollars. His heart beat faster—the entire case could be worth millions. He hurried back, closed the case, and rearranged the jacket over his wrists, then hurried out of the loading bay to the sidewalk, where he continued to walk north, his mind racing. Could this entire incident have been legitimate? Why would a government-sponsored cover operation need to go so far that a real robbery had to take place? Surely the FBI had the means to take over the hotel for a night and fill it with their own people. And free press or no free press, the government certainly had the power to have a newspaper run an FBI-provided story about a holdup. And what of the driver of the van? His actions were the actions of a thief falling out with his partners, just as the shootout in the hotel lobby seemed to be. What a sudden reversal of fortune, he thought, if indeed he had unluckily stumbled into a robbery. He looked down at the case full of jewelry just in front of his legs, and became a little bit surer that it was all real. What should be done with it? It occurred to him that had someone a day ago put him hypothetically into just this situation and asked the question, he would have shrugged and said, in total honesty, that the money was unimportant.

Yet now, he thought, he would ask for time to consider his answer. Hypotheses and reality, he knew, produced very different responses, and real millions provided even an ascetic like himself with food for thought.

When he reached Forty-second Street the Manhattan map he had studied came into sharper focus for him; this street was a New York City landmark whose name he had known since childhood, and so he had searched for and found it on the map first thing, one of the extra-wide cross streets that occurred every ten blocks or so, wherever the oddly angled Broadway crossed a north-south avenue. He came to a halt for a few moments, and was able to visualize clearly the huge rectangle of Central Park that would lay ahead and well to his right, the United Nations Building nearly two miles to his right, Grand Central Terminal a mile and a half in the same direction. He looked over his right shoulder, and was pleased to see the lighted top of the Empire State Building where it belonged. Orienting himself among the landmarks he had fixed in his mind months earlier gave him a lift. He crossed Forty-second Street and saw that Tenth Avenue ahead was more built up. Half a block later he was startled when he suddenly came upon a uniformed policeman standing in a doorway on his left. He kept his eyes straight ahead as he passed within arm's length of the policeman, who had a cigarette in his mouth as he used his hands to remove a small beverage container from a paper bag. At the next corner Cheito turned west, toward the Hudson—the kind of shop or people he might find along a riverfront seemed to hold more promise of getting the handcuffs off. He needed tools; a simple hammer and chisel would do the trick. Even harder to come by, though, he needed someone willing to use them.

Ahead of him, on the corner of Eleventh Avenue, four whores wearing outlandish clothing paraded back and forth across the tiny parking lot of an all-night restaurant. Even from a distance he could see that all of them were exceptionally tall, with huge breasts and bright hair colors and four-inch, spiked heels on which they walked unsteadily. One wore red mesh stockings and a garter belt whose black straps were completely visible below a tiny leather miniskirt. They seemed to be plying their wares to motorists; it was nearly dawn and there were now more cars on the streets. As he approached the corner, a low-slung Porsche stopped at the curb, the driver lowered the passenger-side window, and one of the girls rested her forearms on the roof and bent over to bring her face down to the driver's level. She bent completely from the waist, keeping her knees locked and her legs straight. Cheito estimated her to be five-foot-ten in bare feet and nearly six-two in the heels. Because the car was so low to the ground and she stood on the curb, her legs appeared to be longer than the car was tall. He cast a connoisseur's eye on the scene, and thought, "These are remarkable whores," and found himself eager to get closer and see whether their faces measured up. After a few moments the door of the Porsche opened, the whore got in, and the car drove off. As he walked by the remaining three girls, disappointed with the quantities of makeup they wore, the mesh-stockinged girl, another six-footer, made a great show of catching sight of him. She stepped back, into the overhead lights of the diner's sign, and went into a highly theatrical, hands-on-hips pose.

"Well," she called out in a stage whisper to her colleagues, "what have we here? A tired, lonely business-man going home?"

She began to walk with him, keeping three or four feet to his side and just ahead, half-turned to face him, moving crablike across her lit-up, concrete stage fronting the diner, wobbling dangerously with each step on the ridiculously high heels. In the large, well-lit window behind her that served as a backdrop, a tall, round showcase of crystal-clear glass revolved, showing off cakes with whipped-cream toppings. A small, red neon sign hanging beside it read, OPEN 24 HOURS.

"You make your sale, little fella?" she asked Cheito, then leaned over and patted the bag. "Bringing home the bacon to mama?"

He forced himself to look straight ahead, and kept walking.

"Or you going home to an empty room?" she said, pouting. "You live alone, sweetie? You don't want to face an empty room."

In a lifetime of dealing with prostitutes in several different cultures, he had never seen this level of aggressiveness; there was the undercurrent of a threat in her behavior.

"How 'bout a little hanky and panky?" she teased. "Maybe even a little spanky? Huh? Don't be bashful, caballero; you can tell Darlene."

He cut diagonally across the corner of the now-unused parking spaces that lay between the sidewalk and the diner, on to Eleventh Avenue, and speeded up his pace. Darlene stopped—in her shoes, she could not have kept up if she wanted to—and called after him in a good-natured, teasing tone, "Faggot."

He brightened, pleased with the encounter. It had given him an idea.

As he walked north along Eleventh Avenue, bag in hands, he looked down each side street. At Fiftieth Street, just east of the avenue, two men were bringing garbage cans out of the small apartment houses and setting them at the curb. He turned and walked along the sidewalk opposite them. They worked at two buildings separated by several others, about a hundred feet apart. The first man, a husky *negro,* used a two-wheel dolly to bring metal cans from an alleyway beside his building to the curb. The second, a wiry man in his fifties, Cheito guessed was Latino. He carried each can of garbage by its handles, down the two front steps of his old building, then dragged it by one handle across the sidewalk. Neither man seemed to acknowledge the other.

Cheito decided to gamble on the wiry Latino. He was not about to approach him, though, wheeling several million dollars in jewelry that he was unable to defend. He continued to walk, circling the block. On Fifty-first Street he saw an opportunity; a private sanitation truck stood at the curb, one worker operating the lever that noisily cleared a fresh load from the rear well and compacted it into the body of the truck, the second worker wheeling a large, just-emptied hopper across the sidewalk to its place beside the service door of a restaurant. A minute later the truck pulled away. He pushed his airline bag to the hopper, looked both ways and saw no one walking, then hoped that no one was watching him, and slung the bag up and into the hopper. He let it drop and walked away fast, the jacket still over his wrists. It would be all or nothing with the wiry Latino around the corner, since he doubted that he could retrieve the airline bag from the hopper wearing handcuffs.

He was still putting out garbage cans. Cheito jaywalked across the street, timing it so he crossed the man's path. He stopped punctiliously to yield right-of-way to the garbage can.

"That looks heavy," he said, in Spanish.

The wiry man ran the back of his sleeved forearm across his forehead, and replied in Spanish. A Dominican.

"It is," he said. "These tenants must throw out a ton of garbage every week. It's a wonder they're able to carry so much shit home to begin with, and this doesn't include what they eat or keep."

"You're the superintendent?" Cheito asked.

"I'm not the owner, my friend," the man answered.

"Do you keep a workshop in the building? With simple tools?" Cheito asked. He strove for a soft and friendly demeanor.

"You can't run a building without a workshop."

"I have a problem," Cheito said. "An embarrassing problem. I need five minutes' worth of help and I don't know where to turn."

The superintendent quietly sized him up before nodding an invitation to continue.

"I'm visiting the city. A while ago I was approached by a whore outside the restaurant at Forty-third Street. I'm sure you—"

He was interrupted. "The Market Diner? The diner on Forty-third and Eleventh Avenue? On the corner?"

"Yes."

. "Those are not honest whores," the superintendent said, then added defensively, "Don't judge all our whores by them. There are good whores in New York, too."

"I'm sure there are," Cheito said. "At any rate, you know how it is—a strange city, a long night of drinking, on your way to an empty hotel room."

"I've never stayed in a hotel," the superintendent said, with a blend of wistfulness and resentment. "The floors are carpeted?"

"It's lonely," Cheito said. "Anyway—I blush to reveal this but I can see that I speak as one man of the world to another—I allowed one of those whores to put a pair of handcuffs on me. Foolish, I know. Foolish. She promised—"

"Ayeee!" the superintendent interrupted. "I hope he only stole your wallet."

It took a few moments to register with Cheito. Then he said, "I ran away. But now I'm stuck with these handcuffs. I have no one to turn to."

The superintendent laid a hand on Cheito's shoulder for a moment. "Come inside. I'll have them off in a few minutes. You're a lucky man, my friend. Only half of that Market Diner gang have had the full operation. What we call in the States, the whole nine yards. The others just do the silicone, and when it comes time to part with the dick they've lived their whole life with, they find they're too attached to it. Not so surprising. You know yourself what it is to give up a favorite tie or shirt you've had for years. You must have got one of the whores who had the full change—they're the more gentle ones."

He leaned close to Cheito and lowered his voice, though there was no one within a hundred feet of them.

"They say when the surgeon discards the penis, he discards the anger and violence. There is a substance we men have coursing through our bodies—tetra something—that gives us all our machismo. It's a fluid. Women lack it. When we sleep at night, or are made unconscious with medicine, the fluid all collects in the penis. When the surgeon removes it, that sleeping man is made docile. Forever after, if you slap him, he will cry. But the ones who do only the silicone—they can be vicious. Had you let one of them handcuff you, he would have used you as a woman."

He looked quizzically at Cheito.

"I give thanks to God," Cheito said, "that my whore had been drained of fluid. Can we get these handcuffs off?"

The superintendent led him through a narrow, dark hallway, where the last can of garbage stood beneath the staircase, waiting to be carried to the curb. They descended a flight of wooden steps into a low-ceilinged, dank cellar with foundation walls of rough-cut stone—schist, he guessed—that contained a lot of mica. Cheito wondered if it was rock native to Manhattan, unearthed when excavating for the house. He looked around, and saw that the superintendent was a slob. Along one stone wall, a sturdy, ten-foot-long workbench made of scrap lumber held a jumble of tools, electrical fixtures obviously in need of repair, and old plumbing fittings. One particular piece of brass pipe caught his eye, since it was close in size to the piece he had used to bludgeon both Angel and the thief back in the garage.

"My name is Mariano," the superintendent said, as he tugged on a dangling string until a long fluorescent tube above the workbench lit up. He turned and extended his hand, holding it closer to his body than seemed normal, Cheito thought. It compelled him to extend his manacled hands more than ought to have been necessary.

"Ernesto," he said, and shook hands as best he could.

Before releasing Cheito's hand, the superintendent examined the handcuffs. He nodded gravely.

"The whore got you just where he wanted you," he said, and looked up with a smile. "He must do this often, is my guess. What do you think?"

Cheito felt his gorge rise at the man's insolence but managed a stupid and embarrassed smile. "You may be right," he said softly.

The superintendent took Cheito's wrists in his hands and moved them to a large vise bolted to the front of the workbench. He pulled the little chain taut and set it across the top surface of the vise jaws.

"Keep it tight," he said, then rummaged through the hodgepodge of fittings and tools until he turned up a hammer and cold chisel. He set the blade of the chisel on a link, raised the hammer, then stopped. He laid the hammer down.

"No good," he said. "This will work better."

He spun open the vise, took Cheito's wrists in his hands, and arranged the chain to pass between the jaws then over the top of one of them.

"Better if I clamp it," he said. "This way nothing can slip."

Cheito came close to yanking his hands away from the vise. It took great willpower to leave them where they were, but no matter what, he mustn't turn this man against him. The superintendent tightened the vise jaws, then tapped the handle with the hammer several times to lock them even tighter. The little flourish with which he delivered the final tap of the hammer, as though a significant task had been accomplished, made Cheito realize how firmly he was now fixed to the spot. A picture flashed through his mind, from a book given him on his tenth birthday, a woodcut illustration of the Count of Monte Cristo bound in chains fixed to a stone wall.

Cheito, his heart racing, maintained a stupid smile, and said, "That should hold all right. Hit these damn things with gusto."

The superintendent did not reach for the chisel. He set the hammer down and leisurely took a pack of Marlboros from his shirt pocket. "What's your rush?" he said. "You were happy enough to let the whore put them on." He extended the pack toward Cheito.

"No, thank you," Cheito said. "After these are off, I'd like to buy you a drink, and we can have a smoke together."

The superintendent pushed aside enough of the clutter to clear a small space on the workbench, a few feet from

Cheito, then turned and used the heels of his hands to
boost himself up onto the bench. He sat, and smoked his
cigarette for a bit, his dangling legs swaying forward and
back softly.

"Do you go to male whores when you're home?" he
asked. "Or only in a strange city? Where you can treat
yourself."

"I thought she was a girl," Cheito said. "I've never
seen anyone like that. Where one is fooled so completely."

The superintendent laughed. "Is that from one man of
the world to another? That's what you called us outside."

Cheito felt an urge to strangle him. He maintained his
smile instead, and shrugged.

"Are you with the Cubans down on Lexington Avenue?" the superintendent asked. "The United Nations
ones?"

"I left Cuba thirty-five years ago. I'm a citizen of Venezuela. A businessman."

"What kind of business?"

"We export tropical foods. Canned fruits, mostly."

The superintendent laughed loudly, and slapped his
knee and said, "Tropical fruits! Perfect!"

"Please," Cheito said. "You've had a few laughs. I
deserve it. But please cut through these things."

"I think we should have the whore locked up. We'll
call the police. Let them see what was done to you. How
he fooled you. We should even call a newspaper. So
other innocent businessmen—tropical fruit dealers—
won't find themselves in such a terrible position."

He looked off into space and puffed his cigarette, as
though ruminating on what a good idea that was.

"What do you want?" Cheito asked.

"Respect."

"Meaning what?"

"My services are apparently worth a drink and a
shared smoke. That's what you've offered. Will you buy
me a whole pack of cigarettes? A Cuban cigar, maybe?
How generous!"

"It's been my intention to reward you."

"You did a fine job of keeping it secret."

Cheito realized what a fool he'd been. Of course he should have offered this Dominican money. Ironically, he had avoided it precisely in order to show the man respect, in order not to insult him with payment for a humanitarian act. It had come naturally to him to take that approach. And now he realized how out of touch he was with a society that put a dollar value on an act of kindness. He couldn't explain it to the man, either, for it would be a bona fide insult to tell him now that one can't respect someone who asks for payment.

"I thought it was obvious that I intended to reward you," he said.

"When a rich man intends to give money to a worker, it's never obvious."

"I'm not a rich man."

"Only the rich ran from Cuba when Fidel took over."

Cheito was momentarily dumbfounded—never had he been accused of being anti-Castro.

"They should build statues to the man," the superintendent said. He raised his right hand, forefinger extended, in the stance of an orator. "Fidel is the best thing to happen to Latin America since Simón Bolívar. It's *gusanos* like yourself who caused the revolution to fail. Who ran off with their stolen wealth. Long live Castro!"

"Take what I have," Cheito said, desperately.

The superintendent lifted his chin higher. "*Take?* Do I look like a thief to you?"

"I'll *give* you what I have," Cheito said.

"How much is that?"

"I have fifteen hundred dollars, U.S. Plus a few thousand bolívars, Venezuelan. That's worth just a few U.S. dollars."

"I'll accept your offer." He smiled, and added, "Maybe you brought with you some tropical fruits you can sell to make up your loss."

"Done," said Cheito. "It's all yours, and well earned."

"It must be willingly," the superintendent said. "I'm not one to take advantage of another's bad luck."

"Willingly and happily," Cheito said.

He took the wallet and passport from Cheito's pocket, removed all the money, then ceremoniously put back a twenty and said, "To get you back to the hotel. Your lonely room. Don't spend it on any young boys."

He sheared off both bracelets with just a few sharp hammer blows. The very first thing Cheito did was to reach around with his right hand and scratch his lower back—although it didn't itch just then—first with one hand, then the other. He moaned several times with pleasure, which was, in fact, genuine; the sudden freedom had infused him with energy and confidence that he felt as a physical sensation.

The superintendent watched, obviously pleased with the start of his day. Not surprising; who would expect that putting out garbage would bring such a windfall? Cheito stopped scratching but continued to moan as he groped behind his back on the benchtop in the vicinity of the short length of brass pipe he had made note of even before the Dominican had begun to humiliate him. His fingers found, instead, the wood handle of the hammer. It would do. He clenched it and broke into a smile and said, "Thank you, Mariano. I've needed to scratch my back for the last hour."

Mariano nodded and started to say something as Cheito swung the hammer in a tight little arc, aiming for the center of the forehead, wanting accuracy rather than great force. Even a moderate hammer blow to the right spot would stun this ignoramus sufficiently; the second blow could be counted on to do the real work. The hammer head landed just an inch off-center, above Mariano's eye. It carried enough energy to crack bone. His head snapped back and he stood motionless, hands at his sides, an expression of great surprise on his face, until the next blow fell. He crumpled to the unswept floor. Cheito immediately kneeled on him, and hit him half a dozen more blows than were necessary to take his life. He would have continued even longer, but remembered the airline bag waiting to be retrieved.

XV

Breslin headed north on Ninth Avenue, needing to get off the street, to someplace where he could sit still and think things out. He noticed that the parking rate for special events these days was up to $16.91, which meant an even twenty dollars when the bizarre 18.25 percent tax was added in. He remembered his first trip to the Garden to see the circus, with an uncle who had bitched at paying $2.50 to park. His arm hurt where it had jammed against the steering wheel—one more reason, he thought, why six ounces of vodka would hit the spot just now. The bars had been closed since four, though, and liquor could not be sold again legally until 8:00 A.M., still a few hours away. He knew bar hours well. From age eighteen, during periods of great stress, he would duck into bars in the early morning for two fast hits before facing the day. Nearly always, he had found himself in the silent company of four or five suited-and-tied patrons spaced along the bar, en route to the office, attaché cases set on the floor beside them. Odorless vodka was the drink of choice for all, straight up or on the rocks for the seasoned early birds like himself, in a Bloody Mary or screwdriver for the up-and-coming alcoholics or the health-conscious. He remembered a Martin's Bar on Broadway, across from the Gulf and Western Building, with a large sign in its window: ALL DRINKS HALF PRICE DURING HAPPY HOUR—8 TO 9 A.M. Right now a cup of hot coffee in a quiet booth would be the next best thing, but what was open now in this off-the-beaten-track neighborhood? The Market Diner, he thought. Forty-third and Eleventh. Open all night and a good place to think. His pace picked up now that he had a destination.

At Forty-second Street he headed west and walked the long block to Tenth Avenue. At the corner he decided to turn up Tenth to Forty-third Street, then go west on Forty-third to the diner, but suddenly changed his mind as he noticed a beat cop barely visible in a doorway on Tenth Avenue, container of coffee in one hand, a cigarette in the other. Breslin continued straight ahead on Forty-second Street. He turned at Eleventh Avenue, where, to his surprise, a newly opened all-night coffee shop presented itself, obviously competing with the Market Diner just half a block north on the next corner. It occurred to him that he might want to sit tight for hours, and so he could put both places to use. Which first? He started to walk to the diner—the roomy men's room was ideal for cleaning up—when he noticed the small crew of hookers working the corner. These five looked like a pro basketball team on their night off, he thought; aggressive transvestites, for sure. Who needed these freaks attracting attention to him? He stopped, turned back, and entered the coffee shop, a pleasant enough place. He would clean up there, and use the diner as his second stop if he ended up with a lot of time to kill.

He waited until nine o'clock to call. Lynn picked up on the third ring.

"Can you talk?" Breslin asked. "It's me." Then he remembered Mr. Gordon, her Friday lover, whom Nelson the doorman had told him about, and added quickly, "It's Chuck."

"Jeremy's been gone for hours," she said.

"I need help, Lynn. Badly."

"I was just about to shower," she said.

"What the hell does that have to do with anything?" he snapped, then quickly said, "I'm sorry."

"I told you never to call here," she said.

"I'm desperate, Lynn. You should be able to figure that out just *because* I'm calling you at your house."

She let a few seconds go by then said, impatiently, "What's your problem, Chuck?"

Her tone implied that she was expecting a request for help in securing a reservation at a trendy restaurant.

"I need your help, Lynn. *Help me* is what you can do."

There was another long pause at her end, before she asked, "How?" in the least bitchy tone so far.

"I need a lot of cash in the next few hours. Four or five thousand. Ten would be even better. And I need you to rent a car, too. A monthly deal. Something mid-size and ordinary. You'll get your money back, if I live through this."

She was suddenly intrigued. Her voice became noticeably more southern. "My God, it's serious, isn't it, Chuck?"

"Yes."

"You're asking for a lot of money."

"I'm in a lot of trouble."

"Tell me about it," she said. He could visualize her rearranging throw pillows for a long listen.

"I can't, Lynn. I need you to meet me in an hour at the apartment."

"I haven't even showered," she said. "There is *no* way I could be out this door till an hour from now. Then the bank. And Hertz. And I have a dentist's appointment at noon I cannot break."

He choked off a stream of obscenities that would have culminated in a drawn-out howl, and asked, instead, "How soon can you be there, Lynn?"

"Say, two."

"Beautiful. And even sooner would be better, I'm heading there now. Put the car in the building's garage. If they tell you they have no space hand the guy twenty bucks—nothing less, don't skimp. Tell him it's only for half an hour. Whatever you do, don't leave it on the street. It'll get towed. They look for rentals."

"Are you sure that's a public garage?" she said. "I thought it was only for the building tenants."

"It's public," he said, and wished he was free to add,

"Your Friday john, Mr. Gordon, uses it for his station wagon."

"Two," she said. "I'm hurt, Chuck. You were never this desperate for my loving."

"I was, Lynn. I was. I just kept it hidden so you wouldn't have total control over my life."

"That's the kind of white lie you don't tell often enough to keep a girl happy," she said. "But right now I can't wait to hear every juicy detail of what you're up to. And have a very cold martini ready."

She hung up. Her last words had not been said teasingly; they had carried the slightly authoritative tone she used to convey orders, a tone so subtle it could only have come from someone raised in a privileged family whose power was made clear to her at a very early age. This woman was so self-absorbed, so crazy, that his life-and-death situation was secondary to her shower and her romantic fantasies. He wondered which Lynn would show up today. Given that she would be carrying thousands in cash to one of her lovers about to go on the lam, he guessed it would be one tough cookie who walked through the door expecting her martini.

He hung up the phone and returned to his booth, where he put down a two-dollar tip to cover the long time he had sat. Through the window he saw that the skies had opened up in the past few minutes and a torrential rain was falling. He exhaled a long, deep breath to relax himself, and felt the nervous energy he had been running on drain from his body. Exhaustion set in, brought on, he knew, by the relief of seeing a way out of his immediate mess. With a car and thousands in cash he could spend a few weeks formulating a long-range plan in a far-off city where he knew no one—the safest immediate destination for him, since even the name of his remotest acquaintance might be in his Agency files. He may well have been followed at some period in the past, either for cause or simply as part of a routine. That he had managed a six-month affair with Lynn, without it coming to Cutshaw's attention, he attributed to his already being out of the Agency. Now, though, he could desperately use some sleep. It was a bit past nine. A cab would get him cross-town in twenty minutes, which would give him some four hours to nap in Heide Wrabel's apartment.

After both parties hung up, Timothy Clant stopped his little cassette recorder and set it to rewind. He was seated on the concrete floor of the utilities room in the basement of Lynn Cutshaw's Central Park West building, his back against the unpainted cinderblock wall, just under the telephone panels that served all ninety apartments above. The wall opposite him, which he could nearly touch with the soles of his shoes if he stretched his legs out, supported a dense array of electric meters. The leads of his recorder were alligator-clipped to a pair of terminals on the telephone panel. Another lead, this one coaxial, went from the recorder to a headset that he now removed and placed on top of his small toolbox. He unhooked a compact utility phone from his work belt and clipped it to a set of terminals at the bottom of the panel, which gave him an outgoing line, then dialed Linwood Cutshaw's private number in Virginia.

For six months now, since Lynn Cutshaw had taken up with Chuck Breslin, Clant had spent scores of hours in this particular utilities room, outfitted with a full set of NYNEX-issued tools and equipment, a NYNEX ID tag pinned to his shirt pocket. Whoever was on duty at the door invariably waved him through, usually without a word. The one time early on that a doorman had asked, out of general curiosity, what was wrong, Clant had grumbled, "The usual shit," in a voice that invited no further questions, and continued toward the service elevator.

"Hello," Linwood Cutshaw's voice said on the other end of the line.

"The call you've been wanting just came through," Clant said. "He's expecting her to meet him at two in their usual place. He ought to be there in the next thirty to sixty minutes."

"I'll handle it from here," Cutshaw said.

"Do you need the cassette?" Clant asked.

"No one on earth needs that cassette."

"Done and done," Clant said, and ended the call by squeezing the handset-line clips free of the terminals.

Cutty sat back in his stress-relieving desk chair and decided that things could be taking much worse turns under the circumstances. Eliminating Breslin would be a step toward salvaging the dismal situation that Jay Garrick had reported on just before 6:00 A.M., minutes after closing the door on the dead Cuban and the van in the West Thirty-ninth Street garage. Cutty's first piece of positive news had come just minutes later, when Hank Zivic, Mr. Woodling for this assignment, called from a pay phone in midtown Manhattan for instructions. Cutty had had him go to the garage, load the body into the van, and drive it to a safe house in New Jersey. It was an important lead to have deprived the police of.

He dialed Jay Garrick, who sat beside a phone in the little studio apartment on Irving Place that he had occupied since coming to New York. Garrick's head pounded and his senses were dulled by the Percodans given him by Fenton Blauser, an internist with offices in the New York University Medical Center. Cutty had directed him there when he had called in, still groggy from the Cuban doctor's blow. Dr. Blauser had not uttered a word to Garrick that wasn't part of his succinct medical diagnosis. The good doctor's best guess was that he had nothing more than a concussion, after being told there was no time for a scan.

Now, Cutty gave Garrick the address and apartment number on Sutton Place South. "Breslin should be there in one hour max," he said. "If for any reason things are delayed . . . if it gets to be one o'clock . . . call it off. Clear?"

"Clear. No go after one," Jay said, and hung up.

He thought for a bit about how pleasant it would be to shoot Chuck Breslin, less for crashing into the wall than for duping him so completely on the ride downtown. The question now was why, from the original planning stage, had Breslin been slated to die? Belmonte and Tedesco he had understood from the beginning, but had always wondered, why Breslin? Had the female operative done things right in the lobby, Breslin was to have helped transfer the Cubans and the planted couple into the Town Car, then transport them to a safe house in New Jersey. Mrs. Woodling, as Cutty called her, spoke fluent Spanish and Cutty had hoped that she, in the role of fellow hostage, might overhear something said by the Cubans that would help. But even then Cutty had wanted Breslin killed when they were finished with the Cuban doctor. Why? For just a moment Garrick wondered about himself, then put it out of his mind. He trusted Lin Cutshaw with his life.

Cutty only wished he was in a position to take out Breslin personally. That this St. John's Law School graduate had had the brass to take up with the head-of-the-Agency's married daughter grated on him even now. He had learned of their sordid affair just days after it began, since he periodically put her under surveillance, as he did anyone near and dear to him. Breslin happened to have been ideal for this assignment, and since a lifelong thief and a greedy ex-detective were to be left dead in the hotel lobby as the final proof to Castro that the robbery wasn't staged, tossing Breslin into the pot as a personal indulgence worked just fine. For six long months Cutty had listened to hours of tapes that nauseated him, unable to turn the machine off until he had heard every word, sometimes playing the most awful parts over. It was fitting, he decided, that Charles Francis Breslin meet his end in the apartment used to inflate his own ego and piss on everything Linwood Cutshaw stood for by demeaning Lynn.

The Cuban doctor was the key problem now, but there was simply nowhere to begin looking for him. If that damn woman with her glowing history of successful assignments hadn't allowed herself to be killed in the lobby he might now have a lead on the Cuban. He wondered for a moment whether he hadn't underestimated Dario Tedesco. In any event, there wasn't a single lead, and nothing to do but let it play out. That wasn't a complete disaster, though, since it was clear from the Havana tapes that the doctor's mission was very specific—to stage a small, contained demonstration rather than a major event. Leads for Teddy and Frank, his second problem, were weak. Teddy was surely disciplined enough to stay far from his home or usual haunts, so there was no point, given the limited manpower available for this operation, to covering them. Frank Belmonte was another story—a career criminal, with that breed's penchant for risk blended with a subconscious wish to be caught. He might head home. And while there was really no doubt that Tedesco ought to be put down, too, Belmonte was the more dangerous, the more likely to be picked up by police and decide to tell what he knew. And by now he knew a lot more than he had three or four hours ago. His house was worth staking out, once Jay Garrick resolved Breslin.

Breslin arrived at Heide's Sutton Place South apartment at ten o'clock. Nelson smiled when he opened the taxicab door, his huge umbrella spread over the short, open space between taxi and building canopy.

"Today's Thursday?" he asked disingenuously, then looked at his watch. "And it's early for you, Mr. Begley, isn't it?"

"Don't be overly familiar and crack jokes with your betters," Breslin said. "First rule of doormanning."

Inside the building, Nelson dug out the apartment key from the jumble of keys in his drawer and nodded his thanks as Breslin pressed a folded ten into his hand. As Breslin started toward the elevator it occurred to him that his being in a deep sleep when Lynn arrived at the apartment could actuate one of her sensitive emotional buttons and cause her to spin on her heel and leave, money in pocketbook. He turned, and said, "Incidentally, Nelson, I need you to do a little favor for me today."

"You sure that wouldn't be getting overfamiliar with my betters?" Nelson asked.

"In this case, it's fine," Breslin said. "My lady friend

should be here around two. When she comes in, lean on the bell enough to wake me up in case I dozed off. And don't let her see you do it."

Nelson nodded, and said, "I'll be sneaky. Second rule of doormanning."

"Is there a word in Spanish for smart-ass?" Breslin asked.

"Not really," Nelson said, evenly. "Latins don't behave like that. It's a Anglo thing. Irish, mostly."

Jay Garrick had the cab drop him at Fifty-seventh Street and Sutton Place South, then walked the few blocks to his destination. His head pounded despite the Percodans. He hoped it was nothing more than a concussion—it wouldn't be his first—and if there were blood clots floating around right now, he would never know it anyway. Cutshaw had remained cool on the phone but there was no mistaking the firmness of the marching orders he had issued.

It was just a few minutes after eleven when Nelson pulled open the door for him, prepared to lift the intercom handset, and asked, "Can I help you?"

Garrick took a billfold from his hip pocket and held it at waist level in front of himself, which put it just in front of Nelson's waist as well. He deliberately withdrew a newly issued fifty-dollar bill and inspected it for a moment before asking Nelson, "Does this bill look good to you? I got it in change last night and I'm not sure."

Nelson looked at it carefully, then turned it over for further inspection.

"Looks good to me," Nelson said.

"Put it in your pocket," Garrick said, and took a step into the lobby. "I know my way, and the lady likes to keep her life private."

Nelson folded the bill carefully and put it into his pants pocket.

"That's a wise woman," he said. "The help here do nothing but gossip. Elevator's around to your right."

Garrick rode to the twelfth floor, then walked down four flights. Before opening the stairway door, he removed his Glock from an ankle holster, fitted it with a silencer, checked that the safety was off, then set the weapon into the inside pocket of his jacket, where it wobbled around but would stay put for the fifty feet or so he had to travel. He stepped out into the long, carpeted corridor that ran north-south and walked at a comfortable pace, reading the apartment number on each door. He reached 8F quickly. It was on his right, in the east wing of the building, whose apartments had views of the river and the drab Queens landscape on the far side. The doorbell was the standard New York City manual push-button in the center of the door with a peephole above it, both set in a brightly polished brass escutcheon. He took the pistol from his inside pocket and gripped it as he would a very short rifle, the silencer-encased barrel cradled between his left thumb and forefinger, his right hand on the stock, then held it horizontally and pushed the tip of the barrel hard against the doorbell.

A chime sounded loudly when he pushed; a second, lower-pitched chime sounded as the button returned. He raised the gun the few inches to the level of the peephole and steadied it by pressing his left elbow against the door. Half a minute went by with no sound of movement from inside. He pressed the button again with the pistol, twice in quick succession, then returned the gun to the peephole. He sighted down the short barrel and waited.

Breslin opened his eyes to see the vodka bottle directly in his line of vision, just a few feet away on the coffee table, his empty glass beside it. The door chimes rang insistently. He sat up on the couch for a moment, then pushed himself to a standing position. His mouth was dry. As he walked toward the door the chimes rang again. Lynn must be at her most aggressive to be pressing the bell so doggedly; she generally tapped on the door with a delicacy she believed suitable for a properly raised southern lady. It was like her to overreact here, when he was at his most vulnerable, waiting to be rescued by money she was providing. This was too good an opportunity for her to pass up. It frightened him. Lynn was very capable of turning around and leaving him alone and broke if she didn't find him waiting expectantly, cold martini in hand, dabs of a subtle aftershave on his cheeks.

Just before touching the doorknob he felt a flash of anger as he remembered that Nelson was supposed to have saved him from just this situation by ringing the downstairs bell. The flash of anger was followed immediately by the thought that it was odd of Nelson to have screwed up a task for which he had been tipped. Just that brief thought—that Nelson's behavior was odd—stopped his hand. He never thought it out further, never took the next mental step of considering that maybe Nelson had not screwed up, had not rung the bell because Lynn had not yet arrived. Only the word "odd" stuck in his mind and by itself altered his behavior, allowed his instincts to take over, though he remained unaware of it. His hand pulled back from the doorknob and went instead to the tiny knob that allowed the peephole cover to pivot open.

He would never know if he had moved his head erratically or had somehow reacted as his eye reached the opening or whether the shooter skewed the gun just a bit as he fired, but the bullet simply took a slice off the top of his right ear. He dropped to his haunches and pressed his back against the door. The gun fired once more into the room, the bullet passing through the window at the far end of the living room. It left a clean hole in the pane. The next shot created a different sound and the door shuddered against his back; the shooter had fired into the lower lock, which looked to be disabled. Another thirty seconds and the door would swing open and he would be gunned down cowering in some corner of the apartment.

He had to get out now. The door shuddered again. The windows were the only other outlets. He sprang forward and dashed across the living room to the couch, lifted the wood coffee table up over his head, vodka bottle and glass crashing to the floor, and hurled it through the picture window. The table disappeared into the pouring rain. Long, triangular pieces of glass remained in the sash. He yanked a small floor lamp from its socket and used it as a ram to punch out the remaining glass pieces. A six-foot-by-six-foot opening, wind-driven rain pelting in, awaited him. He looked down quickly. The water, nearly a hundred feet below, was barely visible. He couldn't make out the rocks that he knew were just to his left and some twenty feet from the concrete bulkhead of the FDR Drive. He kicked off his shoes and stepped up onto the radiator cover, then onto the bottom of the window sash. He crouched in the opening. Behind him, another bullet was shot into the top lock. He sprang from his perch, favoring his right to avoid the rocks, trying to gain as much horizontal distance as possible by running in midair, hoping the river was deep enough here to accommodate this high a jump, remembering first and foremost not to tumble—to hit the water feetfirst. He felt for a moment as he once had during the long seconds a chute wouldn't open, until he freed a tangled line at three thousand feet. The wind was much stronger than he had expected—he was being blown north, exactly where he didn't want to go, throughout the three seconds or so of his fall. He looked down and saw the protruding rocks coming up directly at him and could do nothing but react instinctively and pull himself into a tight ball. He squeezed his eyes shut, filled with the terrifying certainty that he was about to die.

XVI

Sally Seventeen's three-year-old Sedan de Ville coughed several times as he maneuvered it off the Williamsburg Bridge into the traffic of Delancey Street. He cursed aloud at the engine; he was a year overdue for a new car. Maybe, if he caught a break in the next hour or so, he could put an order in with Potamkin before the week was out. A few moments later his attention was caught by the neon sign of Ratner's. As always when he passed the big, comfortable restaurant, he reminded himself that it had been too long since he had eaten their soft-as-cotton onion rolls smeared with butter. He liked to polish off an even dozen of them as a starter when he sat down to a meal in Ratner's—two bites to a roll, twenty-four bites in all. A minute later he crossed the Bowery onto Kenmare Street and took a right onto Elizabeth. Half a block later he pulled into an empty stretch of curb at Lambiasi's Pasticceria. Thoughts of Ratner's onion rolls had whetted his appetite and now he looked forward to a couple of sfogliatells and a cup of brown coffee.

Gennaro, dozing on his feet behind the counter, opened his eyes when Sally entered. He nodded almost imperceptibly that it was all right to go back. Gaetano Rossoletto, whose street name since his teens had been Tommy Ross, sat in his usual booth, a *Daily News* opened on the Formica table. Barring drastic events, Tommy could be found where he now sat every weekday afternoon from two to four, open even to visitors without appointments—if they were entitled to visit at all. For thirty years now he had conducted much of his business in this booth, for the past six months much more than he ought to have. Sally stopped a few feet short of the booth and waited to be acknowledged. Tommy finished the paragraph he was reading before looking up and motioning with his eyes for Sally to take the seat opposite him. Sally squeezed himself into the booth.

Tommy pointed to an open half-liter bottle of mineral water. Sally shook his head no, as Gennaro arrived at the table.

"Brown coffee," Sally said to Gennaro. "With milk. And a couple of sfogliatells."

"But it's no wonder you look the way you look, Sally," Tommy said, as Gennaro went off to fill the order. "What do you want to poison yourself for?"

"What's a matter with brown coffee, Tommy?"

"Not the coffee. The sfogliatells, Sally. The sfogliatells. A ton of butter, a ton of cream, and in case your heart still don't want to stop they put in a ton of sugar so you'll get diabetes. You got to be careful what you eat, Sally."

"I'll watch out," he said.

"You got to be what? A hundred twenty, a hundred thirty pounds overweight?" Tommy asked.

"My doctor says eighty."

"Shoot your fucking doctor. He's blind or he's a liar."

"I'll watch out," Sally said.

Tommy was quiet for a few moments, then he closed his newspaper and sipped his mineral water, a sign that the exchange of pleasantries was finished.

"What have you got?" he said.

"Something very nice, Tommy. Sweet. But I'll be up front here—I'm looking for something for myself. Something serious."

"You ever hear of anybody got shortchanged at my table?" Tommy asked. "You been around me what—thirty years? Close to it?"

"Thirty-two. December will be thirty-two years I been around you."

Tommy shook his head slowly and said, "But fucking time flies. Where did it go, Sally? Where?"

Gennaro arrived and set down Sally's coffee and pastries. Tommy watched Sally empty three packets of sugar into his cup.

"So what have you got?" Tommy said.

Sally felt the pang of disappointment he had known earlier he would feel at this point in his pitch to Tommy. This was where he had hoped to get a commitment—before opening up. Where he needed to get a commitment if he was to get one at all. Yet the most he had been able to wring out of him was a mushy statement that no one had ever been shortchanged at this table—this from a man renowned for never having left a dime for anyone at the end of any deal he ever did. And he couldn't raise the subject again; now he would have to show his hand and hope for the best. He swallowed the mouthful of pastry and pointed toward the newspaper.

"This hotel thing," he said. "Fourteen, fifteen mil? Whatever they're calling it?"

"Yeah."

"For sure, Frank Belmonte got the place."

Tommy remained impassive and quiet. Sally knew exactly what was running through the man's mind—tribute. The longer Tommy remained silent, the more morally outraged he would become at being cheated out of his tithe. Frank Belmonte was a neighborhood guy. Although Frank had never in his life asked Tommy for a favor, he was certainly free to. Frank knew Tommy's position. If some out-of-the-neighborhood wiseguys tried to shake Frank down, or worse, steal his money, Frank would undoubtedly come to Tommy to straighten things out. Who else could he go to? This had never happened, but it could. The right thing for Frank to have done was to call Tommy an hour after the robbery, and say, "I've got tribute for you, Tommy. Heavy-duty, too. Ten percent of a lot of fazools. I want you to know it's earmarked. It will be in your hands in a few days. *Grazie,* Tommy." But he had never called. Tommy began to see that he was being screwed. By some run-of-the-mill heist guy with no respect for nobody. By somebody who lived across the street, for Christ sake. Belmonte had ducked him successfully on the Quincy job—which for sure he had done—but he, Tommy, had been fighting a case at the time and let him slide. Not this time.

"You seen Frankie?" he asked.

"I seen him on the phone," Sally said. "Tommy, I got to talk to you about myself here. I'm sixty-seven, Tommy. I ain't getting any younger."

Tommy took a long swallow of mineral water, as though reluctant to say what had to be said. "I'm a little disappointed, Sally. I got to tell you that. You come to my table with an important piece of information, like you're supposed to. You did exactly the right thing. You been around me so many years it's your obligation. What's it been, Sally, thirty years?"

"He's spitting in my face," Sally thought. "Pretending we didn't just go through this. Making me just another around-guy like a hundred others."

He said, "Thirty-two years, Tommy. It'll be thirty-two years in December."

"That's a long time," Tommy said. "You walked in here just like you're supposed to. You tell me how this weasel, Frankie, is trying to duck me. I sit here thinking that Sally Seventeen is a down guy who's always going to have a special place in my heart. Then, bang! Greed rears its ugly fucking head."

"It ain't greed, Tommy. I'm sixty-seven. I been scuffling since I'm twelve. I'm tired. My fucking feet are worn out. I got a car out there coughs all day. The power door-locks don't work no more. I'm ashamed to be in the fucking thing. I'm a busted suitcase, Tommy. For once, I got to think of me."

Tommy nodded his head sadly, a man whose worst fears had been confirmed.

"Me, me, me," he said. "Every fucking yuppie running around the city says, me, me, me. You see how it spreads? Like a disease? My own people are being infected. You're a case in point, Sally."

Sally finished his coffee and looked back to catch the attention of Gennaro, who pretended not to notice; long years of reading Tommy's body language told Gennaro that Tommy was at this moment screwing Sally Seventeen, not the time to approach their table unless Tommy called him.

"I'm willing to listen," Tommy said, magnanimously. "What are you looking for?"

"I want to get made, Tommy. I want to get straightened out. I want a button."

Tommy found himself speechless.

"All these years I been an around-guy," Sally said. "I came *this* close twenty-five years ago when Chubby was alive. Chubby promised me I'd be straightened out. A month later he gets clipped. Three years later J.J. put me up and for sure I would've had the button but that rat bastard Sammy Slippers kiboshed it. The guy had a hard-on for me 'cause when we were kids I was banging some girl from the Village he had the hots for and the lunatic never got over it. A couple a years later the guy flips and goes into the rat protection program—his wife and *kids* wouldn't go with him, she said on *Geraldo* she didn't want to raise rats—so what does *that* say about Sammy? But everybody forgets it was only him had kept me from getting straightened out. Then the books close for a hundred fucking years. Now's my time, Tommy. The books are open and I brought you something here is going to be worth half a mil to you. I deserve to get straightened out."

Tommy reached across the table and laid his hand on Sally's.

"I'm going to see what I can do, Sally," he said. "I can't promise anything—these things ain't as simple as you think. But I'm going to look into it. I'm going to explore the possibilities."

He called out to Gennaro in a tone meant to admonish the counterman for his neglect of an important visitor, "Gennaro! Bring Sally another cup of coffee. And bring him three or four more sfogliatells." Then he squeezed Sally's hand and said, "I'm going to see if I can get you straightened out." He lowered his voice. "No matter what, though, you'll see some green out of this. But about this Frankie B. Where is the bum?"

"I just put it all on the line and I crapped out," Sally

thought, and said, "He's at my place out in Brighton Beach. I got a little studio apartment on the boardwalk. He's holed up there with another guy."

"It's nice out there," Tommy said. "Where are you on the boardwalk?"

Sally thought for just a moment of dodging the question, but knew it couldn't be done. "On Fifth Street. Brighton-Fifth Street." After a few moments he added, "Number two-ninety."

"You got a nice view, Sally? You up high?"

"The view's okay."

"What floor you on?"

"The third. I'm on the third floor."

"It's a big building, Sally? There are a lot of apartments in the building?"

"Not too many."

"Well on each floor. What do they go from? Like, A to J?"

"I ain't sure. There's maybe just seven or eight apartments on a floor."

"Nice," Tommy said. "Not too big. You don't want to be in a place is too big. So which letter is your apartment?"

"They ain't really marked. Like everybody just knows which door is which."

Sally knew that holding back this final piece of information was meaningless—Tommy would locate it easily enough if he wanted to—but to give him the exact apartment was to roll over completely. It was clear Tommy was not going to do the right thing here and so holding back even a meaningless piece of information allowed Sally to maintain the illusion of self-pride. Then, suddenly, as so often happened to him, an uncontrollable desire to please seized him. It was irrational, since Tommy would never appreciate it. Sally would, if anything, lower himself in Tommy's eyes by volunteering, yet he couldn't help himself—he wanted, in the worst way, to make Tommy Ross happy at that moment.

"I just remembered," he said. "There are letters on the doors. There's so much fucking paint been put on them over the years you could hardly read them. But they're there. D. I'm in D."

He immediately despised himself. A moment later, he added, "Tommy, you can't let Frankie know I tipped you. You know, Frankie's an independent. Frankie's never been around a crew. He wouldn't understand."

"Don't worry about it," Tommy said.

Sally recognized that those were Tommy's first sincere words. He was relieved.

"What I'm going to do," Tommy said, "is tell Frankie's mother he's got to contact me right away. Like I don't know where he is. For sure he's in touch with her—Frankie don't take a piss without asking her first. And he'll call me, he ain't stupid. I tell him I put two and two together and he's got to do the right thing. And he will, he's a good kid. Frankie knows the rules."

Gennaro arrived with a fresh cup of coffee and two more sfogliatelle. He set them in front of Sally, who was upset enough by how poorly things had gone that he welcomed the sweets as a mild sedative. If only he hadn't given up the apartment number, he could at least walk away from the table with his head high. Twenty grand—that's what he would wind up seeing out of this. A lousy twenty grand—a ham sandwich. He took his first huge bite of his pastry even before putting sugar in his coffee.

A few minutes later, as Sally, on his way out, reached across the counter to tuck a folded ten-dollar bill into Gennaro's shirt pocket, both Jimmy Eng and his partner, Catherine, removed their headphones and looked at one another with mutual astonishment. Jimmy turned off the reel-to-reel.

"Can you believe these people?" she asked. "Nothing happens in this neighborhood that they don't get a piece of."

She started to walk toward the cassette player near the apartment door, and said, "Time for the baby to cry."

"Wait five minutes," Jimmy said. "I can't take that kid just now."

He stared out the window at the street below, and after a few moments said, "There he goes now."

Catherine moved beside him and watched Sally lumber across the sidewalk and get into his car.

"I don't know what he's bitching about," she said. "None of my friends drive a car that nice. Who, exactly, is he?"

They both lit cigarettes, one of the reasons they liked working together.

"Sally's an associate. An around-guy. And it's all he'll ever be. He's got as much chance of being made as I do."

"What will he get out of this?"

Jimmy shrugged. "My guess? Ten thousand, tops. Tommy Ross will give him a first payment of five, then months later another three, and after that tell him Frankie B. never really came through with what he should have and go into his patented greed-rearing-its-ugly-head routine, but, 'Here's two thou more because I'm a soft fucking touch.' Then he'll chase Sally back out to Brooklyn to work with the Russkies. Nobody ever got rich being around Tommy Ross's crew. It's why, when indictments come down on this operation, some of his people are going to roll and Tommy Ross is going to get a hundred years."

"And how much money will Ross get out of this?" she asked.

"Even allowing for the usual inflated news reports, Belmonte must have taken out ten or twelve million in jewelry, retail. If he fences it sensibly he'll get three or four million for it. Ross will wind up with what the wiseguys call a buck and a half."

"A hundred and fifty thousand," she said softly.

He nodded.

"More wealth than humble peasants like ourselves will ever have a chance at," she said, speaking in the Cantonese dialect both had learned in childhood. They used it rarely, only when some appropriate Chinese maxim carried a subtle meaning less easily expressed in English. The old saw she called up here, familiar to both of them, might be heard hundreds of times each day in Hong

Kong, to justify cutting a moral corner or entering into a shady business transaction, and she gave it the intonation of an old Chinese peasant, greatly exaggerating the tonality. It caught Jimmy's attention—as it was meant to. Inexplicably to him, he responded in Chinese, the first time either of them had used it with the other in extended conversation.

"And humble peasants we will remain," he said. "We have no chance at it."

His Chinese was a touch less fluent than hers. She chose to continue using it; there was something more intimate about it.

"Let me tell you, Mr. Eng," she said, "if I were working here alone I would be awfully tempted to erase that piece of tape and sell the whereabouts of Frank Belmonte and his twelve million dollars retail to some tough, young Chinese gang members for ten percent of what they get."

They were quiet as they watched Sally Seventeen's Cadillac move away in the street below. Then Jimmy said, in Chinese, "If I were working alone, Miss Wu, I would be tempted to do the same thing. If I knew some tough, young Chinese gang members to sell it to."

"I do," Catherine said, in English.

In Lambiasi's, Tommy sat alone at his table and read the *Daily News* account of the robbery. The only information of interest to him were the various numbers given for the take. The guests, he figured, were setting their preliminary estimates of what was missing from their boxes as high as possible since it was all insured, and these were people who would need a day or two to evaluate their chances of successfully robbing the insurance company; the police would inflate those figures even more to make the publicity value of their case greater; the press was tacking on some more because the more money gone, the better. Still, after discounting for each of these, Tommy guessed that Frankie's team had banged the place out for a minimum of ten mil. Retail. Frankie, then, would pedal it for a low of two-five. More like three

since he knew what he was doing. Tommy would give
him the benefit of the doubt, though, and figure two-five,
which put the 10 percent that were his own just desserts
at a nice, round Q-mil. Frankie would try to weasel. That
was okay; the guy was entitled to do that. Tommy decided that if he in fact ended up with just half of what
he was entitled to, a buck and a quarter, it would be
fine. Frankie would feel he got away with something,
which was as it should be. He would give Sally Seventeen
some walking-around money. Seven, eight thousand. Let
the fat fuck get his car simonized. He thought for a moment about Sally's hope to get straightened out and came
as close to smiling as was possible for him. Sally Seventeen a made guy. It was fucking ridiculous. This free-
hole should be out stealing hubcaps.

His problem now was just how to approach Francesca
Belmonte. She was a strong woman knowledgeable in
the ways of the neighborhood—their hybrid Neapolitan-
Sicilian village whose spine was Mulberry Street—more
so than her one remaining son, Frankie, who had never
been with nobody. Tommy knew a bit about the Belmontes because his own father—let him rest—had insinu-
ated himself into the bed of the then-beautiful Belmonte
widow thirty-five years ago, just months after she had
donned the head-to-toe black garments that were to remain her lifelong dress. Gaetano senior had been the
neighborhood's premier snake. It was Francesca's one
moment of weakness and she had never forgiven him or
his blood relatives for it. If Tommy were to approach
her himself, she was perfectly capable of spitting in his
face—the woman refused to acknowledge his presence
when they passed on the street. Yet if she were shepherded around her natural Nabolidon response, she
would quickly see the danger of her Frankie's not com-
plying with Tommy's wish to be contacted. He needed an
intermediary to approach her and the obvious choice was
his nineteen-year-old nephew, his wife's brother's youngest
son, Frank Santini, who was quite close to Francesca
Belmonte. That, however, presented its own problem.

Frank Santini was in his junior year at Columbia, a

physics major accepted into the university at sixteen.
Both his father, Pete, and older brother, Junior, were
soldiers on Tommy's crew. From his earliest years, Frank
had been shielded from even the most indirect contact
with the life that his father, his brother, and his Uncle
Tommy had chosen for themselves. They never feared
that he might want to follow in their footsteps; given the
boy's makeup that was impossible. Rather, he was to be
kept pristine. Even open discussion of their life would
sully this young gift that God had bestowed upon the
Santinis. Frank was remarkably gentle and good-natured
and had struck up an acquaintance with Mrs. Belmonte
when he was ten, running errands for her during a period
in which she was bedridden with a lengthy attack of gout
and her own Frankie was doing a deuce in Auburn for
violating parole. "God sent me this Frankie for while my
Frankie is away from home," she had told her neighbors.
A few dollars for his services had to be pressed on the
young Frank; he enjoyed helping a sick neighbor. On
Francesca's part, since the boy was not a blood relative
of Tommy's dead father, she allowed him to become her
friend. Indeed, she came to love him. He still dropped
in to visit with her for a few minutes at least once each
week.

Tommy could simply have Frank tell Francesca Belmonte that it was important for her son to telephone
Tommy—that he knew not why. The boy would not
really be involved in the business, just deliver a simple
message whose meaning he wouldn't know.

Tommy poured himself more mineral water. To in-
volve his nephew even in such a glancing way was a
violation of the order of things. If found out, it would
be looked on as having sullied this single pure thing in
the Santinis' existence, and both the father and son were
full-mooners where this boy was concerned. That he,
Tommy, was the crew chief would mean nothing to those
two. But young Frank Santini *was* the perfect messenger.
And there was a buck and a quarter at stake.

XVII

Teddy left the building at four o'clock to buy a late edition of the *Post*. The room had neither a television nor a radio. He turned away from the boardwalk, toward Brighton Beach Avenue, the busy commercial street on which business was conducted in the shade and noise of the elevated subway line. A street vendor offered only Russian-language books and all of the conversation Teddy overheard was in Russian. Fruit stands pushed out so far toward the curb that pedestrians passed one another single file. The neighborhood, which Teddy was generally unfamiliar with, was vibrant.

Since waking from his nap half an hour earlier he had thought about the scene in the garage several times, and now found himself doing it again. Breslin had been the planned driver of the van when they left the Montclair and there was no reason for that to have changed. The position of Garrick, unconscious in the passenger seat, reinforced it, so almost certainly the van had left the hotel with Breslin driving, Garrick in the passenger seat, and the two Cubans in the rear. The bumper-to-bumper mechanical check of the van a few days earlier had certainly included the brakes, and so it must have been crashed into the wall purposely. Breslin must have feared for his own life. After crashing the van Breslin would have run. The Cuban doctor must have run, too. Who had killed the doctor's accomplice? It was a puzzle, and Teddy knew from long experience that there were always puzzles in these sorts of incidents, puzzles that were never solved. The bottom line was that Breslin was in the same spot as he and Frank. More important, the

Cuban doctor was loose, either running for cover or trying to carry out his mission alone. He would leave that to the CIA people. There was nothing he could do about the doctor.

The *Post* headline riveted his attention to the stack of papers on the stand. TWO DEAD IN 15 MIL HOTEL HEIST. THREE HOSTAGES TAKEN. Beneath it was a lurid photo of the dead Mrs. Woodling sprawled on the bloodied Persian rug, a hotel towel spread over her face. He bought two copies, folded one under his arm, and skimmed the other as he walked back toward the apartment slowly. The dead woman's name was being withheld until next of kin were reached. Three hostages were taken: the dead woman's male companion, presumed to be her husband; and two Venezuelan businessmen who had been late arrivals and thus were bound, gagged, and blindfolded along with hotel employees held prisoner in the manager's office. The robbery had been carefully executed. Two men who had been guests in the hotel for several days had been joined by two hooded men and proceeded to occupy the hotel. During the three hours they were in control, a porter had been shot in the back for reasons unknown and his body left in a hall closet. Police speculated, off the record, that he had been the inside man in what was likely an inside job, whose accomplices had ruthlessly cut him out of his share. A Mexican alien found huddled in a kitchen bathroom was now under guard in Bellevue Hospital suffering from gangrene. He, too, was believed to be part of the inside team. A second porter, employed at the hotel for six years, had punched in for his usual 11 P.M.-to-7 A.M. shift but had not been seen after that. He was being sought for questioning and was for now considered a suspect. Estimates of the haul ranged wildly from a minimum of $10 million in jewelry to a possible $40 million. According to accounts of employees, able to hear exchanges among the robbers, the robbery was apparently cut short by the thieves' conviction that police in unmarked cars had set up an ambush outside. They decided to leave immediately, with hostages. Gunplay suddenly erupted in the lobby. Police theorized that the same greediness that led to the porter's demise was at work here, with one or more of the robbers slated for execution by his accomplices and the woman caught in the crossfire. It was hoped that ballistics tests on a gun found in the lobby plus the lethal bullet would clarify that puzzling aspect. Meanwhile, police sketch artists were working with hotel employees to produce drawings of the two well-spoken robbers who had posed as guests for two days.

There were two sidebar interviews, the first with the twenty-eight-year-old hotel doorman, John Tannersman, who lived in Maspeth, Queens, and had advanced to the finals in the 1990 Golden Gloves as a member of the CYO heavyweight team.

"They were punks," he had told the reporter. "I would love to meet any two of them at once with no guns."

The second interview was with the night elevator operator, sixty-nine-year-old Brian Cudahy, of Manhattan, who said, "This kind of excitement isn't healthy for a man my age. It's the final straw that's going to push me into retirement." He had appeared shaken and upset but refused medical aid, wanting nothing more than "the comfort and privacy of my own apartment for a few hours, where I can compose myself." Mr. Cudahy went on to say that he finally understood the frequent comment of robbery victims in recent years that they felt "violated," telling the reporter, "To be truthful, I always thought it was just New Age baloney. Young people too sensitive for their own good. But this has been a learning experience for me. It's the same thing as rape. This is going to leave a permanent scar."

When Teddy reached the apartment house entrance he decided to pass it by and sit for a few minutes on the boardwalk, where he could think more clearly than he could in Frank's presence. He found a bench at the front railing, just above the sand, one end occupied by a barefoot old woman reading a Russian-language newspaper. Her bulk, along with the stoicism of her jowled, winter-hardy face and the uncaring way in which her skirt was hitched halfway up her thighs and her knees splayed wide to admit the ocean breeze, as though she had been placed there to anchor the bench forever to the boardwalk, caused him to reflect that Hitler must not have studied these people carefully before invading the Soviet Union.

He sat on the opposite end of the bench and looked out at the ocean. It occurred to him that had he studied Cutshaw and Garrick carefully, he would never have been suckered into his present situation. How could he have not considered that Cutshaw had no reason to trust him once the kidnapping was complete and even less reason to trust Frank Belmonte? The way in which Garrick had planned their exit, with him and Frank coming out last in the company of the female shooter, meant that he and Frank were to be left dead in the Montclair lobby, killed by their accomplices for their share of the loot. It would have given the robbery its final touch of authenticity: a professional jewel thief partnering with a retired-cop-gone-bad had pulled it off and been killed by their accomplices. Even Fidel would buy that.

He should have seen it coming. He had been blinded by the chance to test his mettle as a member of a unit even tougher than the thin blue line of urban police— the cold warriors. Patriots whose courage required not merely the occasional physical bravery of ordinary cops or soldiers, but also the mental toughness to break any moral rule that got in one's way—a challenge demanding enough to have enticed the likes of Donovan and Dulles and in their wake a host of Ivy Leaguers, including Cutshaw. Here was a profession in which machismo could be raised above its usual adolescent level and made worthy of intellectuals, where men who camouflaged their supreme arrogance with professorial clothing could make their own laws. It was the perfect playing field for intelligent egoists—a field in which the more abhorrent the deed, the greater the credit that accrued to the perpetrator, since it was a measure of the lengths to which he would go in the service of his country. A vision popped into his head of the steely-eyed Linwood Cutshaw at a Greenwich Village bar, whiskey in hand, laying a backdoor claim to self-sacrifice by summing up a lifetime in the intelligence business with the hackneyed, understated phrase, "It's dark and dangerous work but somebody's got to do it." It had been accompanied by a self-deprecating smile, presumably to signal Teddy that it wasn't meant seriously, but of course Cutshaw had been deadly serious. The memory was replaced immediately by another from a few years later, of a rookie cop delivering the same line with a straight face in a bantering, locker-room discussion of cunnilingus. At the time, it had caused him to recall his pub crawl with Cutshaw.

His thoughts were interrupted by the appearance of Frank, who took note of the old Russian woman and said to Teddy, "Let's walk." They strolled along the boardwalk, the roller coaster and restored parachute jump of Coney Island ahead in the distance. Occasional cyclists, moving at a sane speed, some of them with trotting, leashed dogs in tow, wound through strollers and joggers as though choreographed, all of it observed by an audience of bench-sitters. Frank never opened the *Post* Teddy handed him, just studied the photo on the front page for a bit, then folded the paper and stuck it in his back pocket, and asked, "So?"

"First off," Teddy said, "there's a dead porter neither of us knew about. Up on one of the floors. Garrick must've popped him while we were all downstairs."

"I clocked that guy for an asshole from the get-go, Teddy."

"He never said nothing to me about a porter."

"Well, what's the paper say about any leads? Between the lines."

"In a nutshell? An inside job. They would bet their bottom dollar on it. And they'll be banking heavily on what their sketch artists come up with. They're figuring two of the perps lived in the hotel for a couple of days so there's a dozen people who saw plenty of them. And under very relaxed conditions. A big plus because you can't believe how witnesses distort stuff if they're under stress when it happens. Forget about inaccuracies or bad descriptions—they see stuff that never happened. And go to their graves *swearing* to it."

"Tell me about it," Frank said, nodding dolefully. "Just about every guy I ever met in the joint who was really innocent—and I grant you they were few and far between—he had been sandbagged with eyewitness testimony. And when you read any of the criminal justice stuff, the scholarly literature, it turns out the prosecutors, the judges, the criminologists, they all know how unreliable eyewitness testimony is. Circumstantial evidence—when there's plenty of it—it's almost never wrong, but juries don't want to trust it. They'll buy eyewitness testimony every time though. They look at a solid citizen on the stand and say, 'Why would he lie?' Never dawns on them he might be making an honest mistake."

He shook his head philosophically and added, "But hey, most of the time it's just twelve little people. Prisoners of their own narrow experience. And not for nothing, Teddy, but the cops don't help neither. They're always influencing witnesses—poking them or coughing or whatnot when they get to the guy in the lineup the cop thinks is guilty or maybe figures got away with so much he ought to take a fall for something."

"It's been known to happen," Teddy said dryly. "Anyway I don't think the eyewitnesses in this case are going to be a big help. You and me, nobody ever caught a peek of. And the makeup Garrick and Breslin had on was as good as it gets, no?"

"I never seen nothing like it," Frank said.

"So they're going to come up with half a dozen solid sketches that all look the same. From people who got good long looks at the two of them for the better part of two days and two nights, and weren't excited or under duress. And they'll use those to do final composites that all the witnesses are going to agree on and the department's going to hang their hat on. And those final composites won't look like Garrick or Breslin."

"So we're in good shape," Frank said.

"I wouldn't go that far," Teddy said. "We're not in terrible shape. But the right move here is for the next couple of days to remember we're on the lam. Stay out of sight. See how things shake out. Behave like lamsters are supposed to behave. I been through enough of these kind of investigations to know things turn up out of the blue."

Teddy wondered whether a connection had been made between the department and Cutshaw. He doubted it but couldn't be sure. The longer he and Frank stayed out of sight, though, the better.

"There's no reason not to go after our jewels though," Frank said.

"I'd love to," Teddy lied. "Just one big problem. Where do we start?"

"Woodstock."

Teddy stopped short.

"What are you talking about?" he asked. "Where'd you come up with that?"

"A little birdy told me."

"What little birdy?" Teddy asked.

"When you left the two spics in the manager's office and went off for more tape to do their mouths. They were already blindfolded, and I sat there just like my mother taught me—with my ears open and my mouth shut. The one spic asked the other one where the *cosas* was—I don't know the word, but the way he used it, it had to mean junk—and he told him it was in a house up in Woodstock. Even gave him directions from the middle of the town. The only thing I missed was the exact name of the road. It was something Lane. A yellow house on something Lane. Can't be too hard to find."

Teddy thought for a moment, then asked, "Which one of them knew where the stuff was and which one didn't?"

"What's the difference?"

" 'Cause I got to know everything," Teddy said. "I'll read people's mail if I get the chance. It's an occupational disease I contracted."

"The younger guy knew where it was. The guy who was dead in the garage. He told the older guy," Frank said, then after a moment added, "That Colombian and

Breslin are up there now retrieving their drug stash. With our jewels as a bonus. Plus the broad's money. These guys hit the lottery here."

"And you remember what you heard?" Teddy asked. "Enough to get to the place?"

Frank smiled. "I cannot forget directions to a big stash of valuable stuff. That's the occupational disease I contracted. I even remember where the key to this house is hidden. The only word I missed was the actual name of this lane."

Teddy would now lay ten to one that Cheito was on his way to pick up the viruses, which were apparently in Woodstock.

"Which Woodstock?" he asked.

"What do you mean, which Woodstock? It's where that big concert was, no?"

"That's just a little ways upstate. Near Kingston," Teddy said. "But there's one in Vermont, too."

"People in Vermont ain't dealing drugs," Frank said.

They walked quietly for a bit. Teddy felt the Russian flavor of the boardwalk evaporating as they neared Coney. It occurred to Teddy that he and Frank were likely the only people who knew the Cuban doctor's whereabouts. If his motivation in signing up for this mission had been anything more than the excitement and the allure of the romantic outlaw role that he had been considering earlier—if, in fact, he wanted to stop the Cuban doctor from killing innocent people—then he ought to try to stop him. While Frank was after his jewels, maybe he, Teddy, could nail the Cuban.

XVIII

Jay Garrick sipped his fourth Jim Beam on the rocks, held the bourbon in his mouth as his forefinger traced a line across his copy of the *Racing Form,* then pretended to drink from his Coke chaser, in fact spitting back the bourbon. He was unwilling to swallow even an ounce of alcohol. The Breslin work had gone poorly. The man was supposed to have been shot through the eye, not smash himself on rocks in the East River, but then, Breslin had been a trained agent. Frank Belmonte was not a trained agent but a common thief, and Garrick was determined that this piece of work would come off letter-perfect. "There's no river to jump into from the top floor of these tenements," he thought.

No one in the rough-and-ready Elizabeth Street Tavern paid him any mind but he continued to stare down at the handicap charts and occasionally circle the name of a horse. Was this a waste of time? What were the chances of Belmonte trying to sneak into his own house? Slim, but real, he decided. The man lived with his mother, for one thing, and for another, he remembered Richie Zito once telling him, "Even smart criminals make a lot of dumb moves. There's some kind of innate recklessness in even the best of them." The bottom line was that Lin Cutshaw wanted this base covered, and so Garrick faked another swallow of whiskey and spit back. He wondered about the Cuban. Maybe Cutty was being honest, and had no clue where to start searching for him, or maybe Cutty was holding back information, which he hoped was the case. His head still throbbed from the Cuban's blow—he would welcome the chance to catch up with him. First order of business, though, was to exterminate this odd little thief. He, Garrick, would be God's ultimate monkey wrench.

His little table at the window gave a good view of Frank Belmonte's building. Richie Zito, whose entire FBI career had been spent running organized-crime informants in New York City—considered by colleagues the best of the Bureau's handful of streetwise "brick-agents"—had also told Garrick that Little Italy was the toughest surveillance job in America. One could get away with a night or two of watching a house but that would be it; ten-year-olds through grandmothers in the neighborhood spotted strangers quickly and spread the word. Zito had added with a smile, "Kids must have been doing that a thousand years ago in some *castello* near Naples—hollering from a watchtower, 'Wake up! Wake up! Here comes an outsider.' "

There was a sudden, minor rumpus at the bar and Garrick turned to watch it. An old man who should have been cut off three drinks ago was cursing out the bartender for refusing to serve him any more.

"Don't make me come out from behind the bar, pop," the jaded young bartender kept repeating as he washed glasses. After a few minutes of fruitlessly searching for sympathy from those around him, the old man weaved to the door and left. Garrick returned to his watch. Just a minute later the light in Mrs. Belmonte's front room went on. It had been off all night, though he knew she had been in the apartment during that time—he had seen her enter the building not long after he took up his vigil. He studied the front windows and after a few minutes saw the figure of a male pass by. He wanted to curse aloud at himself—just that little distraction at the bar and he had missed seeing Frank enter the building. It had to be Frank, since it was now past eleven o'clock. Who else would be visiting an old lady at that hour?

Sally Seventeen put on his turn signal, slowed, then swung off into the tiny strip mall near Rockaway Boulevard and pulled into an empty space in front of Giorgio's

Pizza. The window was dirty, a sign that Giorgio was running out of steam. He had noticed it when he made his stop last week, and mentioned the window in a nice offhanded way to Giorgio, who had spun a Frisbee-sized disk of dough up into the air and said, "Yeah. I got to get to that." Clearly, he hadn't. Now, Sally decided to say nothing about the window, since he knew that Giorgio could no more conceive of a clean window making a bit of difference in his business than he could of a clean, well-lit store with a polished oven making a difference; early on, he had laughed out loud at Sally for suggesting just that, and told him, "But you don't know nothing about a pizzeria, Sally. You know about lending money. People don't come to a pizzeria to sit under bright lights and look out through a clean window. At what, the cars going by on Rockaway Boulevard? People come if the *abeetz* is good. People don't come if the *abeetz* is no good."

Sally had shrugged. A greaseball was a greaseball was a greaseball. Giorgio should have stayed in Calabria—America was for people who wanted to grow.

There were no customers. Giorgio nodded, as he did each week when Sally entered, but didn't smile, another sign that reality was setting in—he was starting to be mad at Sally. Starting to stew over all the money and all the work about to go down the drain. He continued on an outgoing order, pressing a ball of dough flat with his fingertips.

"You want something to eat?" he asked.

Sally hadn't given it any thought. On the drive from Bensonhurst his thoughts, oddly enough, had been on how Frank Belmonte was going to fare. Now he took a deep whiff of the rich, oven-warmed air and realized that he could stand a bite to eat.

"Good idea," he said. "Make me a pie."

"You like a big pie, Sally?"

"A small pie'll do," Sally said. "I'm going to have dinner in an hour."

Giorgio drew a large Coke without asking.

Sally carried his soda to a table that he guessed had

not been wiped down since the 10:00 A.M. opening. Giorgio had been in the store for ten months now. Sally gave him two more months at most, an even year, about average for the five previous owners. Only the second owner, Cosmo, had lasted much longer; eighteen months, after which even his Abruzzese genes could not withstand the grueling hours. The store was a killer, and meant to be. Sally partnered in it with Pete Santini, a soldier in Tommy Ross's crew. Pete owned the little six-store strip mall. He and Sally had set up the pizzeria six years ago with sixty thousand dollars' worth of equipment—the air-conditioning, ovens, and Hobart mixer the biggest-ticket items—and presented it as a turnkey operation to a recent Neapolitan immigrant whose name Sally had long since forgotten. No money down—not one cent. The immigrant bought the business completely on credit, contracting to pay them a thousand a week for four years. They issued him a little book of numbered coupons. It was inconceivable that anyone could reach coupon 208. The business could not sustain itself with that much debt service piled on top of rent plus the myriad other costs of running a small retail business in New York. Only the immigrant's ability to work sixteen hours a day, seven days a week for a prolonged period kept it afloat. Long enough to make his fifty or so payments. After a few months he invariably found room in the tiny kitchen for a cot, and brought in other family members to shore himself up, none of them, himself included, earning close to minimum wage, until finally he threw in the towel and told Sally he would have to take back his store, grateful that he hadn't sunk any family capital—only family labor—into the failed business. America had proven a tougher place than expected. It was time to jettison dreams of ownership and get a job.

Sally sipped his Coke and made a mental note to tell Pete to line up a fresh immigrant, that Giorgio was ready to bust out. He hoped that Pete had scrapped his wacky idea of putting in Chinese as the next owners.

"Chinese we could bump up to twelve hundred a week," Pete had said.

"People don't want to buy pizza off a Chinaman," Sally had said.

"I ain't so sure. The world is changing. We don't want to get left behind, Sally. I was out to Main Street in Flushing a week ago and I seen Chinamen making pizza. And people were paying a buck-forty a slice for it."

"The way the Chinese work they just might keep it going and end up making the last payment. Then what? They would actually own the joint."

Pete had shaken his head in a way Sally recognized as the beginning of exasperation, and said, "That would mean we collected over two hundred large, Sally. There's worse things could happen to us. And anyway, then I would raise their rent."

"Who's going to teach them how to make a pie?" Sally had asked.

"You could."

"I don't know how."

"Anybody eats as much pizza as you ought to know how to make the stuff," Pete had said, losing patience. "Besides, it ain't rocket science. Go learn how. Contribute something to this partnership for Christ sake."

Sally had played his trump card.

"If we up the payments Tommy's going to want more," he had said, lowering his voice though he didn't have to; they were alone. "We send a hundred and fifty of it up to Tommy now. We bump the payment to twelve hundred and mark my word, Tommy Ross will tell us to send up two fifty every week. Maybe even three."

Pete had chewed on that for a bit and hadn't mentioned the Chinese idea again. Sally hoped he had given up on it. He looked across at Giorgio and tried to visualize in his place a short, ninety-pound Chinese in soiled kitchen whites and an orange baseball cap tossing pizza crusts toward the ceiling. It looked ridiculous. The thoughts of Pete Santini made him think of Tommy Ross, which caused him a pang of guilt, not his first since leaving Lambiasi's. He had ratted, plain and simple. Try as he could to paint a better picture of himself, each time during the day that his meet with Tommy came to mind he could not. He was, whatever his faults, never able to kid himself. Frank Belmonte, a nice guy, had put himself in Sally's hands, and he, Sally, had sold him out. And for a ham sandwich. It gnawed at him, and made him regret not having ordered a large pie. He wondered if there was a way of redeeming himself at least halfway with Frankie.

Frank Santini finished his second cup of coffee, then covered it with his hand to keep Francesca Belmonte from refilling it.

"It will keep me awake," he said.

"Eighteen years old, nothing should keep you awake except girls," she said. "You study too hard is the trouble."

He laughed. "I don't study enough, signora."

"Francesca," she said. "You're a young man now. When are you going to call me Francesca?"

"When I'm twenty-one."

"Now you're even going to school at night, Frankie. It's too much studying. It's no good for the brain. God forbid, you could snap."

"It's one course, by a really good professor, and his daytime class is at the same time as another good course. So I take this one class at night. Eight to ten-thirty, two nights a week. It won't make me snap."

"Where do they give you a class at night?" she asked. "There's other people go?"

"There's eighteen students. And it's in my regular school. A Hundred-sixteenth Street and Broadway."

"Oh my God," she said. "How do you get home?"

"The subway."

She sucked air through her lips.

"It's safe," he said.

"No place is safe except your own house," she said.

He looked at his watch and stood.

"It's almost twelve," he said. "I'm glad you're feeling well. I'll see you next week."

He had planned to walk to the door, say good night, and then, as though it were a sudden afterthought, de-

iver his uncle's message. Now he discovered that he had
no taste for the little deception, and knew she would see
through it instantly. Absolutely nothing got by the
woman.

"My Uncle Gaetano asked me to come here tonight
and give you a message," he said simply.

She registered a moment of surprise but said nothing.

"I don't know why, signora, but it's very important for
your son, Frank, to contact my uncle."

He handed her a folded piece of paper.

"There's a number for him to call. Whenever you talk
to Frank, tell him to call as soon as he can." He paused,
and said carefully, "That it concerns his welfare."

He kissed her on the cheek, as he always did when he
arrived or left, and she returned the kiss but remained
impassive, glacing briefly at the paper in her hand. When
he opened the door she said, "Frank. Tell your uncle I
don't know when I'll be talking to my Frankie. But when
do, I'll give him your uncle's message."

"I'll tell him," he said, and closed the door behind
himself.

Just before he reached the street-level hallway he
heard her voice call down, "Frankie! Remember! Careful
on the subway."

He laughed loudly and called up, *"Buena notte,"* and
continued down the last flight of steps.

As he walked from the stairway to the vestibule, across
the tile floor of the darkened hallway, Garrick stepped
out from under the stairway beneath the lightbulb he had
loosened ten minutes earlier, raised his silenced pistol in
the two-handed grip he favored, and shot Frank Santini
in the back of the head with a hollow-point bullet.

Sally found a parking spot on Brighton-Fourth Street,
just around the corner from Oleg's Baseball Memorabilia
Shop, a small but busy store stocked floor-to-ceiling with
forgeries. He was only a few blocks from his apartment.
Oleg kept his store open until midnight or one; Russians
were late-night people and, more important, it was his
base of operations for shylocking and fencing small lots

of hijacked goods. Sally sat in the car for a few minutes
while he consolidated the money he was carrying. He set
Giorgio's $1,000, all of it in worn and often greasy tens
and twenties, on the seat beside him and counted out,
off the top, the $150 to be sent up to Tommy Ross, put
a jumbo paper clip on it, then divided the remaining $850
into his and Pete Santini's share, feeling the usual twinge
of resentment as he set aside $450 for Pete and took
$400 for himself; what Pete called a fifty-fifty split. In the
first week of their partnership Sally had counted out the
shares in front of Pete and split their $850 down the middle,
four and a quarter each. Pete had taken $25 from Sally's
pile and put it on his own and said, "We don't want to
fuck around with change. It gets too complicated. So I'll
pick up the breakage. We'll keep it round and do the
split four and four-fifty." As he pocketed his $450, he
had said, "It's easier this way, ain't it Sally?" Sally had
shrugged, unsurprised; whenever there was less than a
$100 in a split, the change usually ended up with the
made guy. It was one more reason to dream of a button.

He now took money from other pockets, some of it
crumpled, some in rubber bands, some in paper clips. He
totaled that money up and found a few dollars more than
he had figured, just shy of $1,000, accumulated over the
course of the day from working guys paying their weekly
three points on loans of $1,000 or $2,000. Three hundred
of it came from Fred Bosc, owner of Caribou Spring
Water, a company that provided offices and upscale
homes with ten-gallon demijohns of "Crystal-Clear
Maine Water from the Spring of the Caribou." He also
owned, in his wife's maiden name, several car washes in
Queens, where two of his three tank trucks filled up. The
third actually made trips back and forth to Maine. Bosc,
a respectable upper-middle-class family man, was as de-
generate a gambler as Sally and so frequently carried
outstanding loans with several shylocks simultaneously
for weeks or months at a time. All told, Sally had $1,400
for himself; good, and not good.

Good because he had his weekly payment for Oleg
around the corner, to whom Sally had turned for $40,000

several months ago after Michael Jordan had barely reached double digits against the Heat. An $800 payment instead of the $1,200 it by rights ought to be—Oleg had extended a professional-courtesy discount to Sally and was taking only two points in juice every week instead of three.

Bad because after paying Oleg he was left with only $600, which he thought of as gas and food money for the next day. It meant he couldn't bet on tomorrow's Braves game. Unless he took $10,000 from Patty Bronx, which would add another three bucks a week in juice. On the other hand, a Braves win tomorrow could give him some breathing room. He knew, as he returned his now neatly categorized money to his pocket, that he would take the ten thou from Patty—Maddux was going tomorrow; there was no way the Braves could lose. His pocket would be fuller, he thought, if this three-points-a-week system had not made obsolete the nice forty-eight-knock-down system that had been in place forever and he wished were in place now—where money was lent in $48 increments for which the borrower repaid $6 a week for ten weeks. Sally's borrowers had been two- or three-increment guys, with a handful of them taking ten incre-ments—$480, repaid at $60 a week for ten weeks. This three-points-a-week and no knocking the loan down—the borrower had to save up the full amount—came out to less juice. Meanwhile, he thought, along with less juice, he had Pete Santini dipping in for a third of his shylock earnings *after* they had sent up a nice taste to Tommy Ross. The fingers of his left hand felt a bit numb as he opened the car door, and not for the first time in the past few months it occurred to him that after fifty years of busting his ass he had no medical and no pension. He owned nothing. He didn't have two nickels to rub together.

Oleg was not in his shop. Fyodor, a skinny twenty-five-year-old with a pallid complexion, was beside the samovar, leafing through a Russian-language magazine. He had no idea when Oleg might be back. Sally was reluctant to leave the payment with Fyodor. He caught sight of Alex Zotov, now in his late seventies, a legend in the Russian underworld. One of the great forgers of the USSR, Zotov had often been used by the KGB to create eleborate documentation for agents. Now, his hand just a touch less than rock-steady, he sat at midnight in a tiny back room in America, signing the names of dead baseball greats of whom he had never heard on gloves and balls, after which they would be dirtied up and aged in a low-temperature oven for hours. Sally didn't disturb the old man. He told Fyodor that he would stop back in an hour or so; to tell Oleg that he had something for him.

He decided it would be a good move, after all, to go to the apartment. Make a first strike. As he walked toward the beach he formulated an idea that had been kicking around his head for hours. He would tell Frank that Tommy Ross was asking around whether anyone had seen him. That maybe Frank ought to contact Tommy. Frank would see through it easily enough and guess that Sally had given him up, and was there to make it up to him in this small way. He would likely even ask whether Sally had said anything.

"But what are you nuts?" Sally would say. "I figure you might want to talk to Tommy. Nip any crazy ideas he has in the bud. Or do whatever you got to do. I don't know your circumstances in this thing."

Sally spoke the words, aloud but softly, as he walked, practicing the gestures and facial expressions he would use. Both of them would recognize the sham being played, but they would play it through.

"What does Tommy Ross want with me?" Frank would ask.

Sally would shrug, maybe even make a little circular motion near his head and say, "You know Tommy. *Botz,* sometimes. I think he's got it in his head it was you who got that big hotel the other day. You read about it Frank?"

"Yeah, I read about it," Frank would say.

Sally planned to leave a long silence here, so that Frank would know that he wasn't fooling anyone, then say, "Anyway, I thought I'd tip you off. So you can do whatever you have to do."

Sally hoped that Frank would assume he had given him up under duress, rather than ratting him out for personal gain. There was a big difference; no one was expected to stand up to a Tommy Ross grilling. With just a touch of luck—and for sure Sally was long overdue for it—Frank would think him a stand-up guy for bringing him the warning. With just a second touch of luck— even longer overdue—Frank would show his gratitude for the tip-off by giving him a couple of stones from the heist.

He expected they would be big stones; Frank Belmonte was a class act. Two or three big stones could make him well, he thought, as he walked up to his apartment. The painted-over 3D on his door made him recall again his meet with Tommy Ross. It occurred to him that if this was actually turning into his lucky day, then Tommy might reconsider his request to get made. "Like the guy on TV says," he thought, "hey, you never know." And sooner or later a lifetime of hard work had to pay off for him; there had to be that much justice in the world.

He knocked hard, in the shave-and-a-haircut tempo he had mentioned to Frank on the phone early this morning, then opened the door with his key. When he flipped the light switch he was shocked to find four guns pointed at him by young Chinese tough guys. He recognized their type from Chinatown, and wanted no part of them.

"You're going to answer my questions and I'm going to let you live," a twenty-year-old said. "Or you won't answer and I'm going to kill you."

Sally started to respond but was cut short.

"And don't bother telling me whose flag you're under. I don't care. You won't be the first wop I've buried. With their buttons."

XIX

When Cheito walked, unfettered, out of the dim tenement into the dawning day, he experienced for perhaps the tenth time in his life the feeling of having been granted a death-sentence pardon. As he hurried toward the garbage hopper that he hoped still held his suitcase full of jewelry, he let himself enjoy the familiar feeling of joy at having just been granted the gift of life. It was a physical sensation. He had learned early on that for him this was the peak experience of soldiering and that the closer the margin by which he cheated death the more intense his joy. The satisfaction he derived from his scientific work felt good, but only on an intellectual level. It never equaled this. He marveled, as he always did in the aftermath of a close call, that anyone was able to live a life devoid of physical danger.

The airline bag, happily, was still in the hopper. Once it was firmly in his hands and rolling nicely across the sidewalk behind him, he considered his next move. He remembered from his maps that Broadway was nearby, a tourist attraction, where he would be able to buy a map and even comfortably ask directions. Angel had said the village of Woodstock was just a few hours north. Surely there were trains or buses that would take him there. At some point he would need a car, which couldn't be bought or even stolen since he had no idea of how to bypass the ignition lock on these complex cars he saw all around him. He would have to take the car away from someone, and it was best to do that just before he absolutely needed it; the police here must have sophisticated ways of searching for a car they wanted to find.

The car should be commandeered in Woodstock, not here.

His confidence rose as he walked along Fifty-first Street and knew that he was heading east and that the next avenue he would cross was Tenth, and that Broadway lay between Seventh and Eighth avenues along this stretch of Manhattan. He was also growing surer that the robbery of the hotel was bona fide, that he and Angel had been victims of circumstances, and while he would continue with great discipline to behave as though intelligence agents were, in fact, on his trail, he did not have the awful feeling of being pursued by a superior force, of having to keep moving, a situation he knew very well. The city just then seemed not at all threatening. Indeed, these people now on the streets were so purposeful, so clearly involved in their own lives, appeared to be so removed from one another and to lack any common interest, that he half believed were he to announce his identity and his mission, they would continue on their way. Everything conspired to lift his spirits, and his thoughts turned toward the suitcase he was pulling.

The value of the stones so outweighed the value of the melted-down gold or platinum settings that he could, once ensconced in the safety of Angel's Woodstock house, remove the stones and throw away the settings. He would have just a small sack of diamonds to deal with, a sack that would fit in his pocket. The question was what to do with the diamonds when this mission was over. He found it surprisingly pleasant to consider the possibilities as he pulled his fortune along, creating a rhythmic clacking as the tiny wheels rolled across joints in the sidewalk. A life of luxury in the south of Spain or France was nice to contemplate, he thought, but in fact would soon cause him to loathe himself. More important, it would write an absurd final chapter to his career, subverting his accomplishments and lifelong dedication to the revolution. His mind formed a sudden, dismaying image of the inner flap of the dust jacket of *Cheito, Soldier-Scientist*: "The author now lives in retirement on the French Riviera." What seemed appealing at first blush was the thought of living an ascetic life in Cuba, his name known to every schoolchild but he himself out of the public eye sufficiently to slip away unnoticed from time to time, sell off a stone or two, and treat himself to some of the pleasures that had been denied him. It also occurred to him that he might use some of this money to buy himself a liver. Transplants were now routine and undoubtedly half a million of his dollars would buy a healthy young liver, installed and functioning. It would surprise him if a flourishing black market for organ acquisition and transplant did not exist in half a dozen countries, perhaps even a South American country. What the market's source might be for healthy young organs was not his concern. A new liver was a possibility that simply never had crossed his mind—which now surprised him. It ought to have more than crossed his mind years ago, not as a possibility but as one more source of emotional energy for himself. Since it was a procedure available only to the rich, it would have nurtured the long-term resentment he felt at all things in this category. All his life he had collected just these kinds of injustices and from them developed a stock of resentments that could be drawn upon during periods of doubt to keep him true to his ideals.

And now, out of the blue, a new liver was a very real possibility. How might his plans for the rest of his life change if instead of ten more years he had twenty? Or even thirty? It would be a pleasant diversion, when this mission was over, to entertain changes in his life plans. As so often in the past, he found himself amazed at how suddenly one's fortunes turned. Just a short while ago he had been a handcuffed prisoner on the floor of a van, on his way, he believed, to a brutal interrogation. Now he had in his hands the means to extend his life a decade or two, God willing, and even indulge himself from time to time in well-earned pleasures. He enjoyed the irony of it; even for a visitor like himself, here to do harm, the United States was indeed the land of overnight, rags-to-riches opportunity it claimed to be.

* * *

Knowing the interest and even wariness with which strangers are received in a village, no matter the culture, he was prepared to feel his way into whichever role might arouse the least curiosity: businessman, tourist, or professional man researching something. How one got around was what he had to learn first, after which he could locate the house Angel had rented. When he stepped down from the bus, though, he realized within a few minutes that no one was the least interested in visitors, much less suspicious of them. The complete unconcern with newcomers in a place this small was a new experience for him. Young people—the poorest group of Yanquis he had yet seen, judging by their clothes—sat around the tiny patch of green in the center of town, just across from a small church. He assumed they were begging, yet they made no pleas to passersby. Several of them strummed guitars. There were also some older hangers-on who looked very much like the homeless men he had seen on Tenth Avenue, but without the huge plastic bags full of cans and bottles, who seemed to mix comfortably with the teenagers. He was caught completely off guard by the nearly palpable feeling of ease in the air and wondered was this typical of villages across the country, or was Woodstock an anomaly?

He bought a street map, then crossed the road to an open-air pub whose rough-hewn wood walls, mismatched tables, and concrete floor would fit comfortably in any South American village he had ever been in, the only thing missing here a group of locally stationed soldiers in uniform with automatic weapons slung over their shoulders, occupying most of the tavern and well on their way to being completely drunk. He ate a huge hamburger and plate of french fries washed down with draft beer that was tasteless but very cold, the airline bag pushed under the table close enough for his knee to rest against it, the map spread out beneath his plates. It took him just minutes to find Quarry Lane and see that it was a crooked little road whose farthest point was less than three miles from where he sat. When a couple at the next table paid their check, he watched closely enough to see that it came to just under twenty dollars. They left three dollars on the table as a tip. His own check was for eleven dollars and he confidently left two as a tip.

Twice during the first twenty minutes of his walk to Quarry Lane a car stopped to offer a lift. Each time he smiled his thanks and claimed to want the exercise. People's friendliness seemed to carry over to their living arrangements; there were no fences, or even markers, to show where a man's land began and ended. The houses themselves were widely spaced on parcels he estimated as three, four, even ten acres, which calmed a lurking fear he had about privacy. He had expected houses much closer; this was rich country. Why, then, he wondered, so many For Sale signs? Was there some great problem in the area?

He had napped for much of the two-hour bus trip, and now it felt good to be on a country road, even a paved one, and have to slap at a gnat or mosquito from time to time. The pebble-strewn surface was poorly suited to the tiny wheels, and so he carried the suitcase at his side now rather than wheeling it, the pull-handle telescoped closed, changing it from hand to hand often. The extra weight caused him to sweat, another welcome sensation, though he was happy this was not Angola; he would be sweating much harder and moving much slower. He had never been in wooded countryside this far north, with vegetation so much less dense than that of the subtropical forests he had fought in. It struck him that this would be more difficult terrain on which to fight a guerrilla war. Visibility was greater, an advantage for a conventional force, and he could only imagine what it would be like to elude helicopter-supported forces in winter, when the trees were bare and snow covered the ground.

He passed several hand-lettered signs nailed to trees, which said, GARAGE SALE STRAIGHT AHEAD. When he came upon a long stretch of items displayed along the side of a driveway he realized this was the sale and that it consisted of unwanted household items, enough of them to make many Cubans or Angolans or Bolivians consider themselves wealthy. A bicycle caught his eye, a ten-speed outfitted with racing handlebars. It would be a good way to get around until the time came when he had to have a car. He walked across the lawn tentatively and looked it over. It was an old, white Peugeot, well taken care of.

"Does everything on it work properly?" he asked the elderly woman who knitted beneath a huge shade tree, in an easy chair that itself had a price tag dangling from it.

"Try it," she said, without looking up from her work.

He set the airline bag down and rode the bike in little circles on the road in front of the lawn, never out of sight of the bag.

"How much?" he asked her.

"I'd like to get a hundred dollars," she said.

"Will you sell it for eighty dollars?" he asked.

"I'll take ninety."

"You would take sixty," he thought, "if I were able to stand here and bargain as I should."

He counted out her money, then tied the airline bag onto the rear rack. There was a little tool bag hanging off the seat. He used the wrench in it to lower the seat a few inches, then thanked the woman and pedaled off.

Ten minutes later Quarry Lane appeared on his left, running uphill. It, too, was blacktopped. He wondered, were there no dirt roads in this country? As well, did no one, even in this rural area, keep a few chickens? The fifth house on the road was pale yellow, a two-story structure with a single windowed gable on the front. Angel had picked well. It was set back from the road two hundred feet or so, the houses on either side separated from it by a long stretch of heavy woods. There was no walkway from the road, only a driveway—finally, an automobile path not paved. It was, though, topped with a deep bed of crushed rock that would be the envy of a road commissioner in Cuba.

He walked the bike slowly up the driveway and saw that it led not to a garage, but instead turned upon itself to form a tight circle in front of the house, enclosing an oval piece of lawn in the center of which stood a lush, red-leaved tree taller than the house. The grass had been mowed early that morning, judging by the smell. At most, yesterday. He wondered, who did the mowing? Was there a caretaker of whom even Angel was unaware? If so, how often was he here? More important, had he been in the house? Certainly he would have a key. He wished he had pumped Angel for more details of his arrangement with the owner during their ride in from the airport.

A short flagstone walk led him from the driveway to a simple portico. He pulled open the screen door and used the brass knocker. After a minute he walked around to the back of the house, but saw nothing that might be a heat pump, whatever that might look like. Angel had said it was at the back of the house but he could easily have meant one side. He continued around, and found what must be the heat pump, a device about waist high enclosed in louvered sheet metal and resting on a three-foot-square concrete pad set close to the house. Insulated pipes, too small to carry treated air, ran from the machine through the wall of the house; this was simply a remote air-conditioner being used in reverse—it sent heated refrigerant into the house. He reached into the narrow space between the metal shroud and the wall of the house and felt along the sheet metal until his fingers found a small bump, a key held in place with the kind of aluminum-colored tape that had been so difficult to obtain when he was assembling his lab.

He entered the house on edge, instinctively looking down at the floor for tripwires, then remembered where he was. He set the airline bag down behind an easy chair, uncomfortable with it out in plain sight. It took only a few minutes to make a cursory inspection. The house was old, well kept, and sparsely furnished, with polished wood floors and walls painted in pale colors; four bedrooms upstairs, a living room downstairs, beside a dining room that looked unused. There were three bathrooms, the one attached to the largest bedroom more elaborate than any he had ever seen. A huge kitchen with a table for six in one corner had terra-cotta floor tiles that made him think of home, and heavy-duty ovens suitable for serving hundreds. Could this place once have been a restaurant? The biggest surprise, which actually gave him a start when he entered the room, was a huge poster of Che hung on a bedroom wall, perhaps three by four feet—the Alberto Korda photo that was more ubiquitous in Cuba than even Fidel's somber visage. Because of its unexpectedness he paid attention to it for the first time in many years. His old friend wore a red beret with a single, small star on its front, and looked off into the distance with a visionary's gaze that saw the certainty of his future martyrdom at some faraway point behind the viewer. The scraggly beard, surely retouched by Korda or the poster maker, lent a feminine, Christlike side to Che—a saintly acceptance of the road ahead. It was a fine piece of romantic, revolutionary art. *But what in the world was this poster doing in this house?* His first thought was Angel but he quickly dismissed that as absurd. The room itself looked like that of a young person's.

In the center of the large table in the kitchen lay a manila folder with a message on the cover written in red ink:

Dr. Sosa,
  Hope you enjoy your stay. Come Aug. 30 we will have Central Hudson take a meter reading and issue a bill, which we will deduct from your security deposit. Ditto for the phone. A receipt for $12,000 covering rent for July and August is enclosed. A list of numbers you might need (plumber, etc.) is enclosed, also some brochures describing local points of interest, etc. The Maverick Concerts are first rate. Opus 49 is well worth a trip. We expect to be back in Manhattan on Aug. 15, in London until then. Both numbers are enclosed.

Enjoy,
Marc and Jennie Fielding

P.S. Our son, Jeffry (25), may be returning from New Mexico for a short stay with friends during late July. If so he plans to take some things from his room. Of course he will call ahead.

P.P.S. Our good friend's sister is Dr. Louise Crayton, a botanist (plant morphology her specialty?) who is a researcher at the New York Botanical Garden (and teaches, too, we think, at NYU). She's recently been for several years in the Guayana region of your country as part of a biodiversity study. Do you know her? (Your field can't be *that* big.) She spends weekends in Woodstock sometimes, just down the road at Jill and Jerry Gross's. (Number on list on refrigerator door.) You two should likely meet and swap Venezuelan and American plant gossip. She might call you.

Based on the dates, Angel must have seen the letter. He had obviously told them he was a botanist, probably to account for any signs of scientific doings in the house. This was the early part of August and so the twenty-five-year-old son—surely the smiling young man in a framed photo on the bureau across the room—had either been here a while ago or was not coming. In any event the boy was less of a threat than this botanist, who would be curious about Angel's fictitious work and background. Nothing in the note required action on his part. Right now, his immediate task was to locate the virus; he had seen no trace of it during his quick tour.

The door to the cellar was next to the kitchen. He expected to find a dark, low-ceilinged place that housed a furnace, and instead saw that Yanquis lived very well even below ground. The space had been improved to the level of a fine apartment, dry as could be, completely illuminated, air-conditioned, and even carpeted. A small room, set up as an office, held a computer whose cost he could not guess. A full-sized billiard table stood in the center of the main room, and the largest television he had ever seen was set against the far wall. In a corner he saw what he was looking for—a small refrigerator of about three cubic feet. It was exactly the kind of unit he had specified to Angel months ago, and now he saw that Angel had taken enough time from his pursuit of thankful women to follow instructions to the letter, adding a cheap, luggage-quality lock onto the door, beside which was taped an index card with the hand-lettered message:

"Seed Specimens—Do Not Disturb." The lock was tiny enough not to arouse suspicion that something inside required great protection. When he peered behind the unit, he saw that Angel had also rigged the power plug as told—the outlet cover-plate had been removed and a short piece of wire twisted under its anchoring screw and pulled taut, then its other end twisted around the power plug, so that it couldn't be disconnected inadvertently. The refrigerator was simply one more precaution, since the virus would likely keep very well for months at normal temperature. His goal had been to dampen the effects of any minor bacterial contamination during Angel's packaging procedures. He made a quick tour of the basement closets in search of a hammer and found instead an entire workshop whose power tools he literally would have killed for when he was equipping his Zapata Peninsula lab.

The little lock gave way in seconds and he opened the door to find the three small aerosol cans into which Angel had packaged the virus after propagating it. He had obviously removed labels from cans of whipped cream and applied them to these, then clustered the three cans together with a thick rubber band. Cheito closed the refrigerator. Things looked very much in order, and Angel had told him in the car that a test run just days ago had shown the virus to be alive and well. Angel had made the test using a monkey-cell line he had been able to order from a biological supply house here in the States—by mail, no less. Cheito remembered how preposterous that had seemed to him just twelve hours ago, yet he was already accepting such things after less than one full day in the country.

He returned upstairs for a more thorough inspection of the master bedroom, which was obviously the room Angel had used during his two-week stay here. A night-table drawer held a brand-new pair of good binoculars along with a folder full of newspaper and magazine clippings about the Erigena cult. The most valuable item in the folder came as a surprise: a topographical map of the area in superb detail, at a scale of about two and one-half inches to the mile with contours plotted at twenty-foot intervals. He read the various notes and explanations carefully but found his conclusions incredible. Apparently the entire United States was mapped out in this detail, broken up into rectangular parcels of about sixty square miles each. He ran a rough mental calculation, and found it hard to believe. There would need to be about sixty thousand of these maps plotted. And they were obviously for sale to the general public. Even harder to believe. He had fought battles using military maps not one tenth as good. For someone like himself, completely at home with a topographic map, a piece of land could be visualized immediately, in sufficient detail to sculpt it roughly in a piece of clay if need be, and thus the difficulty of a trek across mountainous countryside could be judged with great accuracy.

He refolded the map. Later that evening he would study it at length.

The rest of the afternoon was fruitful, since the little village offered far more than he had hoped for. He found every article of clothing he needed, including good hiking boots; a rucksack, which he filled with food from the aisles of the local supermarket; a compass; a box of hand-rolled Honduran cigars from a shop just off what he learned was called the Village Green; and a disposable camera to hang around his neck. The supermarket impressed him, but not nearly as much as the hardware store. He could have wandered through its aisles for hours, but chose instead to spend the rest of the afternoon moving around, on foot and on his bicycle, eyes wide open, becoming comfortable in these strange surroundings. People drove noticeably slower and more carefully than he was accustomed to, always using turn signals and obeying traffic signs, which he filed away as important for when he had to drive a car. Most of them also wore seat belts, and on the street or in the stores they smiled and nodded a lot and apparently expected strangers to do it, too. They pumped their own gas, which he thought worth learning how to do, so he bought a can of Coca-Cola at a store called, inexplicably, Cumberland Farms, and drank it while standing outside the door studying how people worked the pumps, then went inside to pay. Police seemed to be nonexistent, though he cautioned himself not to become lax, since there were sure to be more of them circulating within the general population than met the eye.

The Hondurans were better than he expected, but not much; still, the smoke was delicious. He brought the folder downstairs and spread the contour map out on the table in the kitchen, then hunted through cabinets until he found a shelf full of liquor in an antique credenza. He chose to stand at the table, his left hand holding the cigar, his right hand skimming across the map as though the contours were printed in braille, but stopping often to bring the glass of Scotch whisky to his lips.

The extent of uninhabited land just a hundred miles from New York City surprised him. It appeared that the government had set aside large tracts as public parks. A lightly penciled-in circle on the north face of Tremper Mountain drew his attention. He took from the folder the packet of newspaper articles and found one from the *Kingston Freeman,* with photos, that described in some detail the Erigena tract of land as "a retreat of three thousand acres on Tremper and Carl Mountains." Certainly the pencil mark referred to the Erigenas and had been drawn in by Angel. He guessed that it marked the location of the buildings Angel had described during the car ride. One could hike up to the spot either from the little town of Phoenicia or the even smaller town of Chichester pretty easily, with a fair amount of zigzagging. A moment later he spotted a light, dashed map line that crossed not far above Angel's little circle, across the twenty-seven-hundred-foot peak then across the high ridge onto the adjacent Carl Mountain. The legend identified it as a marked hiking trail and it started at a roadside point less than a mile south of Phoenicia. A marked trail for amateur hikers—he could crawl up that in torrential rains if need be, something he had done in Bolivia without mark-

ings. Angel's circle could be reached from the trail by
descending about a half mile of fairly steep mountainside. He puffed his cigar contentedly; things could be
looking a lot worse, considering the position he had been
in early this morning. To be standing over a map studying contours, cigar and whisky at hand, needing sleep—
he was a soldier again, for the first time in nearly
seven years.

The crucial knowledge for him—the physical layout of
their buildings—would have to be gleaned from his own
observation the next day. He looked through the literature Angel had assembled on the Erigena cult and absorbed enough of their absurd beliefs to feign an interest
in joining them if that proved necessary. There was nothing more to do until the morning.

Except for the diamonds. The thought of the diamonds
had been lurking in the back of his mind for hours now,
and he had savored the thought of examining them. For
some reason, he enjoyed delaying his first good look at
them for a few more minutes, which surprised him, since
one of his strengths was that he never procrastinated for
even a minute. But now, surprisingly, what came to mind
were several Mozart discs he had admired during his
earlier look around the house. He put the serenade for
strings on the fine sound system, refilled his glass, and
settled into the inviting easy chair beneath a bright lamp,
the airline bag beside him on the floor, and instead of
opening it immediately he reflected for a bit on the idea
of a new liver and brief sojourns on Mediterranean
shores. It became more intriguing with each passing
minute.

When he finally unzipped the bag and lifted out
piece after piece of heavy, exquisite jewelry, their beauty
and obvious value overwhelmed him. His plan had been
to knock loose the biggest diamonds and literally discard
everything else. That was when he had believed the entire haul was worth a few million. Now that he saw it
was worth two or three times that—and so could truly
afford to throw away the relatively bulky settings—he
ought to have been even more willing to discard all but

the biggest diamonds, but knew he could not bring himself to do it. He asked himself, "Why?" And surprised himself by answering, "Because no matter what the value of the big stones alone—no matter how much I have there—these settings by themselves appear too valuable to throw away." His answer amazed him, yet he couldn't deny it. He remembered a night forty years ago, when he had been a secretly committed young Marxist whose leanings were not a great secret to his father's circle of friends. Señor Edwin Higgins-Rincon, a rich tobacco grower, had returned with several friends to Cheito's house from the casino at the newly opened Riviera, exultant because he had won ten thousand dollars. When Cheito had wondered aloud at such happiness over what was, in fact, pocket money for a man of Higgins-Rincon's wealth, these rich men had laughed at his naïveté and said, "The more money one gets, the more one wants, Ernesto. It's human nature." He had loudly disagreed.

Now, he thought, was not the time to analyze the oddities of human nature. Rather than throw away the denuded settings he could bury them, in their airline bag, somewhere in these vast wooded tracts around him—he had buried and retrieved caches of small arms and ammunition in Bolivia with no difficulty.

Why not? Why throw them away? There was nothing lost by tucking them away safely, even though he believed he could never spend in his lifetime the money he would get for the half-a-handful of the largest diamonds alone. His thinking here amazed him but he had no doubt about his conclusions—the more all of this stuff was worth, the less inclined he was to give up even a small part of it, no matter that he had far more than enough.

He decided to divide his treasure into two parts: a small sack of the largest diamonds and gemstones removed from their settings, which he would carry on his person, and the remaining pieces, not broken down, along with the denuded settings, which he would bury. That he would ever return for this buried portion was doubtful, but he knew from experience that life takes odd turns. Why not have it stashed away safely?

He sorted out the pieces worth disassembling and carried them downstairs to the workshop, where he enjoyed prying loose their stones with a variety of needle-nose pliers or a light ball-peen hammer and a bench vise. The vise brought to mind vividly the smirking Dominican who had been such a poor judge of people.

The last stone he wanted loose fell from its setting near midnight. He relit the Honduran—they did not hold a light as they should—refilled his drink, and took stock. In front of him was a pile of good-sized stones, almost exclusively diamonds but with several large rubies and sapphires mixed in and ten superb emeralds taken from a necklace. The size and quantity of the diamonds piqued his curiosity enough to send him into the small office for a postal scale he had seen. They weighed just over a pound. About half a kilo, and he remembered from Angola that there were five carats to a gram. On the little platform of the scale, then, were about twenty-five hundred carats of diamonds. He remembered from Angola that large stones like these could easily be worth four thousand dollars a carat.

He brought the stones upstairs and put them into a man's sock found in a dresser drawer, then tied the sock closed in a tight knot and taped it to his stomach, wrapping several yards of adhesive tape around himself. The stones, he decided, were staying taped to his torso until he was out of the United States.

XX

After Teddy had agreed to make the trip to Woodstock in pursuit of the jewelry, Frank had said, "We need a car. You own one, no?"

Teddy, afraid to go near it for the same reason he was afraid to go near his apartment, had said it wasn't running.

"The on-board computer's screwed up. It needs to go into the shop."

Frank had simply looked up at the gods without breaking stride and asked aloud, "When are we going to catch a break?" then fell deeply into thought—his problem-solving mode—as he continued beside Teddy on the return leg of their boardwalk stroll. When they neared a phone a few minutes later, he had veered off to it suddenly. Teddy had made his way to the front of the boardwalk, where he leaned forward against the railing and looked out at the Atlantic and wondered when would be the best time to level with Frank.

"Never," had been the answer he kept coming up with, but he knew that would prove impossible, and so told himself, "If not never, then as late as possible."

Frank had interrupted his thoughts, his mood noticeably upbeat.

"I got us a car. Come on," he had said.

"Where?"

"Riverhead. Out on the island."

"How'd you swing that?"

"A guy I did time with, a hundred years ago."

"You guys *do* keep in touch, huh? Sounds like our

penal system has a tighter old-boy network than the
Ivy League."

"Fraternity of thieves," Frank had said. "People think
it's bullshit, just a romantic myth went out with the
James brothers, but it exists, believe me. Between guys
who did time together. Unless he wants you to lay down
in front of a truck, it's tough to turn down somebody
you done time with, Teddy. Adverse conditions bring
people together. Anyway, this guy finally retired from
crime and went into the used car business. How's that
for a fucking oxymoron? He couldn't have been thrilled
to hear from me, but he came through. Said he'll hang
dealer plates on something nice we can take for three,
four days so long as we don't use it as a work car."

"And he trusts you to tell him the truth?"

"Habituals are so trusting it's sad. They want to trust
their buddies so bad they refuse to recognize flat-out lies.
Half the guys in the joint are there because of it."

"I thought half the guys were there because cops pressure witnesses into false eyewitness testimony."

"That's the other half."

The sudden little turn of events had put a bit of spring
into Frank's step and caused him to whistle softly as they
walked. Once again, Teddy had been amazed at how
little was required to convince him that life was treating
him well.

Later, as they had left Sally's for the Long Island Rail-
road at Jamaica and a two-hour ride to Riverhead, four
young Chinese entering the lobby door of the building
had yielded no leeway in the narrow vestibule.

"Fukienese for sure," Frank had said when he and
Teddy were out on the street. "Chinese mafiosi. Those
are tough kids. You ever bump heads with them?"

"The department has special units to deal with them,"
he had said.

"They don't respect nothing, those kids," Frank had
said. "Totally unsocialized."

Now Teddy drove the two-year-old Audi slowly along
Route 375, just outside of Woodstock, Frank in an un-

troubled, deep sleep beside him. They had called ahead from the darkened car-lot office in Riverhead and found a place in the center of Woodstock whose owner promised to check them in at any hour. It was 2:00 A.M. when Teddy made a U-turn using the broad driveway of the volunteer firehouse and parked in front of the Staub Guest House, a turn-of-the-century structure whose steeply pitched tin roof warned what Catskill winters could be.

"I guess you didn't run into any traffic, did you?" the owner asked, smiling, while they filled out registration forms. He had the look of a retired blue-collar worker who hadn't exercised since his teens.

"I can put you in a small single upstairs with its own bathroom and squeeze in a second bed—we do it all the time—or I can put you in a comfortable double on this floor where you share a bathroom. Seventy-five a night for the double, fifty-five for the little one."

"The private bath," Teddy said, and glanced at Frank, who nodded.

Mr. Staub walked them through the big living room, barely lit by several night-lights near floor level.

"What brings you to Woodstock at two A.M.?" he asked.

It was stated so directly and unexpectedly that both of them were dumbfounded for what seemed to Teddy a long time but was probably just five or six seconds. Frank answered, and Teddy wished he hadn't.

"You running a fucking survey?" he asked.

Mr. Staub looked Frank in the eye before answering, long enough to make it clear he was not backing down, then said in a completely unapologetic tone, "I was trying to be hospitable."

"He's tired," Teddy said. "And cranky. We're on our way to Rochester and changed our mind about driving all night. Thought it would be a nice break to take a day off and explore your pretty little town."

Mr. Staub nodded and opened the door to their single room, then opened the door to a small storeroom across from it.

"If you two can handle the box spring and mattress I'll take the frame. There's a trick to maneuvering it into the room without hitting the lamp."

"Sure," Teddy said pleasantly.

Frank handled his end of the move willingly enough but was very close to glaring at Staub, who avoided eye contact with him.

When they were alone in the room, starting to undress, Teddy asked, "What the hell was that about? The guy didn't mean any harm."

Frank's mood remained sour.

"Hey, I don't have to take any shit from him," he said. "If I never see another upstate hick with a big belly it'll be too soon. Those are the guys they hire in all the upstate joints. Lousy pay, they do a third of the time every day that the inmates do, but they walk them corridors like pigs in shit. You could tell by his puss—a juicer, and one nosy son of a bitch. That's the other thing about them—nosy."

He opened the window a few inches, then lay flat on the bed, hands under his head. "The guy rubbed me the wrong way," he said.

"Yeah, you kind of gave that impression," Teddy said. He clicked off the little lamp on the night table between them and lay on the narrow mattress, eyes wide open in the darkness, puzzling over Frank Belmonte, who lay just a few feet away. After a few minutes he said, softly, "Can you stand answering a question? Or you going to ask me if I'm taking a fucking survey?"

"Ask," Frank said. "You ain't fat, you ain't a hick, you ain't what the English aptly call a tradesman—which this guy is by the way—butting into your customer's personal life. So yeah, you're welcome to ask."

"If this guy downstairs had grabbed you by the collar and told you to learn some fucking manners—which he came close to doing, believe me—what were you going to do?"

"An honest answer?"

"Yeah."

"I would've used my knee to drive his balls somewhere

up around his tonsils—a technique I mastered years ago—and found another place to sleep. In the car if I had to."

"And if he called the town constable, or sheriff, or whatever they've got here? Another big-bellied hick no doubt who went through grammar school with Staub or Staub's brother and who might find it hard to be a hundred percent evenhanded about things."

"I didn't plan that far ahead," Frank said. "I would've managed the situation if I had to."

"But you're here to get back the biggest chunk of money you've ever had in your hands at one time. A small fortune that will change *the rest of your life*. And you risk it for what? To impress some stranger you're never going to see again? Who you not only don't respect but who you look down on? It makes no sense, Frank."

"There's times, Teddy, when you respond to the emotion of the moment."

"If some stranger pinches your girlfriend's ass maybe. But when the emotion of the moment is about as important as a guy cutting you off in a car, and the stakes are maybe ten million dollars, it's a good time to exercise a little self-restraint," Teddy said.

"It's funny you should pick that example," Frank said. "A guy I grew up with—Willy Red—you know him?"

"I know the name. I never had the pleasure."

"A man's man. Red got cut off on Avenue C by a Pakistani cabdriver who then made the mistake of giving Red the finger when he hollered and made the bigger mistake of doing it when Red was carrying. He pulled the Paki out in broad daylight on C and Fourth and put one into each knee. And maybe 'cause I can't stand to be cut off on the road, I always understood it perfectly. We ain't automatons, Teddy. There are times when it's only human to be a little impulsive."

"How much time did it cost him?" Teddy asked.

"Forty-two months. Light, huh? But he used Kenny Kirsch for his lawyer. Who got it delayed a hundred times. Paid Kenny close to sixty large—then spent another thirty buying witnesses or buying people to intimidate them. So it cost Red close to a hundred on top of his forty-two months, but he told me a number of times that it was all worth it for the look on the Paki's face just before he pulled the trigger."

"You don't find that excessively responsive to the emotion of the moment?" Teddy said.

After a silence, Frank asked, with genuine curiosity, "How long goes by, Teddy, without you doing something completely over-the-top? Where you give in to your emotions a thousand percent? Without thinking for a single second?"

"What do you mean, how long?"

"Six months? A year? How long do you go without doing it?"

"Frank, I haven't made that kind of move since I was eighteen, nineteen."

"You're shitting me."

"I'm not."

Frank remained silent for what seemed like a long time, then asked, "You think that's true of most people?"

"Don't you?"

"Not until you just told me. 'Cause it's not true of the people I know."

"Not for nothing, Frank, but you might want to peruse some of your criminology books again."

"They talk impulse-neurosis but I never thought there was *this* kind of difference. Where people could go for years swallowing their bile or eating a little shit when they're told to because they think things out in such detail no matter what their heart is telling them to do. Don't you ever just cut loose and go with your heart, Teddy?"

"The answer to your question—I guess—is, no. But that's a loaded way of framing the question."

After a short silence, Frank said, "We better catch some zees."

XXI

Cheito woke up early and after two cups of coffee packed his rucksack methodically. The most crucial item was a rig that Angel had constructed with great care in the basement to Cheito's design, which used a nine-volt battery to activate a little solenoid. A spring-loaded lever then pressed down on the aerosol-dispensing valve. He placed it in the center of the rucksack, wrapped in a bathroom towel. The last item packed was a spade found in the toolshed behind the house. He sawed off the handle to a length of just one foot, then used the shop's grinding wheel to sharpen the edges of the blade to a knifelike sharpness. It fit into his rucksack well, the blade padded with a towel to keep it from tearing through. The airline bag of less valuable pieces and denuded settings he tied onto the rear rack of the bicycle.

The start of the hiking trail was along a road called Old Route 28, ten miles as the crow flies from where he was, about fifteen miles, he estimated, of actual travel distance. The map showed hilly sections along the way but nothing he couldn't climb with this bike's gearing. The hiking trail itself was shown on the contour map as a dashed line. He used a razor blade to cut a square, two inches on a side, out of the map, which showed a section of the trail and also the north slope of Mount Tremper, where Angel had penciled in the little circle, and put the little square in his pocket rather than the map. The last thing he did before mounting the bicycle and pedaling off was to check that the sock full of gems on his stomach was firmly in place.

He reached a rustic wood sign that indicated the start

of the trail at nine o'clock, after two hours of pedaling at a comfortable pace. Just across the two-lane road, on the creek side, was a stretch of widened shoulder with room for half a dozen cars to park, but only a lone, rusted-out pickup truck sat in the space, with what he would swear was an empty gun rack on the rear of the cab. The truck also carried a puzzling little sign pasted on the rear bumper stating that great beer bellies are made, not born. That would be the owner, Cheito decided, wearing rubber coveralls and standing in the fast-flowing Esopus Creek, which ran on the other side of the road, casting for whatever fish lived there. The attraction of the sport eluded Cheito, but then the only sport that had ever tempted him was trapshooting. After trying that only once—with great success for a beginner—he had found it too boring to pursue. He made a small adjustment to the straps of the rucksack, then hoisted the bike so that the crossbar rested on his shoulder, the airline bag still tied to the rear rack. It was heavy and uncomfortable but he would manage easily enough for the fifteen minutes or so it would take to hike well away from the road.

The trail rose steeply for the first thousand feet but because it was cleared the going was easy. After that it snaked much more, accommodating itself to the contours of the land, and thus the grade diminished and the going got easier, so much so that he continued to carry the bike for longer than he had planned. Finally, a particularly lush clump of bushes just off the trail presented itself. He untied the case from the rack and hid the bike in the bushes. Although he was sure he would recognize the spot instantly on his return trip, experience had taught him how foolish that assumption could be if he ran into bad luck and was being pursued. He used a pocket knife to mark a nearby white birch, then continued on, scanning the terrain for a good place to bury the airline bag. A quarter mile later an outcropping of shale that formed a long, nearly vertical wall the height of a man presented itself, distinctive enough and certainly permanent enough to serve as a landmark. After study-

ing the lay of the land for a few minutes, he settled on
a huge pine tree as his starting point. He laid a hundred-
foot tape measure from the base of the thick trunk
toward the face of the outcropping on a line perpendicu-
lar to it. At the eighty-foot mark he had passed through
enough foliage to shield him from the trail while he dug;
the ground looked inviting, and there was a large boulder
nearby that would do nicely as a second reference point.
He took the sawed-off spade from his rucksack and dug
quickly, thankful that he had taken the time to sharpen
its edges. Half an hour later he tamped down the last
shovelful the hole would accept, scattered the remaining
pile of earth, then used a pocketknife to cut a deep notch
into the trunk of the pine tree at knee height. He took
from his shirt pocket the little square of contour map he
had cut out and estimated where on the trail he was,
crosshatched in a little symbol to show the position of
the outcropping, then turned it over and carefully drew
a tiny map that included the outcropping itself, the huge
pine tree with the eighty-foot dimension marked, and the
boulder, twelve feet from the buried bag. The position
of the treasure itself he marked with an X, which brought
a smile to his lips as he remembered reading *Treasure
Island* as a little boy. His final note on the map was
an arrow indicating north, which he determined with his
compass. He was satisfied that anyone using this map
would have no trouble locating the airline bag, though
he could not imagine who on earth he might give it to.
Drawing it this precisely, he knew, was the result of his
years as a soldier and his obsessive attention to detail.

He moved faster now, and reached the peak of
Tremper Mountain at eleven o'clock. A watchtower, apparently unused, stood at the highest point, a wood structure rising perhaps fifty feet into the air, with a steel
staircase rather than a ladder. The staircase seemed ex-
travagant to him, as did so much else he saw in this
country—for the use a tower like this might get, a simple
ladder would do, and would be far more economical. The
staircase, with its switchbacks and landings, could serve
a well-trafficked building. A sign warned people to stay

off the tower. He thought about climbing it but decided to push on instead, and rested for just a few minutes before starting out again. Now it would be downhill, and if Angel's marking on the contour map was at all accurate, he would reach the cultists' encampment by one o'clock.

Teddy and a surprisingly upbeat Frank left the guest house early—Teddy relieved that Staub was nowhere to be seen—and sat down to a hearty breakfast at a small place near the Village Green that catered to an eclectic mix of natives. They bought a *Daily News,* which carried police sketches of Breslin and Garrick.

"I've been in a position to criticize a lot of police composites over the years," Frank said. "And this is the bottom of the barrel. That makeup worked."

Teddy agreed.

"No one's collaring either one of them from these sketches," he said.

Frank opened the paper to page three, and said softly, "Jesus Christ. That broad was a *cop.* A fucking *cop* had to check into our heist. That's why she was packing." He skimmed quickly. "Janet Stein. They got a little column about her here. Forty-four years old. Lived in Arlington, Virginia. Twenty-year veteran of the Washington, D.C., Police Department . . . 'who, fellow officers said, always carried her firearm when off-duty.' Twat should've left it home. Never married, so the guy with her, who was taken hostage, must have been a traveling companion. That surprised neighbors who described her as . . . 'quiet and private almost to the point of being reclusive. She used her seniority with the department to take three or four brief vacations each year, though both co-workers and neighbors had always believed she traveled alone.' "

Frank skimmed the rest of the page quickly.

"No sign of three hostages . . . Police fear for their lives. . . . Relatives of the two Venezuelan businessmen not yet notified . . . police withholding their names while working with the embassy to identify them. And the guy in the kitchen is an illegal knows nothing about nothing, they're shipping home to Mexico. Guy'll be back in the States in a week."

He mumbled through a dull stretch, then brightened. "Jesus, look at this. That porter who disappeared? Guy punched in and was never seen again and the cops had him figured for an inside guy? Turns out that for the past three years the man held down a second job a few blocks away in a restaurant on Lexington Avenue as the midnight-to-six porter five nights a week. He'd punch in at the Montclair, duck out to the restaurant, then hustle back to the hotel in time to punch out every morning. The other porter—the one that asshole Garrick popped— he'd work hard enough to cover for him. The two of them were splitting three salaries down the middle."

He folded the paper and said, "But is there *anyone* out there don't have an angle, Teddy?"

Teddy waited for Frank to raise questions, but "Mrs. Woodling" being an off-duty D.C. cop seemed not to dissuade him from his earlier theory of a drug-deal rip-off. It seemed to him that given his own role in the robbery, why should it? Instead, Frank surveyed the many beards, ponytails, bandannas, and sandals approvingly, and seemed to include even the extensively tattooed, unhurried waitress in the little sweep of his hand.

"Town's a time warp," he said. "These people are definitely not ready to bust their asses in the raging global economy."

"You got up on the right side of the bed," Teddy said, while Frank skillfully used his knife to construct on his fork a neat little pyramid of scrambled egg, bacon, and a large home fry.

"New day, clean slate, and I have a gut feeling we're going to recover our stolen property," he said, while he managed to move the heaping forkful to his mouth intact.

Good mood notwithstanding, Frank had nothing further to say until his plate was cleaned and he had started on his second cup of coffee, at which point he sat back with the satisfaction of someone who had the world on a string, and asked, "If we get back our swag, Teddy,

what are you going to do with your end? The two of u
split down the middle now. Four, five mil apiece
minimum."

"A lot of fazools for a retired cop," Teddy hedged
though it happened to be his honest feeling about it. "I'l
be fifty before I turn around. What would you advise
Frank?"

Frank shook his head, puzzled. "How did you ever
take the giant step across the line into heavy-duty crime
after a lifetime of being a thousand percent legitimate'
More than a thousand percent legit—being a *cop.* How
do you do that without a dream that's driving you? Solid
citizens who go after that once-in-a-lifetime score do i
because they have a dream."

Teddy had no stomach at the moment for an elaborate
lie, which would be exposed as such all too soon anyway
if the two of them caught up with the Cuban doctor. He
simply shrugged, and motioned to the waitress for a
check. "I want a little nest egg for my old age," he said
and motioned with his head toward a wall clock. "It's
after nine. We should pick up a street map of this town
and get rolling."

Left alone for a few minutes while Frank used the
bathroom, it occurred to him that it would be pretty
sweet to be sitting right now with that jewelry. Money
had never been a driving force for him, past the poin
where it provided security and a decent quality of life
and so he had never given any thought to what he migh
do with his share of the loot. One thing was certain—a
few million dollars right now would not be a burden
He wondered if maybe there wasn't some way to track
down Breslin.

It was ten-thirty when Teddy swung the car onto DeLisic
Lane, their first destination. Frank had their map opened
on his lap, marked with an array of short, orange ink
squiggles, each one highlighting a lane in the town o
Woodstock. They had expected there to be six or eigh
short thoroughfares designated as lanes, but found twenty

eight of them. It had taken a while to mark each one of
them and plan an itinerary.

Teddy slowed to a ten-mile-per-hour crawl toward the
roadway's dead end, already in sight just a short way
ahead. The houses were simple and set close to the road.

"Whoa," Frank said, and pointed ahead to their left.

"What?" Teddy asked.

"A yellow one."

Teddy stopped in front of the small clapboard house
Frank pointed to. He studied it for just a few seconds,
then turned and studied Frank for a few seconds.

"What are you, color-blind?" he asked.

"Of course not. You telling me that ain't yellow?"

"It's beige."

"Teddy, that spic wasn't an interior decorator. He
didn't say a canary-yellow house or a lemon-yellow
house. He said yellow. And not for nothing, but what
we're looking at here ain't beige, it's a buff color. A little
weathered, but buff. Which is in the yellow family."

"Finding this house could take a long time," Teddy
said. "We've got twenty-eight lanes to look at, spread
over fifteen or twenty square miles. We've got to limit
ourselves to yellow houses. *Distinctly* yellow. Or we
could be here a week."

After a few moments Frank shrugged, and said,
"You've got the experience doing this kind of stuff."

Teddy cruised to the end of the lane and made a U-
turn.

As Cheito made his way down a steep incline, the longhouse that Angel had described in the car came into view
first; moments later an octagonal building could be seen
just to the east of it. This would be the temple Angel
had recommended as the best killing room. There was
no sign of life around the buildings. He continued down
the slope and into the clearing, where he shouted out
several hellos.

A husky young man with short-cropped hair appeared
in a doorway of the longhouse, wiping his hands on a
stained apron that hung well below his knees.

"I didn't see you come up," he said, with some surprise. "From the kitchen window I see a long stretch of the path."

Cheito pointed to the top of the mountain as he unbuckled his rucksack and eased it to the ground.

"I came down off the hiking trail that runs across the crest."

"Are you lost?"

"Aren't we all a little lost?" Cheito asked plaintively, then after a few seconds smiled with satisfaction at his own cleverness, as he imagined a cult member would do, and said, "I know exactly where I am. I came to find out more about your group."

"Come inside," the young man said. "Have a cool drink."

They entered the most spotless kitchen Cheito had ever seen. The young man poured each of them a glass of water from a jug in one of several large, sliding-door refrigerators.

"It's from our own spring," he said. "Febronia is working the farm today. She's our spiritual leader. She's the person for you to talk to."

"What is the octagonal building I passed?" Cheito asked.

"Our temple."

"Do you use it often?"

"Every day."

"Regularly?" Cheito asked, with great interest. "Do you have a set schedule, or is it flexible?"

The young man smiled, and gave off precisely the aura of self-satisfaction Cheito himself had striven for a few moments earlier.

"Nothing here is flexible. Everything we do follows a set schedule. A rigid schedule. It's the only way to free your mind of trivia, and concentrate. We assemble in the temple at two o'clock each day for exactly an hour, and again at seven."

Angel's information had been correct. It crossed Cheito's mind that everything Angel had done had been even better than correct—had been first-rate. The selection of this place, the Quarry Lane house, everything. It was too bad his leg had been hurt in the crash of the van, which was pretty much a matter of luck. Cheito had seen scores of comrades who had run into just a bit of bad luck in the field, and inevitably, as with Angel, it had cost them their lives.

"May I go into the temple?" Cheito asked. "For the feel of the place?"

"That's what it's for," the young man said. "The eight sides will make you feel secure and protected. See if I'm not right."

Cheito left him to his food and his dishes and walked the short distance to the temple, along the way retrieving the rucksack from where it sat on the ground. He carried it in one hand, by the straps.

The temple contained no altar, only a low octagonal platform of highly polished marble just a few inches high, in the very center of the room. Three rows of simple, backless benches arranged octagonally faced it. The walls were windowless, the only light entering from small skylights, one in each of the eight pie-shaped sections of roof. Seven life-size statues stood around the periphery of the room, each in the center of its wall panel; the eighth panel was unoccupied because of the door. He recognized Christ, Muhammad, Buddha, and a personage he took to be Moses, but could not identify the others. He sat on the third-row bench opposite the open door, directly in front of Muhammad, and set his rucksack on the floor, then quickly unbuckled the flap, installed the aerosol into the dispensing device, then used both hands to lift and guide it out gently. A small, nine-volt battery was taped to the side of the can. He pulled it loose and inserted it into the holder, forcing himself not to hurry, looking up every few seconds to see if someone was coming, taking the extra time to double-check that he was installing it with the correct polarity. The battery clicked snugly into place and the tiny digital timer came alive. It registered 0. He checked his watch: 1:45. They would be in here from 2:00 to 3:00. Five-past-two seemed a good time to go off, and so he set the timer for twenty minutes. He reached back and set the device on the floor in the narrow space between Muhammad and the wall behind him.

Done. Now he would return to the kitchen and offer to help, until Febronia returned, then beg off the group prayer. He would observe the temple through binoculars, from a position well upwind, and when he was down off the mountain later this afternoon he would call the Centers for Disease Control in Atlanta and get through to Dr. Lane MacArthur, the authority on hemorrhagic viruses down there, who would grasp things and act very quickly and quietly to seal this area off. Cheito hoped to be able to speak directly to Dr. MacArthur, to express admiration for the fine papers he had published over the years, and acknowledge the help they had been in his own development of Kaongeshi-Zaire.

It was three-thirty when Teddy and Frank reached the start of Quarry Lane, the halfway point of their itinerary. Since they set out, four houses had been deemed yellow enough to investigate, but at each, forthcoming occupants or neighbors who seemed thankful for unexpected visitors had vouched for the house's innocence.

As Teddy went into his ten-mile-per-hour mode, Frank studied the generously spaced homes and said, "These are not poor people."

A minute later Teddy slowed even more when he spotted a two-story yellow house set well back from the road, then pulled into the long driveway. As they drove slowly over the finely crushed rock, peering forward for signs of life, Frank said, "You may have twenty years of police work under your belt, but I still don't like this MO— driving up to the front door like this."

"You park on the road and walk up a driveway in a rural area, you attract more attention. Everybody drives up like this."

"And what if Breslin's watching us right now from one of them upstairs windows?" Frank asked.

"He'd watch us walking, too. Pay attention to the house, please. See if you can spot anybody peeking out."

They stopped halfway around the circle, at the beginning of the flagstone walkway, and sat in the car for a minute before getting out.

Teddy banged the brass knocker hard for a long time, then said, "No one home. It figures—there's no car in sight."

They walked around the building and tried to peer into each window, unsuccessfully; every blind was tightly closed.

"He said a key was taped to a heat pump," Frank said, and walked to the unit on the side of the house. He felt around thoroughly, then said, "Nothing."

"Let's talk to some neighbors," Teddy said.

The Fieldings were away until late August, Mrs. Layton, the neighbor to the east, told them through a haze of cigarette smoke on the front porch, while behind the screen door some kind of lapdog barked unrelentingly. As for the house being for rent, she doubted it; Teddy must have been told that before the Fieldings rented to the Venezuelan scientist, Dr. Sosa, whom she had met two months ago—an attractive fellow who was expecting to be joined by a colleague about this time. She, incidentally, just assumed it was a gay relationship. Which she sure didn't have any problem with since her sister, Willa, who lived down in Armonk, marched up Fifth Avenue every year beside her oldest boy in the Gay Pride parade, holding a sign, and for another thing Woodstock had been an arts community since 1902 so not much shocked the natives—if Teddy and Frank could have seen the goings-on among Byrdcliff Colony artists in the 1920s, it would turn their hair—and one more thing, she had yet to hear of a gang of drunk gays beating up some fellow because he was straight, and finally, this was America wasn't it, for Christ's sake? But gay or straight, it was her guess that either the colleague or Dr. Sosa or both of them had moved back in yesterday, since there were lights on in the house last night for hours.

Teddy saw Frank's eyes widen.

*   *   *

At one-forty-five acolytes began arriving at the clearing from whichever workstations they had been assigned to that day. A colorless lot, Cheito thought, and, as one would expect, a passive lot as well. He wondered if the canings Angel had described were not more frequent than the cultists acknowledged. What in the world would bring young people to a place like this? Only a society with no core beliefs. The single acolyte with a spring to his step was called Alan. He had what Cheito thought of as the youthful super-Yanqui look, brought about, he supposed, by the never-ending availability of antibiotics at a moment's notice along with generous portions of vitamins since infancy and an endless supply of nutritious food munched on by a perfectly maintained set of teeth; a self-confident, two-hundred pounder undoubtedly able to push basketballs downward through hoops, who knew nothing of the real world other than that it was a wonderful place for himself. The only oddity that Alan exhibited was a hint of hardness never present in the young super-Yanquis Cheito had seen previously. If there were supervisory positions in this group, Cheito thought, Alan held one.

A few minutes later Cheito felt himself being scrutinized again, this time by Febronia Orbelian herself, religious leader to these others, past drug addict, heiress to millions, a woman who certainly had been beautiful in her youth. The toll taken by drugs and prostitution and whatever private demons had possessed her was apparent. She was a woman in her mid-fifties with dark hair cropped short in a style that he normally disliked more than he did here. She wore the same loose, khaki fatigues they all did, and no makeup. Her skin was smooth—an important feature for him—with an olive cast that must have come from her Armenian side. Nothing special, he thought, a girl whose beauty had had no staying power, an early fader lucky to have run across her desert guru before her thirty-fifth birthday; her ability to earn with her body—the standard by which he measured any woman's desirability—would have left her destitute at a fairly young age. She was also far less spiritual, he thought,

than Brian, the young man in the kitchen, though it occurred to him that he might be wrong, and that perhaps
she was simply less naive than Brian. He could never
help but equate spirituality with naïveté.

"You're the second Venezuelan we've had here in the
past two months," she said, after they had talked for a
few minutes.

"There are more of us in the country than people realize," he said.

"Ah," she said, with no conviction. "And what is it
that brings you here?"

"I'm at a point in life where I'm searching for answers.
I thought your group might have some."

He sounded unconvincing to himself.

"I meant, what brings you to America?" she said.

"I'm visiting my sister in New York."

"Where does she live?" she asked.

"You're familiar with the city?" he asked, while he
struggled to bring a street to mind.

"Pretty well."

"Tenth Avenue."

"And where?"

"Thirty-seventh Street," he said, and immediately
thought it a stupid choice. "It's industrial. Not a very
good neighborhood."

"This week it might be a very good neighborhood indeed," she said. "You'll be right around the corner from
the bizarre ritual known as an American political
convention."

He had no idea what she was talking about and was
afraid to fake it. He remained noncommittal.

"You might even get to see the President," she said.

"The President," he repeated, then decided quickly
that this was worth knowing more about.

"I don't pay much attention to the news," he said,
with a self-deprecating shrug. "Why would I get to see
the President?"

"New York is where the convention is being held this
year. At Madison Square Garden. Not far from your
sister's house."

"And the President attends?" he asked, in great surprise.

"You're not familiar with our political conventions?" she asked.

"I'm not," he said.

She finished explaining them ten minutes later, during which he listened, amazed, at the number and importance of those attending. He interrupted frequently to ask questions, and to his delight learned that delegates would be there from all fifty states, more than four thousand delegates in all—this in a huge enclosed space. Perfect for the big one he had dreamed of, the one he needed for the final chapter that would marry Cheito the scientist to Cheito the soldier. A hall big enough to hold the thousands of people this woman claimed would be there, *must,* in this country, be air-conditioned. It would have air-conditioning ducts large enough to walk through upright. And, if this pitiful handful of people around him whose deaths were to serve as a demonstration were to be left alone, the government here would have no reason to expect this kind of attack at their convention. Fidel would never okay the big one, but that was because there was no more steel in Fidel. Fidel was a tired, loud-mouthed old man for whom having come close to his goals, having done better than expected, having secured a place as the great Marxist of the Americas, was good enough. Fidel had lost the drive to win it all.

He saw young men and women converging on the temple, and looked at his watch: three minutes before two. He needed to turn off the timer. Let these fools live; they meant nothing. This mission on an unimportant little mountain in rural New York was unworthy of him and of the revolution he stood for. The convention was the challenge worthy of his talent.

He hurried toward the temple but was stopped at the door by Alan, who lifted his hand to chest height.

"It's a private service," he said.

"I need to get something," Cheito said, and started to step around him.

Alan took a short, fast sidestep that put him directly in front of Cheito, who bumped up against him.

"Private," he said. His tone of voice made it clear that he was very happy it was private.

A second young man whom Cheito had seen earlier at a distance rose from his seat and joined Alan, placing himself shoulder to shoulder with him. Both their faces were impassive but their eyes were the eyes of strong young men for whom the practice of nonviolence was a great effort, who would be enormously grateful to be backed into a corner where their only rational choice was to hit him, where they were *forced* to hit him, for the most justifiable reason imaginable—to protect their sacred temple. It would release in one moment who-knew-how-many years of pent-up aggression. He was no match for them. Febronia stood and walked to them. She carried herself at a purposefully slow pace, very erect, head held higher than it had been a few minutes earlier, her eyes focused on some distant point well behind Cheito. The aura of superiority she cast set off in him a burst of anger. He felt it in his stomach. This bitch, who had once rented her pussy to strangers on the street for drug money, fancied herself as royalty. And the dozen or so weak, stupid acolytes treated her as such.

"This is a private time for us," she said evenly.

"I *have* to get in. For just a few moments."

"For what?"

"For a few moments, *God damn it!*" he said. "For your own good!"

She turned to the two husky followers and spoke as though he weren't present, her tone softer, gentler, and even more affected than during her talk with Cheito.

"If he won't leave quietly, just throw him out," she said, then turned immediately and walked toward her bench.

Alan gave him no chance to withdraw on his own. He placed his palm against Cheito's chest and pushed hard, driving with his legs. Cheito went reeling back across the bare dirt surface on his heels for several steps, arms extended in an unsuccessful effort to keep his balance.

He went down, raising puffs of dust when he hit the ground in a sitting position. Alan studied him for a few moments then pulled closed the heavy temple door.

"Idiots!" he screamed, in Spanish. "Religious idiots! I'm trying to save your lives but you deserve to die!"

He stood and brushed the palms of his hands clean, then checked his watch: 2:02. His mind raced. Good! Three more minutes and they were all doomed. Good! Let them crawl around disintegrating while Kaongeshi-Zaire appropriated their bodies. She would beg then. He wished he could stay long enough to watch—to tell her she had crossed the wrong man. But these fools dying would ruin his big opportunity. He wasn't throwing away his chance at the President in order to punish a band of lunatics.

He sprinted to the kitchen and grabbed the largest carving knife in sight, then ran back to the temple door, threw it open, and ran in, brandishing the knife in circles, willing to decapitate whoever stood in his way. Half hoping Alan wanted to play hero. Screams filled the room as he leapt over benches onto the low marble platform. Febronia, he was pleased to notice, cowered against a wall. He went directly to Muhammad, squatted beside him, and managed to claw the battery out of its holder with the fingernails of his left hand without taking his eyes from the little group, who ran to the door as though caught in a fire. For insurance, he yanked loose one of the wires going to the tiny solenoid that would open the dispensing valve. He picked up the device and cradled it against his body with his left arm, and saw that Alan was the only one left, lingering in the doorway, unwilling to attack but reluctant to concede defeat. Cheito moved toward him fast, knife held high. Alan turned tail and ran to the others, who stood at a distance in a small group, wide-eyed.

Cheito passed his right arm through the straps of the rucksack, knife still in hand, and set the straps on his shoulder. He walked fast across the clearing, checking behind several times, and began his return through the woods to the hiking trail. Another quarter mile or so and he would stop to repack the dispensing device into the ruck-sack, after which he could pick up his pace. He wondered how many seconds—surely it was well less than a min-ute—were left on the timer. Twelve, he guessed. That was how close he had likely come. But it might very well be two seconds. Or forty. A two-second reading, he knew, would send a physical thrill through his body. A forty-second reading would leave him feeling cheated. He walked quickly for a bit, paying attention to low-lying branches, then reached into the device nestled in his arm and without looking down to read the timer, pressed the reset button to return it to zero.

XXII

Frank was ecstatic as they left Mrs. Layton's driveway, but only for the short time it took him to consider that the Venezuelan might already be gone; then his mood darkened.

"Ball's in your court, boss," he said.

"We bust in," Teddy said.

He drove past the yellow house until he was well out of sight of anyone in or near it and parked on the narrow shoulder, then raised the hood. They walked back.

"Jesus, Teddy, enough knocking. There's no one in there," Frank said, while Teddy pounded with the brass knocker one last time before walking around to the back. They punched out a tiny pane of glass in a kitchen-to-patio door and opened the simple slide bolt. Frank stopped for a minute to push the broken glass on the floor under a cabinet with the side of his shoe.

"One of us has got to stand lookout at the front," Frank said. "Rule number one on a thing like this. You take the post, I'll go through the place."

"You take the post," Teddy said. He could think of no good reason to give Frank for it.

"Teddy, I can give this place a toss twice as fast as you can. Believe me."

"I want to," Teddy said stubbornly.

"What is this, a fucking ego thing?"

"No," Teddy said, and turned away. "Watch the front."

As he hurried upstairs Frank called after him, "Close everything after yourself—it's always worth the little extra time."

Teddy went through each bedroom in a methodical

routine: dropping to his knees for a quick peek under the bed; opening the closet and pushing back the hanging clothes with his forearms while he scanned the floor, then checking the top shelf for anything that looked peculiar; last, the dresser drawers. He took the bit of extra time to close each drawer behind himself. Throughout, he wondered what a batch of deadly virus would look like.

Downstairs, Frank got over his momentary anger. Ego, he thought. Everybody's got it, cops more than most. He looked around and guessed that this floor was going to yield nothing. Anything hidden would be upstairs or in the basement. On his walk around the house a few minutes earlier he had noticed there were small basement windows at ground level—until the kitchen door presented itself, he had intended to kick one of them in. Now, he realized that he could have a look around the basement and still keep an eye peeled for anyone coming up to the house, if not a floor-to-ceiling search a pretty good look around. It couldn't hurt—Teddy might be experienced at going through places with a search warrant in his pocket but this kind of thing was not his stock-in-trade. He hurried down the basement steps and surveyed the place. It was sparsely furnished, with few nooks and crannies. The workshop caught his attention and he quickly opened and checked out the two large steel storage cabinets that were packed with hand tools and supplies. They were the only enclosed spaces in the room; hundreds of items were hung on pegboards that covered the walls. He took a minute to survey the walls carefully—people sometimes hung valuables out in plain sight, usually to no avail.

His attention was caught by tools lying on the workbench: three different sizes of needle-nose pliers and the lightest ball-peen hammer a shop like this would likely have. They lay helter-skelter near the vise, the only items in the shop not set in place neatly. What kind of work called for three sizes of needle-noses and a light hammer? He looked closely at the serrated vise jaws and saw telltale traces of gold. His heart beat faster. Each pair of pliers carried the same sign. Now, he had to hope that the thieves would return. To have come this close—to have missed them by only hours—would be unbearable. He took a quick look in the small refrigerator, which had once been provided with a lock and used to store seeds—sensimilia marijuana he guessed. He was disappointed when he saw nothing but cans of whipped cream—people loved to hide valuables in refrigerators. Almost reflexively, he shook each can briefly, expecting there to be no tinkling sound but knowing that people could find a way to seal diamonds into cans of whipped cream if need be. He returned to his post at the front door and decided to let Teddy finish his search. There was no doubt in his mind that the first-grade detective would miss the workshop evidence, and he was going to enjoy rubbing it in a little.

Teddy found nothing upstairs. Downstairs, the only items of interest were Cheito's neatly folded maps on the table in the kitchen. When he opened out the topographical map, the carefully cut-out little section on the north slope of Tremper Mountain puzzled him but he forced himself to set the map aside quickly and continue searching. In the basement his attention was caught first by the hasp on the refrigerator and the little message that it held seeds. He opened the door and saw two cans of whipped cream, the only items on the glass shelf other than a thick rubber band that apparently had been used to bunch cans together—three or four cans, he decided, since it was too big for just these two. He would bet his bottom dollar these cans just a few feet below his nose contained a virus—he found himself holding his breath, knowing it was meaningless but still unwilling to inhale until he had closed the refrigerator door. When it was closed, he remained still for a bit. He had found the virus, or what looked to be some of it. It was what he had come up here to do and he had done it. It gave him a sense of satisfaction he had not felt since leaving the department. That the stuff was here meant the Cuban would be back. But was he off having a cup of coffee? Or off with the missing cans to the place that was cut out of the map? Waiting here for him to return was not the smart move—finding out what was on the side of that mountain was, which meant it was time to bite the bullet.

"Frank!" he called out.

A few moments later Frank hurried down the steps expectantly.

"I've got something to show you," Teddy said, and indicated the refrigerator.

Frank came across the room, puzzled.

"Not what you're looking for," Teddy said, as he opened the door.

Frank peered in, as though seeing it for the first time.

"Whipped cream," he said. "So what?"

"It's a virus. As deadly as it gets. And there's enough of it in those cans to kill off all of New York if it was disseminated just right."

"What the fuck are you talking about?"

"Listen close, Frank, and don't interrupt. We only have a few minutes before I've got to leave here to stop this guy and you have to decide whether you want to come with me. I lied to you from day one. Jay Garrick and Chuck Breslin work for the CIA. I was working for the CIA, too, for this one operation. The robbery was staged, just to nail this terrorist and his partner. Everything fucked up and the CIA guys tried to kill you and me. No question but that they're out to kill us now, so in fact, my friend, we are on the lam, the two of us. I don't really think I fucked you, Frank, even if I misled you a little. It wasn't like you were going to get hurt—you were going to keep your end of a ton of money. The CIA was going to catch a bad guy. Everybody was going to go home happy. Right now the terrorist is loose. On the side of a mountain near here if my hunch is right, about to infect people. I'm leaving out all the reasons for things happening the way they did—I've got no time for it. I'm going to try and stop him. I'd like you to stick with me here—it's a lot to ask but this is a situation where two of us is way more than twice as good as one of us. I've got no time for *mea culpas* and if I did I doubt

I would give them. If you've got any questions I can answer quick, ask."

Frank responded instantly.

"Where's my fucking jewelry?" he said.

"I don't know."

"I think this guy's got it," Frank said. "For sure he's got half of it, even if he already split with Breslin."

Teddy started to say there was no way the Cuban could have the jewelry but caught himself up short.

"Then you ought to come along with me," he said.

"I will," Frank said. "Just one thing."

"What?"

"The Belgian," Frank said wistfully. "Never existed, huh?"

"No, Virginia," Teddy said, "the Belgian was bullshit."

Teddy wanted to play it safe and do *something* with the two cans of presumed virus other than let them sit in the refrigerator. He took them to the shed, a small board-and-batten structure, and stood in the doorway looking for a nook or cranny that would be overlooked by any casual user in search of a garden tool.

"Come on, for Christ sake," Frank called.

Teddy laid the cans inside one of two snow tires hung on the rear wall of the shed, then hurried back to the house to retrieve the topographical map with the little cut-out square.

Cheito pedaled back from the mountain at a much faster pace than he had set going there. While he guessed Febronia would not leave her retreat to file a complaint about the threatening behavior of a visitor, one never knew. She and her acolytes had to wonder what it was that he had first placed inside, and then carried out of the temple. His only concern, though, was whether there were police now combing the roads for him and setting up checkpoints. He doubted it, and since he had no alternative to the bicycle, it was best not to dwell on the possibility.

He felt a little chill of excitement each time he thought of this convention in New York City. Had he gone ahead with his mission—had he not, for the first time in his life directly contravened his orders—he would now be calling Dr. MacArthur at the CDC. Government people would be all over Tremper Mountain in the next few hours, sealing off the Erigena compound and confirming for the State Department that this virus threat of Fidel's was the real thing and God help the country if it were to be released in a crowded area. Fidel would indulge himself in an orgy of gloating, never recognizing that the battle he had just won had cost him the war. He would welcome the miserable crumb the Yanquis would throw onto his outstretched plate—an end to the blockade. And that, Cheito believed—in spite of loathing the realities about human nature from which his reasoning stemmed—would be the end of Cuban socialism. If there was an end to the blockade, Fidel would soon find that what he had won was the opportunity, before he died, to kneel at the altar of the free market, squeezed in among every other Marxist leader alive. Perhaps, with hand-tailored fatigues and neatly trimmed beard, he could do television commercials for the American Express Gold Card. The young, revolutionary Fidel, Cheito fantasized as he pedaled, would have pulled out all the stops from the beginning. No warnings. No demonstrations. No bargaining for concessions. The man was already in the marketplace. The young Fidel would have sent Cheito here to wreak havoc where opportunity presented itself. Would have left him in place for years to come—one could be an agent in this country without bothering to hide. He, Cheito, had presented Fidel with a weapon beyond a weak country's wildest dreams and the impotent old man chose to wield it as though it were a flyswatter.

His decision a few hours earlier to abort this foolish little demonstration was the right one. Had he infected them, it would have precluded his going ahead on his own and wafting Kaongeshi-Zaire through the convention; the security measures taken in the aftermath of the Erigena incident would be impossible to penetrate. Now, however, with no hint of his presence in the country or of the existence of the Kaongeshi-Zaire, he could not imagine that they would be on guard against an attack like this. Bombs and firearms are what they would be guarding against at this convention, and if their much-heralded profiling systems were at work, it would be Arabs, not Latins, they would be watching for.

He was approaching the huge entry gate to a Zen monastery he had passed earlier—were these Catskill Mountains some sort of spiritual magnet?—where he would turn off onto Route 212. His watch said five o'clock. He ought to be back in the house by six, where he would polish off the remaining whisky, get a good night's sleep, and take a bus to New York in the morning.

Teddy and Frank arrived in Phoenicia at ten past five. Main Street was just a few blocks of two-story buildings, with half a dozen Harleys angled at the curb in front of the town tavern. Teddy stopped and called out to the bikers on the sidewalk, "Fellas! Who would have the best selection of local maps?"

"Mueller's," one of them said, and pointed. "Another couple a hundred feet."

The store was a throwback to the 1950s, Teddy thought—a big stock of quality goods sat unobtrusively on shelves or hung on pipe racks waiting to be found by customers who had come into the store knowing exactly what they wanted. Most of the space was given over to fishing equipment and apparel. There was a large rack of maps near the cash register, where an elderly man sat reading a paperback book and puffing on a bent-stem pipe clenched in his teeth. Teddy took note of his big belly.

"A little self-restraint here, please," he said softly to Frank.

"Relax," Frank said. "This guy's okay. How are you going to get mad at somebody smokes a pipe? Especially those Sherlock Holmes jobs. It's like wearing a sign that you're a passive—that you're happy to be second fiddle—just like an ape who don't want trouble with another ape looks down at the ground or hangs his head or covers his balls with his hands. Whatever. That's what them crooked pipes do."

Teddy smiled at the storekeeper and asked, "Do you have a Geological Survey map of the immediate area?"

The storekeeper set the open book down on the glass-topped showcase that served as a counter, removed the pipe from his mouth, and said, "Number six one six eight, southeast. Phoenicia quadrangle," then produced one, rolled up, from the storage area beneath the showcase. It was identical to the map now folded into Teddy's back pocket, which he left there. Teddy opened out the fresh map and located the area cut out of the Cuban doctor's copy. There were no roads or structures shown, simply the uninhabited north slope of the mountain.

He indicated the area with his forefinger and asked, "Is there anything up here that's not shown?" he asked.

The storekeeper pointed to the notes at the bottom as he read them aloud, moving his finger along beneath the words so there could be no misunderstanding.

"Topography from aerial photographs taken 1942. Revised from aerial photographs taken 1968. Field-checked 1969." He looked up. "There are two buildings went up since then. Part of the Erigena Derivation goings-on."

"Who are they?" Teddy asked.

"A cult. They don't like to be called that but it's what they are. What they do up there is anybody's guess, but they keep to themselves and they don't try to weasel out of paying taxes on the property with some hoked-up religious exemption. They pay."

"A big group?" Teddy asked.

"About a dozen. Twice that on weekends."

"Can we get up there?"

"You have a four-wheel drive?"

"No."

"Then you walk. Take you close to two hours."

They reached the longhouse at seven o'clock, where Febronia received them coolly until Teddy said he was a private investigator working for the family of a Latino dentist from Queens who had gone out for cigars after dinner a week ago and never returned.

"People in Phoenicia saw him headed up this way," Teddy said.

She seemed relieved by the information.

"He was here this afternoon," she said. "He told me he was from Venezuela. Visiting his sister in New York."

"A lie," Teddy said. "Or a delusion. His wife is worried that he's delusional. That he's a danger to himself."

"The way he waved one of our kitchen knives around, he was more a danger to us," she said, then described the scene that had taken place just five hours earlier. "I've seen more than my share of crazies when I was young—schizos, acid-trippers, you-name-it-I-knew-it—and he didn't fit that part. He was fiddling with something in there. I would swear he planted a bomb and then changed his mind."

"You didn't call the police?"

She smiled sweetly, and said, "We live without a telephone here. And if someone threatens us, it's our responsibility to dissuade them. One human being to another. As we did with your dentist, by the way. I believe he rationally changed his mind."

"What could have done that?" Teddy asked. "What happened?"

"You know, even lunatics have sudden flashes of sanity. That's what I think happened here. Perhaps just the human contact. He and I were talking. And I was trying to be friendly and encouraging—I'm not always as good at that as I should be. But I must have been calm and nonthreatening enough to bring on that sanity flash."

"What were you talking about?"

"About Manhattan. He said he was staying on Tenth Avenue and Thirty-something Street and that it wasn't a very nice part of town and I said this week it might be the best part of town for a visitor—that he would have all the excitement of the convention just a couple of blocks away. That he might even get to see the President."

Teddy chewed on that for just seconds, then asked, "Do you have any kind of vehicle up here?"

She smiled sweetly again, and her voice took on a

patronizing tone. "We believe that any mode of transport other than walking is inherently exploitive. We use our legs."

"Two hours to get up here," Teddy thought. "We ought to make it down in an hour and a half. Figure we can be back to the house by nine."

Cheito walked his bike up the driveway at six-thirty. He leaned it against the rear of the shed, keeping it out of sight of the road on general principles. Once inside, he set the rucksack, intact, on the foyer floor—when he was ready to leave, he would add the two additional cans from the refrigerator. What he did immediately was pour a generous double Scotch and light a cigar, both of which he carried up to the spacious bathroom, along with a bus schedule he had been given in the terminal. He soaked himself in a hot bath, kneading first one calf, then the other; his legs had started to cramp the moment he got off the bike, one more sign of the physical deterioration he had undergone while being chained to his laboratory. A bus left Woodstock at nine tomorrow morning, which would get him into New York at eleven, a comfortable, almost leisurely, schedule. And why not, he thought, as he blew smoke toward the ceiling—there was no rush.

Half an hour later he was downstairs again, where he filled his glass a second time and put on Vivaldi's *Four Seasons*. A first-rate sound system such as this was a worthwhile thing, he thought, then nestled himself more comfortably into the easy chair when it occurred to him that the smallest stone in the sock taped to his stomach would buy this system many times over. When the Vivaldi piece was finished and his thoughts returned to the real world, he realized that he was hungry and went into the kitchen to make sandwiches of the cold cuts he had brought in the day before. As he laid out four slices of bread, the phone on the wall above the counter rang.

He froze. He had no plan for this—a pure oversight. It rang again. His mind raced. The owners? Neighbors? If neighbors, they may have seen him enter and know he was here. It rang again. People hunting him would not call first.

He picked it up and said, "Hello."

"Hi. I'm looking for Dr. Sosa?"

It was a young voice.

"This is Dr. Gomez," Cheito said. "His colleague."

"Hi. I'm Jeffry Fielding? Marc and Jenny's son? I'm here on a visit from New Mexico?"

"Your parents left a note that you might come by."

"I'd like to pick up a few things from my room?"

"When would you like to do that?" Cheito asked.

"Now? I could be there in five minutes, I'm at a friend's house?"

Why was everything the boy said a question, Cheito wondered.

He paused for a few moments, then said, "Tomorrow would be more convenient for me, if it's not inconvenient for you."

"I was hoping maybe I could do it now? I'm driving up to Margaretville later, to a girl's house? And there are some bootleg Springsteen tapes I'd really like to bring, but they're in my closet?"

"By all means come over," Cheito said.

"I'll be there in five minutes?" the boy said, and hung up.

Cheito replaced the handset and thought for a moment of what might be out that the boy should not see. Only the maps. He walked to the large round table on which the map was spread out, its little missing square a prominent feature even from a distance. As he passed the door leading to the rear patio, the short, white curtain caught his attention. It wafted inward a few inches—held there for seconds—then collapsed back against the door. As he studied it for a few moments, puzzled, it moved again, this time even more noticeably. He reached out and lifted the curtain and saw the broken-out pane, one jagged corner of it still in the frame. A surge of adrenaline coursed through him. He squatted and saw tiny shards of glass on the tiles and larger pieces that had been pushed under a wheeled cabinet beside the door.

He forced himself to exhale deeply, and relax. No one was waiting outside to capture him; they would have done it when he came in. What would they have found in here? He bounded down the steps to the basement and nearly trotted across to the refrigerator. Empty! His heart speeded up as though it had been jolted electrically. He stood still for only seconds before hurrying upstairs. In the kitchen he realized that whoever had taken the virus had taken the topographical map with the cutout—it had been on the table. Someone seeing that and wanting him would go up to that side of the mountain. Which would take them hours. And then return here, he thought. But if he were being pursued, it would be a group pursuing him, not an individual, so why would there not have been people stationed here when he returned? Whatever was going on, the only course of action was to abandon the morning-bus plan and get out of here quickly, with the single can of virus in his rucksack. He was back to needing a car.

The front door-knocker sounded.

He glanced out the living-room window as he walked to the front door. Whoever was knocking was not in his line of sight, but a dirty Volvo station wagon was. It stood on the circular driveway just thirty feet from him, at the foot of the walkway. He opened the door to find a skinny young man with blond hair tied in a ponytail that hung to his waist. He had once suffered from acne and now attempted to hide it behind an ineffective, scraggly, blond beard. The young man smiled and extended his hand.

"I'm Jeffry Fielding?" he said.

"Dr. Gomez," Cheito said, and opened the door wider.

Jeffry stepped in, then pulled up short. Something had surprised him. He sniffed deeply, and said, "Wow!"

Cheito was puzzled.

"Mom always puts in a nonsmoking clause when she rents? Man, she is going to go through the roof when she smells this."

"I'll air the house out thoroughly," Cheito said. "I wondered why there are no ashtrays."

As Jeffry bounded upstairs, Cheito went into the kitchen and selected a five-inch boning knife whose blade was especially narrow but rigid, part of an extensive set of professional-quality cutlery. He took a magazine from the table and used it as a sheath, sliding the knife into the pages so that it was completely hidden, then held it in his left hand, beside his thigh, as he would carry a book. The question was, how quickly would the boy be missed? And what to do with the body? Best to assume that the intruders—whoever they were—would be back at any moment and would raise an alarm if they found a body. But maybe raising an alarm was meaningless. He only needed the Volvo long enough to get to New York City, a few hours. It *must* take that long for the wheels of any police department to turn, even in the United States. He wanted to curse aloud in frustration—he was operating in the dark, completely ignorant of technology here. Could they have police on the highway looking for this Volvo so quickly? It didn't seem realistic, yet these people went back and forth to the moon at will, and in the few days he had been in the country, each time he had happily convinced himself that he was overrating Yanqui technology some miracle would occur before his eyes to change his mind. At toll plazas during the trip up he had watched from the bus window as cars in the lane next to his slowed, but never stopped, and simply glided through their toll booth. He had assumed these were the cars of government officials using a lane reserved for them, until a young Egyptian beside him, an engineering student in the country only a year, had explained that it was something called E-ZPass, employing a system of transmitters, receivers, cameras, and computers so complex that Cheito had thought at first that the Egyptian was having fun at his expense. Though the Egyptian was convinced otherwise, Cheito believed that the government must also be using the system to catch criminals. Surely every lane had a camera and sensor that could be signaled from the central computer to alert an operator when a particular license plate passed through—how could a police department with this technological capability not use it?

He squeezed the handle of the sheathed knife and told himself that the conservative course of action here was to assume the police would have an efficient dragnet out for the Volvo just minutes after finding the young man's body, and to act accordingly, to not let them find the body too soon. He walked back toward the front door as the young man came down the stairs.

"Did you find what you want?" Cheito asked.

"They were on the shelves where I left them?" He held up a handful of cassettes. "There are a couple of lamps and like, hundreds of books? If it's all right with you, I'd like to pick them up in the next few days?"

"Fine," Cheito said, as he opened the door for him. "Tell me, what is the year of the Volvo you're driving?"

"An 'eighty-two," he said enthusiastically. "My parents bought it new? I've had it for eight years—put a hundred and sixty thousand on it? It's only six thousand short of three hundred? I keep a bottle of champagne that I'm going to open on the day the odometer goes to three and all zeroes?"

"Can I look at it?" Cheito asked. "My sister has an old Volvo—I think even the same year—and she's willing to give it to me."

"Take it, man. Take it. It's like its own little classic?"

As Cheito followed him down the walkway he said, "I noticed a poster of Che Guevara in one of the bedrooms."

"I used to be into Che? Like when I was fifteen? We had a teacher who was really into revolutionaries?"

"Here's my baby," he said, and patted the car. At Jeffry's behest Cheito sat behind the wheel. The manual shift was completely familiar to him—Jeffry warned him against an automatic—but he asked about the accessories: headlights, turn signals, windshield wipers, even the kind of gas one selected for it here in the States.

"You've convinced me," Cheito finally said, as he walked back to the rear door. "How does this work?"

Jeffry demonstrated the door, his back to Cheito, who

stood behind him. He lifted open the flap-door and turned.

"How's that for—"

Cheito drove the knife up and forward from waist level in a straight line to a point just below the sternum, where it penetrated the young man's body at an angle that would allow several inches of the blade to pierce the heart. It was a perfect strike, Cheito thought, as he watched his victim's mouth fly open and his eyes widen. He pressed his weight forward against the knife, and pushed the young man backward, down onto the deck of the station wagon, then waited a minute to withdraw the knife, thinking that the procedure had been close to surgical in its economy.

He packed in minutes, then carefully set the full ruck sack on the floor in front of the passenger's seat and spread several heavy blankets across the body. The safest place for it, he had decided, was in the car. Let it be discovered along with the Volvo, which he would abandon somewhere close to the city—he had no desire to enter Manhattan as a driver. If he were stopped for any reason he would have to fight his way out or be captured, body or no body. He fashioned a makeshift scabbard from rolled-up newspapers and taped it to the outside of his right ankle, the boning knife inside. Before getting in the car he debated with himself for just moments, then spent the few minutes needed to carry the bicycle from its berth behind the shed twenty feet farther into the woods, where he laid it flat, out of sight.

The car started easily. He would need gas before he got on the main highway at Kingston, and was pleased that he had paid attention the previous day to figuring out how self-service gas stations worked. His observations of the natives' driving habits had also been time well-spent. He buckled up his seat belt before putting the car in gear. A few moments later, when he swung the Volvo out of the driveway onto the blacktopped Quarry Lane, he was more relaxed than he ever would have expected, but he took it as his due—one more example of how planning ahead always paid off.

XXIII

Free of any immediate threat, Cheito forced himself to concentrate on becoming comfortable behind the wheel of the Volvo. Whatever had gone on back at the yellow house was, for now, behind him—the immediate task at hand was to reach New York City safely. Just as in leading a guerrilla squad, one had to expect to move from one pocket of danger to another and in between not dwell on the past one. He was pleasantly surprised at how quickly he settled into the highway rhythm; the darkness, rather than being the hindrance to driving in unfamiliar circumstances he had feared, contributed instead to the sense of security he felt. As did the dense cloud of cigar smoke that filled the little station wagon, and the presence of the body just behind him, concealed beneath the blankets. He complimented himself on what a wise decision it had been to keep it with him. Had he left it behind he would be fretting constantly, wondering had it been discovered and a manhunt begun. Oddly enough, the corpse also served as company. Surely, he thought, it was because he had been around death so often and for so long that the dead did not seem to him nearly as far removed from the living as they did to most people. While lighting his cigar at the entrance to the thruway he had recalled the arrogance of the wealthy young Jeffry, and pivoted his head a quarter turn to say, over his shoulder, "Don't worry, I'll air your car out thoroughly," and had derived the same dollop of satisfaction that he would have had Jeffry been alive and tied up. Since his first days in the Sierra Maestra he had decided that the ability to be comfortable in the presence of death was more than a necessity; that learning to do so was an opportunity to mold himself into a better soldier. Che himself had said to him, "If you turn away from staring death in the face—your own as well as others'—you open the door to self-deception in everything else, and self-deception is the revolutionary's great siren song." That was long before Che himself had heard the sirens calling from the jungles of Bolivia.

His feeling of comfort, he realized, was enhanced by the cloak of anonymity in which everyone in this country seemed to be clothed, whether they liked it or not, the newest newcomer included. It provided someone like himself, as it must provide native criminals, he thought, a wonderful protective shield. This seemed to be a society in which there was no way to recognize a stranger, and no particular need or desire to do so in any event.

Relaxed now, he kept the car at a steady sixty miles per hour and considered the break-in. Could it have been genuine burglars who were frightened off? Or, for that matter, not frightened off but successful? Came in for something specific, a valuable possession of the Fieldings about which the burglars knew, and having found it, left? Then why were the two cans of virus missing? Could it have been teenagers who, having got what they came for, then took along what they believed was whipped cream? It seemed so unlikely, yet most things that were puzzling turned out to have unlikely explanations. Most important, any intelligence agents pursuing him would have nothing to gain by delaying his capture, and so he had to discount that possibility. The analysis left him dissatisfied. The possibility occurred to him that it might be traceable to Angel. Could he have stupidly told someone about the house? Or, more likely, brought women there? One of the appreciative ones who sent gifts the next day? Could something have caught her eye about which she told a boyfriend or a brother? Perhaps that was why she was so free with gifts. Still, this didn't explain the missing virus.

As he moved along steadily in the right lane and marveled at the quality of the highway, he slowly came to

believe in the teenagers-taking-whipped-cream explanation. He felt a nagging fear, however. It was, unfortunately, the explanation that provided him the most
comfort, and whenever that was the case it left him
doubtful of its truth—he found it analogous to trusting
favorable results of a clinical trial that was not double-
blind. After a while, having explored the possibilities, he
put it out of his mind—there came a point in any analysis
where one had exhausted the realistic possibilities and
moved into the realm of pure speculation. It was time to
forget it and move on.

The Modena rest stop, promised by a sign a mile back,
now appeared. He moved into the lane that materialized
on his right and rolled easily into the parking lot, occupied just then by a dozen or so cars. He checked that
the blankets covering Jeffry were in place, locked the
car, then surveyed the huge parking area. Off to his right
was a long line of eight or nine tractor-trailers, several
of them tandem hookups. As he walked to the building
he looked across at the trailers and wondered if the
Western European countries were anything like this, with
untold millions of pounds of goods being moved around
the clock, gasoline stations like the one just ahead of
him with row after row of pumps, and highways built as
extravagantly as the one on which he was traveling, with
shoulders of concrete poured in a washboard pattern to
create enough noise and vibration to alert a driver who
began to wander off the road. The USSR was the only
other industrialized country he had been in and it had
impressed him greatly. What he had seen in the past two
days overwhelmed him. The numbers heard and read
over the years were one thing—automobiles manufactured, television sets consumed, millions of tons of grain
grown—but to *see* it, along with the myriad other things
not included in the numbers, was another. Inside, he
marveled most at the size of the men's room. As he
stood in the center of one of several long lines of urinals
he wondered, did Yanquis have weak bladders? Could
there be a real need to accommodate so many men at

one time or was there some terrible overproduction of things like urinals, quietly absorbed by the government?

He had brought his map in with him, from which he planned to select a place to ditch the Volvo before having to drive in Manhattan traffic. It had to be close enough so he could use public transportation into the city. He looked forward to the little respite from driving, during which he would put food into his stomach and study the map in leisurely fashion at one of the many tables in the restaurant. There were five or six food vendors side-by-side offering a variety of items, but the McDonald's appealed most. He would look at his map over two Big Macs. When he stepped away from the urinal, it flushed itself, and he realized after staring back at it for a few moments that it had been actuated by some sort of electronic sensor.

He paid the Tappan Zee Bridge toll at ten-thirty, a reminder that he would soon be in the Bronx, where he would part company with the Volvo and Jeffry. It had seemed to be the ideal compromise—about as close as he could get to Manhattan without encountering such intense traffic that he risked being stopped for some infraction. After parking the car he would first try for a taxicab but was not sure how readily available cabs were. If not, he would make his way to whichever subway or bus went into Manhattan. His maps, unfortunately, did not show subway or bus routes but he remembered walking past a subway kiosk on his way to the Port Authority Bus Terminal, whose sign listed the Bronx as a terminus. In any event, there had to be a way for him to get from the Bronx to Manhattan.

A large green sign welcomed him to the Bronx. The driving was already becoming a challenge, enough to affirm his decision not to drive into Manhattan—there was more traffic here and each of the three lanes in his direction felt a bit narrower than they had a bit earlier. Most noticeable was that the distance between fast-moving cars diminished enormously—sometimes to less than a single car length—and drivers now weaved in and out and even across lanes. He would be happy to get off this road, but the surrounding area looked so heavily wooded that he could not conceive of a subway or bus line running through it. Brakes suddenly screeched all around him as traffic was forced without warning to slow from fifty-five to zero, then creep around a car stalled in the center lane. Its hood was up and a young man stood in front of it peering into the engine compartment. If one of the speeding weavers was to plow into the back of that car, Cheito thought, the man would be dead or crippled for life. As cars crawled past it on both sides drivers appeared to want to look into the engine compartment themselves; once past it by just a few yards they pressed their accelerators to the floor in what must have been frustration at the five-minute delay, some of the younger drivers causing their tires to spin on the road until they gained traction, apparently testing how fast they could go from near zero to full speed. There was a touch of madness to it all that seemed out of place for Yanquis. He had to get out of this traffic. The next exit, Fordham Road, looked good. It was urban and crowded, with apartment houses close to the highway and pedestrians crossing the overpass—cabs or subways ought to be plentiful here—but the short exit ramp was upon him too soon. Uncharacteristically, he became confused for a moment and found himself past the exit, and now in a lane that would soon put him on the George Washington Bridge with signs warning him not to change lanes. He became angry at himself—sudden firefights never caused him to panic like this. He forced himself to calm down but found that he was now angry at everyone around him. Where the hell were all these people going at this hour? In spite of drivers who stared straight ahead but refused to yield an inch he finally edged his way across a solid white line into the lane on his left—still dedicated to bridge traffic—then into the extreme left lane, which continued south. An exit for Yankee Stadium appeared and his mind flashed to newsreels he had seen over the years of long home runs hit to right field in which an

elevated train passed by in the background, very close
to the stadium.

He swung into the exit lane quickly and found himself
following a series of loops and curves that felt like a
driver's training course. He finally emerged into a wide
street adjacent to the stadium. The streets were lighted
and packed with people, tens of thousands of them leaving a game that clearly had just ended. He recognized
the voice of Frank Sinatra blaring "New York, New
York" from speakers powerful enough to carry for several blocks. There were uniformed police everywhere, simply standing alone or in pairs, their demeanor relaxed and
friendly. He had to stop at a red light, where pedestrians
crossed in front of his car six abreast. Just a stone's throw
away a mass of people ascended a wide staircase enclosed
by steel bars. He wondered for a moment where these
wide stairways might lead, then a loud, rumbling noise
from above drew his attention. He looked up and saw a
subway train rolling into the station directly above him.
When the light turned green, two policemen, one at each
curb, held back the crowd and motioned Cheito and the
car beside him to move on. As he passed under the structure it crossed his mind, not for the first time during the
past two days, that he was running in very good luck
here in the States. As if to punctuate his thought, a block
ahead, beside a seemingly official, granite building, lay a
stretch of parking spaces now being vacated by people
leaving Yankee Stadium.

He emerged from the subway at Forty-third Street and
Lexington Avenue, having learned in the crowded car
that the Yankees had beaten the Orioles in eleven in-
nings. The streets here were nearly deserted. He walked
south on Lexington for a long way, passing two small
hotels that looked to be cheap. Both were full and both
clerks told him to try a place on Madison and Twenty-
seventh Street. The clerk there sized up his rucksack
then rented him a tiny room on the sixth floor that
shared a bathroom down the hall with three other guests
for seventy-five dollars a night. Cheito was certain the

clerk was pocketing half of it—this rate was too absurd to be genuine—but he was in no position to argue. It was going on 1:00 A.M. and he needed to sleep. He tried to peer out of the filthy little window to see where he was, and first had to slide open an interior steel grate that was locked against burglars. A key to the grate hung from the ceiling, out of reach of an intruder but suspended on a chain long enough to reach the grate in case of fire. The window looked out on a dark, ten-foot-square air shaft that held a fire escape. The country was a land of contrasts, he thought. He wondered if he would be disappointed with Madison Square Garden, which he would investigate in about ten hours. He had heard the name for years—his father had been a fight fan, and a devotee of Kid Gavilan—and there was something a bit magical about it.

Teddy accelerated smoothly as he and Frank pulled out of the Modena rest stop into the long approach lane, then blended comfortably into the light, 10:00 P.M. traffic.

"You think this guy is headed straight for Manhattan?" Frank asked.

"Most likely. No matter; it's our only lead."

"How far in front of us?"

"Hard to say. From what Febronia Whoever said, he left her compound at two. Give him two hours to get off the mountain. That's four o'clock. He drives back to Quarry Lane, four-thirty. That's the earliest. We got back to the house at nine, so he's got a four-and-a-half-hour lead max. If he hiked back to the house or hitchhiked, he could be just minutes ahead of us."

They were silent for a bit, then Frank belched loudly, and grimaced.

"Jesus, but you'd think these places could put out better food," Frank said. "They give the concessions to chains is the trouble. McDonald's, Carvel, Domino's. Crap. Why couldn't they let some mom-and-pop operations in there? Local people, who would put out some real home cooking."

"I didn't know you were into solutions-for-a-small-planet stuff," Teddy said. "Maybe these local folks could grow their own organic produce, too. Haul it to the res stop on a horse and wagon. Singing some kind of appro priate harvesting songs."

"You're a cynic, is your trouble," Frank said. "You look around and see what is, Teddy, and I look around and see what might be."

"Where'd you rob those lines from?"

"Who remembers. I read them somewhere years ago In the joint."

"The place is clean and the food won't make you sick," Teddy said. "Isn't that what our mothers told u was the best we could expect from any American restau rant? Don't become a leftist malcontent. They're out o fashion."

He set the cruise control for sixty-two and pulled hi right foot back to a comfortable position near the seat The Cuban—in particular, the Cuban with virus in hand—could be his salvation. If, God willing, he and Frank could nail him, he would deliver him to the deputy inspector running the NYPD contingent, almost certainly Francis Ahearn, and make it clear that there was more than enough credit and publicity here to be shared among Teddy, Francis, and the department. The country would take to its bosom a hero ex-cop who saved the President's life. That kind of notoriety would provide al the protective shield he needed against Cutshaw and would cover Frank as well. The case would be closed and whatever reason Cutshaw now had for wanting him and Frank dead—worry they would someday rat, likely— would evaporate. Heroes don't defile their own heroic deeds. And if, God forbid, the NYPD ever began to link Frank and himself to the Montclair robbery, they would look the other way sooner than lose their share of the credit in capturing a terrorist. The Cuban undoubtedly was his and Frank's best insurance policy.

He didn't understand Frank's thinking on the jewelry As fanciful as Frank's original scenario of Breslin part nering with the two Latinos had been, one could see how he had arrived at it. Wishful thinking, perhaps, but there was a certain bizarre logic about it. But having been told that the entire robbery had been a sham, that the conversation between the two Latinos had to do with a virus, that Breslin had been working for the CIA—how could he be self-deceptive enough to believe that the Cuban now had the jewelry? Another facet of the contradictory criminal mind, Teddy thought.

Suddenly and unexpectedly, it occurred to Teddy that he ought to level with Frank. The man had been honest to a fault with him and a lot more accepting of his duplicity than Teddy would be if their roles were reversed. He felt he owed it to himself to behave decently.

"There's absolutely no way this Cuban could have your jewelry, Frank," he said in a level tone.

"Our jewelry," Frank said.

"Our jewelry. Breslin's got it, Frank, and Breslin's not with the Cuban. I can guarantee that. And as much as I want you with me in the Garden, I don't want to con you into it. I did that once. You're deluding yourself if you think the Cuban can lead you to the jewelry."

"Count me in anyway," Frank said.

They paid the Tappan Zee Bridge toll at eleven-thirty, crossed the Triborough Bridge forty minutes later, and found a parking space on Brighton Beach Avenue at twelve-forty-five. Teddy let out a long, slow yawn as he exited the car, and stretched his arms toward the sky.

"I'm going to be happy to hit Sally's mattress," he said, "broken down as it is. Tremper Mountain was a little more than I'm used to."

They walked the few blocks to Sally's building.

Just before they opened the street door Frank pointed toward the ocean and said, "Listen."

With no city noise to mask it, the sound of the surf was clear.

"Nice, huh?" he asked.

Teddy shrugged.

Frank reached out and pinched the short sleeve of Teddy's shirt, then tugged on it several times.

"Hello," he said, in an upbeat tone. "You got to learn

to stop and smell the flowers, Teddy. Or listen to the Atlantic Ocean just a few hundred feet away. Life ain't all that grim, unless you let it be. There's millions of people in this country would love to be able to hear the ocean this close, and you got it. There's kids in the Midwest never seen any hunk of water bigger than a lake."

"Every night I'm in Atlantic City I look at the ocean," Teddy said, and stepped past him into the building. "But right now I'm tired."

As they climbed the stairs, Frank continued, in a monotone that signaled a mild talking jag, the result, most likely, of his nap.

"The way you were just unconscious outside there?" he said. "It proves what I've said for years—being a cop is a brutal job. It dulls the senses. Day in, day out, the filth and vomit of New York. How many abused kids you see in twenty years?"

"Don't ask."

"That's what I mean," Frank said. "I maintain cops should get sabbaticals. This idea of academics getting every seventh year off—to *renew* themselves—is crap. Cops need it. To get a fresh viewpoint on life."

"What about criminals?"

"We see less bad stuff than cops do—those of us who are professional thieves. Psychos are another matter. And anyway, we get our sabbaticals."

Teddy turned his key in the lock and pushed the door open. He snapped on the overhead light. A nude, obese white male sat on a chair in the center of the room, head slumped forward so that a small, round bald spot on top of his head faced the door. His lower legs were bound to the chair with loops of thick, brown, old-fashioned hemp.

Teddy moved forward into the room. When he reached the side of the chair he saw that several loops of the same thick hemp encircled the man's torso—they couldn't be seen from the front, being completely swallowed up in the monstrous folds of fat.

"Let me guess," he said to Frank, who remained just inside the door.

"Yeah, it's Sally," Frank said. "Look at the poor bastard. He ain't been out in the sun since he's a little kid."

Teddy placed his hand against Sally's back.

"Eight or ten hours minimum. Could be a lot more."

Frank's posture made it clear that he had no intention of moving closer.

"Don't you have to feel his heart?" he asked.

"His heart?" Teddy said lightly. "You want to reach into this mountain of fat looking for a heartbeat? There might be a fucking bear trap in there, there's no way to know. He's room temperature, Frank, and he's stiffening up. Mr. Seventeen has departed this vale of tears."

"Is there blood?"

"No," Teddy said. "This guy's heart stopped, is my guess. And if you look at the workload it faced every day it had a hell of an incentive to throw in the towel. He was tortured is what he was. These little pairs of marks on him are from a taser gun. A stun gun. Somebody hit him with fifty thousand volts plenty of times and my experience with this kind of thing tells me you'll find numerous pairs of stun-gun burn marks on Sally's scrotum. In this case I believe I'll leave that for the coroner to determine."

"Fucking Russkies," Frank said. "They play for keeps. I've heard of this stun-gun shit in Chinatown, but I didn't know the Russians are into it. Technology spreads all right. We're in a global village."

Teddy walked across the room and joined Frank. He kept a straight face, and said, "You know, Frank—I don't think we ought to sleep here now."

"Are you fucking nuts! Sleep here?"

He opened the door and stepped into the hallway ahead of Teddy.

"That's sick," he said. "This is proof of my theory on sabbaticals."

As they walked down the stairs Frank asked, "What's the next move?"

"Into Manhattan for a hotel. Sleep for six or seven hours. First thing in the morning we buy ourselves some fresh clothes. Late morning, or maybe even for a lunch date if he's free, we get some scientific consulting from a brilliant young genetic researcher you're going to love. Then I pull some strings to get us into the convention."

"Sounds good," Frank said, and smiled. "You know something funny—I never even been in the new Garden."

"The *new* Garden?" Teddy said. "It's been up and running about thirty years."

"Yeah. Well there's been nothing there I wanted to see. And for anybody was ever in the real one—Forty-ninth and Eighth—this'll always be the new one. But there's still something special just about the name—Madison Square Garden."

XXIV

Cheito awoke to the soft but insistent cooing of doves. A half-dozen pigeons roosted side by side on his narrow windowsill, visible through the grimy glass in silhouette. He stood up, fully alert, and leaned forward to peer out. Dozens more of the birds perched along the railing of the fire escape, whose metal slats, he saw, were encrusted all over with an inch of droppings. There was no way to know whether the day was cloudy or sunny, only that it was not raining. Uncharacteristically, he lay down on the bed to relax for a bit, where his attention was caught by the bars of the steel window grate, which formed a pattern consisting of rhombuses, if he remembered his high school geometry correctly. As a boy he had been consumed by geometry for the better part of a year, had immersed himself in it to the near exclusion of everything else, nurtured by his teacher, the animated Señor Ochoa, who believed he was molding a future first-rate scientist or mathematician. Years later the then-retired teacher had fallen off a raft and drowned while fleeing his homeland for Florida. A week never passed without the memory of him surfacing.

When his thoughts returned to the present, he found himself unconsciously probing his liver with the fingers of his right hand, pressing just under his lowest right rib to see how enlarged it was. It dawned on him that this was why he had lain down—to relax his abdominal muscles and manipulate his liver. This was the second time he had done this in the forty-eight hours since his first heady fantasy—and the even more heady recognition of the utter practicability—of buying a liver for himself.

Normally, months passed without him bothering to examine himself. Now, his liver felt mildly enlarged, as expected. He moved his hand to the tape on his belly and checked that it was secure, then allowed his fingers—they moved seemingly of their own accord—to go to the sock itself and squeeze it lightly along its length. He closed his eyes for the next ten minutes and allowed himself to doze, thinking of long-ago incidents in the Sierra Maestra and Angola, recalling comrades mostly gone, remembering the final, nightmarish days in Bolivia and the relief upon crossing into Chile and seeing the welcoming face of Salvador Allende at the border—another physician desperately trying to heal society—waiting to take them under his wing, just six years before he was murdered by the CIA. Teachers other than Señor Ochoa came to mind, and men who came regularly to his father's huge study to play dominoes into the wee hours and laugh loudly over rum and fill the house with cigar smoke. He would lie in bed and listen. Sometimes, when he pretended he couldn't sleep, his father would put him on the leather couch, close to the card table they used, and let him quietly watch their goings-on until he dozed off.

Throughout his reverie his hand remained protectively on the sock, fingertips searching out the especially big stones beneath the thin cotton fabric. When he found one, he would squeeze it gently, as he had done with mother-of-pearl rosary beads received for first communion, back in the days now surfacing so often as memories in which he took great pleasure.

Hours later, he completed his fourth tour around the exterior of Madison Square Garden and crossed Eighth Avenue to the long, low building that ran from Thirty-first to Thirty-third streets, where he sat on the imposing set of nearly-two-block-long steps, one of many using the steps as a viewing gallery for the passing traffic. Above him, letters two feet high cut into the stone face of the building spelled out a message that stretched for hundreds of feet—that NEITHER SNOW NOR RAIN NOR HEAT

NOR GLOOM OF NIGHT STAYS THESE COURIERS FROM THE
SWIFT COMPLETION OF THEIR APPOINTED ROUNDS. It had
puzzled him when he noticed it on his first walk around
the Garden since it didn't quite apply to soldiers or police or firemen—his first candidates—then it dawned on
him that this must be a public-health center employing
the counterparts of Mao's barefoot doctors—idealistic
young Yanquis who carried lifesaving medicines to infirm
people living in the city's slums. On his second go-around
he had discovered that this classic building was, in fact,
Manhattan's main post office. Could this stirring tribute
conceivably be meant for mailmen? Was there some tra-
dition in this country by which children aspired to be
letter carriers? He guessed that climate created greater
cultural differences than he had ever realized.

The newspaper he had read at great length this morning devoted page after page to the convention, though
he had passed that by in favor of the Montclair robbery
coverage. The two Venezuelans taken hostage had still
not been definitively identified. Only one of them was
listed on the passenger manifest of a Caracas-New York
charter flight, whose arrival at JFK fit the time frame of
the robbery. The second Venezuelan, authorities speculated, might well have already been in New York. Since
there was no word on any of the hostages, police privately concluded they had likely been killed, and homicide detectives were now assigned to the case. Cheito
had wondered for a few moments about this third hostage—he hadn't been put in the van with Angel and
himself. He guessed that the other two thieves had taken
the man along. If the first pair had wanted hostages, the
second pair would have, too. The possibility that this
robbery was an FBI cover for his own abduction had
long since been put to rest. The value of the diamonds
and the death of the woman precluded it. He had recalled, with near amusement, his own rationale when
taken hostage that had the FBI wanted to abduct him,
surely they could have faked a robbery like this with the
hotel's acquiescence and had the newspapers publish a
government-composed story. Here, after his mere fifty-

four hours in the country, he sensed that it couldn't be done, that this vaunted openness was not quite the sham he had always, in his heart of hearts, known it to be.

Finally, the only item of importance to him had been the news that the President would address the convention at nine-thirty tonight. Having learned that, he had spent the rest of the morning investigating the environs of Madison Square Garden, walking back and forth between Fifth and Ninth avenues along each street from Thirtieth to Thirty-fourth, not because he expected to learn anything useful that far from the Garden but because it couldn't hurt. It was nice, too, if on the run, to know what lay around the next corner. He had also spent time in Pennsylvania Station, which was well patrolled by uniformed police, there for the convention, he guessed. The streets had more uniformed police than he had seen anywhere else. How many security people in civilian clothes were on the streets and in the station he could only imagine, but he really didn't care—ten thousand policemen around the Garden would have no effect on him.

His watch showed noon, which was what he'd been waiting for. A few minutes later he made out small clusters of men clad in gray work clothes walking south on the sidewalk across the street. They had just turned onto Eighth Avenue from Thirty-third Street. He walked quickly to the corner of Thirty-third and looked east. The groups of gray-clad men were emerging from a Garden entrance halfway up the block. It confirmed his earlier guess that it was an employee entrance. The scores of workers entered any one of the dozen self-service places within Cheito's field of vision—delicatessens, a Burger King, pizzerias, falafel counters, nondescript luncheonettes. He watched a large number of workers, singly or in small groups, enter a place on Eighth Avenue that advertised, by means of a huge, green-neon sign overhanging the sidewalk, BAR. Of all the places patronized by the Garden's workmen, this one by far drew the largest number of loners. He walked to it.

A small, red-neon sign in the window, readable when

he was closer, advertised FRESH SLICED SANDWICHES. He entered a cool, smoky room far bigger than he had expected, with a bar along the left wall some fifty feet long. Behind it were three bartenders wrapped in long white aprons and behind them a mirrored backbar that displayed, from floor to top shelf, well over a thousand glittering bottles, all of the opened ones topped by brightly polished chrome pouring spouts faced in the same direction. It had the effect of a mural or a huge collage. All but a handful of the dozens of workmen standing or seated at the bar had food in front of themselves as well as beers. There were fewer customers drinking whiskey than he would have expected. Along with the Garden workers, whose gray shirts, he realized, constituted a uniform of sorts, there were many postal workers, distinguished by a U.S. POSTAL SERVICE patch on their sleeves, and a large number of what could only be construction workers for some project nearby. Cheito guessed it was a building he had passed a few blocks away to which huge steel beams were being delivered that looked as though it was destined to rise forty or fifty floors. These must be the steelworkers.

On the wall opposite the bar, immediately upon entering, was a short counter at which Cheito pointed to a blood-red joint of roast beef, from which the sandwich man sliced the makings of a sandwich that in Cuba would feed four grown men, then dropped onto the plate beside it two pickles and a little paper cup of coleslaw. The cashier took five dollars. Cheito followed the lead of those before him and carried his plate to the bar, where he ordered and paid for a mug of beer, then wandered, mug and plate in hand, among a sea of Formica-topped tables, each of which seated six or eight, scanning the diners who wore Madison Square Garden gray. A large sign on one wall informed him that OCCUPANCY BY MORE THAN 190 PERSONS IS UNLAWFUL. He wondered, briefly, how and by whom that was determined; then his eye was caught suddenly by what looked to be the perfect opportunity—a lone Garden worker, almost surely Latino, with empty chairs beside him. Cheito moved to the table unhesitatingly.

The worker was prepared to ignore him, as everyone seemed to do when a stranger took the seat beside him, but Cheito hesitated at the table for the few moments needed to attract the man's attention, then nodded toward an empty chair and raised his eyebrows questioningly—a gentleman whose old-world manners were never put aside, even in a workingman's bar. The man nodded and motioned to the chair.

He was perhaps thirty-five, built just a bit stockier than Cheito, wearing a wedding band and displaying small tattoos on both forearms, easily visible because of the short-sleeved Garden shirt. He had a pleasant enough face despite not having shaved that morning.

"Buenos días, señor," Cheito said, with a cultured formality that caught the young man off guard.

"Oh, buenos. Sokay. No problem. *Agarre un asiento,"* he replied, in what Cheito considered the most atrocious Spanish he had ever heard. Every fifth or sixth word was in English, yet the Spanish portion of his speech—by far the bulk of it—was anything but stumbling. It flowed so fast that one word slurred into another. This was Spanish as spoken in some remote corner of which Cheito knew nothing.

Cheito continued to use Spanish.

"Is this style of restaurant common here in New York?" he asked.

The man shrugged, then chewed his food thoughtfully for a bit before saying, "There used to be more of them now that you mention it."

He took another bite of his sandwich and continued to think, then nodded emphatically.

"You know something? There used to be a *lot* more of these places," he said. "I don't know what the hell happened to them. This is the only one left around here. All along Sixth Avenue, Eighth Avenue, there were loads of these. Where you have six kinds of meat to pick from and draft beer and they don't skimp on the sandwich."

He looked critically at Cheito's sandwich, and fell into all English.

"Jerry shortchanged you a little," he said.

Cheito saw that his own enormous sandwich was noticeably smaller than his companion's, which looked to be freshly cooked ham.

"Did you put half a buck in the glass on the counter?" the man asked.

Cheito switched to English, too.

"I never saw a glass on the counter," he said.

"Then forget about it," the man said, and shrugged. "Nothing's for nothing." He indicated Cheito's sandwich and said, "Just watch yourself—if you rubbed him the wrong way up there he might cut a hunk of gristle would choke a horse into your sandwich. Jerry does that sometimes."

He chewed for a few moments, then asked, "Where you from?"

"Caracas."

"That's Venezuela, right?"

"Yes."

"I never been there."

Cheito carefully wiped his right hand on one of the paper napkins given him at the sandwich counter, then extended it.

"Ernesto Gomez," he said.

The man shook it.

"Benny," he said. "Benny Ramos."

"Tell me," Cheito said, in a tone of intellectual curiosity, "What is the origin of your Spanish? Did you learn to speak it here?"

"It's like, mostly Spanish," Benny said. "Spanglish, some people call it. Spoken by Nuyoricans. When I was a little kid I shuttled back and forth between San Juan and the Bronx so much I never knew where I belonged. In Puerto Rico my uncle would smack me on the side of my head if I used English and in the Bronx my mother lived for years with an illegal immigrant—an Irish bartender had shot an English soldier over there—who'd smack me on the side of my head for speaking Spanish.

I was the only punch-drunk ten-year-old on Brook Avenue."

Cheito nodded sadly, and mixed together Spanish and English in precisely the way Benny might were he saying it.

"Life, *es difícil para* . . . for everybody," he said.

Benny laughed.

"That's pretty good," he said.

Cheito reverted to English.

"Am I right in thinking you work in Madison Square Garden?"

"Maintenance," Benny said.

"How long have you been there?"

"Eleven years."

"I take it you know the place well? I mean physically. What goes on behind the walls that people never get to see. What it takes to keep a place like that running— the heating or air-conditioning, the lighting, the electrical systems, the plumbing. The way things must have to be moved around."

"You kidding me, or what? Do I *know* it? Hey, I'm one of the guys makes it happen. *Comprende?*"

He became more animated.

"You have any idea what it *takes* to keep the Garden going?" Benny asked. "You got your special events— like the convention is on now—your basketball, your hockey, your concerts, your boxing or wrestling, your Westminster Dog Show, track and field, all kinds of trade shows, tennis, the ice show. *The circus.* You know what that takes? It's us does the rigging—MSG workers. That ceiling you see when you look up in the Garden, it's false. A drop ceiling, for looks. And that's sixty-eight feet high. Stuff gets rigged off the steel above that. You got to go up to the tenth floor of the building just to get access to the steel up there."

He took a long drink of beer, then said, "So when you ask me do I know the place well—the answer is yes."

Cheito smiled broadly.

"This might be my lucky day," he said.

"Why's that?"

"I assume you've never heard of the *Manolito* magazine. I write for them. I'm a journalist. I do a regular series of feature articles called Behind the Scenes, where I go to a famous arena or a famous event—*and I ignore the event itself completely.* I am there strictly to give our readers a behind-the-scenes look at what it takes to make the place function, and I do that by interviewing a workman who knows it perfectly."

"What do you know," Benny said.

"I've done the Academy Awards," Cheito said.

"You're kidding."

"Do you know Yankee Stadium well?"

"I've never been to a baseball game."

"I wrote a piece on it two years ago. People have no idea of what's required to make those places work."

"Hey, Ernesto," Benny said. "No disrespect, but a ballpark where that's all they do is baseball is pure bullshit next to the Garden. What's there to do? Winter they put the place to sleep, right? The Garden never sleeps."

Cheito's face lit up with a smile.

"You just gave me the title for my piece," he said. "The Garden never sleeps."

Benny nodded, and said, "I like it."

"If you had to," Cheito asked, "sometime in October, could you get off from work on a Friday and a Monday? So that you'd have a four-day weekend? Is that possible in your position?"

"Sure," Benny said. "Why?"

"The Manchosa Company—they own the *Manolito* magazine—also own Caracas Broadcasting, the biggest TV station in Venezuela. After the magazine article runs, they like to fly in the key worker—the worker who contributed to it—and interview him on television. It's a Sunday program called *The Men Who Make It Work— Los Hombres Que Los Hacen Trabajar.* The Yankee Stadium key worker was probably the best we ever had."

"And the TV station pays for the tickets?" Benny asked.

Cheito laughed, and patted his forearm. "First-class tickets for two. Limousine service to and from the airport. A suite at the Macuto Sheraton, which is on the beach a few minutes from Caracas. And a thousand-dollar honorarium. The Manchosa Company knows how to treat a guest."

"How do you pick the key worker?"

"I think I already have," Cheito said, and smiled. "How late do you work tonight?"

A worried look came over Benny's face. "Till midnight at least. There's a ton of overtime on this convention. We do double shifts. But I could duck out early if I have to. Someone'll cover for me."

"No need to. Do you get a dinner break?"

"Seven o'clock. An hour. But no one'll shoot me if I come back fifteen minutes late."

"Let's meet for dinner," Cheito said. "I'll take notes of all the important information I need—emergencies you've been involved in, all that kind of thing. An hour is plenty of time for that."

He smiled and patted Benny's forearm again. "Then comes the interesting part. Where your expertise earns you your night's cash bonus."

"What cash bonus?"

"Five hundred dollars. It's our standard practice."

"That's beside the honor money for going on TV?"

"Of course. The thousand is paid in Caracas. The five hundred is paid here and now. For your time at dinner and for knowing how I can slip in there for a few hours behind the scenes. Into the heart of the Garden."

"You want to get in there yourself?"

"It's imperative. I can't write a piece without first being in there."

"Shouldn't be tough to do," Benny said quickly. "Any other time I'd just tell the guard you're with me and he'd wave us through, but with this convention there's a lot more security bullshit. But hey, it's no big deal."

XXV

It was a few minutes past noon when Teddy, Frank, and Lars Manwaring settled themselves into a booth in Hank's Place, a small restaurant near York Avenue, just a short walk from Rockefeller University. All three ordered rare hamburgers, Teddy and Lars with mugs of draft Brooklyn Lager, Frank with "a thin glass of the lager. Put it in anything except a mug."

"I hate drinking beer out of a thick glass," he explained to Teddy and Lars as the waitress left their booth. "Funny, ain't it, but I don't mind wine out of a thick glass. Fact is, I like drinking wine out of a water glass. But not beer."

He directed his attention at Lars and said, "I'm kind of surprised you'd order a hamburger, the work you do. Especially rare. You're not afraid of the mad cow? Or the *E. coli*?"

"You have a better chance of hitting the lottery," Lars said.

"And he knows something about odds," Teddy said.

Lars smiled with sham modesty.

Teddy had met him five years ago, shortly after the then-twenty-four-year-old blond scientist had come to Rockefeller to do research on bacteriophages while pursuing his doctorate. Along with a master's in microbiology from UCLA he brought with him a great talent for up-close magic—sleight of hand performed within five feet of one's audience—developed enough so that any number of fine magicians had encouraged him to turn professional. He had chosen to put his ability to work with his version of past-posting at the roulette tables in the King Tut.

One busy night on Lars's third visit to Atlantic City the eye-in-the-sky people had buzzed Teddy, who was cruising the floor at the time, and told him to check out the good-looking blond kid on table six for past-posting. They were puzzled since he seemed to be working alone, which was all but unheard-of. Past-posting was by far the most common form of cheating in the casinos, but invariably it was worked by a pair—one fellow created a slight distraction as the ball nestled into its slot while his—very often, her—partner slid the stack of chips onto the board. For a single scammer to create a distraction *and* move the chips seemed impossible. Teddy had studied Lars for the better part of an hour and *knew* that he was past-posting because the chips were not on the board when the croupier called "No more bets," yet were on the board number when the dealer announced the winner, *but he had never seen Lars move the chips onto the number,* and had he been required to testify under oath and chosen to tell the truth would have to have said, "No sir, I did not see the defendant move any chips out onto the board after the croupier called 'No more bets.' " The video cameras, used not only to analyze a cheater's moves—as often as not by the dealer or croupier—but to have a record for prosecution, could catch nothing definitive on Lars. Apparently, he moved his body in a way that blocked out an overhead view. The ultimate proof that he was cheating was that over a period of seven hours, *without betting wildly,* he consistently built up his winnings. The man was in a steady, grinding, chip-for-chip contest against the house and was winning. Money was flowing consistently from the house to him— for seasoned casino professionals analogous to a physicist watching heat flow from a cooler to a warmer body. He was clearly an independent and it was more trouble to prosecute than it was worth so that the casino manager, John Byrne, made the smart move—he submerged his anger at having this smart-ass, long-haired kid outsmart him and acted pragmatically. Teddy had escorted Lars to Byrne's live-in, penthouse suite, where the video-room chief, a retired Asbury Park lieutenant, had joined them.

"The party's over," Byrne had told him. "And you're going to have to play ball or your picture goes to every casino in *America*."

Byrne had handed Lars a dozen fliers of casino cheats, with their photos and detailed MOs.

"How much you ahead?" he had asked.

"You mean your video people don't keep track?"

"Don't be a fucking wise guy here," Byrne had said. "I'm trying to be civil."

"About thirty-four hundred dollars. I didn't think it was enough to attract attention."

Byrne had leaned forward and said, "Pay attention. In a small, dark alley once, in Reno, when I was a neophyte in this business and casinos were not owned by publicly held corporations but by quiet individuals with very low thresholds of financial pain, I watched a fella about your age have every one of his fingers broken under the heel of a Tony Loma cowboy boot. One by one—all ten. He had sat at a dollar minimum blackjack table and bet a dollar a hand, and sometimes two dollars a hand. Never more. After six hours he had ground out a ninety-dollar profit—fifteen bucks an hour. The fella was an early card counter, before a mathematician named Baldwin and some cohorts of his at MIT published an article in a learned mathematical journal called "An Optimal Strategy for Blackjack" and a college math professor at the University of New Mexico named Roderick Thorpe read it and—being a man who enjoyed weekend trips to Las Vegas—saw that if you used Baldwin's strategy *and counted cards,* you could beat the dealer. The professor wrote a book called just that—*Beat the Dealer*—and the floodgates opened. The card counters came in like cockroaches and the casinos went to multiple decks and frequent shuffling and said, count all you want. But this kid in Reno was before all that and the casino manager, Buddy Archer, busted his fingers because a steady fifteen bucks an hour for six hours on dollar and two-dollar bets meant he was cheating. Period. Bust his fingers.

"So my point, young man, is that thirty-four hundred bucks—*on your size bets*—is more than enough to attract my attention. Now because I'm a mature adult, we're going to let you walk out of here with your stolen money—*if, and only if*—you promise never to do it again anywhere in the United States, and if you demonstrate for us here and now exactly how you do it."

Byrne had produced a stack of chips from a desk drawer and set them on the coffee table.

The scientist in Lars had surfaced.

"Can you give me one minute to process all this?" he had asked. "And make a decision?"

"Take two minutes," Byrne had said, and pointed toward a side bar. "Would you like a drink while you're processing?"

"A Jack Daniel's would be nice. Neat."

Byrne had walked across the room to pour it himself, and on the way had sweetened up the pot.

"What's your name?" he had asked.

"Lars."

"If I'm really convinced you're not holding back on us, Lars, I'll give you a bonus—a one-night full comp. No going near the roulette but you can play blackjack and craps as long as there's no hanky-panky. Full comp— room, food, beverage. A suite, ocean view. You and your girlfriend."

Lars had looked from one to the other of them, and said, "But I don't have a girlfriend," then settled his gaze on Byrne and said, "Unless you know someone."

Byrne had laughed louder than anyone in the room had ever heard, and said, "I could learn to love this kid."

Lars had then given a demonstration of professional, close-up magic, including a bent-spoon sleight-of-hand gag that caused their jaws to drop open and remain that way for the next few minutes. He had then explained his late-posting roulette scheme.

"I bet small amounts on red or black or a number, just to keep me in action on the board. But my working number is sixteen, which is on the edge of the board layout, in front of me. That's the number I do or don't late-post to. There's thirty-six numbers plus the zero and double zero. So every time that ball bounces the odds are just one in thirty-eight that it'll fall into a given number. And the house pays off thirty-five to one on a number—the player's working against a house edge of about eight percent. But when I see the ball get very slow— which is after the 'No more bets' call, I can't tell exactly which slot it'll fall into, but I've become good enough to know which segment of the wheel—which quarter—it'll fall into *most of the time.* Eighty percent of the time, actually. And that's all it takes to give me a big edge. I have a segment of the wheel marked out in my head that represents about ten continuous slots, with the sixteen-slot right in the center of that segment, and I know— eight out of ten times—when the ball is going to end up in that segment. So when I see a situation where the ball's heading for my segment my sixteen-slot is no longer one of thirty-eight slots it might fall into, but it's one of about ten slots it might fall into. When I slip my money out onto the sixteen, I'm betting on a ten-to-one shot for a payoff of thirty-five-to-one. I've got a three-hundred-fifty-percent advantage on the house. Since I'm only right eighty percent of the time about which segment the ball's going to end up in, my edge is reduced to about two hundred eighty percent. Still not bad, huh?"

Teddy had watched Byrne wince involuntarily when the two-hundred-eighty-percent figure was spoken.

"How did you learn to do this?" Byrne had asked.

"I bought a used, full-size roulette wheel in an antique shop in Carson City when I was driving east to start at Rockefeller."

"A place in the bottom floor of a house a couple of blocks from the capitol? The other side of the street?" Byrne had asked.

"Yes."

Byrne had pointed to a nineteenth-century portable faro board on the credenza and said, "I bought the faro board there. The guy's got beautiful stuff," then asked Lars, "You practiced on the roulette wheel?"

"Three or four hundred hours."

"I got to see this," Byrne had said.

The four of them, along with a croupier, had gone to a room in the casino used for training or sharpening personnel, where the croupier spun the wheel two hundred times. On each spin, a few seconds after the croupier called "No more bets," but while the ball was still spinning, Lars would instantly call out, "Bet!" or "No." On fifty-six of the spins the ball landed in what was referred to as, "Lars's segment." Lars failed to bet on only six of those, and in eight other cases he called, "Bet," but the ball landed out of his segment. Byrne had spent a lot of time shaking his head in astonishment. When the final spin was finished, he had totaled up the marks on his paper and said, "Fifty-eight bets—fifty of them in his segment. That sure enough puts him into his two-fucking-hundred-and-eighty-percent ballpark edge on the house." He had turned to Teddy and said, "Take this kid to Rudy and see he gets a full comp. Tell Rudy he's going to have to make a *shidduck* here, too," then had shaken Lars's hand and wished him well.

"Do the world a favor, kid," he had said. "Throw away your wheel and go into cancer research. We need a cure fast."

Frank had been surprised at Lars's appearance when they were introduced outside the restaurant; his hair hung almost to his shoulders and he wore a World War II vintage Hawaiian shirt that might well have belonged to his grandfather, a pair of nondescript chinos, Birkenstock sandals, and—as Frank would say later to Teddy—"Out of left field very close to the foul line a 1930s Patek Philippe watch that belongs in a Swiss museum, plus the *kicker*—a pinky ring that John Gotti could love. We're not talking jade or opal in some Navajo silversmith's handcrafted creation for counterculture tastes. This kid's sporting your basic wiseguy pinky ring—a two-carat diamond surrounded by baguettes set in half a pound of gold. Meanwhile he's wearing Birkenstocks. Is this a split personality we got here, or what?"

Now, Lars spoke through a mouth full of rare hamburger, in answer to Frank's statement that "I can't believe I never heard of Rockefeller University."

"It's been around since 1900. Called Rockefeller Institute then. For biomedical research. Very basic stuff. Now there's seven or eight hundred researchers. In the fifties it became a university as well. Just for graduate degrees. I research viruses that infect bacteria. Bacteriophages, they're called. Interesting stuff. You want to walk around the lab and all after lunch?"

"Another time," Frank said. "I'd love it."

"You ever been in Madison Square Garden?" Teddy asked Lars.

"I have season tickets for the Knicks," Lars said, "that I split with three other guys."

"Well suppose for a minute you're a terrorist," Teddy said, "and you have in your possession a deadly virus."

"Why not?" Lars said, and winked surreptitiously at Frank.

"And you want to infect the President."

"How is it transmitted?"

"Let's say it's airborne," Teddy said.

"Good," Lars said. "If I'm trying to infect our President, airborne is better than bodily fluid exchange, no? Just how close can I get to him?"

"Not very. He's at the convention tonight and you manage to get yourself into it. That's it. You have no special access."

"Do I have associates?"

Teddy thought for a bit, then said, "No."

"Is this a known pathogen?" Lars asked. "Something the CDC could deal with once they know what it is?"

"It's brand-new."

"How fragile floating around in droplets?"

"Take your best guess," Teddy said.

"Can't be too fragile or I wouldn't be doing it this way, right? And it must stay alive long enough for the same reason. Am I myself inoculated against this virus? Have I got a vaccine that I gave myself?"

"What do you think?"

Lars raised his eyebrows for just ten or twelve seconds

before saying, "No," then asked, "Am I willing to commit suicide doing this?"

"Yes," Teddy said.

Frank broke in.

"Does a yes or no there make a big difference?" he asked.

"Huge," Lars said.

"Then I file a dissenting opinion on that," Frank said. He addressed Lars. "I don't believe you're ready to commit suicide. For sure, you're not planning it that way. You may—I repeat, may—be willing if there's no other way. I doubt even that. I believe you want to get out of the convention alive and well."

Teddy was surprised.

"Why?" he asked.

"I have good reason to believe it," Frank said.

"Would you care to share it with me?" Teddy asked.

"I think not. But if you're smart, Teddy—and I think you are—you'll recognize that I'm not one to offer strong advice on a question this crucial unless it's based on something solid."

"Tell me what you think you know," Teddy said.

"It's not in my own best interests," Frank said.

Teddy turned to Lars. "You're willing to commit suicide."

"All *right*," Lars said, with sham enthusiasm. "I make up a little virus grenade. Two or three is even better. Little devices. And I don't even need an explosive. I need a container made out of thin glass—something between a Christmas tree ornament and a very thin wineglass. Something that's sure to break if I toss it, even if it lands on somebody's head or shoulder."

His face lit up.

"A light bulb is what I'll use. Drill a small hole through the base. Use a syringe to fill it with our medium—a suitable liquid, a buffer—loaded with virus. Fill up the little hole with Krazy Glue. Bingo—I have a couple of virus grenades."

He was pleased with himself.

"Nobody pays attention to me walking around a convention carrying a couple of light bulbs, because I put them in the little cardboard jackets they're sold in. And from what I've seen on TV, I can sure get close enough to the President to toss a couple of them. And I don't have to be too accurate—anything close and he's done."

He lifted his mug in a small, silent toast to himself and took a long drink.

"And if you're not a suicide bulb-thrower?" Frank asked. "If you got something worth living for and want to get out with your hide so you can't have glass busting all over and ten Secret Service men sitting on you in seconds? If you want this to be a silent killer?" He turned to Teddy and said, "Like he would if he was operating in a little church upstate just trying to infect a dozen people. Except now he's got thousands." He turned back to Lars and said, "Give us an alternate theory."

"Let me mull this over for a minute," Lars said, and seemed to concentrate on his beer, while Teddy quietly studied Frank with a puzzled expression.

"What kind of bee is in your bonnet?" Teddy asked softly.

"I believe our man is carrying those items that right-fully belong to you and me. I believe he's taken the trouble—back there in the yellow house—to break those items down. That's not the way a person acts if he's going to sacrifice himself in the next day or so."

Teddy shook his head in sad disbelief, and said, "You have a talent for self-deception, Frank, that's staggering. It's no wonder—"

He was interrupted by a suddenly awakened Lars.

"Legionnaires'," he blurted out.

They both waited for more.

"The way to get a virus moving around a place like the Garden is through the air-conditioning system. Like the first outbreak of Legionnaires' in Philly in the seven-ties. That's a bacterium by the way, but man, would those ducts do nicely to disperse a virus. I mean, they're *made* for it. You hear engineers talk about designing ducts to *dump* cold air out so that it tumbles—that's the way they describe it, the cold air tumbles—out of the duct down onto the people. If I don't want to give myself up, then that's the way I do it. The air-conditioning system. It's as good as it gets."

After leaving the restaurant Teddy and Frank returned to their room at the Gramercy Park Hotel, where Teddy called a longtime friend in the Deployment Section at One Police Plaza and was given the name of the top-ranking officers assigned to the convention detail. As he had guessed, Deputy Inspector Francis Ahearn was in charge. The second-in-command, George Hudler, a captain in Midtown South, had worked with Teddy years earlier. Teddy got a number for him.

"This guy'll let you in, Teddy?" Frank asked.

"If I tell him I'm on a case," Teddy said. "Professional courtesy. Lot of guys when they retire end up in the security field. Independent private investigators freelancing for lawyers. Guys become employees of insurance companies. Retail chain operations—looking for employee theft. The captain will cover his ass, but he'll find a way to get us in."

"Who am I going to be?" Frank asked.

"My associate at the casino. Frank Scalfani."

"And what do we have to get in the convention for?"

"We're tracking a guy with the Jersey delegation. In hock to the casino for big bucks. We don't have to be too specific. It'll be understood we do nothing in the Garden, just keep him under surveillance and follow him out if he leaves. And George'll insist we go in there unarmed—guy's got captain's money at stake. Maybe seventy-five thousand a year. And in case this Cuban does show up here and we nail him, you're going to do a disappearing act. I'll bring him to the right people."

"Why?"

"Your résumé doesn't fit our requirements here."

Teddy was quiet for a moment, then asked, "What makes you think this Cuban was breaking down the jewelry back at the house?"

"You're finally asking me why—really asking—instead

of telling me I'm nuts for thinking so?" Frank asked. "With your cops-know-it-all voice? You do that sometimes, Teddy. You—"

Teddy interrupted. "Not for nothing, Frank, but there's no way he could have your jewels."

"Yeah? Remember the workshop in the basement? Three different sizes of needle-nose pliers laying next to the vise? They might have escaped your notice, Teddy, you being a detective for just twenty years or so. Thieves are more observant, 'cause our livelihood depends on it. And we're freelancers—entrepreneurs. You guys are civil service. Well, the serrated jaws of the pliers and the vise, too, all had gold in them. Gold."

He let that sink in, then said, "I don't know just how this Cuban ended up with our jewelry, but he's got it."

"You're sure about the gold on the pliers?" Teddy asked.

"And the vise. No. Maybe it was brass, I can't tell the difference. Give me a fucking break, Teddy."

XXVI

Cheito folded up his five pages of notes, finished his after-dinner coffee, and looked at his watch: quarter to eight. Benny, seated across the table, was working methodically with a soup spoon on a large ball of chocolate ice cream set beside a piece of blueberry pie. He had not yet told Cheito how he intended to get him inside the convention. Indeed, he had not so much as mentioned it during the forty-five minutes they had been at the table. It had required discipline not to ask him—to sit there as Cheito had done and duly fill page after page with notes of Benny Ramos's behind-the-scenes adventures at Madison Square Garden, but Cheito had not wanted to seem anxious about it. Now, he took an envelope from his pocket and slid it across the table to a position beside Benny's plate.

"I've got my notes," Cheito said. "And they're terrific. So you've earned most of your money. This is the five-hundred-dollar payment I mentioned." He kept his hand on top of the envelope, and in as offhanded a voice as he could muster, asked, "There's not going to be a problem arranging my behind-the-scenes peek?"

Benny concentrated on his food, lifting one side of his plate so that the ice cream that had melted ran to the opposite edge, where he soup-spooned it up with great efficiency. He smiled.

"All set."

He opened the envelope, flipped through the five $100 bills in a businesslike fashion that Cheito found distasteful, given the apparently friendly relationship they had, then put it into his trouser pocket. He reached across to a large, brown paper bag on the chair beside him and opened it so that Cheito could see the contents—gray fabric.

"Your uniform," he said. "I told my buddy, Jimmy, that my wife's brother is up from P.R. and wants to see the convention. You're going to punch in for him. His ID badge is on the shirt."

"Is there a picture on it?"

"Forget about it. They like glance at the pictures from six feet away. I don't know what you can do with your own clothes, though. You can't bring them in. The one thing the extra security people got eyes for on this convention is packages. They're scared of bombs."

Cheito started to say he would throw away his clothes, then realized it would seem more legitimate to show some concern about them.

"You don't know anyplace I might leave them?" he asked.

Benny shrugged, then said, "Tip the bartender a five. He's on till closing. He'll stick them behind the bar for you."

Cheito hesitated. Would the bartender wonder what was going on? With the convention just around the corner might he not report to the security forces that someone had changed into work clothes and left his street clothes behind? Did people in the States report this sort of thing, or anything, for that matter? He was afraid to ask Benny, even indirectly, since it could only raise questions in his mind, yet there was no choice but to put himself into Benny's hands. It was an uncomfortable place to be, given the man's mediocre intelligence.

He changed quickly, in a stall in the men's room, reading some of the dense graffiti as he did so. Not a single statement was political. The clothing, thankfully, was on the loose side. He carried the small canister of virus, in its dispensing device, at the inside of his ankle, tucked vertically into the top of his sock then anchored securely with several turns of adhesive tape around his leg. The uniform pants concealed it as well as his own pants had, and he was able to blouse out the shirt enough to conceal the sock full of diamonds taped to his belly. What if the sock couldn't be concealed, he wondered? What if there was no way to get into the convention with the sock on his person? Where would he leave it? Not in his clothing, along with the hope that the bartender would not look into the bag. Certainly not in another garbage hopper— that was fine when his freedom had been at stake and it had not yet occurred to him that the diamonds represented a new liver. Would a sane man leave a healthy young liver in a garbage hopper?

Almost as important a factor in his changed attitude toward the diamonds was that they had now been reduced to a small package. Earlier, they had been in a bulky suitcase. Now the same treasure had been compressed to three or four handfuls and somehow its greater density made it far more valuable, not only because it was, in fact, more portable—in economic theory, a real increase in value—but, less rationally, because each cubic inch of what one looked at now glowed with more intensity. When they were compacted into a single sock on one's belly, he thought, one had the sense that their loss was less justifiable. He attributed it to human nature—a negative aspect of human nature, but an aspect not to be denied. It fascinated him that in a city such as this, it might not be possible for a stranger to safely hide something as small as a sock full of diamonds. Thank God he was able to keep them on him when he went into the convention.

As he left the stall, carrying the brown paper bag that now held his own clothes, the question *"But what would you do if you had to leave them behind? What if that were the cold, hard reality?"* demanded an answer. He told himself to answer—to choose something definite. It was one of the demands he had put upon himself over the years as a part of his ongoing self-improvement program—never to evade unpleasant questions, even hypothetical ones. Try as he did while returning to the table to wring an answer from himself, he was unsuccessful.

* * *

Cheito tensed as they approached the employee entrance
on Thirty-third Street, actually a wide driveway able to
accommodate trucks as high as twelve-feet-four, according to a sign painted in bright yellow letters above
the wide-open garage door. It was now being used only
by returning workers entering two and even four abreast.
Benny had timed their arrival for a few minutes before
eight. As he had promised, there was a backup of workers punching the time clock, which was twenty feet or so
inside the building. At the side of the open garage door
the regular uniformed guard stood at his post, beside him
a Secret Service agent focusing on no-one-knew-whom
from behind dark sunglasses. Two New York City cops,
one male, one female, stood farther inside the entryway,
leaning against the concrete wall, the female taking quick
puffs of a cigarette cupped in her right hand and held
beside her thigh. She and the young male cop were in
serious conversation, too interested in what one another
had to say to be regular partners, Cheito guessed. He
had his gaze fixed on them as he listened, smiled, and
nodded to Benny's rapid-fire Spanglish as they shuffled
in the center of the slow-moving crowd past the guard
and Secret Service man to the rear of the time-clock
line, where the cop-couple in blue appeared to be falling
in love.

Benny punched in his card, pausing for a few moments
before inserting it into the slot to laugh and say something to Cheito, beside him. It gave Cheito more time to
locate the fourth-row-over-five-slots-down card of James
Navarro, who was by now at a girlfriend's house while
collecting time and a half, according to Benny. Cheito
slipped the card and removed it, saw that it was 8:04 P.M.,
and quickly located Navarro's slot on the rack past the
clock. He dropped the card into it, breathed a sigh of
relief, and walked after Benny. The President was due
to address the convention at 9:30. It seemed enough time
for Benny to show him the place and for he himself
to find one of the air-conditioning ducts best placed for
his purpose.

"Didn't I tell you no problem?" Benny said, as they

walked down a long, windowless hallway that felt to
Cheito like the bowels of some huge structure.

"You did. You did," Cheito said, and slapped him several times on the shoulder, at the moment flushed with
genuine affection toward his new *compañero*.

Teddy and Frank crossed Seventh Avenue, then threaded
their way across the wide, crowded sidewalk. As they
continued up the few steps onto the expanse of concrete
surrounding the entrance of Two Penn Plaza and made
their way toward the lobby that normally held the box
office, Teddy scrutinized the dozen or so uniformed cops
strung out along the outskirts of the crowd, spaced forty
feet apart, backs to wall. They were halfway through
their shifts, bored and unable to sneak a cigarette or pair
up for conversation—scores of roving news video cameras made this a high-visibility assignment. Teddy steered
Frank toward a young, apparently Irish-American cop
very close to the entry gate itself. His name tag said
BRENNAN.

"Captain Hudler said to have one of the patrolmen
out here buzz Sergeant King," Teddy said. "I'm detective Tedesco."

"Sure," Brennan said, and used his walkie to reach
the sergeant.

"Are there two of them?" the sergeant's voice
squawked out.

"That's right, Sarge," Brennan said. "Two."

"Have them wait close to the gate," the sergeant said.
"I'll be right down."

The sergeant showed up, as promised, within a few
minutes. Teddy noticed that it was eight-fifteen. He was
a dark-skinned African American about as young as a
sergeant could be, whose easy-to-get-along-with manner—which would evaporate quickly, Teddy sensed, if
tested by an antagonist—reminded him of Ben Ward,
with whom he had worked briefly well before Ben made
commissioner. King gave each of them a visitor's badge
to pin on their breasts, one imprinted DARIO TEDESCO,
the other, FRANK SCALFANI.

"Cap says to tell you he's up to his neck in bullshit," King said, as he led them past the phalanx of security people at the gate.

"I figured," Teddy said.

King rode with them on the escalators up to the arena floor level. He mentioned, as though commenting idly, "The captain said you're down in Atlantic City."

"The King Tut," Teddy said.

"My wife and I run down a couple a times a year. She fattens up the machines, I leave it on the crap tables. Never enough to spoil a good time, though."

Frank nodded, and said, "That's most of our customers."

"Look me up next time you come down," Teddy said. "I'm out of cards right now but you can ask any of the pit bosses for me. I can get you comp tickets and drinks for the show. I can't guarantee just when I'm there or not, but give it a shot. The Tut."

King thanked Teddy, then left them on the floor of the convention.

Cheito and Benny stepped out of the elevator at the tenth level, Cheito carrying a toolbox, Benny a pipe wrench. The tools were Cheito's idea when Benny had said their only worry was a foreman stopping them to perform some quick task.

"If we carry tools, it looks as though we're on our way to fix something," Cheito had said. Benny had seemed impressed with his resourcefulness.

The tenth-floor level was deserted. A number of doors along the inner wall of the hallway that circled the periphery of the building gave access to an area that Cheito had learned existed between the actual roof of the building and a false, hung ceiling that covered the huge, circular space of the arena itself. Benny led them through one of the doors, onto a catwalk made of heavy-gauge steel grating. They were in a huge, oval space that spanned hundreds of feet in each direction with some twenty feet of headroom between the actual roof and the hung ceiling, which was just below the catwalk. The space was

packed with catwalks, bundles of electrical conduits, and
air-conditioning ducts. As Cheito had guessed, the ducts
were large enough to crawl through and then some—the
smallest of them perhaps three feet by three feet, the
largest close to six by six. All of them contained a small
access door along whichever side bordered a catwalk.
Cheito was about to ask how often the ducts were
cleaned but realized it was a foolish question—why show
any more interest than necessary in the air-conditioning
system?

Although there was no way to view the scene below,
Cheito knew his position accurately in relation to the
podium, from which the President would begin his
speech in about fifteen minutes. He had kept himself
oriented since entering the building, no matter the twists
and turns they had taken—something he could have done
blindfolded. The podium, he had noted, was set at the
center of the south, or Thirty-first Street, wall. He and
Benny were now on a catwalk along the east, or Seventh
Avenue, side of the building. Looking through the labyrinth of metal, Cheito spotted exactly what he wanted—
a long, medium-sized duct that dumped air down almost
directly over the podium. He made his way along the
catwalks in that direction, jotting down brief notes in the
small steno pad he had been using for his journalistic
notes.

"You got to stay up here long?" Benny asked.

Cheito thought he detected a hint of irritability in Benny's voice. He hoped so—it might cause him to leave
and thus save his life, and Cheito would be pleased to
spare him. Why, he didn't know. There was nothing
about Benny that ought to endear him to Cheito, yet
obviously something had, enough so that Cheito found
himself with a preference not to kill the man. As they
neared the duct, Cheito was tempted to encourage Benny
to go, to tell him he wasn't needed for a while. "Don't,"
he quickly warned himself. "An emotional decision—the
worst kind." This was not the time to change the habit
of a lifetime—don't reduce the chance of success by even
a little bit.

Benny would be on his own here.

Cheito turned to a fresh page of the steno pad and said, "I'm going to sketch this scene. For our artist. He produces a pen-and-ink drawing to lead our piece. You might as well find a place to sit—this is going to take twenty or thirty minutes."

He turned away and started to sketch, while beside him, Benny shifted his weight from foot to foot on the catwalk grating but made no move to leave. It angered Cheito—this fool *wanted* to die. He glanced at his watch; Benny had five minutes more. If he was still here, Cheito decided, the man would have to be killed. Benny sat on the grating, his back against the side rail, and lit a cigarette while Cheito sketched the duct in which he intended to work, and decided upon how to finish the man off. The pipe wrench was the logical choice.

A few minutes later Benny scraped out his nearly smoked cigarette on the side of his shoe, then stood.

"You don't need me here, do you?" he asked.

"No."

"I'm going to show my face," Benny said. "How long you going to be up here?"

"Half an hour," Cheito said. "And if you're not back, I'll wait. I have nowhere to go."

He watched Benny walk back the way they had come, and found that he was annoyed at him for leaving—Cheito had become so irritated at his lingering that he had come to relish the thought of hitting him with the pipe wrench.

Frank stepped off the elevator at the tenth level. Teddy had exited on the eighth, to see whether there was access to ductwork there. They had guessed that any ducts at that level would be for return air, and thus unsuitable for the Cuban's purpose, but Teddy had decided it was prudent to check it out, and for them to split up in any case, in order to cover more ground. Frank went to his left along the gently curving hallway, heading, he realized, toward the Seventh Avenue side of the building. He was certain, after a minute, that if he kept walking he

would return to his starting point—this hallway formed
a huge oval around the perimeter of the building. The
convention floor itself would be below the space behind
the inner wall of the hallway. A minute later, a door on
that inner wall presented itself. He opened it just a crack
and peered into the dimly lit space, then pushed it open
farther, just enough to slip through sideways. He closed
the heavy, metal door softly and stood still for a bit while
his eyes adjusted to the light. Here were the ducts the
Cuban would want, if, indeed, he planned to use the air-
conditioning system—if, for that matter, the Cuban was
in the Garden at all rather than, as Frank would bet,
en route to more luxurious and hospitable climes with
his jewelry.

A catwalk circled the place. He followed it, walking
quietly, peering into the maze of pipes and sheet metal,
watching for movement or some other telltale sign. Suddenly, from far below, a huge cheer filled the Garden
and reverberated in the pancake-like space between ceiling and roof. Music played. After a bit the noise faded,
then stopped.

The familiar voice of the President came up clearly:
"My fellow Americans . . ."

The President's voice was the signal Cheito had been
waiting for. He unscrewed the four wing-nuts that secured the access door—actually a sheet-metal panel—
and peered in. His hair blew forward against the sides
of his face. To reach the front grille, where he wanted
to place the device, he would need to crawl only fifteen
feet or so forward of the access opening. He saw that
the opening admitted enough light by which to work.
Before crawling in, he untaped the canister from his
ankle and set it on the grating, then felt his shirt pocket
for the nine-volt battery but left it where it was—inserting it into the device was the very last thing he would
do before crawling back out of the duct. Once in place,
it would initiate the timing cycle as well as provide power
for the tiny solenoid that would actuate the plunger on
the aerosol can.

Now he had to set the timer, though it wouldn't start running until the battery was in place. The question was—how many minutes to dial in? For maximum safety, always his first choice, he ought to give himself enough time to get out of the building, even though the probability of a virus drifting into the service areas through which he would be moving was perhaps one in a million. Fifteen minutes ought to give him plenty of time, and the President would certainly remain on the podium that long. It flashed into Cheito's mind that if it were Fidel speaking down there, he could set the timer for five or six hours and leave confidently. The thought relaxed him—all his life, when caught in deadly serious circumstances, he had been able to entertain greatly incongruous thoughts, which, he knew, relieved the moment's stress and improved his performance. The only argument against a fifteen-minute delay was the general rule that with things mechanical, sooner is better. He decided to trim his personal factor of safety by setting the timer for five minutes.

He set the timer and crawled into the duct. His shoulders just cleared the access opening. Once inside he turned, on hands and knees, and faced forward in what was a wind tunnel about four feet high by three feet wide. He reached as far forward as he could without moving, and set the device down carefully on the floor of the duct, well downwind, then crawled forward until it was just in front of him, at which time he picked it up, reached far forward, and set it down anew a few feet in front of himself. Sure-handed as Cheito was, this was the safest way to transport the virus forward. Suddenly, a sharp, intense pain struck his right knee. He jerked his leg up and fell away to his left, against the wall of the duct, and felt a stabbing pain on the outside of his left bicep, and willed himself to freeze in position until he figured out what was happening. He peered at the walls of the duct around him, and saw that he was at a joint in the ductwork, where the sheet metal screws used to fasten two lengths of duct together protruded into his passage-way—dozens of skinny, inch-long pointed spears

ready to tear or puncture skin unmercifully. Pulling back
a bit, he saw that the screws followed around the perimeter of the duct, protruding along each of the four walls
to form a rectangle through which he had to pass. He
examined his knee as best he could in the dim light and
could make out a small circle of blood on his pants leg,
surrounding a tiny hole where the screw had pierced
through. His knee hurt enough for him to worry that he
may have hit his quadriceps tendon. When he was safely
past the screws he again moved the device forward, then
continued to crawl toward the grille, much more carefully now.

Frank walked at a steady pace, hearing the amplified
drone of the President's voice and the frequent bursts of
applause but unmindful of the content, scanning the
ducts ahead as they came into view. Something odd
caught his eye—an opening in the side of a duct? He
stopped abruptly, just long enough to make out the
sheet-metal cover on the catwalk grating, leaning against
the side of the duct, then went forward, unconsciously
hunching over into a semicrouch. When he got close he
felt the blast of cold air and saw a small notebook flat
on the grating, wing nuts lying on top of it. He knelt,
saw that the notebook contained a drawing of these surroundings, then peeked into the duct. A man was inside
it, on all fours, still close enough so that Frank could
very nearly have reached in and slapped him on the ass
had he chosen to. Thoughts raced through his head. He
had never thought out just what to do if he found his
quarry here in the Garden. Did this Cuban have the
diamonds on him? And besides the diamonds—what
about the virus? He had, until now, never really factored
that element into his thinking. When he and Teddy had
looked over the convention floor, it had dawned on him
that a deadly virus released in this crowd would be a
disaster hard to fathom. Until this moment, he had simply envisioned getting hold of the Cuban, eliminating the
virus threat, recovering his diamonds, and returning hap-

pily to Mulberry Street. But what to do *now*? If this even *was* the Cuban in there and not some worker doing repairs. He considered quickly bolting the panel back in place and going for Teddy, but if the Cuban was releasing virus in there, they would only capture him after the fact. He could wait for the Cuban to half emerge from the opening and crunch the back of his head with the pipe wrench lying near his feet, but again, the virus would have been released. What he had to do, he decided, was to stop thinking and simply *do something*—that's what he was here for. If that was a mechanic inside the duct—well, the guy was in for the surprise of his life.

He inserted his head and shoulders into the duct, then pulled himself in completely. The intense noise of the airflow would easily mask any noise of his own. When he was fully in the duct, kneeling, he reached back out and picked up the pipe wrench. Ahead, Cheito slowly inched away from him. Frank moved toward him on hands and knees, the wrench clasped tightly in his right hand, which, with each advance, he had to set onto the floor of the duct knuckles first, like an ape. The bottoms of his legs grew cold immediately from the rush of air that ballooned out his pants' cuffs. The rattling of sheet-metal panels combined with the high-pitched sound of fast-moving air was annoying enough for him to wish he had earplugs. He saw that because of the tight quarters he would have only one good swing of the wrench—and even that would deliver only a fraction of the power he could generate with enough headroom to extend his arms fully. Unable to reach far enough forward to deliver a head shot, he would aim for the lower spine. An accurate hit there ought to let him get in close enough for short, choppy head shots able to finish the job even with very little force behind them. He moved close, supported his weight on both knees and his left hand, and swung for the lower spine.

Cheito had just run into another row of protruding screws and decided to set the device down well past them. As he reached forward his forearm hit a screw and caused him to cry out softly and pull to his left just as a tinny sound of metal on metal filled the little tunnel around him and something struck his right kidney and caused him to collapse onto the bottom row of screws, which punctured his chest and stomach. He was only dimly aware of the pain as a blast of adrenaline reached his heart and caused him to kick hard and straight at whatever was attacking him. Frank cursed himself softly—his arm had extended a hairsbreadth too far, just enough for the tip of the wrench to glance off the top of the duct and rob the blow of even the limited power it might have built up in the tight quarters. He guessed he had missed the spine but couldn't be sure in the dim light. He pushed forward to press the attack and everything suddenly flashed white as a sharp pain struck his jawbone and ear.

Cheito felt his very first kick land solidly against something. He realized a moment later that it was his attacker's head. His instinct was to turn as best he could in the tight duct and finish the man off but he was also instinctively protective of the virus. He fished the battery from his shirt pocket and managed to insert it with very little fumbling. The pain in his kidney was intense. He wondered whether he would be able to walk—if and when he escaped from this tunnel. When the battery nestled into place, he put his hand on the timer knob. The thing to do was to twist it counterclockwise fully—to zero. The solenoid would actuate instantly and the virus escape into the airflow and out of the duct to do its work. It would not even be suicidal—given the position of the device downstream in a fairly strong airstream his chances of being infected were low. At any moment of his entire adult life he would have sacrificed himself instantly to deliver this blow to the United States. More than once he had stepped forward into a situation where he apparently *was* sacrificing himself, yet he had never hesitated. Why now? Much to his own surprise, he did not want to die. He felt no fear, no shame, no sudden epiphany. He simply wanted to live. He left the timer set for five minutes and poised himself for another kick to his assailant's head.

Instead, Frank came alive and grabbed Cheito's ankles. He pulled him hard and Cheito let out a subdued scream as the screws tore well into his stomach and chest, harder this time. He kicked out frantically and stunned Frank once again. The thought crossed Cheito's mind that there might be others outside the duct, and if not, on their way. He wanted out of the claustrophobic space and managed to snake his way forward, pausing just long enough to punch Frank several times behind the ear, then crawling fast for the opening. He exited headfirst, arms extended straight down to support his horizontal body as he emerged, and breathed a sigh of relief at seeing no one else waiting for him as his feet landed on the grating of the catwalk. This assailant could not possibly be alone, Cheito thought. He paused—unless he went back this agent would likely deactivate the virus. But others could be here at any moment. Without consciously deciding, he found himself trotting to the nearest door, the thought of the diamonds on his stomach flashing across his mind for a split second, after which he began planning ahead—he would go down one of the service stairways he had made note of, and he would go down it fast.

Frank's head cleared and he scrambled out of the duct in time to see a door in the near distance closing. He rubbed the back of his head and took a few steps forward, then stopped—his diamonds had just gone through the closing door but *the virus device was back in the duct* on top of an arena full of people including the President, whose voice reached him clearly.

"Not my affair," Frank told himself. "I'm a thief. Those are America's heartlanders down there, looking to lock up me and mine."

A burst of applause interrupted the President and Frank visualized for a moment the sea of faces he had passed through on the convention floor an hour earlier.

God didn't make them any squarer than that. He stared
at the steel door some fifty feet away, closing very slowly
against its pneumatic door-check, and sensed that if he
did not make a move toward it before it clicked shut he
never would. The shaft of light, thick with floating dust
particles, that entered through the opening grew narrower and narrower; at the moment it narrowed to nothing he imagined that he heard the door close, with a
distinct *thunk.*

He reluctantly climbed back into the duct and made
his way forward on hands and knees with great trepida-
tion, stopping a few feet short of the device to study it.
Nothing. It sat silently, a lever poised just above the
aerosol-can valve. He reached forward and flicked out
the battery with his fingernails, then studied the components in the dim light. Its workings were easy enough to
follow—when the timer reached zero the solenoid pulled
in and released a spring-loaded lever that then bore
down on and opened the aerosol-can valve. He decided
that he ought not leave the duct without first disarming
the device more surely. The wrench. The thin handle of
the wrench set into the gap of the solenoid would jam
the works perfectly. He spotted the wrench where he had
dropped it a little ways back, close to the line of screws
at the duct joint. He picked it up, then held it with both
hands at its working end and extended it handle first,
hoping that the narrow shank would fit into the solenoid
gap. It had to be coaxed in, his hands quivering a bit
because he was working uncomfortably, arms extended
too far. When it was nestled in place, he released it gently and let out a long, slow breath, then leaned closer
for a final check. Sitting in one of the long, trenchlike
hollows of the wrench handle was, unmistakably, a fair-
sized, polished diamond. For a moment he firmly believed it was a mirage—the spring of water seen by sun-
stroked desert travelers he had read about as a boy. He
reached forward and touched it with the tip of his index
finger, half expecting it not to be there. It was. He picked
it up and held it close—a beautifully cut stone of about
five carats.

He moved back and scanned the floor of the duct around the row of screws. Scores of tiny light reflections sparkled up at him. His heart beat faster. These were his diamonds. Hundreds of them. He began picking them up, quickly at first, until it occurred to him that the Cuban was on the run and certainly wasn't coming back for these—there was no hurry. Now he was able to take pleasure in each stone he picked up, rolling it for a moment between thumb and forefinger, both for the sensual enjoyment it offered and to judge its size. One large, European-cut diamond in particular he was sure he had identified just by feel—the centerpiece of an art deco emerald and diamond pendant necklace that had come out of the first box he had opened, 202, which belonged to the rich old clotheshorse, Mrs. Holbruncke.

After a few minutes he found that he was softly humming, "Volare," though he couldn't hear himself at all in the fast-moving, cold air, which was no longer annoying enough to make him wish for earplugs. He ran his fingers over the floor of the duct, left to right and back again, from one wall to the other, slowly and methodically, in a pattern that would cover every square inch from where the now-deactivated aerosol can lay, back to the access door. He paid special attention to the joints, feeling carefully around each screw. It was important to him not to leave a single stone behind, not for the lost value but because he wanted to leave no clue that the Cuban had ever had the diamonds—better that their disposition remain a mystery. Teddy might very well be right that the CIA people had no interest in the diamonds, that it had been understood from the start that any loot was to be split among the four guys who went in. And Teddy might well continue to show little or no interest of his own in them, but life had taught Frank Belmonte that when millions of talked-about dollars that no one was interested in suddenly materialized *on the table,* people paid attention fast. Teddy had been completely focused on stopping the Cuban, but now that the Cuban was out of the picture, might not Teddy suddenly focus on the diamonds? "Go to sleep on it," Frank told himself.

As the stones accumulated, one by one, in his breast pocket, he remembered that Teddy had never believed Cheito had the diamonds—that was how little the stones had interested him. Teddy had doubted the gold on the vise jaws that Frank had told him about. And Teddy, until the last possible moment, had not been up-front with him. That was, in fact, putting it in its best light— the cold, hard truth was that Teddy had duped him completely. A cop, who, along with some federal cops, used him from the start. Lied to him from the minute he had walked into Lambiasi's and paid off their old hundred-dollar bet.

"Frank Belmonte was being fucked over from the get-go," he thought, as he continued to find far more stones than he had hoped for five minutes earlier. "If anyone deserves a pocket full of diamonds, it's the guy who was lied to. And who was it liberated them from the safe-deposit boxes in the first place?"

Now that the presence of the diamonds relieved his anxiety about walking away from the biggest heist of his life with nothing, he was able to think more clearly. For the first time he wondered about just how things had gone awry in the hotel lobby. Certainly, both he and Teddy were meant to be left there dead, but just how much had Teddy known? Maybe Teddy had been in on the plan to leave Frank Belmonte dead, but when the time came Teddy's cohorts had unexpectedly turned on him, too. With each stone dropped into his breast pocket it seemed more and more likely to Frank that Teddy had been ready to see him killed. And now? Was Frank Belmonte supposed to run downstairs like some free-hole to share a fortune with an ex-cop who had been ready to watch him die? Didn't it make more sense to close up the access door, walk downstairs, and modestly toss off, "That can of virus you're so worried about, Teddy? It's tucked away in a duct upstairs. Safe and sound. Deactivated. Go ahead and call whoever you got to call." Low-key was the ticket. Why distract the man with a show of the very same diamonds that he had been so reluctant to believe in?

Twenty minutes later, at the end of a bar a few blocks down from the Garden, Frank sipped a Glenlivet neat, while ten feet away Teddy dialed the hot-line number and listened to clicks and tone changes that meant the call was being forwarded somewhere. Cutshaw picked up on the first ring and simply said, "Uh-*huh?*" managing to give it a distinctly southern intonation.

"There's a can of virus in Madison Square Garden," Teddy said.

There was just a momentary pause before Cutshaw said, "Who's got it and how do I stop him? Fast, Teddy."

"Nobody's got it. No one's in danger. It's been deactivated and it's sitting quietly waiting for your people to retrieve it."

"You're positive?"

"Yeah."

There was another pause, this one a few seconds long; then Cutty said, "You give me one minute after we deal with this virus and I'll explain the snafu back in the hotel lobby. Right now, where's the can of virus?"

"The virus isn't going anywhere, Linwood. So why don't you explain the . . . what did you call it? . . . the snafu? Back in the hotel lobby."

Cutshaw said nothing for what seemed a very long time, but Teddy was able to keep from breaking the silence. He waited. When Cutty spoke, his drawl was more pronounced.

"I'm *sorely* tempted to tell you that Jay Garrick set up you and Frank on his own." He paused, then said, "But for one thing I don't believe you would buy that particular concoction, and for another, it just ain't the truth. No, God's own truth—the un*relenting* truth—is that for the robbery to play real in Havana—and everything turned on that—there had to be a cold, certifiable body left behind. Like your buddy Frank. Perfect, no?

His background? Hell, it don't get much better than that, does it. But I can't say leaving Frank back there dead was the plan either. Same reason I can't give you the renegade-Garrick scenario. Mainly 'cause it ain't true either. It's a cold, hard world I chose to live my life in. It's rock-hard. And when the stakes are as high as in this operation . . . well it's what you New York fellas say . . . I got to do what I got to do. So this is anything but an apology. You're a big boy, Dario. Been around the block and then some. The best piece of proof we could give Fidel—the clincher—was to leave behind Frank Belmonte and an ex-New York cop gone bad. Not the worst two picks, either. No children being orphaned. No grieving widows left behind. Two lone fellas killed in a holdup. One of 'em pretty much deserved it anyway 'cause he was just there to steal, the other one an anonymous patriot sacrificed his life for his country. Lord knows I've seen more of them than I care to remember. And for one thief and one patriot we get to stop the worst threat this country's faced since October 1962. A no-brainer, Dario. Business. Hunnerd percent business."

Teddy remained silent, though he wasn't sure why. None of it surprised him.

"It's about what I figured, last couple of days," he said.

" 'Bout what I figured you figured."

"Where do we go from here, Linwood?"

"Hell, Teddy, we just stay put. We're done. Once you point me to this virus and I debrief you for anything you might know about Dr. Ernesto Rivera that I don't."

"And I should just relax and trust you not to clip me— and Frank—first chance you get," Teddy said.

"Why would I want to?"

"To sleep better at night."

"There ain't much keeps me awake, Teddy. And for sure, not you and Belmonte. I've had a day or two to chew on this. You two took part in a armed robbery left a porter and a innocent female guest dead. Take my word for it that no one's ever going to trace her to me.

And incidentally, turned out she did for me what you and Belmonte were supposed to—sold the robbery in Havana. No, you and your buddy got every reason to just cash in your stones and quietly go on with your lives. You're not going to hear from me."

"For whatever record you're not keeping, Linwood, we don't have the stones."

"Couldn't care less. Small potatoes, Teddy. Them stones are small potatoes in this particular picture."

It made sense to Teddy, but he harbored more than a shadow of a doubt.

"Sounds good," he said, "but I'll be a lot more comfortable with an insurance policy. What I—"

Cutshaw interrupted. "You're about to tell me you're going to write it all down. Leave it with a trusted person, et cetera, et cetera."

"Pretty much," Teddy said.

"Think about it, won't you?" Cutshaw asked, in his most sincere tone of the conversation. "We all like to be well insured but that's one hell of a document to have floating around. People—even the best of them—read stuff they're not supposed to. This day and age . . . tabloids paying a couple a three million for front page stuff . . . well, there's a whole lot a things can mess up. Think it out. And you'll see there's no reason for me or my people to worry about either of you. And none of us need to worry 'bout a deadly piece of paper—including yourself."

Teddy gave him specific directions to the air-conditioning duct, then returned to Frank. He dropped a ten on the bar and said, "Let's get out of here."

They walked downtown on poorly lit Sixth Avenue, in no hurry, past a mixed bag of mostly closed shops toward the flower district.

"He thought we had the jewels," Teddy said.

"His lips to God's ears," Frank said. "Where do we stand? We got to look over our shoulders here?"

"I don't think so," Teddy said. "I planted a bee in his bonnet about leaving a letter with someone. Just enough so he'll leave us alone. I think he would anyway."

"You going to write a letter?" Frank asked.

"And who do I leave it with? I couldn't come up with anybody who would harbor us when we were on the lam. Forget about it."

"What are you going to do now, Teddy?"

"Before I go back to work I'm going to visit that priest in Massachusetts. See what he can tell me about myself."

When Cutshaw finished passing on the virus location to Fielding Bryam at the Centers for Disease Control, he hung up the phone and thought for a few moments about his earlier conversation with Teddy. That man would never write out a letter, much less put it into anyone's hands. He was perfectly free to have Teddy and Belmonte put away. Should he? Almost certainly, those two would never create a problem, but from long experience in these matters he knew that nothing granted him a sounder sleep at night than the participants' deaths, allowing him to rise refreshed each morning, with no sleeping-pill hangover. He would see how well he did sleep in the next weeks or months. And how bright-eyed he was each morning. If he needed to have Teddy and Belmonte put down, it ought to be done as a single piece of work, while they were together. He yawned, and decided he was tired enough to retire for the night. "Twenty years ago," he thought, "I would still have four more hours in me. Garrick. Jay Garrick. Another possible source of insomnia. Maybe Garrick ought to go. Wrong background to engender long-term trust. California Valley kid. Alcoholic father and an unstable upbringing. Loyal to a fault, but one close call and this time next year he could be en route to an ashram and wanting to cleanse his conscience first. Likely Garrick ought to go. Tim Clant is the man to do that work. Solid and reliable. When I told Clant to destroy the tape of Breslin's phone call to Lynn . . . Lynn, Lynn, will she ever mature? . . . Never wondered for a minute whether Clant would get it done. And done right. Clant's the operative you want to be the last man standing. No one ever lost a minute's sleep with Tim Clant the sole survivor."

He rose from his chair and started up to bed.

Teddy, Belmonte, Garrick—off his mind for good. It was worth considering.

XXVII

On Elizabeth Street, Tommy Ross climbed the four
flights to Francesca Belmonte's apartment, on one
of the few endeavors of his life that would, if successful,
cost him money. Francesca had, two days earlier, locked
her door and unplugged her phone after being interviewed by homicide detectives about Frank Santini's
murder, to spend nearly all her waking hours on a chair
behind the curtain of her living-room window, from
which she observed who came and who went from Lambiasi's. Even from her silenced fourth-floor vantage point
she knew that people were abuzz with young Frank's
death but naturally careful to subdue their curiosity to
the properly respectful level for one whose father,
brother, and uncle were made men. The extraordinary
shock felt by the neighborhood was due to the common
knowledge that Pete and Junior Santini had kept Frank
completely walled off from any contact with wiseguys.
They had long ago issued an edict. Even neighborhood
bookies and numbers runners were forbidden to deal
with him in the unlikely event he might have wanted to
play. In these kinds of killings the neighborhood generally knew within a day who had ordered it, who the
shooters were, what they had done or even eaten just
before and after, and why it had happened—all of it
passed on even at kitchen tables in less than whispers,
with mere mouthings of actual names, from which the
recipient had to read the other's lips, as people of Francesca's generation still mouthed the word "cancer" to
one another.

She took her time when Tommy knocked on her door—

she had seen him enter the building, surprised he had not come sooner. Her stomach turned when she opened the door and saw him face-to-face, as it always did, but she not only invited him in, she poured a cup of brown coffee for him and put out a plate of biscotti—unless she were willing to spit in someone's face at the door, she felt obliged to pour coffee for anyone who entered her home. She listened patiently to Tommy's preliminary jawing; then she patted her chest and breathed deeply, which brought him to the point.

"Signora. Did Frankie say anything to you on his visit here? Anything . . . unusual?"

She shrugged. "School. The subway. Did I need anything." She shook her head. "Nothing else."

"That's it?" he said.

"That's it."

"Nothing else?"

"Nothing."

"You're sure?"

"I'm sure."

He drank his coffee nearly to the bottom and surveyed the apartment.

"You make a delicious cup of coffee."

"Grazie."

"And you have a beautiful home."

She nodded modestly.

Tommy could have shouted for joy. As he had hoped but not expected for the past two days, young Frank had not carried his message to the old *puton*. He was not only off the hook with the two *Santinis*—both lunatic enough to kill their skipper—but he could still exact tribute from the son. He indicated his surroundings.

"Your son Frank is able to take good care of you, signora."

She saw it as a perfect opening. She had intended to wait until he was out of the door and then go through a stumbling memory routine, but his mention of Frank was made to order.

"My son Frank," she said, and squinted. "My son Frank. You know—my memory's not what it was, it comes back slow now—but when your nephew was here he said something about my Frankie." She watched his face change. It drooped, then fixed itself into a tiny, wan smile. "Somebody wanted my Frankie to call them, I think." She let long seconds pass in silence while their eyes locked on one another's. Then she said, "But maybe I'm confused. You weren't looking for my Frankie, were you?"

"You *cagna astuta*!" he thought, but only shrugged, and showed no sign of disappointment. "What would I want with your Frankie?" he asked.

"I must be remembering wrong," she said. "All the excitement."

"You must be. I'm sure my nephew never said nothing to you about your son."

She nodded, and said, "That makes more sense. If you had wanted to talk to my Frankie, you wouldn't have sent your nephew," then sipped her coffee and studied him over the rim of her cup.

"We have a deal," he thought, and it was worth losing Belmonte's hundred thou to be out of the sights of the Santinis.

He wondered whether to give her the envelope. Would she be insulted? He had just let her son off the hook and they both knew it—it ought to be enough, but five thousand in cash never hurt. He set his envelope on the table.

"I want you to treat yourself to something, signora. Something nice. Something that will give you pleasure," he said, wishing that his father had killed her instead of fucking her thirty-five years ago.

"*Grazie,*" she said, and smiled.

She watched from behind her curtain as Tommy walked into Lambiasi's, and down Elizabeth Street, on his usual weekday schedule. He would be gone for about an hour, then return for his stint in Lambiasi's. She picked up the phone and dialed Pete Santini's house, and told him to come over right away, to say nothing to nobody, that she had news for him about his son.

                    *   *   *

Forty minutes later Pete Santini left her apartment and hurried downstairs, where Junior waited for him in front of the building.

"What's the story?" Junior asked, as they crossed the street.

"Act natural," Pete said. "We're just passing the time of day. Is Tommy in Lambiasi's?"

"Not yet. He's due in five, ten minutes."

"We'll wait for him."

They took the three steps down into Lambiasi's Pasticceria. Gennaro came out of his near-perpetual doze and said, "Tommy's not here, Pete."

"Bring us two espresso," Pete said.

The Santinis sat in Tommy Ross's booth, side by side, leaving Tommy's bench free, and remained silent until Gennaro set down their two cups of coffee and returned to his post near the register.

"So what's the story here, Pete?" Junior asked. He had not called his father by anything but his first name since being inducted into the Garragusso Family and assigned to Tommy Ross's crew, ten years earlier.

Pete ran through things carefully to his son, who typically took a while to absorb them. Junior was almost as mentally slow as his dead brother, Frank, had been fast.

"Rat bastard Tommy dragged him into some kind of shit. The poor kid was scared to tell us. Figured we'd wind up in a mess with Tommy, so he told the old lady how scared he was and that he thought somebody was following him."

"She told you that?"

"Of course she told me, how else would I know?" he said, then added, "She said she never seen Frank so close to crying."

"Frankie told her what Tommy wanted from him?" Junior asked.

"No. The kid was a nervous wreck."

"So what's the story?" Junior asked.

"The rat bastard was just up to see the old lady. Gave

her five large in an envelope. To forget anything the kid said the other night."

He waited for Junior to nod his understanding before continuing.

"You can't let Tommy get a whiff of *anything* here. Capeesh?"

"Yeah."

"We're going to clip this cocksucker."

"Here?" Junior asked.

"What's a matter with you? We clip him here and what? Clip Gennaro, too? Then maybe walk out on Elizabeth Street and ask everybody not to tell the big guy we whacked our skipper? What's a matter with you?"

"So tell me where we clip him."

"Tonight. We'll figure it out for tonight. Dump a quarter kilo of *babanya* in his car like drug dealers done it. Nobody'll miss the cheap fuck anyhow. Nobody'll look too hard."

"So what're we doing here, Pete?"

"Just don't let on nothing. He's sharp, this rat bastard. I'm going to ask him nice and easy whether he got to talk with the old lady. If he lies, I drop it. And we whack him later."

"What if he don't lie?"

"Then I go back and talk more to the old lady."

A few minutes later, Jimmy and Catherine, their baby-machine turned off, each lit a cigarette and watched from the window for Tommy Ross's arrival. Their reel-to-reel had been running since the Santinis walked into the *pasticceria*.

"Call it," Catherine said.

"Tommy's going to lie."

"And they'll clip him?"

"You bet."

"Our whole case goes down the drain?" she asked.

"God willing," Jimmy said. "Closed up and done with. So Sally Seventeen never becomes of peripheral interest to anybody."

"You realize, if Tommy lies and the Santinis clip him, we've got them on tape admitting it?" she asked.

"Who cares. That tape gets erased like a lot of others. I'd love to close this out and go on to bigger and better things," he said.

She shifted into Chinese, and said, "We could shake the Santini tree for a lot of money, with this tape."

He answered in English.

"We took our shot. If we walk away whole we're doing fine."

"Just kidding," she said, in English.

Tommy Ross appeared in their line of sight and bounced down the three steps into Lambiasi's.

"Court's in session," Jimmy said. They walked close to the recorder.

"Hey, Pete. Junior," Tommy said. "What do you hear?"

"Nothing," Pete said. "We're going out to Brooklyn. To the pizzeria. Guy's ready to throw the towel in."

The sounds of Gennaro setting down plates came through the wire.

"I swear," Jimmy said, "it's gotten so I can tell a serving of cannoli from sfogliatells by the sound of the plate on the table."

The sounds of Tommy chewing and drinking came through.

"He deserves to be whacked just for his table manners," Catherine said.

They listened.

"You ever get to talk to the old lady?" Pete asked, offhandedly. " 'Cause I can't reach her. I'd love to hear what she's got to say."

"I been on the lookout for her," Tommy answered through his mouthful of pastry. "You can't crash the door down neither, Pete. When she comes out she comes out. Meanwhile . . . I ain't caught a glimpse of her."

XXVIII

The bus moved north on the uncrowded thruway at a constant speed that Cheito estimated to be in the high sixties, past huge apple orchards planted nearly to the shoulder of the road. On his previous trip along this route the Egyptian engineering student who had been seated beside him, after explaining the futuristic toll system, had drawn his attention to these trees and said, "We grow excellent apples in New York." His voice had conveyed the unabashed pride that Cheito had come to recognize, despite his brief time here, as that of a recent immigrant from a poor country enlightening someone even more newly arrived than himself. In particular, the young fool's emphasis on the word "we" had tempted Cheito to point out to him the absurdity of identifying as his own a country in which neither he nor his parents before him had been born. The future engineer had gone on to extol other virtues of his adopted country, which had irritated Cheito more and more. Now, just ten days later, as he studied the efficiently shaped dwarf trees weighed down with unnatural quantities of deep-red fruit, he concluded—with so little reluctance it surprised him—that the young man had been right. About more than just the quality of the fruit. Even from his vantage point on the moving bus it was clear that these fields were cultivated to produce maximum yields per acre despite the surfeit of land available everywhere he looked, and to reduce the labor costs enormously—the dwarf trees needed no ladders for picking. One could say that everywhere he looked, things were done right.

He shifted in his seat and winced at the pain in his

kidney, where the pipe wrench had landed. For the past week he had nursed his wounds, watching the quantity of blood in his urine decrease daily. His guess was that it would disappear completely in a few more days. He closed his eyes and tried to visualize the contents of the buried airline bag. It surely held close to a million dollars' worth of small stones and settings. The sock tied to his waist—actually two socks now, one within the other—held another million dollars' worth of stones. Four or five million in large stones must have been left behind in the duct, but he was able to put that out of his mind easily—he had never been one to cry over spilt milk. He found himself very nearly dozing and was both surprised and puzzled, not for the first time since leaving the Garden, by his lack of regret at failing to carry out his self-assigned mission. That he would be able to buy a new liver seemed to act as a sedative. Not since he was a little boy could he remember feeling so free of anger. "It's money," he thought wryly, "not music, that soothes the wild beast." Mission fulfilled or not, the original purpose of his coming here would be realized anyway—Fidel would get whichever meaningless concessions he wanted from the United States. Whoever his attacker at the Garden was, the man had not been ignorant of Cheito's identity. Why he would be operating alone was a mystery, but he had certainly entered that duct knowing what Cheito was up to. By now the Kaongeshi-Zaire virus had been in the hands of people at the CDC for a week, and when they gave their analysis to the President he would be happy to give Fidel what he wanted and then some. Without any demonstration. Killing off Yanquis would have meant nothing in the long run, since what Fidel truly wanted was little more than an end to the blockade. The old man had better pay attention to the adage that God punishes people by giving them what they wish for. Having seen the States now, even for just twelve days, Cheito had no doubt that Fidel would come to regret any easing of relations—the Cuban people were not about to resist these enticements. Certainly the Russians hadn't, though now that he had seen for himself the levels of wealth and comfort this system generated their behavior was a bit more understandable. In the final analysis, people the world over were bourgeois. A picture of the Russian with whom he had found the virus in Zaire flashed across his mind—not the man's face but his back, specifically the nape of his neck covered by the filtered hood, which Cheito's bullet had pierced.

"So much for dwelling on the mission," he thought, and put it out of his mind for good. Kingston was now twenty minutes away, and after a five-minute stop there, it would be only half an hour more to Phoenicia. There was a tiny hotel on the main street from which a forty-minute walk would bring him to the start of the trail where his treasure was buried. The life that he envisioned for himself after that was not at all bad. He would return to Venezuela and from there find the best country for obtaining his transplant, then return to Cuba or not, depending upon conditions. He could, after all, write his biography as well in South America as in Cuba—certainly in far more comfort. Thoughts of retirement, along with the motion of the nearly empty bus, lulled him. As he dozed off, his mind, for whatever reason, wandered to the many incidents of violence in his life, those of the past few days in particular. The thought that violence would no longer be a part of his life he found oddly comforting. It was ironic, he thought, that several million dollars and only twelve days in the land of his archenemy had been enough to corrupt and convert him from forty years of revolutionary zeal. And so what? Compared with his compatriots—including Fidel—he was simply a few years ahead of the curve. The Yanqui phrase he had heard several times occurred to him—"Hey, that was then. This is now."

He fell into the deepest sleep his circumstances had permitted him in a long time.

Epilogue

Teddy stepped out of the brightly lit casino onto the boardwalk and breathed deeply several times before walking across to the railing. He remembered that the Almanac column in the *Atlantic Monthly* he had skimmed earlier at the lobby newsstand said that tonight Mars, Venus, and the waxing crescent moon would be broadly grouped in the southwestern sky. They were. The atmosphere was clear enough so that even to his naked eye the reddish cast of Mars was apparent. He studied it for a few minutes, then lowered his gaze to the horizon and scanned it slowly from left to right, enjoying the light ocean breeze.

"Waiting for your ship to come in?" a voice behind him asked softly.

He turned and saw Frank, who flashed the tight, almost wistful smile Teddy recognized as the strongest expression of happiness this recidivist was able to muster even in moments of great joy. They hugged, thumped one another's back, then exchanged kisses on both cheeks—all this for the first time. The surge of pleasure Teddy felt at seeing the face of his recent war buddy was completely unexpected. He was still surprised at Frank's behavior in Madison Square Garden, not so much his first decision to go into the duct after the Cuban, since at that point Frank still was after the diamonds—but his second decision to forgo the diamonds by going back into the duct to disarm the virus grenade. It was an unselfish act by someone not expected to act unselfishly

and Teddy both admired Frank for it and regretted that
when all the dust had settled on this operation, the man
had come away with nothing. He, Teddy, had gone into it
not for gain but for excitement in a noble cause, and had
seen less nobility and more excitement than he had bar-
gained for. Frank was the only one of them who had
been recruited strictly for the money.

"I remember you saying you took a stroll on the
boardwalk at ten o'clock, rain or shine," Frank said.

"Creature of habit," Teddy said. "You feel like
walking?"

They walked east, along the quieter length of the
boardwalk, close to the railing. The surf pounded softly
off to their right.

"So what's doing?" Teddy asked.

"Same old grind. What's with you?"

"I got a decision to make," Teddy said. "The guy
down here was head of security, George Klewski, got
himself mugged on the boardwalk six weeks ago. *Morto.*
Pralt just offered me the job. Pretty big bucks but full-
time. And a heavy dose of responsibility compared to
what I do now."

"I thought you were comfortable," Frank said. "First-
grade detectives go out on lieutenant's pay, no? Plus
your part-time gig here. What do you want to go back
to pissing your life away on a nine-to-five for?"

"It's a challenge," Teddy said.

"So's leading a full life. With time to think and nobody
ever over your shoulder."

"It's what I keep telling myself. But it's tempting."

They walked silently for a bit, then Frank asked, "Did
you ever get to visit that priest up in Massachusetts you
told me about? The guy was supposed to know something about your real parents?"

"Father Gangemi," Teddy said. "I spent hours with
him—an old greaseball came over when he was eight or
nine years old. He's in his eighties now and still hearing
confessions Saturday morning. Nabolidon—he knows
how to talk a lot but not tell you nothing.

" 'I knew Gaetano and Gina when I was at St. Francis

in Brooklyn,' he told me, 'even though I didn't see an awful lot of him. Your father was from the school that if the man works hard week-in week-out, then when the wife goes to mass on Sunday it counts for the husband, too. Argued it to my face—the wife goes, the husband's covered. I baptized your older brother in Bensonhurst, and I said a funeral mass for him three months later. I got transferred here about then—I suffered from weakness of the flesh as a young man. Something we all get over whether we want to or not. You say you were born in Boston just three months after your brother died. What can I tell you—take it as proof that miracles happen.' Then he pours out two more big glasses of his homemade wine, talks a few minutes about how his little mechanical press is on its last legs but how at his age you're not so fast to replace things, then leans a little closer and all of a sudden says, 'Hey, Dario—how important are biological parents anyway? It's who shelters you and loves you and teaches you that counts. It's who sits next to your bed all night when you got a hundred and four. You're suffering from more curiosity than is good for you. God never meant for man to know every last thing—it's why Adam got thrown out of the garden. Tonight, kneel down by your bed and say a rosary. All fifteen decades. You'll sleep like a log. Tomorrow morning start fresh without worrying about things that don't matter. Life is full of mysteries.' He put his hand on my forehead and blessed me in Latin, then said, 'Thanks for coming by.' Four hundred miles round trip and he says thanks for coming by. We both knew he wasn't kidding me. Says no, but he knows."

They stopped, by some kind of unspoken, mutual consent, and leaned against the railing, listening to and watching the moonlit breakers disappear against the band of smooth sand at the water's edge.

After a minute, Frank said, "Offer him a lot of money. For his church. Parishes like that are starving. He'll think for a few minutes about all the good he can do with a hundred thousand bucks—you could remind him out loud, too—and he'll see that telling you is no skin off anybody's ass this late in the game and he'll open up wide, Teddy."

"It's probably a good idea. You got a hundred grand, Frank?" Teddy asked, with a smile.

"Yeah," Frank said, and squeezed the back of Teddy's neck affectionately. "As a matter of fact, I do. A hundred grand and then some. It's what I came down here to talk to you about."

They started to walk again, at a very slow pace, back toward the casino.